Praise for The Dirt

"Hoover presents a sprawling world populated by charming heroes, like Jaclyn, and lovable oddballs, like Eduard (an eloquently snooty math whiz). Hoover also creates fragile, heart-stopping moments that launch his narrative above the average kids' adventure… his narrative is a concert of striking events and complex emotions. A remarkable debut enlivened by heroic portions of silliness, spirit, and depth."

— Kirkus Reviews (Starred Review)

"…Hoover combines outstanding characterization and a vivid narrative to create a poignant and delightful young adult mystery novel."

— BlueInk Review

"This young adult mystery features fast-paced action, a complex maze of clues, and high stakes, all leading to a satisfying, cinematographic climax."

— Foreword Reviews

"Move over Hogwarts and Harry Potter! There's a new school with a lot of mysterious events going on and there's a new kid who is as much a hero as Harry, only he's a detective, not a wizard… There are only bad stories, okay stories, and great stories. This one is great."

— Readers' Favorite (Five Stars)

"I feel like I cannot say enough positive things about this book and I am hoping for more to come from Hoover. I would definitely award The Dirt Bike Detective by Douglas L. Hoover 4 out of 4 stars. I look forward to seeing this book (and many more) on the shelves one day."

— Online Book Club

THE DIRT BIKE DETECTIVE

DOUGLAS L. HOOVER

Iconicon
Denver, CO

The Dirt Bike Detective

Copyright © 2016 by Douglas L Hoover
All Rights Reserved.
No part of this book may be used or reproduced by any means, graphic, electronic, or mechanical, including photocopying, recording, taping, or by any information storage retrieval system without the written permission of the author except in the case of brief quotations incorporated into critical articles and reviews.

This is a work of fiction. Names, characters, businesses, places, events, localities, and incidents are either the products of the author's imagination or used in a fictitious manner. Any resemblance to actual persons, living or dead, or actual events is purely coincidental. All fictional characters and places created by Douglas L Hoover remain as intellectual property by the author.

ISBN: 978-0-9966709-3-7 paperback
LCCN: 2022912236
Cover artwork by Douglas Hoover
Edited by Elizabeth Zack

Printed in the United States of America

Iconicon
Denver, Colorado

"Appearances are often deceiving."

—Aesop

PROLOGUE

The following writings are my eyewitness accounts of the happenings at Raven Ridge Academy and the surrounding area. What you are about to read is beyond top secret. In fact, just reading it brings great danger to you. But such a risk must be undertaken in the fight against the forces of darkness.

Continue reading at your own risk, but understand that this is as true of a story as true fiction gets. Tell no one of its contents, especially the ending; otherwise, you may find your own ending. And remember: Trust no one. Everyone is a suspect, even you.

Believe what you believe.
-Oliver Teller

CHAPTER ONE
THE POCKET WATCH

MY NAME IS Oliver. I am twelve years old. My best friend is Chase—the greatest detective who ever lived. This is his story.

I will never forget that dog of a day when I first met Chase. My uncle once told me that the days near the end of summer are called *the dog days*. I never really understood why. I used to think what people really meant to say was *hotdog days*, but just shortened it to *dog days*. That still didn't make sense to me, so I think it might be because dogs lie around in the heat, or something. What I did know for certain: It was unusually hot in Colorado; "record-setting heat," the weatherman said, which translated to me that summer was not over, and the start of our school year came too soon. Not only was it hot, but no rain had fallen in a month either, leaving the land a dry, brittle brown. It was so hot and dry that hotdogs could be cooked on the pavement.

Maybe that's where *dog days* came from.

It was the first day of the new school year, and I had mixed feelings about my return to Raven Ridge Academy. There were teachers and kids who I wanted to see, and others I didn't want to see—or even hear—but I had no choice, seeing as how my mom had worked hard to get me into Raven Ridge Academy, which she reminded me of always.

Raven Ridge is the small, simple town in Colorado where I live, but my school building was anything but simple. In fact, it looked nothing like a school at all; rather, a giant red castle, minus a moat and drawbridge. Some rich guy named Horace Tanner, who owned a silver mine back in the cowboy days, had it built out of large red sandstones brought up from southern Colorado. Even the front steps were made from the giant red stones, which led up to an entrance of massive oak double doors banded in black iron.

The building sat by itself, far out of town on a hill at the base of the Rocky Mountains, which helped give it the look of a fortress. Its massive bell tower and turrets could be seen for miles. The school had pointed silver rooftops that glistened in the sun, and giant stone gargoyles perched on different corners of the roof. The windows looked as though they were carved right out of the stone walls. Neatly manicured grounds covered in green grass and bushes surrounded the school, and a flower garden flourished in a small area to the south. Wild woods bordered the outskirts of the school grounds, creating a dense boundary and encasing the school.

Some people say Horace Tanner built the castle just because he could, to show what his money could buy. Other people say that it was intended to be a university, meant to rival colleges back east. Honestly, I don't know who would want to come all the way out to the small town of Raven Ridge to go to a university. If the place were mine, I would have dug a moat around the castle, installed a drawbridge, and lived in it.

But it didn't work out that way for Horace Tanner. His silver mine went bust; people moved away, and the building sat empty for years. That is, until someone got the bright idea of restoring it and turn it into a charter school. The main section of the Academy is the original building, but the rest of it was updated, expanded, and added onto in recent years. The owners got things approved, like a gymnasium and more classrooms, instead of useful stuff, like a moat and a drawbridge.

If it's a castle look you're going for, the place should have a moat and drawbridge.

The school I go to is pretty large and houses several grade levels. Some of the kids I liked, but most of them I didn't. And that's why I was getting off the school bus that early morning feeling anxious.

I started spotting some familiar faces from last year when I noticed an unfamiliar one on the steps of our school. It belonged to a skinny kid with a thin nose and mouth, and blond hair spiked in the front. He was wearing bulletproof eyeglasses—or at least they looked like it, being that the lenses were so thick. His head was cocked, and he seemed to be gazing up at the stone gargoyles that peered down at him from the roof. He looked lost, or maybe just impressed with a building that looked more like a castle than a school.

No doubt about it: He was a new kid, and new kids have a hard time making new friends. Making friends is a hard thing to do anyway. Trust me; I know. I always have a hard time with it. Not because I didn't want to, but because of my face.

My uncle said one time, "Children can be the cruelest of creatures," and I had grown up with the cruelest of them all—Johnny Ricker. If ever I could forget about the large birthmark on the right side of my face, Johnny would remind me.

I hated Johnny. I hated to see him. I hated to smell him, and I especially hated to hear his voice. I hated Johnny almost as much as I hated my birthmark. And both of them wouldn't go away.

I debated introducing myself to this new kid; maybe I could show him around a bit. But, since I didn't know him, I thought he might be another mean kid, sent here from the forces of darkness to antagonize me yet further. *Best I keep to myself,* I thought. Yeah, I wasn't the most popular kid in the school, but I had friends. Well, I had *a* friend—Gio.

Gio was short for Giovanni, and Gio was short. Shorter than any of the other students, but he didn't seem to mind. He had short brown hair and green eyes, and talked in a high tone, especially when he got excited. I guess you could say even his voice was short.

But Gio's biggest disadvantage was that he'd been born with only one and one-half legs. He used a fake leg that strapped onto his thigh, but it wasn't noticeable until he walked. But that was the problem for Gio—walking. His slight limp made it even more difficult for Gio to run and do many of the things that kids like to do. So Gio got left out of a lot—and so did I. Maybe that's why we became friends.

It was Gio's familiar face that I was looking for; I wanted to see what classes we would have together. I hadn't seen him for the last few weeks because he and his dad had been in California visiting his older sister and her husband. His sister just had a baby, and that makes him an uncle. It's kind of weird that I'm friends with an uncle, but I guess that's a part of getting older.

Gio was nowhere to be found, and I was beginning to worry that he hadn't come back from California.

I started to think, *Maybe his dad decided they should stay out there permanently. Maybe there was a plane crash. Maybe some gang kidnapped him and was demanding a ransom. Maybe he joined a gang.*

No—of course not, I thought. *Gangs don't accept people with one-and-a-half legs, no matter how much rap or heavy metal they listen to.*

I tried to reassure myself that Gio was simply late, but without him around, I felt like the last piece of pizza left in the box: alone and getting colder by the second. No better time for me to run into the one person I wasn't looking for—Johnny Ricker.

It had been three months, two days, sixteen hours, and twenty-six minutes since I last heard that loud, obnoxious donkey-of-a-voice that I dreaded to hear. Why couldn't his parents have decided to move to California—*permanently?* Why couldn't the teachers have held him back in kindergarten—*permanently?* Why couldn't he fall down an uncovered manhole, which the city would then unknowingly seal shut—*permanently?* Why did it seem that he would always show up to torment me—*permanently?*

"Hey look, it's *Freak Face*!" Johnny shouted.

I looked away and tried to start walking in the other direction, but Miles Webster, one of Johnny's stupider-than-stupid goon friends, was standing in my way.

"You in a hurry, Freak Face?" Miles asked.

Miles was a tall, skinny kid, with messy brown hair and messy clothes. Always at Johnny's side, he did everything Johnny did; skateboard with the same skateboard, eat the same gross food, say the same stupid things, dress the dumb way he dressed, and be as nasty as nasty Johnny could be.

I didn't say anything; I just looked down. By now, other kids were starting to take notice. Everyone in our school knew exactly who Johnny was and what Johnny did. This was Johnny and his friends picking up where they left off last semester. Because he was the biggest kid in our class, and the vilest, everyone was afraid of Johnny. He towered over his classmates with a barrel of a chest and squinty black eyes—the kind sharks have.

My uncle says sharks have black eyes because they are evil, soulless creatures—and I believe him.

Johnny also had curly reddish hair, a short nose, round cheeks, and freckles.

My mom tells me freckles are marks left from angel kisses—and I don't believe her.

"So, Freak Face, did your mom send you with extra underwear this year? You know you have a habit of getting them ripped," Johnny said with a stupid snicker.

"Yeah, your undies feeling a little tight?" Miles chimed in.

This was the precursor for the inevitable wedgie that was their trademark: pulling someone's underwear up their butt so far that it ripped. And yes, my undies were starting to feel tight. Johnny and his friends had done it to me enough times that I could imagine the pain and the rip before it even happened. It was enough to make me not want to wear underwear, but then Johnny and company would just de-pants me and throw my jeans onto the roof of the school.

If only there was an open manhole around, I thought.

Miles pushed me back, and Johnny grabbed my backpack. I knew the drill. Give Johnny something he wants out of my pack, or suffer the butt-cracking rip and humiliation in front of the rest of the kids.

"So, what's in the pack, Freak?" Johnny asked.

On any other day, I probably would have given my pack over for pilfering, but today I had something that I wasn't willing to part with—my great-grandfather's pocket watch.

Today, I would be getting a new pair of undies before the second period.

Then I saw her, the most beautiful twelve-year-old who had ever graced the earth with her footsteps: Jaclyn Jones, the girl of my dreams. Her friends simply called her Jax, and I was her greatest admirer. Her hair was straight and jet-black. Her flawless skin was a slight chestnut-brown tone. Her eyes were blue and seemed to emit a glow from beneath long, dark eyelashes. Her pinkish-red lips were a perfect shape, and her cheeks looked soft and radiant. She smelled like flowers when she walked by. She always stood tall and proper, and she dressed nicely every day, wearing a sundress whenever she could.

She was *perfect.*

It was just my luck that she happened to be walking by and looking in on what was going on. I couldn't allow the butt-rip wedgie in front of her—how humiliating! How would she ever think I could protect her from terrorists brandishing AK-47s after witnessing that? On top of it, I had Superman undies on; they were my only clean ones. No—I couldn't let that happen, so I had to let Johnny open my backpack.

"Mechanical pencils, notebooks, sketch pad, deodorant? Paperback—*Crime and Punishment?*"

Johnny sounded disappointed. I knew what he was looking for—candy, money, or a music player, which he would then ask to borrow and never return. If I said no to what he wanted to take, the Superman undies would be lodged so far up my butt only the Man of Steel himself could pry them out. It was because of Johnny that I didn't keep any of those things in my pack now, which made me wonder why I wrapped my great-grandfather's pocket watch in tissue and placed it inside there this morning. After all, I wasn't even supposed to touch it, let alone have it. If my mother found out that I took, or worse—*lost*—her grandfather's watch, I would be walking to Switzerland to get a new one. Not that it would do any good because this watch, handed down through generations, was special in more ways than one.

My mother didn't have many mementos of her family's heritage; she didn't have much of anything. A single mom raising my annoying little brother Adam and me, Mom did her best to provide for us after my dad left. She often said that she "… only had the things she cared about the most, and that's all that mattered."

The fear of my mom having one less thing that she cared about started to race through me, and I prayed that Johnny wouldn't see the hidden tuck-away zipper that held the pocket watch.

Why didn't I have nun-chucks packed inside, instead of low-fat yogurt and celery sticks?

Time stood still as I listened to every single click of the zipper's teeth as Johnny started to discover what I most didn't want him to find. I pondered the watch falling into the hands of evil.

Those dirty, grimy fingers of smelly, rotten Johnny Ricker can't touch my family's history, I thought. Without thinking, I reacted with a quick, "No!" and lunged forward to grab the watch Johnny now held in his hands.

I was met with a forearm to the chest from Miles, and a new perspective looking up from the grass. I could see Johnny laughing, but what I heard was, "Hey, you big jerks!" coming from an angelic voice behind me.

I looked around to see Jaclyn kneeling down beside me, and our eyes met for the first time. I, of course, had always known who she was, but she didn't know who I was. I don't even think she knew I existed before now. I quickly looked in the other direction towards Johnny and Miles, instinctively hiding the right side of my face from her.

"How much is this piece of crap worth?" Johnny snickered at me.

"Nothing," I said instantly. "It doesn't even work."

"Well, I guess you wouldn't mind if I borrowed it for a while. Maybe I'll fix it for you."

Fix was Johnny's code word for "break it into a bilgillian pieces for you."

Now my predicament was even worse than I had imagined: Johnny not only had my great-grandfather's pocket watch, but he was planning to dismantle it beyond recognition—providing the local pawnshop turned it down, of course. If I tried to fight Johnny and Miles, I would end up with both a broken watch *and* a broken nose—no telling which would be in more pieces. However, if I let

Johnny walk away now, Jaclyn would think that I was a coward, even though it was the best chance I had of getting the watch back in one piece.

Where was a teacher when I needed one?

But that's when everything began to change.

"What the.... What's all this gunk on it?" Johnny sneered as he began smelling at his already smelly fingers.

That *gunk* was the watch's tarnish, and the reason I had wrapped the watch in tissues, so it would not stain my pack. That tarnish stuck to everything *but* the watch.

Suddenly, an unfamiliar voice shouted from the crowd, "Gosh, I hope that stuff's not poisonous."

Glaring at the mob of kids, Johnny barked, "What? Poison? It's not poisonous!"

"You never know," the voice said. "Here, you better let me have a look at it."

There was a bit of a parting in the crowd, and that same skinny, blond-haired kid with bulletproof glasses who I had noticed on the school's steps this morning walked fearlessly up to Johnny. He pulled out a magnifying glass from his back pocket and used it to examine the watch in Johnny's hand. The crowd of kids fell silent with curiosity, including Johnny and me.

Could that stuff really be toxic? How did this kid know? Where did he get that magnifying glass? Who was *this kid, anyway?*

I knew everyone was thinking the same thing.

The new kid made a few *hum* noises and raised his eyebrows before finally saying, "Definitely looks poisonous, but my examination is inconclusive. More tests should be done to determine its safety."

Johnny stood for a second, then, as if regaining his cruel senses, murmured, "You're kidding, right? I'm not buying it, Four Eyes."

"Well, suit yourself. Makes no difference to me if you want to take your chances and wind up lying on the side of the street stiff with rigor mortis."

Johnny squinted at the new kid. "Who's Rigor Mortis? And why don't you use your eyeglasses instead of that magnifying glass—they look thicker!" he chuckled.

Miles laughed, adding, "Yeah, I hope you don't lose them on the schoolyard! They'll magnify the sun and start a fire."

Miles should know; he and Johnny had burned ants in the field during recess one day. They were magnifying the sun's effects using a pair of thick eyeglasses they had found when they "accidentally" set the entire field on fire. Luckily for them, the fire department got the fire out before it could do any real damage. Unluckily for them, they both got suspensions from school.

"I'll keep that in mind," the new kid nodded, dismissing Miles. He quickly turned to Johnny, asking, "Hey, aren't you that kid from the skateboarding commercial?"

Of *course,* Johnny was *that* kid from the skateboarding commercial for 360 Boards. *Everyone* knew that!

Thirteen years old and the best skateboarder in the state, Johnny had it made for the rest of his life because of his skateboarding ability. He got free skateboards, free hotdogs, free soda, free t-shirts, free whatever. He even got free money for doing nothing, because every time they showed his picture on the TV, he got paid!

"He's the greatest skateboarder in the world, that's who," Miles boldly touted.

"Dude, you've got some kinda skill on that board!" the new kid beamed, becoming animated.

As if Johnny needed more ego sauce poured on him.

Johnny's posture changed and became less aggressive; he obviously liked the recognition. But he still was Johnny Ricker. "Who are you?" he snapped back.

"I'm Chase," the new kid proudly replied, standing tall. "Now,

I'm sure the rumors about your jumping skills with your skateboard are untrue—aren't they?"

"What rumors? That I can jump anything? It's true," Johnny smirked.

"No, actually, the rumors are that it's all trick photography, and you can't jump over anything," Chase answered.

"Are you kidding me? Who told you that? I can jump anything!" Johnny snorted.

"Yeah, Four Eyes. He can jump anything," Miles affirmed, puffing up his chest.

"Well, it would be awesome if he proved it to us nonbelievers," Chase casually suggested.

"Everyone here knows my skills; I don't have to prove anything," Johnny said as he started walking away.

"Listen, I'll tell you what. Let's prove it with a bet… say… oh, I don't know… I'll bet you that you can't jump over, say… these ten pennies in my pocket without a ramp."

Miles stepped in front of Johnny as he retorted for him, "Ten pennies? Ha! He can jump over a *million* pennies, sucker!"

Johnny pushed Miles aside with an annoyed sneer. "What do you want to bet *for*?"

"If you *can't* jump in *one* leap without a ramp over these ten pennies that I stack on the ground, then I get your skateboard," Chase said.

"My skateboard? Against what of yours?" Johnny shot back.

"My dirt bike," Chase said as he pointed to an old dirt bike in the distance chained to a bike rack.

It was black, dirty, and old-looking. Even from a distance, you could see that the seat and handgrips were worn down. There were no logos on the frame, but rust instead. The tires looked as though they didn't match. The bike seemed as if it had been pieced together.

"Looks like junk to me. Where'd you find that? In a scrapyard?" Johnny chuckled.

Miles gave the obligatory laugh, as did a few of the suck-ups in the crowd.

Chase smiled and shook his head. "You have no idea what you're talking about—it's vintage."

"Vintage? I never heard of that brand. Just looks old to me," Johnny quipped.

"They don't build bikes like that one anymore. It's a custom job," Chase proudly replied.

Miles jumped in here. "They don't build them because they *suck.* Who rides a dirt bike, anyway? Everyone skateboards."

"I ride a dirt bike—that's who. So, do we have a bet?" Chase prodded.

"Are you kidding me—that piece of junk? It probably doesn't even work, and I'm no fool. This skateboard is worth a thousand of your broken dirt bikes," Johnny huffed, turning to walk away once again.

"All right, if you're afraid of losing your skateboard, then perhaps we bet something else. Something like—say, my broken-down dirt bike, which is not broken by the way; it's awesome—against—oh, I don't know, maybe that broken-down pocket watch contaminated with toxic chemicals?"

Johnny angrily turned around and snapped, "I'm not afraid of noth'n, especially you and your stupid dirt bike."

"It's a bet then. My awesome dirt bike for that contaminated watch. I'll place these pennies on the ground, and we'll see if you can jump over them in a single hop or not. Only one try—agreed?"

Johnny shook his head in agreement before giving Miles a smirk, as if this new kid had played right into his hand. I agreed with Johnny; after all, how stupid was this kid, anyway? Even I could jump over ten pennies, and I couldn't even stand up on a skateboard.

Chase began to stack the pennies one on top of the other on the sidewalk. He counted them aloud as he stacked each one: "One, two, three, four, five."

Then he stopped. Standing up, he walked about thirty feet from the stack of five pennies, squatted down, and counted aloud as he stacked the five that remained.

"What do you think you're doing?" Johnny demanded.

"You said that you could jump over these ten pennies in a *single* hop with no ramp, only one try. Now let's see you do it," Chase challenged.

"You're cheating—you can't spread them out into two piles! No one can jump over them spread out like that! You can't do that!" Johnny sputtered.

"Uh, yes I can. I clearly said you have to jump over these *ten* pennies I stack on the ground in *one* hop. I'm sorry if you didn't ask how far apart they'd be, but you did say you could jump over *anything*, and I took you at your word. A bet is a bet, and I'm sure you're not the kind of guy who doesn't pay up. So—if you can't jump over all these pennies in one hop, then I guess you can just give me the watch."

"I'm not pay'n noth'n to a cheater like you," Johnny grumbled, straightening to his full height.

Miles walked over and kicked at one of the stacks of pennies on the ground.

The next voice that rang out was unmistakably that of an adult. "Excuse me, gentlemen, but am I interrupting something?" it said.

Standing behind me was Mr. Doyle, our history and political science teacher. Besides him? My trusty friend, Gio.

Yes, I thought. *My prayers had been answered!*

Mr. Doyle was very tall and skinny. Everything about him was long; his nose was long, his ears were long, and his legs, arms, and fingers were all long. Even the front bangs of his hair were long, which he combed back over the entire top of his head. And when he spoke, it was in long sentences with long tones.

In fact, Mr. Doyle was the reason that I had brought my pocket watch to school today. He loved history, and the watch was old, so I wanted to show it to him.

Ha! Now, I would get my watch back and not have to fight Johnny or get in trouble. Perfect, I thought.

"We wouldn't be gambling on school grounds now, would we?" Mr. Doyle said, folding his long arms.

"No, sir," Johnny replied smartly while giving Chase and me the *if-you-say-one-word-you're-dead* look.

It was the same look I give to annoying little Adam when I don't want him to tattle-tell on me.

"I should hope not. Gambling is a wicked art, and once practiced, it can lead to dark places and wreck a person's world," Mr. Doyle said. He patted at the sweat on his forehead from the morning heat with a handkerchief.

I noticed that Mr. Doyle was wearing khaki pants and a white dress shirt with a brown tweed jacket, which probably made him hotter than it already was.

Unexpectedly, Jaclyn spoke up. "Johnny took that watch from Oliver's pack, and then that kid over there with the glasses was trying to cheat him to get it."

What was that? She knew my name! And she stuck up for me!

Suddenly, I forgot about the pocket watch. Paralyzed by her beauty, I focused all my attention on her.

Mr. Doyle looked at me, and then at Johnny, asking, "Is this true?"

Johnny squinted at Jax. "No, Oliver *gave* me the watch; I didn't take it. *Right, Oliver*?"

Johnny accentuated the, "Right, Oliver?" to make sure I was in cahoots with him.

"Well… well…." I started to stutter. It was hard to focus, and I didn't know how to answer.

"Actually, she's right—well, kinda right," Chase chimed in, "It's true; Johnny and I did make a wager. But I didn't cheat him. I won that watch fair and square. So now it's my watch, you see."

"You cheated!" Johnny quickly responded.

"You won the watch?" Mr. Doyle asked, raising an eyebrow. "Or, did you swindle the watch?"

Chase folded his arms and replied, "Well, it's more like I performed a great public service. That pocket watch may be covered with toxic poison. I was merely trying to keep my classmates and everyone else safe."

Mr. Doyle rolled his eyes, combed his long fingers through his long hair, and put out his hand. "Give me the watch."

With a frown on his face and an evil stare at Chase, Johnny reluctantly handed over his latest booty. Mr. Doyle examined the watch, moving it back and forth from his eyes. "Hmm—interesting," he mumbled.

I knew the watch like the back of my hand. Underneath the tarnish, the pocket watch was encased in brass. The hands were made of gold, and there were small crystals or diamonds in place of the numbers 12, 3, 6, and 9.

Flipping the watch over, Mr. Doyle began rubbing the tarnish away to reveal the inscription on the back of the watch. He half-whispered as he read aloud, "Time waits for no one." Raising his eyebrows afterwards, he gasped out, "Where did you get this watch?"

Every kid there recognized that tone—the tone of *serious, serious, trouble.*

Mr. Doyle's eyes shifted back and forth from kid to kid. This was about the time when I knew that things were not going to get better for me—but worse. I had seen that inscription before, but I didn't know its significance.

Obviously, Mr. Doyle did.

"I… I… I…" Johnny stuttered, all the while pointing at me.

Mr. Doyle's glare landed directly on me—but I couldn't utter a word.

"Mr. Doyle!" a low, gruff voice called out. "Mr. Doyle, I need to speak with you!"

The voice belonged to Frank, the school's maintenance man. Frank was a bald, heavyset guy with a wide face. He was of average height, but he looked bigger, maybe because of his build. His neck, thick with rolls of skin, sat upon broad shoulders. Every day, he wore the same dark gray uniform. It always seemed too tight for him: The shirt never stayed tucked in the pants, and his thick arms bulged from underneath the sleeves. His belly hung over his belt, and sometimes, when he wore his tool belt, the weight of his tools pulled his pants down just enough to where his butt crack would show when he bent over.

"I'm in the middle of something, Frank; it'll have to wait," Mr. Doyle replied in an annoyed tone.

Frank walked in his direction with determination. "I need to speak with you right now—it's important. It's about the basement."

Mr. Doyle looked startled, and he glanced at Frank before pointing his long finger at Johnny, Chase, Gio, Jax, and me. He then said, "I'm needed right now, but all of you report to Principal Sterns' office after school, where we'll get this straightened out. I mean it—*all* of you."

I gulped. Life, as I knew it, was about to change: Now my mother would find out about me taking her grandfather's pocket watch, Johnny would kick my butt, and Jax would never marry me. Not a great start to the school year.

Maybe I should find an open manhole and crawl down in it, I thought.

The crowd of kids surrounding us scattered off in the uneasy quiet. Johnny Ricker gave Gio, Chase, Jax, and me one last evil glare as he and Miles slowly walked off to the school building. Jax shrugged her shoulders and tugged her cute mouth to the side before she also walked away, leaving the three of us standing by ourselves.

Chase tapped me on the shoulder and whispered, "I wonder what this is about?" He nodded at Mr. Doyle and Frank, who were facing each other, and did not appear at all happy to be in each other's company.

"I don't know. Doyle's usually a mellow guy in the classroom. I've never seen him so uptight," I mumbled back.

Chase lit up. "This might be fun to watch; maybe they're gonna fight? If so, my money's on the bald guy."

I agreed with Chase. Frank not only looked like a tough guy, but he also had a reputation for being a hothead. Frank always had an opinion on something or someone, and he didn't mind sharing it with whoever would listen.

I knew this because, at our school, each student was required to stay after school for one hour once a month for *school duties*. Frank was on hand to delegate these, and they usually involved cleaning. I figured out quickly that to get out of that work, all I needed to do was talk with Frank about something he was passionate about, like politics, history, or the way people acted nowadays. He then would lose focus on the task at hand and start ranting and raving. Before he knew it, it was time to quit, and I had escaped doing any of the work.

In front of me, Mr. Doyle flung his long arms up into the air. "What is this about? I'm a busy man."

Frank flexed his shoulders and raised his chin. "There's been vandalism in the basement. Some antiques down there are missing too. Do you have any idea where they might have gone to?"

"What a ridiculous question! Why would I have any idea?" Mr. Doyle spat back.

"You are one of the few people with access, aren't you?" Frank challenged.

"What are you accusing me of—vandalism and thievery? I went down there to conduct inspections for the plans, nothing more. Why would I vandalize the school, or take items?"

"I'm not accusing you… I just thought maybe you knew someone short on cash. Maybe they took a few antiques to sell and then messed with the electrical panels to set back the plans?"

"Is this some kind of setup? Did Sterns send you here to try to intimidate me into changing my mind? Well, it won't work!"

Frank folded his enormous arms. "Listen, I'm just doing my job. It's my responsibility to take care of this building."

"Ah yes, custodian of this building, and keeper of its secrets, isn't that what you always say? Well, I say you are just a spreader of rumors and gossip," Mr. Doyle snorted as he stuck his long nose into the air. "As for me, I'm a custodian of history, and that history must be preserved for the future. So, it will take much more than baseless accusations and petty intimidations to get me to change my mind. Now if you will excuse me, janitor, I have history to teach—something you know nothing about."

"At least the students would learn something if I was teaching!" Frank replied in a voice that was a bit of a growl. "You're about as good of a history teacher as you are a gambler—and not a very good one at that, from what I hear."

"You know nothing of what you speak of, Frank, and so I suggest you stick to your ghost stories and stay clear of office lies and gossip. Oh, and while you're at it, take out the trash and leave the history to me."

Obviously done with what he had to say, Mr. Doyle spun about and angrily stalked away.

Frank stood for a moment before he hauled off in the opposite direction from Mr. Doyle.

Gio, Chase, and I looked at each other in total silence before I let out a deep sigh of disappointment. "So much for my pocket watch," I said.

Gio put his head down as if he were ashamed of something. "Sorry, Oliver. I thought Mr. Doyle would help you get it back!"

"It's all right," I replied, but my words couldn't conceal the uneasiness I felt inside. "Let's not think about it right now. What class do you have first?"

"Literature, you?"

"Math," I said with disappointment, since my only friend would not be by my side.

"I've got Professor Wetherby after that, how bout you?" Gio said.

"Yeah, me too!" I said back with more enthusiasm in my voice.

"I'll see you then; it's time for me to get going. Sorry again," Gio said before he limped off.

I watched him go, and I could tell that he felt bad. But he had just been trying to help me by bringing in Mr. Doyle.

Chase tapped me on the shoulder to get my attention. "Don't worry; we'll get that pocket watch back."

Why was this kid involved at all? I wondered. *What was his stake?*

I looked at the new kid with a frown. "You want my watch for yourself?" I questioned.

"Me? No, no. I was trying to help you out. Let me tell you something about me: my name is Chase, and I'm a detective, specializing in the paranormal. Doesn't matter whether it's ghosts, the undead, aliens, or any creatures of the night; I investigate them all. But I don't focus on that kinda stuff exclusively, and right now, I'm into getting your pocket watch back."

I didn't know how to respond to this. "Well... thanks, I guess. My name's Oliver, and—"

"This is a pretty cool school you've got here, Ollie," he

interrupted. "I've been to a few, but this one looks like it has many paranormal happenings here."

These words got my attention. "What do you mean?" I asked curiously.

"Well, for starters," Chase said, "look at the gargoyles perched on the roof. They are a classic example of paranormal activity."

"Uh, those are statues. They, uh, don't, uh, move," I said.

Inside, I was thinking, *How dumb was this kid?*

"Maybe not at this exact moment. But how do you know what happens when you're not looking directly at them? Or at night?" Chase replied. "Besides, they were put here for a reason. Gargoyles are meant to scare away the evil spirits—and where there's smoke, there's fire."

I looked up at the gargoyles on the roof. The giant stone creatures with their dog faces, horns, and wings were exposing sharp granite teeth. Suddenly, they seemed to peer down at me, and not in a friendly way. They seemed ready to spring to life—and attack at any moment.

Chase's words now bothered me. When I was younger, my uncle had told me stories about these stone creatures coming to life, flying down, and snatching up any children who were late for school. After hearing that, I always made it to school on time.

Truth was, the building my school was in was scary—and not because it was old. It… just… had a feeling about it. A feeling as if there were someone watching you, looking over your shoulder.

All of us students knew the stories about the school being haunted, and how the old spirits didn't like the fact that the building had been renovated and expanded. There were countless stories of a gambler ghost clicking his poker chips; a crazy woman who screamed and cried at night; and an unhappy miner who got lost and was buried alive.

There was a mysterious light that went on at night in the school's bell tower, and a face that could be seen looking out of the window there. All these stories had been talked about for years, but it was the story of the dead boy Charlie Hackett—who vowed to have his revenge on the school and drag everyone into the darkness—that totally creeped me out.

"You mean to tell me that because there are gargoyles on this building, spirits and ghosts are also around?" I asked cautiously.

"Yep, and other things too. I wouldn't be surprised if there's a werewolf in the area as well," Chase said in a matter-of-fact voice. "We have a lot of work ahead of us, Ollie."

"*We* do?" I questioned.

"Yep. And it starts with getting your pocket watch back," he said, nodding his head. "Now, let's coordinate our schedules."

Before I knew it, I was wrapped up in his planning—and I had a new friend.

CHAPTER TWO

FIGURES NEVER LIE

CALL IT FATE, coincidence, or both: Chase and I had most of our classes together, starting with dreadful Miss Crabtree's dreadful math class.

I had Miss Crabtree last year, and she was strict—because, as she put it, *"Numbers are strict. There are only two answers to any problem—the correct answer, and the incorrect answer. Numbers are perfect and demand perfection. Figures never lie, and liars always figure, so if you don't study, the numbers will tell on you, and if you guess on your tests, the numbers will tell on you."*

Not only was dreadful Miss Crabtree the strictest teacher in our school, but she was also the youngest. She dressed in the trendiest clothing, with her black hair worn up in a professional style. Sometimes, she wore old-fashioned horned rimmed glasses, which were more for looks than for looking. Miss Crabtree frequently checked her reflection in a small compact silver mirror that she kept inside her always-nearby stylish purse while we were busy completing our assignments.

Miss Crabtree was famous for her ironclad classroom rules: no talking, no whispering, no gum chewing, no food chewing, no drinking, and no thinking outside thoughts. No anything but math—and math only.

Miss Crabtree had a way of squinting at us when she was displeased, sometimes tightening her lips before she spoke. If I didn't know better, I would say that she hated kids. If evidence need be provided, look no farther than the homework she gave out—pure torture.

As I led Chase up the stone stairway to Miss Crabtree's third-floor classroom, I caught his eyes quickly taking note of the school's architecture—carved stone doorways, odd-shaped windows, and red stone walls—and the old photographs and paintings that hung on them.

"Kinda creepy, isn't it?" I asked him.

"What?"

"The school—it's kinda creepy looking, don't ya think?"

"No, it's awesome. I love it."

"Oh," I said, taken aback. "Uh, where'd you move from?"

"From Denver, with my mom and sister Aspyn. My mom wanted us to move away from the city."

Hmmm. Maybe his dad wasn't in the picture either.

"What about your dad?" I asked cautiously but curiously.

"My mom and dad are split up—divorced. He hasn't shown his face in forever. So, I'm the man of the house," Chase said in a proud tone.

I nodded quietly. His life was something like mine.

When we arrived at Miss Crabtree's classroom—her "torture chamber," as I liked to call it—I led Chase towards the back. It's where I always sat. Except Chase stopped and took a seat in the middle of the classroom.

"Chase—back here," I whispered loudly.

"No, we need to be in the middle," he called over as he made himself comfortable. "This way, we are in the thick of things and able to observe everything around us."

His words set me into a panic. The seats we chose today were *critically important* because where one sits on the first day determines where one sits the entire semester.

"But wouldn't it be better in the back, where we can see everything in front of us?" I asked in a, well, *begging* tone.

"Oliver, we have to use all of our senses, not just our eyes. Being in the middle allows us to be in the center of everything."

"And just what are we supposed to be looking for?" I grumbled as I moved up and uneasily took a seat next to him.

"Abnormalities," Chase said, looking around. "Anything out of the ordinary."

I shook my head. The only thing abnormal here was me sitting in the middle of the classroom. I liked to sit in the back where few kids could see my birthmark, and I could keep to myself. Besides, the farther away I was from Miss Crabtree, the better.

Class was about to begin, and as the other students filled the seats around us, I couldn't help but feel as if everyone was staring at me. Well, my birthmark. But since my only friend was Gio, and he wasn't in this class, and no one else here would talk to me, I decided to take my chances with Chase, who had been nice so far.

As the starting bell rang, Miss Crabtree entered the classroom like a fashion model on the runway. She was carrying a briefcase and a cup of coffee. The purse, which was flung over her shoulder, matched her short skirt and jacket.

"Good morning, students," she said in a crisp tone. "Welcome back. I hope all of you kept up on your math skills during the summer break. This year will be much more difficult, so it's important that you study and pay attention during class. Let me remind everyone right now: no horsing around, talking, or daydreaming. You are here to learn, and learn you shall."

She set her coffee down on her desk, plopped her purse on her chair, and opened her briefcase. Pulling out a stack of papers, she walked up to every desk to hand each student one. She looked each of us squarely in the eye as we reached out to take her syllabus.

"Many of you struggled last year, and you may find yourself struggling again if you don't study and pay attention. Numbers don't care if you struggle or how hard you try. *Trying* doesn't count in this class. Two plus two doesn't *try* to be five. The correct answer is four, and nothing else. Only the *correct answers* to the problems given count, and the only way you're going to get the correct answers is to study and pay attention."

Just as Miss Crabtree marched back up to the front of the room to write on the blackboard, the lights in the building flickered. On and off. On and off.

"Oh—not the power," she murmured.

Chase looked at me and said, "Something's happening. Keep alert, Ollie."

Keep alert for what? I looked around the classroom for anything out of the ordinary. *Nope, nothing out of sorts, other than the lights flickering.*

"Mark the time down. This might be some supernatural abnormality," Chase whispered to me.

Mark the time down? Was this kid trying to make some kind of joke since I had lost my watch? After all, he was joking when he called himself a detective this morning—wasn't he… or was he?

Despite this thought, I found myself looking at the wall clock. I opened my journal and jotted down:

Thursday, 8:15 a.m. — math class: Power outage.

I quickly closed my journal up.

Miss Crabtree looked up towards the lights and said under her breath, "Please don't let the air conditioning go out."

On hot dog days like today, air conditioning in this old building wasn't a luxury, but essential for sustaining life. The school's air conditioning units had been running all morning to keep up with the rising sun outside. If the power went out, the air conditioning would go out, and then the school would soon turn into one giant sweatbox—a giant *dark* sweatbox.

This new possibility led me to wonder, *if the power went out, perhaps they would cancel class or the entire school day. After all, we couldn't be expected to learn in the dark, could we?*

This thought gave me hope. I began tightening my jaw and focusing all my will as if I had some kind of supernatural power to force the power out. Suddenly, the lights quit flickering—but stayed on. Miss Crabtree gave a sigh of relief, but the students' sighs were those of disappointment.

I shook my head. *Of course,* I thought to myself. *I wish for something, and the exact opposite thing happens! Just my luck. I should have willed the power to stay on, and then it would have gone out for sure.*

At that moment, a big thud rumbled through the building, and the lights instantly went dark. A groan came from Miss Crabtree, and a cheer arose from the students. The power, along with the air conditioning, was out.

Yes! I thought.

My joy was short-lived as Miss Crabtree moved towards our classroom's four large windows.

"All right, students, let's control ourselves," she said in an annoyed tone. "I'll open the windows to let some light and air in before it gets too hot up here. Open your math books to page twenty and begin reading."

The classroom quieted down to the flipping of pages and

Miss Crabtree's defiant high heels marching to the windows. She unlocked the first window, and after several prying attempts, she wrenched it open with a huff of satisfaction. Heated from the exertion, she took off her jacket, ready for the next battle.

Walking to the second window with more determination, she unlocked it and, widening her stance, gave a hearty grunt as she put all her weight and force behind her to rip it open. However, this window was not stuck shut from years of paint. Well-greased, it sprang up with a thunderous crash. Everyone expected to see glass shatter across the floor, but miraculously it did not break. Quick bursts of laughter floated through the room, only to be quickly silenced by Miss Crabtree's icy glare and pressed lips.

Miss Crabtree carefully examined the third window before she attempted to open it. She gave it a short testing tug, then pulled harder. It did not budge.

The class remained silent with anticipation as she prepared to muster all her strength to force this one open.

A loud hiss echoed throughout the room.

Sssst-oo-pppp.

Miss Crabtree froze and looked over her shoulder. My eyes grew big. I looked at Chase, who was rubbing his chin.

"Did you hear that?" I whispered.

"Um-hmm," Chase confirmed, looking up into the air.

Without warning, a big thud rumbled through the building. The lights flickered back on, followed by the sound of motors whining through the air ducts as cold air hissed into the classroom. Miss Crabtree gave a quick smile and sighed with relief.

"What was that noise—it sounded like a voice?" I whispered to Chase.

"That, Oliver, was evidence," he replied. "Document that. This school seems to be haunted. We'll need to start investigating."

My heart picked up a beat. *Could it be true?* I wondered to myself. *Was this school actually haunted*? I recorded in my journal:

Whispering voice heard during power outage—unknown source.

Now a clicking noise came from outside the hall.

Click-click-click.

A deep voice followed the sound. "Good morning, Miss Crabtree. Mind if I come in?"

Miss Crabtree looked up over her glasses to the figure in the doorway. It belonged to our principal, Principal Sterns.

I always thought that Principal Sterns seemed too young to be a school principal. He was fit and tall—taller than most of the teachers in our school, so maybe that's why he was the boss. He had thick, always perfectly combed, black hair, an angular face, and a square jaw. He wore a suit and tie every day.

"Oh! Good morning to you too, Principal Sterns," dreadful Miss Crabtree said in a high, soft tone. "Please come in. I was just opening the windows to let some air in when the power went out; it can get terribly hot in here. Now that it's back on, we were just about to get started with our lesson."

"Yes, you do look hot in here," he said with a smile.

I guess trying to open that window had made Miss Crabtree even hotter because her face turned bright red. She cleared her throat and changed her stance to a different angle as Principal Sterns, twirling an ink pen between his fingers, walked towards her.

"Class, you all know Principal Sterns," she said.

Of course, everyone knew—and hated—Principal Sterns. He was mean. He never took the side of any student who got in trouble. He was the judge, jury, and executioner for all matters related to student behavior. One time, he suspended a kid for accidentally shooting a rubber band at a teacher, who then spilled her coffee onto her computer, erasing the entire year's class grades—like that was the *kid's* fault?

Principal Sterns stood in the hallway during passing periods, monitoring the students like he was a sheriff, keeping order in a small town. He had a way of making you feel like you did something wrong, even when you didn't.

And that stupid clicking noise he always made with his ink pen, constantly pressing his pen's button in and out? It was *completely* annoying. At least you could always hear him coming, if not smell him. The cologne he drowned himself with had a spicy, musky smell.

My mom didn't let me wear cologne. But I managed to convince her to let me wear deodorant, even though she said I was still too young to need it.

"Well, good morning, students," Principal Sterns said as he gave a head nod towards the class. "How was everyone's summer break?"

"The students are excited about our new year, and especially about math. Isn't that right, students?" Miss Crabtree said with a smile as the big, fat lie came out of her mouth.

I knew for a fact that I *wasn't* excited—and *that* was the correct answer.

Chase held up his hand, saying, "I don't know if I would say I'm 'excited' about math, but I am curious about this power outage. Have you investigated if there's a paranormal cause?"

The class chuckled, and Miss Crabtree's smile turned into a frowning glance.

Principal Sterns cracked a smile. "I can promise you that while the cause is not normal, it is nothing to worry about. And as far as your excitement towards math, well… maybe that will change. Miss Crabtree is an exciting and fabulous teacher," he replied, turning his gaze towards her. "She's fabulous at many things, in fact."

Miss Crabtree must have gotten something in her eye because she started blinking a lot.

Principal Sterns turned back to the class and continued, "I want to assure all of you that we are working on the power outage problem. This is an unusually hot spell we're having, and our air conditioning units are having a hard time keeping up. Plus, it's an unfortunate thing to report to you, but someone has vandalized the electrical panels in the basement, so they are not running efficiently.

"Now, if anyone has information as to the perpetrators of this vandalism, please report it immediately to the main office. Of course, we will keep your identity confidential. We also welcomed anonymous tips. Frank, our facilities manager, has been hard at work fixing the problem that has resulted, so if we experience brief power outages throughout the day, it is no cause for alarm."

Principal Sterns walked back and forth in front of the class, twirling his pen between his fingers. "On another topic, I'm not sure if all of you are aware the President of the United States will be visiting our school next week to recognize one of our students, Ana Rahela Balenovic, for her award-winning national essay."

How could anyone who lived on our planet *not* know that the President was coming to our school? It was the only news all summer long here—about how Ana Rahela Balenovic won a national contest for the best essay on *why she's thankful to be an American.*

It had shocked me to hear the news; her paper wasn't well written. Mine was much better. Heck, she hadn't even done it for literature class—it was for Mr. Doyle's boring history and political science class, and what did that stupid class have to do with writing anyway? Plus, I was sure Mr. Doyle submitted her essay to the contest only because she's his favorite.

"This is a tremendous honor for this school and the community at large. We will have an assembly in the gymnasium for the

President to present this prestigious award to Ana Rahela. The President will also sit in with Ana Rahela during Mr. Doyle's third-period class. There will be television and newspaper reporters here documenting this event, so make sure to dress your best and be on your best behavior. We wouldn't want the Secret Service hauling anyone away, now would we?" he smirked.

Miss Crabtree rolled her eyes at this remark. "I see. Do you have anything else for the class this morning, Principal Sterns?" she said.

I think she wanted to get on with her math lesson.

"Uh… just that I will continue to announce further details of the President's visit in the coming days. Now students, remember to prepare for additional outages, and to show patience while we work on the air conditioning and power issues today. Again, welcome back, students, and study for the future—or the future will be studying you. Thank you, Miss Crabtree, for your class's attention."

Principal Sterns walked out while clicking his pen again.

Click-click-click.

"Class, continue with your assignment. I'll be just a moment," Miss Crabtree announced before she followed Principal Sterns out of the classroom. They started talking in the hallway, and it almost sounded as if they were arguing.

"Oliver," Chase whispered, "can you hear what they are talking about?"

I leaned forward in my chair and cupped my hands behind my ears. I thought I heard them mention Mr. Doyle's name, but I was leaning so far over trying to hear that my desk tipped, knocking my books, papers, and me onto the ground with a loud crash. The class started laughing out loud, bringing Miss Crabtree storming back into the classroom.

Even upside down on the ground, I could see Miss Crabtree's icy stare and frowning lips. I was convinced I would not make it through the day.

When the end-of-class bell rang, I bolted towards the door; I couldn't wait to get out of there. Chase wasn't far behind.

I wasn't sure if it was my imagination or not, but I felt like I could breathe easier in the hallway.

Chase looked down at his schedule, and then at me, asking, "Looks like we've got science class next, right?"

"Yeah, Wetherby's class—he's got a few loose screws, but he's all right."

I didn't mind the role I had taken on with Chase: He was a new kid, and I was the one giving him insights into the classes, teachers, and kids. It made me feel important to have someone listen to me.

"The rumor goes that Wetherby was once a brilliant professor at a big-time university like Harvard or something until he freaked out. He got all crazy about some theory he developed," I explained to Chase as we walked down the hall. "He became obsessed with patterns of numbers, which he believed held some hidden code to the universe. His coworkers laughed him out of his job and ruined his career or something like that. Now he teaches science here. Whatever you do, don't ask him questions about his theories. He'll turn on the *extra-boring switch*—as if his normal class lecture isn't boring enough."

Chase tapped me on the shoulder and pointed down the hall. "Hey, isn't that the guy who confiscated your pocket watch this morning?"

I looked in the direction he was pointing and saw Mr. Doyle walking down the hallway. My heart gave a jump in my chest, and I said enthusiastically, "Maybe he's cooled down now, and I could ask him for my—"

A high-pitched shout coming from behind interrupted me.

"Mr. Doyle! Mr. Doyle, wait!"

I turned to see our art teacher, Mrs. Huntley, running down the hall. She was moving so fast that she practically trampled over us.

Middle-aged and slightly plump, Mrs. Huntley had short, stick-straight reddish hair and bright blue eyes that twinkled when she smiled. The color of her hair complemented her plump rosy cheeks.

Mr. Doyle paused and looked over his shoulder before ducking down his long neck and head as if trying not to be seen by her.

"Charles! I see you! Wait for me," she chided.

"Oh, Mildred," Mr. Doyle said, acting startled. "What a pleasant surprise."

As we moved down the hallway towards our next class, Chase and I remained within the earshot of the two of them.

"Please, Charles, it's really not a surprise. I work here, remember? And it's not pleasant either. Did you think I wouldn't find out?" she said in a low voice, full of anger.

"I… I… what do you mean?" Mr. Doyle said back.

"I know you used your influence to stop production on the project! How *could* you? You know how much this meant to me. After all the years we've been friends, and I've loaned you so much money too! Is *this* how you repay me?"

"Please, Mildred, I can explain! And actually, I was going to repay you today. But… well, you see, I *should have* won. But I received bad information, and those responsible will—"

"My dear friend, *when* are you going to learn that *you* are the one responsible, and not to mess with the dark side? Look at you! You've lost your soul, and now I'm sure you're in even more debt and out of options." Mrs. Huntley shook her head. "But what I don't understand is your obstruction of this monumental project. Tell me, what is it you're afraid of? Is it something alien that frightens you? There's no toxic threat to the environment, and everything will return to its natural state when it's over. Can't you see this is not just about the transformation of the earth, but of minds as well—the minds of our youth?!"

"It's complicated, Mildred. It wasn't me who—"

"Oh then, who else? Tell me, was it *her?* Is *she* the reason you stood in the way?"

"No, of course not! Leave her out of this," Mr. Doyle said defensively.

"My dear friend, if only you could have opened your mind. We have been friends for so many years! But if this project doesn't happen as a result of you… well, then, don't worry about repaying the money you owe me, for you will be dead to me, Charles," Mrs. Huntley bluntly said before she stalked off.

Mr. Doyle was left looking somewhat stupefied. Shaking his head, he pulled out my pocket watch from his pocket and stared at it before walking off with a distant expression on his face.

I said dismally, "I guess now's not the time to be asking him for my watch back."

"Wow, that exchange was interesting," Chase said. "Oliver, you'd better record the details of that conversation! Whatever this guy's involved with is not good."

Why write all that down? I thought. *So, they argued—people argue all the time. Nothing weird or interesting about that.* I wasn't sure if Chase was serious, but he was my new friend, and I didn't have many, so I did like he asked.

Thursday 8:55 a.m. — school hallway:

- *Mrs. Huntley seen arguing with Mr. Doyle about canceled project and money he owes her.*
- *Mrs. Huntley said not to be afraid of something alien, and the earth will be transformed along with the minds of youth with no toxic effects on the environment.*
- *She threatens Mr. Doyle, saying, he'll be dead to her if the project doesn't happen because of him.*
- *Mr. Doyle said it's not his fault.*

Somewhere from behind me, an obnoxious voice cried out, "Hey, where's my watch, Four Eyes? With Freak Face here, I can't see it. Miles, get out the magnifying glass."

We turned to see Johnny Ricker and Miles Webster walking towards us.

Miles pretended to pull a magnifying glass from his back pocket and look through it.

"Wait a minute—I see some barf. Oh, my mistake; that's not barf, it's your freaky face! Ha-ha-ha!" Miles laughed at me.

Chase nudged me to head down the hall. I started forward.

"Hey, where you going, Four Eyes? I'm talk'n to you!" Johnny sneered as he stretched out his chest. "You think that little stunt you pulled this morning was funny?"

"Are you talking about the watch I won?" Chase asked.

Steam puffs came out of Johnny's ears when he shouted, "*You cheated!*"

Chase shrugged casually. "Seeing as how Mr. Doyle has the watch now, I'm willing to forget about it. Not sure that the principal is going to feel the same way, though."

"Listen, Four Eyes, if you two even think about telling Principal Sterns that I took that watch, you're gonna have four black eyes!"

"Well, unless you mean to give me sunglasses, technically only my two eyes would be black," Chase said as he nonchalantly pointed to each of his eyes. "One plus one equals two, so perhaps you should ask Miss Crabtree to help you with your math skills."

Johnny's face grew as red as his hair, and he made a fist while cocking his arm back.

Click-click-click.

The noise came from behind Johnny. It was loud, and it cut through the din of the students talking as they moved along the hallway.

It was the reason that Johnny lowered his fist.

"Are we having trouble finding our classrooms, students?" Principal Sterns asked Johnny in a slow, measured tone.

"No, sir," Johnny answered back.

Principal Sterns gave him a hard look.

Chase spoke up. "Since I'm new here, Johnny was kind enough to tell me the school rules and help Oliver and me with our schedules." Chase looked down at his schedule. "Looks like I have science class next! Can't wait."

"Ah… yeah. Us too," Johnny said, glancing at Chase. "We'll show you where the classroom is."

Principal Sterns raised his eyebrows. "Well, I'm glad to see students helping students. Hurry along then."

Awkwardly, we walked off under the suspicious gaze of Principal Sterns.

CHAPTER THREE

THE MAD SCIENTIST

PROFESSOR WETHERBY'S SCIENCE classroom looked like it had last year: one big disorganized mess. It lived up to the vision of a mad scientist's laboratory.

Scribbled equations covered the chalkboard; microscopes, electronic equipment, test tubes, and beakers with wires sprouting from their tops were scattered on tables. Mounds of papers and books formed a barricade around the top of the professor's desk.

Wetherby looked the part of a mad scientist too. He was an older gentleman with wavy white hair, a wrinkled face, and a pale white complexion. Since he constantly ran his fingers through his hair, it was a complete mess most of the time.

He always wore a bow tie—*seriously*, a bow tie? Most days too, he sported a jacket of some sorts—a suit jacket, or a lab coat jacket, even though I always thought he belonged in a straitjacket.

Wetherby would always take his jacket off during class and

roll up his sleeves if we were about to perform some messy experiment. He had a habit of chewing on his pen or pencil, and if he were really involved in some distant thought, he'd crunch it in his mouth. Sometimes, the ink of the pen, or the lead from the pencil, would stain his lips.

"Wow!" Chase said as he entered the classroom and looked about in amazement. "Look at this guy's equipment!"

Chase looked as if he was about to drool with pleasure.

What's the big deal? I thought to myself. *It's science class.* Science class might be cool if we actually did something exciting, like blow things up. But most of the time we had to listen to Professor Wetherby's drawn-out lectures on gravity, space, and time: *Blah, blah, blah.* Sometimes I think he forgot we were kids, not college students.

"Are you kidding me? Look," Chase said as he pointed to a table by the professor's desk. "He has an EMF meter!"

"A *what* meter?" I asked, puzzled.

"Electromagnetic field meter. It's used in paranormal investigations to detect ghosts," Chase said proudly.

"It detects ghosts? How?"

"Ghosts give off an electromagnetic charge. With an EMF meter, we could locate ghosts around this school. All paranormal investigators have them."

"Okay… awesome!" I said, trying to sound like I understood what he was talking about. But honestly, I had no idea, and I turned my attention to Gio, who was waving to me.

I was glad to see Gio in class. He was already sitting near the back, where he was supposed to be, and saving me a seat at his table. I nodded to him before I moved in his direction. Chase quietly followed after me.

Johnny Ricker, with Miles in tow, was finding a seat at a table on the far side of the classroom.

Gio gave me a smile as Chase and I walked up to his table.

"By the way, Chase, Gio is one of my best buds. Remember Gio from this morning?"

"Sure. Gio, nice work getting that teacher while I distracted that turd. I knew all along you could make it happen," Chase replied.

Gio smiled. "Yeah, no problem. I hate Ricker."

I understood what they were saying. When Chase saw Johnny taking my pocket watch this morning, he grabbed Gio, who was walking by, then told him to find a teacher while he delayed Johnny, and that teacher just so happened to be Mr. Doyle.

Chase mumbled, "I was hoping that Ricker kid would end up being the one in trouble. Looks like we've got to move to phase two now."

He said it as if we had a plan. The problem was, I didn't know what that plan was.

Class was starting, and since Gio had saved a spot for me, I plopped down beside him. But since the tables in Professor Wetherby's classroom were designed for two students each, Chase now had to sit with someone else.

I motioned for Chase to sit at the table in front of us. There was an empty seat beside a skinny black kid with large glasses and perfect clothing—Eduard.

Chase asked Eduard if he was saving the seat. Eduard turned his head slowly with his nose up, and ever so slightly gestured—no.

Eduard always made me chuckle inside because it appeared he went out of his way to show the rest of us how sophisticated he was. His top-notch clothing and arrogant tone in his voice reinforced to everyone that he came from money and that we, the common people he was forced to deal with, were beneath him.

Eduard prided himself as *the* smartest student in school—straight A's. He was partly right: No one in the school knew more about computers than he did. Sometimes he'd help me with my homework and let me copy answers from his math assignments, all the while lecturing me, *"Oliver, success comes with a price, and the payment is hard work and effort."* When he did so, his voice always rang with a know-it-all tone.

However, my writing skills were better than his. If I were to write a short story, he would offer to review it for mistakes before I turned it in. But after he did, he would simply declare, "Job well done" when he handed it back to me, unable to come up with any mistakes. Sometimes, he'd ask for me to read his stories, which I was happy to do, but I was always careful about giving him any constructive criticism. I didn't think he would take it too well.

Many kids resented Eduard, either because of the way he acted or because they were jealous of his money. I never had any of those feelings towards him. I felt Eduard was a really good guy. Even though he seemed to talk down to me, he talked that way to everyone, so I never took offense. I guess you could say we were friends—not close friends, but friends.

Professor Wetherby cleared his throat in the front of the class. "Good morning, ladies and gentlemen. For those of you who don't know me, I am Professor Wetherby," he said right before he turned to write his name on the small bit of empty space remaining on the blackboard. "I will be your teacher for all branches of science since I am the only faculty member here capable and qualified in teaching all degrees of science."

Wetherby was the only teacher at school who wanted to be called "Professor," probably because he imagined he was still teaching at a university. He had a slight English accent and somewhat pretentious tone—similar to Eduard's. His command of vocabulary was impressive, and he liked to hear himself talk. He often rambled, losing his train of thought as he stared outward into space or some other dimension that no one else could see. It kinda seemed to me that he wasn't in touch with the world—the real world, that is.

The Professor wasn't up on current events, like what movies were playing. He knew nothing about new music, video games, or even TV shows. I often wondered if he knew what day of the week it was. His mind was constantly preoccupied with other thoughts, as if he was working on something bigger than what he was teaching at the time.

"I will take attendance. When I call your name, please respond," he said with a pencil sticking in his mouth.

He went through the roll call and then pivoted to the blackboard.

"This semester, we will build upon the lessons you've learned and advance your overall understanding of the varying disciplines of science. On Mondays and Wednesdays, we will study the intricacies of biology. On Tuesdays and Thursdays, we will tackle various properties of the cosmos, physics, and the mysteries that surround them—my specialty. On Fridays, we will explore the discipline of chemistry."

Professor Wetherby began walking back and forth with his hands clasped behind his back; this was his trademark style.

"Now many of you who have taken my classes in the past will have some measure of understanding of the principles and style taught, and for those who have not, you will quickly come up to speed. Note-taking is *not* optional," he said, stopping to look intently at the class. "It is *essential*."

He resumed walking. "We will explore some of the theories of the universe, their properties, and," he said, pausing, "*their possibilities*. Today, we will begin with cosmology. I encourage all of you to take notes as I give a brief overview of our topic."

He turned back to the chalkboard, and, finding another bit of empty space, wrote, *"THE UNIVERSE."*

"Now, this is a broad topic. In fact, there is no other topic with such infinite possibilities," he said, chuckling out loud.

The class remained silent as we all wondered what he was laughing at.

The Professor cleared his throat and became serious again. "Now, speaking of infinity, who knows its symbol?"

The earth stopped as Johnny Ricker raised his hand.

"Um… Mr. Ricker?" Professor Wetherby called out in surprise.

Johnny smiled. "It looks like the number eight, only sideways."

Professor Wetherby raised his eyebrows in disbelief. "Correct," he said.

I sat silently in shock, along with the entire class. Never in all the years of classes I had with Johnny did I ever see him raise his hand, let alone get a question right when a teacher called on him. Johnny Ricker's stupidity was world-renowned. He had more Fs than fifty flying flocks of falcons.

When Professor Wetherby turned around to draw the symbol on the chalkboard, I watched Johnny turn over his notebook to show Miles a sticker underneath. I narrowed my eyes until I could see that it was an Infinity Snowboards sticker—with the very infinity symbol now on the blackboard.

Of course. That's how Johnny knew the answer. I could breathe easier now that the Earth really wasn't about to explode.

"Infinity means 'without end.' It's something that goes on forever and ever, never stopping. Our universe—outer space—expands infinitely outward and inward," Wetherby said with a dramatic flourish of his hands.

Everyone began writing down the definition of infinity in their notebooks. I wrote down my own definition.

Definition of infinity: this class.

The Professor resumed pacing with his hands behind his back. "Yes, I know it's hard to wrap your mind around, but as far as we can see out, we can see as far in. These two theories will converge at times as we journey down our path of discovery." He stopped and looked at the blank stares coming from the class. "Questions so far?"

Chase raised his hand. "Your EMF meter—you must use that for paranormal experimentation?"

"What?" the Professor said, a bit startled as he looked around the room. Then he spotted the piece of equipment Chase was talking about. "Oh, my tri-field meter—of course," he said as he walked over to the meter and picked it up. "We use this in a variety of experiments involving electromagnetism, which we will conduct during this semester. Impressive you recognized it."

"Any paranormal investigator would," Chase replied. "Are we going to be experimenting with supernatural mysteries?"

"Mysteries of the universe are only mysterious because we do not yet understand them. Our task, ladies and gentlemen, and our quest, is to investigate and uncover the truths of this universe."

Oh great, I thought. *I told Chase not to ask questions. Wetherby could go on for hours now.*

Gio raised his hand, asking, "Are we going to be learning about black holes?"

"Ah… yes. Although the science community has varying opinions on gravity," the Professor answered.

Gio followed his question up with another. "Is it true that the gravitational pull from a black hole is so strong that not even light can escape?"

"True—it's called an 'event horizon.' Some believe black holes are doorways to other dimensions," Wetherby said as his eyes sparkled. "Gravity, ladies, and gentlemen, is the all-powerful force of the universe."

I had a question I wanted to ask now: *Would the gravitational pull from a black hole be powerful enough to suck in Johnny Ricker and hold him there forever?*

Chase raised his hand again, and Wetherby nodded to him. This is what excited Wetherby: questions about science and his knowledge of the universe.

"What about aliens—are we going to talk about them?" Chase asked.

"Aliens?" Professor Wetherby responded, looking as if someone had poured a bucket of cold water on him. His happy train ride of science questions had come off the tracks. "Well, umm… no. While in theory, the possibility of other life forms in the universe does exist, in class we will explore the scientific properties and nature of the universe itself, from the evidence that science has given us."

Chase held out his hands in appeal. "What about the alien abductions of humans? I'm sure there's evidence we could study."

"I admire your enthusiasm, but the idea of aliens traveling through space from distant galaxies is quite improbable. It would require years of travel at the speed of light," the Professor said.

Gio kept the conversation going by saying, "I saw a movie about traveling through another dimension by going through a black hole."

"That is possible only if the aliens could survive the gravitational forces of the black hole itself," the Professor replied. "I do not mean to stifle your theories, but there are basic laws of physics that we all must obey—aliens and humans alike. And that, ladies and gentlemen, is precisely where we shall begin today," he said with a smile.

Now that Professor Wetherby had everyone's attention, it was time for him to put us all to sleep.

"When we think about infinity, we must ask the question, 'When and where was the beginning?' Which then leads to the question, 'When and where is the end?' With infinity, there is no beginning, and there is no end. But how can this be, you ask? It is an age-old question *'Which came first—the chicken or the egg?'* Philosophers have spent centuries debating over this. Does one event cause another?"

The Professor erased an equation so he could write "CAUSALITY" on the blackboard in large letters.

"The question is: are there random happenings? Or does one event precipitate another, and yet another?"

The Professor walked over to a beaker of water sitting on his desk.

"If I were to drop this blue piece of chalk into this beaker of water," he said as he dropped the piece of chalk into the water and it changed color, "the liquid will turn blue. The water did not change color on its own, or by accident, but because of my action of dropping the chalk. It's cause and effect at work. It stands to reason that if one event is caused by another, then there are no such things as random happenings. And if there are no random happenings, then there must be a blueprint in place, a code for what is to happen next—a code that, if unlocked, contains all the answers to the future."

The Professor walked back to his blackboard and pointed to some long equation in chalk.

"If one knows all the factors leading up to an event, one can then formulate an equation to predict the outcome—thus predicting the future. Just as I predicted, the water would change its color to blue once I dropped the blue piece of chalk into it. Nothing happens on its own. Cause and effect, ladies and gentlemen—*causality.*"

He continued pacing in front of the blackboard and chewing on the end of his pen.

"Ladies and gentlemen, you may find yourself ostracized, laughed at, and ridiculed for thinking differently. Maybe it was because you asked the *wrong* question—a question that approached a problem unconventionally. Or, perhaps because you didn't follow what is believed to be the *right* way of thinking—not following the established premise. Pursuing your own theories not aligned with those of your peers comes, at times, with great peril.

Here, I began drifting in and out of consciousness. Wetherby now was rambling on about Einstein and some theory of relatives. What he was saying couldn't have been important, anyhow. It made no sense to study family in science class.

Finally, the alarm clock went off. Uh, the end-of-class bell.

As the class emptied out, I said to Chase, "See what I mean? Wetherby's a crack."

He shrugged his shoulders. "I didn't think he was too bad. Besides, all that equipment in there—microscopes, telescopes, test tubes—might come in handy with our paranormal investigations."

"I guess so," I said, nodding my head as though I agreed. But at this point, I didn't quite know what to make of Chase. Either he was a cool kid sarcastically making fun of things, or he was just a big nerd with a big imagination. Most boys our age were interested in girls, music, movies, skateboarding, and sports. But Chase kept talking about paranormal investigations—not exactly the kinda stuff the cool kids were interested in.

As I shouldered my backpack, I said to Gio, "Well, Chase and I have Mr. Doyle's history class now—how about you?"

"No, I have Miss Crabtree this period. How was she this morning?" Gio answered.

"Strict and dreadful as ever. She came up with new rules this year," I huffed.

"Well, I better not be late. See you at lunch?" Gio said.

"Yeah," I smiled. "We'll save you a seat."

When Gio turned to go in the opposite direction, Chase tapped him on his shoulder. "See ya later, G."

Gio half-smiled back at Chase before walking off down the hall. I could see that it bothered him that I was hanging out with Chase. Before this semester, Gio and I had almost every class together; now, it was Chase who was in most of my classes. I'm sure Gio was feeling left out.

As Chase and I made our way to the next class, I noticed something else: All the girls we walked passed were quickly, and sometimes not so quickly, giving Chase the up-and-down glance. When I looked back, I could see them whispering to each other and giggling. Chase had all the girls gossiping; maybe they thought he was cool, or maybe they thought he was strange.

"Hey, I've got to use the bathroom," I said.

I only kinda needed to go. Really, I wanted to check my hair in the mirror since the girls were looking our way.

"Yeah—go ahead," Chase said, his eyes fixated in the distance. "I've got something I need to take care of. I'll meet you in class and save you a seat."

"You sure you don't want to wait for me?" I asked. I tried to see what he was looking at, but there was just a hallway full of kids shuffling about to their lockers and classes. "Do you know where the room is?"

"I'll find it. See you there," he said abruptly, then walked away without even looking over at me first.

I suddenly didn't feel the need to use the bathroom anymore. I wanted to follow him. But I'd look insecure and needy if I just went wherever he went, so I went to the bathroom anyhow.

It's not as though we had a lot of time during passing periods for him to make a new friend anyway, and besides, who cares if he did, I told myself.

I was quick in the bathroom, checking my hair in the mirror, and not giving my birthmark any time to taunt me. Flying out of the bathroom, I looked around. Chase had disappeared, and the hallway was emptying of kids who were shuffling into class.

Did he get lost trying to find the classroom? I wondered. *Or was he already in there saving me a seat?*

I know it had only been two classes, but I felt a bit lost without my new friend. I looked down the hall once more for Chase before shrugging and entering Mr. Doyle's classroom.

My mind shifted to my task of convincing Mr. Doyle that this morning was just one big misunderstanding—and that visiting Principal Sterns' office after school would be unnecessary.

CHAPTER FOUR

HISTORY REPEATS ITSELF

I HADN'T TAKEN more than a few steps into the classroom when I saw it: my great-grandfather's pocket watch in Mr. Doyle's hand. He was fiddling with it, but then he placed it on his desk. I stared at the watch as he turned his back to me, engrossed in a conversation he was having on his phone.

My mind became enamored with the opportunity this presented: *Could I simply walk by and put it in my pocket?* Mr. Doyle might not realize it was gone until after class—and then I would be off the hook. It was my watch anyway, so it's not as if I would be stealing it.

After all, the only reason I had brought the pocket watch to school was to show Mr. Doyle. I knew Mr. Doyle prided himself on his collection of antiques and his historical knowledge of them—so surely, an old relic like my great-grandfather's watch would bring him great joy to see. And yes, maybe Jessica Blake's family broach from the Civil War, which had impressed him enough to help her grade last semester, had something to do with my motives.

Since Mr. Doyle already had my great-grandfather's pocket watch and had time to admire it, perhaps he might end his call, and now give it back to me with a big smile saying, *"Wow, thank you, Oliver, for showing me this precious family artifact. This has made my day, and please let me know if I can help you, or your grade, during this next semester."*

But it was apparent that my pocket watch hadn't had that effect on him.

Mr. Doyle was walking back and forth behind his desk, arguing on his mobile phone with someone—someone who was making him furious. His face grew red between sentences, and he clenched his jaw; I knew instantly this wasn't the time for him to offer me some praise and return the watch.

Besides, Mr. Doyle seemed completely oblivious to any of the students swarming into the class. He was totally focused on his conversation.

"Yes, I know, but you know I don't have those kinds of resources!" he said to the person on the other end of the phone.

He tried to muffle the volume of his voice, but I could hear an intense note in it. His long fingers swept through his hair that had been combed back so neatly before—now it was a long, tangled mess. He had black marks all over his forehead, too.

The class chatter quieted as Mr. Doyle's voice got louder. He continued in pieces, "I can't do that!" and, "No!" Those utterances were followed by, "You don't understand!" and then finally, "I can't talk right now; I've got a class. We'll meet later."

The bell rang, and Mr. Doyle ended his phone conversation. He looked down at his desk, picked up the pocket watch, and looked up to notice me standing near his desk. He raised his eyebrows.

"Oliver, are you going to sit down, or might you be teaching the class today?" he asked softly.

The class chuckled. I had been lost in the fantasy of retrieving my pocket watch, and I had forgotten to take a seat.

"Uh... yeah, sorry," I said.

I turned to sit. The classroom was now full, except for only two seats. Scanning the faces for Chase, I spotted him nowhere. One of the empty seats was in the front, next to Jax. This was fate—a perfect opportunity. I hadn't seen her since this morning's episode with Johnny, and I had never thanked her. Destiny was bringing us together now. My heart beat faster, adrenaline rushing through me.

My birthmark, however, had different plans, and instead dragged me, kicking and screaming inside, towards the other empty seat near the back. The one time I wanted to sit in the front, my birthmark wouldn't allow me to. I cursed my birthmark, said goodbye to my opportunity with Jax, and took the other seat.

This seat was behind, wouldn't you know, Ana Rahela Balenovic. This was more like my luck: Ana Rahela was Mr. Doyle's favorite student, and the national essay competition winner, as I mentioned before. She had medium-short brown hair, big brown eyes, and a big mouth—yes, I'm serious; she had a big mouth. She spoke with a slight accent, being from another country. But beyond that, she was just annoying. I mean, with that three-name thing, *Ana Rahela Balenovic,* as if one name wasn't good enough. How about just plain *Ana?* Or even *Ana Balenovic?*

Mr. Doyle shuffled through some papers before producing an attendance sheet. He cleared his throat and began calling names.

"Ahbrea Ames?"

"Here," a voice squeaked.

"Kelly Anderson?"

"Here," said another voice.

He paused, and with a smile cracking his face, happily sang out, "Ana Rahela Balenovic?"

"Present!" Ana Rahela quickly answered, thrusting her hand into the air.

'Present?' *What's wrong with, 'Here!' like everyone else?*

Probably she couldn't wait to hear all three of her names called out.

Mr. Doyle was about to call out the next name when Chase slid in through the doorway.

"Excuse me?" Mr. Doyle quipped, annoyed.

"Whew! Thought I was going to miss this class," Chase said. He straightened up, came to a stop, and looked around the room before catching my eye.

I shrugged my shoulders; obviously, there wasn't a seat around me since he wasn't here before me.

Chase calmly walked over to the empty seat in the front next to Jax, saying, "It's tough both working a job and going to school at the same time."

"And you are?" asked Mr. Doyle.

"Chase Sullivan—new kid."

"Ah, yes—the charlatan from this morning," Mr. Doyle observed.

"No, actually, I'm from Denver, Colorado," Chase answered as he casually sat down next to the most beautiful girl in the world.

"Well, please see to it, Mr. Sullivan, that you make it to class on time from now on; otherwise, you will be marked absent."

"I'll do my best," Chase nodded.

"I certainly hope you're not working during school hours," Mr. Doyle said, sounding concerned.

Chase held out his hands. "Mysteries of this world never take time off, so neither can I. But this job was just a case of some kid forgetting his locker combination." He proudly folded his arms and looked over at Jax. "Quick work of my services," he boasted.

The class giggled, and I could see Jax rolling her eyes.

Mr. Doyle shook his head, quickly finished roll call, and began the class. "Students, this is an exciting year. The President of the United States is coming to visit our school and recognize Ana Rahela Balenovic for her essay!"

Mr. Doyle beamed like a ridiculously proud father.

Enough already, I thought. *How many times are we going to have to hear about this? The next thing you know, the school will be selling copies of her autographed essay in the lunchroom—and they would sell zero, by the way.*

Chase raised his hand. "Do you think the Secret Service will come with him?"

"Well, of course, they travel with him everywhere," Mr. Doyle answered.

"What kind of guns do you think they have?" Chase countered.

Mr. Doyle frowned. "I'm sure they have the very best. No need to worry about them. And you shouldn't be interested in guns anyway."

Isaac Steininger, a smart-aleck kid in our neighborhood, sarcastically blurted out, "They're not supposed to bring guns into schools. So, I guess they'll have to wait outside."

Blake Williams asked, "What about grenades? They'll probably have grenades."

"And Chinese throwing stars!" Jack Thompson added.

"Chinese throwing stars are used by assassins, not by the Secret Service," Chase corrected.

"That's enough, Class!" Mr. Doyle hollered, the redness returning to his face. "The focus should not be on what type of weapons the Secret Service carries with them, but that one of our gifted students will be recognized by the President."

Mr. Doyle walked by each student's desk while handing out a paper on the history of the Presidency. Each kid looked at his or her copy funny, puzzled, or disgusted—and when I got mine, I realized why. There were black smudge marks and fingerprints on the tops or corners, and sometimes through the print of the handouts.

Where did he get these copies—out of the trash? Was it grease? Dirt? Whatever it was, Mr. Doyle seemed like he didn't notice or care.

"Read through this handout on the history of the Presidency, and answer the questions on the back," he said. "This will not count towards your grade. It's merely to see how much you know, or think you know."

I looked over the handout—three pages of boring historical babble. In front of me, Ana Rahela Balenovic was pouring over the papers like she couldn't get enough of it. *I bet they wrote this handout together,* I thought.

I just wanted this class to be over with, so I could talk with Mr. Doyle about my great-grandfather's pocket watch. I kept looking at him sitting behind his desk; he was holding the pocket watch, staring at it as if it had hypnotized him. He rubbed the back of it with his thumb—and that's when it hit me.

The smudge marks on the papers were from the tarnish on the watch. He had been rubbing it the entire time he was on the phone, not realizing the impossible stains it left on one's fingers, not to mention clothes, papers, walls, and whatever else your hands came in contact with. It was the explanation for the black marks on Mr. Doyle's forehead.

I would be doing him a service by taking it off his hands before it stained anything else, like the upholstery in his classic yellow car. The car was his pride and joy, and he had spent a ton of money and time to restore it to its original condition. He parked it far away from the other teacher's cars in the faculty parking lot just to keep it safe from scratches.

Of course, Ana Rahela couldn't see fit to keep her foreign-accented mouth shut. She turned to me and whispered, "I have all the Presidents memorized. I spent all summer studying them. I can help you out if you want."

Of course, she studied them all summer long; she had nothing better to do. I spent the summer doing more productive things, like reading, writing, and practicing the deadly art of kung fu.

"I think I'll be okay," I said back.

I read over the handout and took the quiz on the back, then handed it in. Mr. Doyle graded the papers on the spot and handed them back.

Mr. Doyle smiled while giving Ana Rahela Balenovic her paper. She turned it so I could see her perfect one-hundred percent correct test score. *She wouldn't be so smug if Mr. Doyle wasn't here,* I thought.

Mr. Doyle didn't smile while giving me my paper. I got eighty percent—eighty percent wrong. I failed. Anna Smarty Pants Rahela looked over her shoulder at me and raised her eyebrows.

I shrugged my shoulders at her and said, "He said it doesn't count; it was just to see how much we knew. I didn't even try. I took this test with my eyes closed just to see if I could do it."

The problem was, I did try. And x-ray vision wouldn't have helped me.

"Now, students, we have this great honor of the President's visit next week, thanks to Ana Rahela Balenovic's hard work and effort." Mr. Doyle paused to smile at his most precious student. "We will prepare for this historic event by studying the office of the Presidency, its history, and the men who have occupied this highest office in the land. Please take the time to study and put forth your best effort. As you can see through Ana Rahela Balenovic's example, hard work and determination can achieve anything."

Ana—*I'm So Proud*—Rahela—*Smug*—Balenovic sat tall in her chair, smiling with her big mouth.

Mr. Doyle continued, "You must make yourself the strongest possible person you can be! Self-reliance is what this country was built on." His smile disappeared, and he began to take long strides with his long legs, back and forth in front of the class as he continued to lecture. "There is no substitute for hard work, no shortcuts. Rolling the dice to get ahead, in an effort to get rich quick, will only put you in the poor house."

The class sat silently, watching our once-calm, always boring teacher now raising his voice with emotional tones. As he walked over to his desk to pick up a copy of the handout he had just given us, I heard someone whisper over my shoulder. I couldn't understand what he or she said, and I turned to see who it was. But no one was speaking to me.

Was someone playing tricks on me? Was it my imagination? Was I falling asleep? I know I had been under a lot of stress, but I didn't need to be imagining voices now.

Just then, the lights flickered. Everyone began looking around—except for Mr. Doyle, who was in the middle of a rant.

"Some of you took the time to read and understand this handout, answering the questions correctly. Some of you did not, relying on the advice of others or copying answers from the person next to you—perhaps to your advantage—or disadvantage."

The light seemed to pulse with the same frantic energy coming from Mr. Doyle. His eyes flashed white and then dark again—*and so did the lights.* It was as his energy controlled if the lights!

Our once docile, dull, and drawn-out history teacher lashed out in quick and passionate tones, the veins in his head and forehead pulsating and throbbing as he talked. *Has he gone mad?* I thought.

"Relying on other's work doesn't always work out in your favor. What if they're wrong? Then what? I ask you, who's the greater fool—the one who acts the fool, or the one *who listens to* the fool?"

His outburst slowly subsided, and so did the flickering of the lights.

The class sat in frightened silence as Mr. Doyle picked up my great-grandfather's pocket watch off his desk and rubbed it while saying in a depressed voice, "We often think that if one thing, *just one thing*, fell into place, then the rest of our plans would work out perfectly. However, when things go wrong, who's to blame? Was it that one piece that didn't fall into place? Or was it the poor decision to rely on that one piece in the first place?"

He looked back over his now lost classroom of students. "No one can predict the future—no one! No one."

He set the watch back down and ran his long-blackened fingers over his long forehead, leaving long black marks. "Having something and losing it is much worse than not having something to begin with—remember that."

We all sat motionless—silently staring at our history teacher, who was now wiping the sweat from his smudged brow. He mumbled a few words to himself and then looked back to the class as if catching us spying on him. "Well, what are you all waiting for?" he asked with surprise. "Open your books and get reading—there's no time to lose!"

Textbooks flew open as we all flipped to the pages written on the blackboard. No one wanted to reignite his anger.

Mr. Doyle sat back down behind his desk. Picking up the pocket watch, he began mumbling, "Just as Santayana said, *those who cannot remember the past are condemned to repeat it.*" He continued fiddling with my pocket watch while staring at it.

When the end of class bell rang, it was time to plead my case. Gathering my books, I walked towards his desk.

The intercom rang out, ***Mr. Doyle, please contact the office—Mr. Doyle.***

Mr. Doyle looked up at the ceiling and muttered, "What now?"

The news seemed to agitate him. His latest bad mood made me hesitate, but I decided I needed to try. After all, the worst he could say was "no."

I moved forward towards his desk, but then Jax walked by me. The sight of her caused me to stop and forget everything around me. She was so beautiful and smelled like flowers; I could watch her all day long. *Why didn't I take that seat next to her?*

Just then, Mr. Doyle yelled towards the doorway, "Wetherby! Wetherby! Stop! I need to talk with you!"

Professor Wetherby glanced in at Mr. Doyle from the hallway, but then turned and hurried in the opposite direction. He was acting as if he didn't hear his name being called.

Mr. Doyle jerked his head high as if a bee had stung him, threw some papers together, and stormed out the classroom with my pocket watch in hand.

"Mr. Doyle," I hollered. He ignored my call, so I blurted out again desperately, "Mr. Doyle!"

He glanced back, put one finger in the air to signify *just one minute,* and dashed after Professor Wetherby. Chase was by my side as we followed him.

Mr. Doyle caught up with the Professor, and they began a heated argument right in the middle of the hallway. Chase and I watched and listened to them from a short distance.

"This is your fault!" Mr. Doyle yelled. "*You* said it would work!"

"I said there were no guarantees," Professor Wetherby corrected, shaking his head back and forth. "Only a high degree of probability."

"You and your irresponsible equations. Do you have any idea what you've cost me? Of course you don't, you fool. I should have never listened to you. What am I supposed to do now?" Mr. Doyle spat out.

"Unfortunately, I don't have a remedy," Wetherby said in a sober tone.

"No, of course not—why would you have a remedy?" Mr. Doyle flung his long arms high into the air. "You only have the poison!"

Mr. Doyle stormed off through the hallway, leaving Professor Wetherby chewing on the end of a pen.

Chase whispered to me, "And so the plot thickens—better document that conversation. More people with more problems for Mr. Doyle."

"I guess so," I muttered back. This interaction hadn't helped my cause, and I began to realize that my visit to Principal Sterns' office was inevitable.

Out of the corner of my eye, I saw Johnny and Miles walking in our direction. "Come on, let's get out of here," I said as I started rushing down the hallway. "Gym class is this way."

CHAPTER FIVE
THE DARKNESS

OUR GYMNASIUM WAS one of the newest additions to the school, built with the money donated by a former student who was now a professional basketball player.

The gym was set apart from the main building and, from the outside, resembled a giant aircraft hangar. Inside was a large space with bleachers on both sides of the center floor we used for a basketball court. We also used it as a running track when the weather outside was bad. Climbing ropes hung from the ceiling on the north side of the space next to a fifty-foot-high climbing wall. Some kids didn't like the climbing wall because they were afraid of heights, but I did.

On the south end of the gym, two sets of blue double doors led to an equipment storage room that housed mats as big as a car and thicker than ten feather beds. When you jumped on one, you sank ever so gently as the air slowly whooshed out of it. I'm sure someone could jump from the roof of the school onto one and be perfectly fine. If I could, I would make one of those mats my bed at home.

Today, Chase and I entered the gym to find Coach Conley near the center of the polished floor. He was swinging a whistle on the end of a string.

Dressed in black athletic shorts and a gray t-shirt with *"Property of Raven Ridge Academy"* on the front, Coach Conley was young, with short-cropped black hair. He had an athletic build, but was not overly muscular. His skin was a tan bronze, as if he had just came from the beach.

I was not the most athletically gifted kid, but I liked gym class. Coach Conley made it enjoyable. He focused on activities that required hand-eye coordination, running, jumping, and climbing. He found a way to bring out the competitor in every kid, and it didn't matter to him who won the contests. Coach Conley appreciated whoever gave their best effort, and so I always tried hard.

As the starting class bell rang, he loudly blew his whistle, silencing any chatter. I looked at the group of kids in our class and saw stupid Johnny Ricker and Miles. I didn't feel my usual apprehension when I saw them, but maybe that was because Chase was here, and he made me feel less vulnerable. Besides, Coach Conley didn't put up with any kind of name-calling.

"For those of you here today who don't know me, I'm your athletic instructor, Coach Conley," our teacher said, deepening his voice like a drill instructor. "Now, in this class, it is of the utmost importance that you listen to me, be safe, and always do your best. Your grade at the end of the semester depends on these three things."

Here, he put his hands on his hips before continuing. "It's not how many push-ups or sit-ups you can do, or how fast you can run. It's effort, ladies and gentlemen, that will determine your grade, and the responsibility for that rests solely on you. Don't blame others for any losses you endure. You must take responsibility for your own actions."

Coach Conley then barked out orders for us to form six lines of three kids. Chase fell into line behind me.

Coach walked in front of the lines like a general reviewing his troops.

"First, we begin by stretching our muscles," he said. "Spread your feet wider than your shoulders, and with your legs straight, place your hands flat on the ground if you're able to—ready?" He blew his whistle once for us to begin.

I put my hands on the ground and looked between my legs at Chase from my upside-down perspective. I noticed he didn't quite have the flexibility that I had. He couldn't quite put his hands flat on the ground.

Coach Conley's whistle blew twice, a sign it was time to stop.

"Next, stand up tall and grasp your hands behind your back, to stretch your chest," Coach ordered, blowing his whistle again for us to begin. As we were stretching, a thud echoed through the gym, followed by a now-familiar flickering of the lights, and then darkness, as the power completely went out. This was met with cheers and squeals from the class. Since the gym was our tornado shelter in an emergency, it had no windows to the outside. The room was completely dark now, save for the exit signs above the building's doors. The little light they provided cast our entire class into shadowy figures that giggled and wiggled.

Coach blew his whistle to silence us.

"That's odd.... The emergency floodlights should have come on," he said in a curious voice that bordered on worry. "All right, well, I'm sure the power will come back on at any moment. But for now, I want all of you to sit down where you are. *No horseplay,"* he instructed. "Someone could get hurt in this darkness."

We sat down on the floor in the middle of the gymnasium. The class buzzed with excitement because of this unexpected break in the normal routine.

Chase whispered over to me, "Three times in one day? Something's going on."

"Nah," I objected. "It's just because it's so hot outside. The air conditioning units can't keep up and are frying the breakers."

I knew this because, during one of my after-school sessions with Frank, the janitor, he had complained about how he lost a fight with the school over its plan to install A/C units on the roofs. The teachers wanted their classrooms cooler, but they had built the original building before air conditioning. Frank had tried to explain to them that retrofitting the old section with A/C units couldn't possibly keep up with the actual demands. But the school didn't listen to him.

"Maybe, but maybe not," Chase replied. "We can't always accept obvious explanations for obvious problems."

Suddenly, a loud crash came from behind the equipment room doors on the other end of the dark gym. Everyone jumped, and some of the girls screamed. Coach blew his whistle, instructing us, "Quiet down! I'm sure that was nothing."

Chase whispered to me, "Nothing? No, that was *some*thing."

"These power failures we've had today have only lasted a few minutes, but if the power doesn't kick back on in the next minute or two, we will take our class outside," Coach said. "Now relax."

I spied the faint outline of Miles pointing toward the dark, far corner of the gym, near the equipment room. In a startled whisper, he said, "I think I saw something moving! Over there—"

The class went silent in an instant. Everyone strained their eyes to see what Miles was pointing to in the dark, shadowy gymnasium.

"There! A shadow! It flew up in the corner! Did you see it?" Miles demanded.

"Where?" said one kid.

"I don't see anything," said another.

"I think I saw something!" Christi Patrick's frightened voice blurted out.

"What was it?" asked Alyssa Gonzales.

"It looked like... Charlie Hackett," Miles whispered. "He's come back to kill us all!"

"Oh! I think I saw him too!" Cammie Davis screamed.

"That's enough!" Coach Conley shouted. "There's nothing over there; it's just your eyes playing tricks on you. *Settle down!*"

I moved uneasily in my spot. It was just like Miles to bring up Charlie Hackett—the young boy found dead at the footsteps of the school and whose ghost, people said, haunted the school's hallways.

I looked to where Miles had pointed, but saw nothing except darkness. Then again, I didn't want to see anything *except* darkness.

Except the darkness could see into my mind, bringing a feeling that someone was watching me. The air hung heavy with evil, causing goosebumps on my skin.

My imagination took control. Any moment I was sure I would hear screams and feel the wet stickiness of pools of blood around me as, one by one, we were slaughtered in the dark. Only then would Charlie start laughing while wiping the gymnasium walls with our blood.

"Who's Charlie Hackett?" Chase whispered to me.

"A student who died years ago when he jumped out of... or, was pushed out of, the bell tower," I quickly whispered back.

"Really? Why did someone want to kill him? Or why did he want to kill himself?" Chase asked.

"I don't know," I said in a high, agitated tone. "Charlie claimed he could hear voices inside the school building talking to him. He talked with these invisible people all the time. The other kids teased him because he did this, and soon, he became withdrawn.

Everyone avoided him, including the teachers. They say even his parents stopped liking him.

"One time, the other students locked Charlie in the basement as a prank. He couldn't get out and was down there for the entire night. His parents didn't even notice him missing! The janitor found him the next morning, clinging to the basement door at the top of the stairs. He said Charlie was pale as a ghost and kept repeating, *'Darkness, darkness—you'll all be pulled into the darkness.'* The next day, they found Charlie sprawled on the front sidewalk of the school, dead.

"Some say the constant teasing was too much, so he jumped. Others say another student or teacher murdered him by pushing him out a window. Some say the darkness consumed him… forcing him to jump. Now they say his ghost haunts this school, plotting its dark revenge."

I strained my eyes, staring at the equipment room. Indeed, if Charlie Hackett's ghost wanted to harm us, this was the place to do it. We were trapped in the middle of the gym with only two ways out: the exit by the equipment room, leading back into the school's main hallway, and the exit behind us near the climbing wall, leading to the outside.

Suddenly, a creak and a moan came from behind us. It came from around where the climbing wall would be if we could see it.

"You are all going to die in my darkness!" a low, eerie voice echoed through the gym.

Immediately, the class turned in unison. We spied… a shadowy figure floating in the air!

Screams sprang out everywhere. Even Coach Conley let forth an involuntary burst! Kids jumped to their feet, running and stumbling in the dark towards the exit near the equipment room.

I ran with everyone else as the shadow flew back and forth through the air. I glanced around for Chase, but couldn't see him in the dark gym filled with bloodcurdling screams of panicked kids trying to find their way out of the dark.

"Chase!" I screamed. "Chase, this way!"

Instantly, sunlight shot into the gymnasium! The outside door flew open near the ghastly figure! Shining like a spotlight, it revealed a boy hanging from one of the climbing ropes.

It was no ghost flying through the air. Johnny Ricker had put on one of the climbing harnesses and then pushed himself off the rock-climbing wall to swing back and forth. In the dark, he had been a shadow—a ghastly figure of a ghost.

Chase stood holding open the outside door with a look of satisfaction on his face. The class was cowering in a huddled mass now, Coach Conley in the middle.

Coach looked more scared than any of us.

Miles helped Johnny down as the two laughed.

Johnny gave Miles a high five. "Ha, they totally believed you saw a ghost, Miles."

Miles laughed. "And they totally thought you were the ghost of Charlie Hackett! Ha-ha!"

Coach Conley glared at Johnny and Miles and yelled, "Johnny Ricker and Miles Webster! Both of you are in big trouble!"

Chase propped open the door with a rock to continue letting light into the gym, then walked over to me.

"How did you know that was Johnny and not the ghost of Charlie Hackett?" I asked.

Chase grinned. "When Miles was pointing towards the equipment room, I noticed he wasn't next to Johnny. Since he sticks to Johnny like glue, I wondered where Johnny went. At first, I thought Johnny might be making the noise in the equipment room, but I quickly ruled that out. Since everyone was looking in that direction, we would have spotted the outline of his shape when he headed over there. This left the other direction.

"In the commotion, Johnny must have slipped past everyone and attached himself to the harness. Once he climbed the wall, he pushed off, swinging back and forth. When I spotted the swinging figure, I knew it wasn't a ghost. A ghost would never fly back and forth; it would fly forward, in one direction only. This led me to the conclusion that the figure was Johnny. A pure hoax that I simply *shed some light on*," Chase said proudly, folding his arms.

Wow, I thought to myself. *Chase really was a detective, and brave.*

Just then, a clicking noise came through the inside hallway exit door near the equipment room. I could see a thin beam of light bouncing back and forth. It grew in size as it came closer.

The class was still jittery from Johnny's prank, so some of the girls started crying. The rest of us knew this was no ghost coming down the hall, but something much scarier.

"Everything's fine—don't worry," Principal Sterns said, popping his head around the corner. "We are just experiencing another minor power outage. Our maintenance crew is working on the issue now, and we should have power back soon. Until then, sit tight. I assure you we will work out this problem."

Coach turned, blew his whistle, and told us to form one line.

"All right, let's go outside now. Follow me," he said, taking the first step toward the sunlit exit way. However, before we took even two steps, a low thud shot through the air, followed by the lights quickly flickering on and off like strobe lights.

That's when I saw it... the figure of a boy standing in the corner of the gym. However, when the lights stopped flickering and stayed on, *no one was there.*

Shivers went through my skin as I let out a startled puff. *I'm seeing things,* I told myself. *It's just my eyes adjusting to the light and playing tricks on me. It was nothing.*

Johnny stuttered, "T-th-there. Over there... I saw Charlie Hackett. It was him!"

"Very funny. But the joke's over," Coach barked in an annoyed tone.

"No! I'm not joking this time! I saw him in the corner, over there!" Johnny hollered as he pointed to the same corner I had seen the boy's figure in.

The rest of the class shook their heads, rolled their eyes, and muttered under their breaths about how stupid Johnny was to try the same trick twice.

Should I tell everyone I saw the same thing? I thought. *Should I back Johnny up? Then they'd probably think I was in on his joke, or even worse, think I believed him.*

The answer was clear. I kept my mouth shut, told myself it was the lights playing tricks on my eyes, and let Johnny look stupid in front of everybody. After all, I was more mature than Johnny Ricker and knew that there were no such things as ghosts.

But I did see something—didn't I? I asked myself.

Coach looked at his watch. "Well, we lost a lot of our class time, but we can still do a few exercises inside here before class is over. Johnny and Miles, you'll be doing extra laps for your little prank."

When the end-of-class bell rang, Coach Conley blew his whistle long and hard. "That's a wrap!" he said. "I'll see all of you tomorrow. Be ready to work twice as hard since we missed time today. Johnny and Miles, I want to see the both of you."

I hoped they would get in trouble for their stunt. But knowing Coach Conley, the two just got a talking-to.

I was starting to get hungry and changed my attention towards lunch, forgetting the two troublemakers. Heading to the hallway exit, I said to Chase, "Lunch time. You bring yours?"

"No, my mom gave me lunch money."

"Well, I've got mine in my backpack here, but I need to stop by my locker."

That's when Mr. Doyle almost knocked us over. He stormed past us into the gym, yelling, "Conley! We need to talk!"

Coach shook his head at Mr. Doyle, then said, "Johnny and Miles, I'll speak with you later."

Johnny and Miles wasted no time slipping away, shoving their shoulders into Chase and me on their way out. When we regained our balance, Chase put his finger in the air, motioning to me to pause, and not go another step further. We both looked back in the gym, where Mr. Doyle had gotten close to Coach's face.

"You gave me bad information! You are to blame!" he shouted at Coach.

"It wasn't bad information! *What you did with it was bad.* I can't predict the future! If I could, I wouldn't be here," Coach Conley responded, his voice tense.

"Well, you've got to talk to them and get me some more time. They're your people; you understand them. They'll listen to you," Mr. Doyle said.

"They aren't *my* people. I'm not a part of that world anymore, and I told you not to drag me into your problems. I want nothing to do with this," Coach replied.

"*My* problems are going to be *your* problems if you don't help me, you dumb jock!" Mr. Doyle hollered.

"Be careful who you throw threats at. This '*dumb jock*' isn't the one in trouble. I've got nothing to do with this," Coach said, his face getting red under his tan.

"It would be a shame if people found out what you've been doing—giving terrible advice to fellow teachers who are broke," Mr. Doyle hissed at him.

"Just a minute! You wanted my opinion, and I gave it to you—that's all. I didn't tell you to gamble your life away. In fact, I'm the one who told you not to get involved with them in the first place!

But you did, and now you have to deal with the consequences," Coach Conley said.

"You'll pay for this, Conley," Mr. Doyle spat out before he stormed off.

"No, I think it's you who'll pay more," Coach mumbled right before he swung his whistle and walked out through the gym's other exit.

It was obvious to Chase and me that Coach was completely unaware we were by the hallway and listening.

Chase looked at me, his eyes wide. "Uh, Oliver… I hope you write all that down."

"Already on it," I said proudly, showing him the pencil clutched in my hand.

But I didn't tell Chase that my hand shook as I wrote down what was important about the conversation.

CHAPTER SIX

OUT TO LUNCH

AFTER STOPPING BY our lockers, Chase and I walked down to the cafeteria. Once again, I was feeling pretty miserable. Talking with Mr. Doyle after class had been my last hope of getting my watch back before Mom found out—and now that hope was gone. There would be no getting around Principal Sterns' standard: *call the parents* when there was a problem.

Chase tried to reassure me. "Hey, I'm sure you'll get that watch back after school. I'll tell the principal everything was my fault. Plus, he's not going to believe anything Ricker says."

"Thanks for that. But I'm more worried about him calling my mom."

"Right, because that pocket watch isn't really yours, is it?" Chase said.

"Yes, it is...." I blurted. "Well, kinda. It's my family's."

"I thought so," Chase said, his voice soft. "But your mom

doesn't know that you took it this morning, does she? And she'll be furious with you even if you were planning on putting it back when you got home."

"Yeah, that's right," I answered, startled at how perceptive my new ally was. "How did you figure out that it wasn't truly mine?"

"The way you reacted when Doyle asked you about it. You acted like you were in trouble, and you wouldn't be in trouble if you were supposed to have it. And it was Jax who told the truth this morning; you remained silent. Plus, you've been obsessed with it all morning, wanting to get it back before the end of the day—before someone notices it's missing, maybe. And if it were yours, going to the Principal's office wouldn't be such a big deal to you," Chase said. "But the super-obvious clue was, *what kid has a pocket watch anyway, especially an old one like that?*"

The corner of my mouth rose involuntarily. "Yeah," I agreed. "It's my great-grandfather's pocket watch, actually."

Wow. This kid sure was a good detective!

"I don't know the principal at all, but maybe we can avoid Sterns phoning your house if all of us, including Jax, explain what happened in the same way. No reason the principal shouldn't just let the matter drop and give you back your watch," Chase said.

"Jax? She'll be there?" I gasped, my eyes widening as I imagined her fabulous face.

"Yeah, she was there and saw what happened, right? And we were *all* told to go to the principal's office after school, remember?" Chase laughed. "So, she and I talked about you during Doyle's history class, and I know for a fact that she's on board with us."

"You talked with her—about me?" I mumbled, my eyes the size of manhole covers. "What did she say?"

"Not much," Chase said, shrugging his shoulders. "Mostly that she hated Johnny Ricker and wanted to help you get your watch back."

"Anything else?"

"Not really," Chase winked. "Why? Do you like her?"

"Me? No… well, I mean, I think she's cute and all, but I never really put much thought into it," I scoffed.

Any thought into it? She's the only thought going through this spinning head of mine! Wow, I thought, *Jax was on my side, talking about me and thinking about me. Maybe this wasn't such a bad situation after all. If I lost the watch but got Jax for my girl, I might be willing to live with the consequences!*

When Chase and I reached the cafeteria, tides of kids were already spilling into the lunch line, filling tables, and drowning the cafeteria with noise. Even though my mom had packed me a lunch, I jumped into the lunch line with Chase, since he was buying his.

Gio hadn't made it to the cafeteria yet, and I kept a sharp eye out for him, like a lifeguard watching the shoreline. Jax was also on my watch list.

That's why I was able to spot trouble in the ocean of kids. I eyeballed Johnny Ricker's cap as it broke the surface and circled like a shark smelling blood. *No one was safe while he was around.* I watched where he claimed his territory—that was the area to avoid.

As we neared the front of the line, Chase asked, "What's good here?"

"Depends on what you like. The pizza's okay, I guess, but I think the rest of it's gross. School food's never any good."

There were four cooks at our school, and I thought they might be brothers since they looked so much alike. Big men with broad shoulders and huge muscles beneath white t-shirts and aprons, they all had pale white skin, black hair, and broad faces. They spoke in broken English, but I couldn't tell from their accents where they came from.

I could see them in the back of the kitchen, swinging big cleavers, chopping the meat with such force that it sent chills down my spine. I had visions of them coming to my house in the middle of the night with their meat cleavers and saying, *"You don't like our cooking? Is that why you bring your lunch to school? Let us prepare a special meal for the students tomorrow—Oliver soup."* Seriously—they were that scary.

Today, the cooks appeared upbeat, dishing out food with quiet thuds, not the hammer-pounding thuds the spatula or ladle usually made when finding our trays. They were definitely preoccupied.

Maybe they all got a promotion. Maybe they actually made something that tasted good. Maybe they were going on a vacation back to wherever it was they came from.

Whatever the reason, they weren't angry, and that was odd. They didn't smile, though. Then again, they never smiled.

Gio wormed his way into the line with us; he was also buying. "What's up with the cooks? Did they actually cook something that tastes good?" he asked sarcastically, keeping his voice low.

"Beats me. Maybe they're happy to be out on parole?" I mumbled.

Pizza and spaghetti were the choices for Chase and Gio. Unfortunately, that came with a side of cooked spinach that caused involuntary nose crinkles.

Seriously, why do adults think kids enjoy cooked spinach? I mean, could there be anything grosser?

But even Gio and Chase's outright expressions of disgust from the slimy weed hitting their trays did not seem to upset the giant enforcers of eating. *Something was very off today.*

A deserted island of a table far away from Johnny Ricker's is where I found seats. Chase didn't seem to care either way, but Gio supported our traditional lunchroom protocol: *Sit as far from Johnny Ricker as possible and stay out of sight.*

But since Chase was a new face at our school, he unintentionally drew attention to us—especially from the girls. I began to wonder if this was what popularity felt like. I was used to receiving attention only for the wrong reason—my birthmark—and I didn't like how that felt.

"Gross, what do they put in this food?" Chase coughed as he choked a bite down.

"Yeah," Gio agreed with a mouthful of food. "How can you mess up pizza?"

"That's why I bring my lunch! No need to risk food poisoning," I proclaimed as I unwrapped my PBJ.

But what I said was only half-true. Sometimes I really did want to buy pizza or mac-and-cheese instead of bringing my sandwich. However, it was cheaper for my mom to send me with a lunch. She would only give me lunch money when her tips from waitressing at Jam'n Joe's Bar the night before were really good.

"What's up with your leg, G?" Chase asked suddenly.

Chase's out-of-the-blue question surprised me.

"Shark attack," Gio said in a pirate's voice. "I managed to kill the shark, but not before he took me leg."

"Wow. But how did you kill the shark?" Chase asked.

"I reached through the shark's gills and pulled his heart right out from his cold body," Gio answered.

All three of us started laughing.

Gio had never known two real legs, so I guess it didn't bother him to joke around about it. He never felt sorry for himself or asked anyone else to. He was just who he was.

To be honest, I never really put much thought into him only having one and one-half legs because it's how I always knew him to be. The only time I thought about his missing leg was when we did some activity he couldn't do.

"I was born with it," Gio said once he stopped laughing. "But I didn't always have this prosthetic. It's new."

Chase furrowed his eyebrows. "How does it work?"

"I just strap it on to my upper thigh, and when I walk, I swing my hip around so the knee bends."

"What's it made of, titanium?" Chase questioned.

"Some of the joint parts are metal, but the leg itself is high-impact, lightweight plastic. This upper portion is hollow," Gio said, knocking on that part of his leg to make an echo to support what he had just said.

"I'm sure that could come in handy if you were giving a round-house kick to someone's face," Chase said.

"Sure," Gio said, making a casual shrug.

"Maybe you could be outfitted with a special bionic leg with all kinds of secret weapons hidden inside it that would allow you to jump super-high," Chase said. "Then you could be recruited by some spy agency and perform top-secret missions."

At first, I chuckled at his comment, thinking it was a joke. But then I realized I was not so sure.

When I met Chase earlier this morning, I thought he could be one of the popular, cool kids, someone who Gio and I had a real chance of hanging out with. But more and more, I was beginning to think he was a big detective-type geek with a big imagination who talked with big confidence.

The first clue was the magnifying glass in his back pocket: What popular kid carries something like that around? The second clue was his interest in ghosts, werewolves, and aliens. And as for all his paranormal talk? None of that would be the topic at the cool kids' table.

But I liked Chase. Even if he was a big nerd.

Gio swallowed some food and asked Chase, "So, what's your story?"

"I moved here from Denver with my mom and sister, Aspyn. I've been working on several paranormal investigations lately."

"Paranormal investigations?" Gio said, raising his eyebrows.

"You know, hauntings, alien abductions, and stuff like that," Chase casually said as he took a drink of his milk.

There was no doubt that Chase believed what he said—and I think Gio believed what he said as well. I knew I was a lot more mature than they were, but after what I had seen and felt today, I was starting to believe in all that stuff a little bit, too.

"I've already started investigations on what's going on at this school. There's plenty of evidence to support paranormal activities here," Chase said in a completely serious tone.

"Investigations of this school?" Gio asked.

"I've been collecting data all morning, paying close attention to the supposed power failures, the noises, the teachers' conversations, the eyewitness accounts, and the history of this building," Chase said as he took another bite of his pizza. Pointing to my journal, he directed, "Oliver, show him the data."

A tinge of excitement went through me as I realized I was the keeper of this important information! I quickly put down my sandwich and opened my journal for Gio to see my notes.

While Gio sat looking at my journal, Chase said to me, "So, you told me about the ghost of Charlie Hackett. Any other stories about this building I should know about?"

"Tell him the story of the gambling ghost," Gio said in a voice that squeaked. He looked over at Chase. "Oliver tells it best."

I looked around to see if anyone else was listening. Nobody was, nevertheless, I lowered my voice. I didn't want anyone else to think I actually *believed* these things.

"A long time ago, this guy named Horace Tanner owned the most profitable silver mine in the West," I started. "He said there was no end to the silver it could produce. That's why he called it *The Endless Mine*. He constructed our school building, his house, with the profits.

"Horace loved playing poker, and he hosted poker parties

regularly. But Anastasia, his wife, disapproved—saying that it was unsophisticated to gamble. So, he began holding poker parties down in the building's basement to appease her.

"The story goes, that one time, one of his guests who was winning kept clicking his winning poker chips together throughout the games. Horace was having an awful night, losing every hand he played. The constant clicking drove him *crazy.* The gambler knew this—and only clicked them even more.

"When Horace asked the man to stop, the gambler simply replied, *'Why don't you win them back from me? Then I'll have nothing to click.'* But no matter what hand Horace Tanner was dealt, the clicking man always had the better hand.

"It grew near the end of the night. Horace had run out of money at the table but had been dealt a hand he was sure would win. The clicking man knew Horace was out of money, so he raised his bet with all his chips. Convinced the clicking man was bluffing, Horace wagered *The Endless Mine.* The clicking man accepted Horace's bet. When the cards were turned over, the clicking man had won the hand. Horace had lost his endless mine.

"Horace congratulated the clicking man by giving him a glass of whiskey. Then he insisted on taking him to see the silver mine he had just won. The clicking man, completely drunk on the whiskey Horace had been serving all night, followed Horace into the mine.

"Once inside, a terrible accident happened. The clicking man lost his footing and fell into a mineshaft. As he fell, the clicking man yelled back to Horace, *'Bad luck will haunt you!'*

"No one knows whether or not Horace pushed the gambler into the mineshaft, or if the drunken man actually slipped and fell. Nevertheless, the sheriff accepted Horace's account of what had happened.

"People say the clicking man's ghost wanders the halls of this school, still clicking his poker chips and looking to make a wager with some poor soul. They say if someone makes a bet with the ghost and wins, they win a fortune of silver. But if they lose, then the loser must spend eternity inside the mine—condemned to the same fate as the clicking man."

I concluded my re-telling in as dramatic a tone as I could muster.

Chase nodded. "Murder… revenge. Sounds like a classic haunting. So, what ended up happening to Horace and the mine?"

"Because the clicking man fell into a mineshaft, Horace Tanner kept the silver mine. To further the story, Horace said it was discovered that the clicking man was cheating. Nevertheless, just as the clicking man had predicted, Horace's bad luck got worse. Soon after, Tanner's Endless Mine went bust. Then, his wife, Anastasia, mysteriously disappeared. Depressed, he wandered into his Endless Mine with a few of his possessions and never came back out."

Gio confided, "People say they hear his wife Anastasia crying in the school's halls. There are stories of a light and a face in the bell tower at night—maybe her ghost?"

"Quite possibly… maybe one of many ghosts, in fact. We'll have to analyze all the evidence as it comes in," Chase answered, giving Gio a smile.

I sat silently for a moment, thinking about the whisper over my shoulder I heard in Mr. Doyle's class, and the figure of a boy I saw in the gym's corner when the lights were flickering. *Do I tell Chase what I saw and heard? Or do I keep it to myself?*

I wasn't sure. It could have been my imagination at work. I figured it was best to let Chase discover his own evidence for now.

Suddenly, a fresh breeze swept into the lunchroom. I spied Jax walking across the cafeteria. She moved daintily, as if walking on pillows of clouds.

I imagined the two of us standing in the lunch line together, chatting and laughing about stupid Mr. Doyle. When the cooks tried to be mean to us, I would back them down with my menacing stare. Then, I would pay for her lunch and escort her to a private table. We would sit together, feeding one another celery sticks from my bag and gazing into each other's eyes. At recess, we would run off holding hands, laughing as we jumped on the merry-go-round.

My dream turned into a nightmare the instant Johnny interrupted my line of sight. Thankfully, he didn't notice me at my table. He was too busy harassing the students around him.

Jax sat down at a far-off table with her friends. All the girls who had been glancing over at our table began giggling. Jax looked over her shoulder towards us, and I immediately sank my head down.

Were they talking about me, I wondered, *the three of us—or just Chase?*

Now I couldn't see anything, so I peeked up through my eyebrows. That's when I saw Johnny Ricker put a forkful of slimy spinach behind his back and flick it towards Jax and her friends. The girls met the green splatter in the middle of their table with a shriek. Johnny and his goons huddled together and laughed.

I narrowed my eyes. My mind filled with visions of me running over to Johnny's table, grabbing Johnny by the shirt collar, and stuffing that horrid spinach down his throat. I'd glare at his friends, my forceful look saying, *Leave the ladies alone… understood?* Then Jax would spring up and throw her arms around me while her table of friends cheered wildly.

Unfortunately, school rules only allowed me to glare in Johnny's direction.

"So, now what?" Gio asked. "How are we going to get Oliver's watch back?"

His words got my attention back.

Chase took another bite of his lunch. "Well, if we're going to avoid the principal's office, we somehow need to persuade Mr. Doyle to return it to Oliver before the end of the day," he said.

"I have Doyle next hour!" Gio's voice rang with excitement.

"I could tell him what happened, explain everything. Maybe he'll believe me?"

Chase pointed in the air as he spoke. "Yes, soften him up. You'd be a good character witness. Then, Oliver could talk with him before going into Principal Sterns' office. Who knows? Maybe he'll give it back and forget everything."

"Yeah, but what if he's set on telling Principal Sterns?" I said.

"Then we'll just convince Principal Sterns that you were supposed to have the pocket watch all along, and there's no need to make any phone calls—no big deal," Chase drawled.

"Doyle made a big deal about it this morning—like that pocket watch was something really important, and he knew it. And he's been looking at it all morning," I said.

"He's just excited to see old stuff, that's all," Chase said. The fact that he didn't agree with me made me feel pretty good. "Probably reminds him of his grandfather or something. But I feel there's much more going on with this Mr. Doyle than just having your pocket watch."

"Like what?" Gio asked.

"He's been in arguments with practically everyone he's come in contact with. We need to watch him closely."

Finished with our lunch, we headed outdoors to the schoolyard for recess. It was so hot outside that it almost made us want to go back to our classes with air conditioning.

Almost.

There was rock throwing, pushing, chasing, and shouting. A few boys started a two-hand-touch football game on the grass field.

Nick Briggs, a kid in our neighborhood I knew since kindergarten, caught sight of us and waved. Carrying the football, he ran across the grass towards us and yelled, "Hey! Wait up!"

Nick was a muscular kid, almost as big as Johnny. He had

short brown hair and narrow green eyes. All the girls thought he was handsome.

Nick was, by far, the most popular kid in our school. But even though I'd known him since kindergarten, we weren't actually friends. He hung out with the cool crowd, other kids who liked sports, and even occasionally with the likes of Johnny Ricker—which I never understood. But Nick got along with everyone.

Nick was great at all sports, and probably the most athletically gifted kid in school. It only helped that his mom had enrolled him in almost every team sport possible.

My life wasn't like Nick's. My mom never allowed me to participate in team sports because she thought I'd get hurt. I wondered why Nick was coming to talk to us now.

Nick walked up to Chase and said, "Hey, thanks again for helping with my locker this morning. I can't believe I forgot my combination. I really owe you."

"Anytime," Chase shrugged.

"Where'd you learn to pick locks like that?" Nick asked Chase.

"Just a little skill I acquired. Comes in handy every now and then," Chase said casually.

"We're putting a football game together. I brought my autographed football my dad just gave me for my birthday—want to play?" Nick asked Chase.

"Awesome!" Chase said. "You got room for Oliver and Gio?"

"Well…." Nick said, pausing.

I saw Nick glance at the two of us. Gio and I were not the athletic types and never were picked for any teams—especially Gio.

Before Nick could answer, Chase blurted, "They'll be on our team. Oliver can kick off."

I didn't even know how to catch a ball, let alone kick one. I hoped Nick would say no. Instead, he shrugged his shoulders and smiled. "Sure, sounds good to me. Let's go!"

We divided into two teams: Nick, Chase, Gio, me, and a few other boys. Johnny Ricker, Miles, and some other nasty boys were on the other team.

Nick handed me his football to kick off as the other team backed up into the field.

Johnny Ricker yelled to his teammates, "Hey, look! Freak Face is kicking off! We should all move in closer. I'm sure he kicks like a baby."

Miles shouted, "I bet he misses the football and falls on his butt!"

His entire team started laughing.

I squinted with fury. Adrenaline mixed with anger, coursed through my veins. No longer was I afraid to kick the ball. Now, I couldn't wait to kick the ball with a kung fu kick.

I took a few steps, dropped the ball, and swung my leg as hard as I could. A loud *SMACK* rang out as my foot made solid contact, rocketing the football into the air. Everyone squinted up into the hot afternoon sun. My eyes were big, but my smile was bigger. I had done it! I had kicked the football.

I had kicked the football so high that it shot out of the schoolyard. Out of the schoolyard, and into the faculty parking lot, hitting—Mr. Doyle's classic yellow car.

It smacked the hood with a loud hollow thud, causing a collective, *"Ohhh,"* from everyone in the schoolyard.

I could see the dent even from where I was standing.

"Not good, man," muttered one kid.

"Sucks to be you," said another.

"Wrong car to hit," Nick said.

Johnny and Miles laughed wildly.

Yes, of all cars, that was the wrong one to hit. It could have hit Mrs. Huntley's red Volkswagen Beetle. It could have hit Coach

Conley's Jeep. It could have even hit Principal Sterns' Jaguar. But *not* Mr. Doyle's pride and joy.

The instrument of destruction, Nick's autographed football, lay beside the classic car. It needed to be retrieved. A chain-link fence separated the teacher's parking lot from the school grounds, but there was a small opening between the fence and the school building.

Nick tapped me on the shoulder. "Don't worry—I'll get it. Good kick."

He looked around before squeezing through the opening and running towards his ball.

As Nick got close, a white work van with the lettering, *"Central Air"* pulled into the parking lot. It moved right alongside Mr. Doyle's car… right over Nick's football.

There was a loud pop—from the football, and from everyone's mouths.

The van stopped. The driver, a thin young man with black hair and a gold earring, stepped out. He looked at Nick before he reached under the van and pulled out the deflated football.

"Oops," he said as he tossed it to Nick. "You're lucky that wasn't your head. I guess that will teach you not to play in the parking lot, won't it?"

Nick stared at him, then looked down at his father's gift. Complete silence reigned on the playground. The only sound came from the three other men exiting the passenger side of the van, all wearing the same gray coveralls as the driver.

One of the men, who looked the oldest because of his gray hair, snapped, "Let's go, Finnegan. We're on the clock. There's work to do."

The driver looked over his shoulder at him. "Yeah, yeah, Murdoch. Stupid game, anyhow."

The two other men were opening the back doors of the van and gathering tools. One of them, a bald man wearing dark sunglasses, slung a work belt over his shoulder. "What's the matter, Finnegan? You don't like football?" he said.

The other guy, a man with dark skin and wavy black hair, clipped on a tool belt. He said with an accent, "Vincent, in my country, football is a sport where you *kick* the ball."

"Yeah, Santos, it's called *soccer*," the bald man named Vincent answered. "What Finnegan here just ran over is a *football*. It's the most popular sport in America."

"Why don't they call it *throw-ball?"* Santos asked. "You throw the ball, not kick it with your foot."

"How about *stupid-ball?"* the driver snorted. "You see, this is what's wrong with this country, Santos: its obsession with sports." Finnegan turned back to Nick, who was speechless and looking at his flat football. "You should be more worried about the deflating world around you instead of your football, kid. Pay attention to your classes and leave the sports alone."

"Quit playing around, morons; the time's ticking," the workman with gray hair barked angrily as he walked towards the school building. "Vincent, come inside with me; you other idiots hurry and get ready." Silently, the workmen followed his directions.

Deflated ball in hand, Nick slowly walked back and squeezed through the fence. All of Nick's friends gathered around him silently, and then collectively tossed me a dirty look. Chase and Gio stood by my side.

I didn't mean to kick the ball over the fence, I didn't mean to hit Mr. Doyle's car, and I certainly didn't mean for those workmen to run over his football! I thought. Even so, I was pretty certain I wouldn't be picked for anyone's sports team in the future.

Just then, as if he was abiding by some *bad-luck-for-Oliver* schedule, Mr. Doyle walked out of the building and into the teacher's parking lot toward his car.

Did he see what had just happened? Did he know who did it?

Chase and Gio stayed beside me as everyone else ran off in all directions, not waiting to get blamed. I prayed that Mr. Doyle would think the four workmen who had just pulled in with their white van were responsible. They certainly deserved to get the blame more than I did.

Sticking our bodies like bubblegum against the school wall near the space in the fence, Chase, Gio, and I made sure we were just out of Mr. Doyle's line of sight. However, Mr. Doyle didn't get more than five feet into the parking lot before a voice called out to him.

Clearly annoyed, Mr. Doyle stopped dead in his tracks. He lowered his head before turning around to talk with our principal.

We could see Principal Sterns waving a piece of paper in his hand as Mr. Doyle flung his hands into the air. It was clear that Mr. Doyle was not having any pleasant conversations with anyone today.

Perfect. Mr. Doyle's already mad, and he's only about to get madder. Not only would I get detention, but I would be grounded at home until I was in my thirties for taking my great-grandfather's pocket watch. Oh, and I'd have to work the rest of my life to pay for the dent in the hood of Mr. Doyle's car. Could my day get worse?

Some of their conversation floated over to us as their voices became louder.

Mr. Doyle said sharply, "Did you really think your antics would frighten me?"

"No. But I thought you'd be smarter than this!" Principal Sterns replied. "Can't you see this is for the greater good? A chance to make history."

"I want to *preserve* history, not make it," Mr. Doyle shot back.

"That's the difference between you and me! You live in the past, and I live in the future. All things evolve over time. Change is inevitable, and in the process, we can do very well for ourselves."

"Don't you see what monsters they are? They will destroy everything—you, along with it—despite the promises they've made. They'll leave nothing for future generations! Our very future depends on learning from history," Mr. Doyle replied.

"Wouldn't it be nice to have a little extra to pay your debts?" Principal Sterns asked, changing the tide of the conversation. "I hear they are quite hefty."

Mr. Doyle huffed. "That stupid janitor is always running his mouth, spreading lies and gossip. Frank has never liked me." Mr. Doyle then lifted his long chin in the air. "But I too know about the skeletons in *your* closet, and it'd be awful if anything about your *visitors* were to leak out to the press."

Mr. Doyle's tone was threating and caused Principal Sterns to bristle.

Principal Sterns folded his arms and looked through his eyebrows at Mr. Doyle. "That, my friend, would be a terrible gamble on your part. But then again, you are a poor gambler, aren't you?" Principal Sterns said in an arrogant tone. "Funny, I would never have pegged you as a gambling man. A respected history and political science teacher by day, but a high stakes roller by night."

"You know nothing about me, Sterns, or what I'm capable of. This cover-up will haunt you," Mr. Doyle threatened with a growl while waving his long finger in the air.

"Desperate words from a desperate man," Principal Sterns responded with a huff. "Very well, then. I'd like to have you on board when this takes off, but this must go forward. I have to do what I have to do."

"And so must I," Mr. Doyle growled.

Doyle turned and stomped off towards his classic car.

This is it, I thought. *Will Mr. Doyle notice the dent? Will he see us here, against the wall of the building?*

When in doubt—run.

With Mr. Doyle's back now to us, the three of us wasted no time running around the school and back inside the cafeteria.

"That was close," Gio panted once we stopped.

Chase caught his breath. "Did you both hear that? Oliver, document it immediately. This guy, Doyle, and Principal Sterns are involved with something. Did you hear that part about 'this cover-up will haunt you?'"

"And Doyle said something about skeletons and visitors too," Gio huffed. "What do you think's going on?"

"At this point, I think we are looking at a case of a ghost haunting cover-up here at this school. Mr. Doyle is threating to tell the press something that Principal Sterns doesn't want him too," Chase answered.

As the end-of-recess bell sounded, Chase gulped in another breath. "Guess we'll have to sort it out later. I've got art class with that Huntley lady next hour, Oliver's got literature, and G—you have Mr. Doyle's history class now, right?"

Gio nodded. "Yep. I'll try to talk to him about this morning, to soften him up."

"Okay, and keep an eye on him. Write down any suspicious behavior. Oh, and try to figure out if he noticed the dent. Then we'll all meet right after school outside Mr. Doyle's classroom. Maybe we can convince him to give Oliver his pocket watch back, so none of us have to see the principal. After all, we now know that Doyle doesn't like Sterns either," Chase pointed out.

"And if Mr. Doyle doesn't give it back?" I asked.

"I'll think of something," Chase promised me.

We nodded our heads in agreement before going our separate ways.

CHAPTER SEVEN

TRAGEDY AND TRIUMPH

AFTER RECESS, CAME a much-needed break—my advanced literature and language arts class. This was the only reason I came to school—well, this class and Jax. Reading and writing were my passions. I ruled in this class.

The room was on the third floor, and the teacher was Miss Ivy. Tall and slender, Miss Ivy had delicate features: soft, milky-white skin; fair hair that she wore back; light blue-gray eyes; and cheeks with a natural pinkish hue. Her thin lips never seemed to wear lipstick. She wore reading glasses that sat on the end of her nose when she read.

She spoke beautifully, pronouncing every syllable with velvety tones. It didn't matter what came out of her mouth—it always sounded like pure poetry.

Miss Ivy was my favorite teacher. I'm sure I was her favorite student too, as I received straight A's in her class every semester.

Miss Ivy said that maybe someday I could get paid for my writing, like Johnny got paid for skateboarding.

"Talent not used is worse than not having talent at all," Miss Ivy always said.

I took a seat in the middle of the room this time; Chase had broken me of my habit of always sitting in the back. Sure, I had only met Chase this morning, and he was now in a different class, but I did it anyway.

Eduard's pretentious walk into the classroom cracked a smile on my face. He took a seat next to me on my right. Nick was also in this class, and he awkwardly walked by me, clearly still upset about his flat football. I glanced up at him with an apologetic look.

I'd make it up to him somehow.

Since this was *advanced* literature, I didn't have to worry about the harassment of Johnny Ricker here. He was probably off in a class for foul and disgusting idiots and goons. But of course, this class wasn't free of annoyances—in walked stupid Ana Rahela Balenovic. She wasn't the teacher's pet in here, though. Miss Ivy was *my* ally.

Brilliant rays of sunshine pushed away the dark storm clouds gathering in my mind. Into the room radiated Jax. There just happened to be a seat open next to me on my left, and she saw it.

This was the time and place for our love story to begin, I thought. *She could whisper in my ear during class, asking me all sorts of questions. Perhaps I could help her with her homework after this long day at school and then take her out for ice cream or lemonade. We could work on class projects together, co-authoring a novel or screenplay about two young lovers.*

As she looked down my row of chairs, I got flustered. I leaned over and acted as if I were rummaging for something in my backpack. I was so nervous I couldn't look up. By force of habit, my birthmark kept pulling my head down.

Eduard tapped on my arm and asked, "Oliver, do you have a pencil in there I could borrow? I misplaced mine."

I glanced at him out of the corner of my eye. "Uh, I think so. Let me see," I answered.

Out of the corner of my other eye, I saw the open chair next to me move. I froze; my head was practically inside my backpack. I couldn't look up. I couldn't move.

Could this really be happening? I thought. *Jax chose the seat next to me?*

She chose me! This was the best day of my life!

Now that the greatest moment of my life had arrived, I didn't know how to act. This was my chance; I couldn't blow it.

Play it cool, Ollie, play it cool.

I took three long breaths in and out before I finished pretending to look in my backpack. I dragged out the pencil for Eduard and straightened up before slowly turning up to look at Jax with some cool expression on my face—as if it were *no big deal* she was sitting next to me.

There was only one problem. This was now the worst day of my life.

Jax had not taken the seat next to me. Ana Rahela Balenovic had.

Jax was sitting across the room near the front with some friends.

I felt like marching myself to Principal Sterns' office and turning myself in, saying, *It was I who dented Mr. Doyle's car. And the pocket watch, which I'm not supposed to have, is my great-grandfather's. Suspend me, send me to jail, but please don't make me sit next to Miss Know-It-All in one more class.*

I handed Eduard the pencil with a frown.

Miss Ivy took attendance in her soft, velvety voice. Pure English rolled off her tongue, and I couldn't have cared less. I could only think of one thing—well, two things: stupid Ana Rahela Balenovic and an open manhole.

Miss Ivy turned to the class and began with a poem. It was her custom. The class fell silent, listening.

Our remedies oft in ourselves do lie,
Which we ascribe to heaven: the fated sky
Gives us free scope, only doth backward pull
Our slow designs when we ourselves are dull.
-William Shakespeare

Then she looked around at the class.

"Good morning, everyone. Welcome to Advanced Literature. Over the course of this semester, we shall read and study several works by famous authors, but we will begin this semester by studying one of the greatest writers of all time—Shakespeare."

Miss Ivy wrote, *"Tragedy"* on the blackboard.

"Who can tell me what a tragedy is?" she asked.

Miss Ivy looked around the room before calling on Ana Rahela Balenovic, who couldn't keep her arms down.

"A tragedy is when something bad happens to someone," Ana Rahela Balenovic said in a smug tone.

You mean like having to sit next to you? I thought to myself.

"Yes, I suppose so," Miss Ivy said. "Tragedies in our world are when unfortunate circumstances meet one another: a plane crashes while carrying relief supplies to victims of a natural disaster; a young father on his way to work is killed by a car, leaving his family to struggle without him; a young girl is diagnosed with leukemia and her parents have no money to pay hospital bills. Tragedy is associated with disasters.

"However, tragedy in literature is a genre unto itself. It usually involves the main character upon whom some misfortune befalls, either of his or her own doing or by way of the environment. This misfortune is then followed by a series of missteps that only worsen the character's predicament as the story continues."

Miss Ivy wrote on the blackboard, "*Shakespeare: King Lear—Anthony and Cleopatra—Macbeth—Hamlet.*"

"Perhaps the tragedy is a *flaw* of the character—a weakness that can't be overcome and ends up leading to the character's demise or downfall. Or, maybe the tragedy stems from a *misunderstanding.* A misunderstanding that becomes bigger and bigger until it's out of control.

"Such stories touch us because we can relate to their very nature. At times, we may be confronted with our own mistakes or unfortunate circumstances, and our own efforts to deal with them—even if fueled by very good intentions—may wind up making matters worse. Our efforts might bring about the very outcome we were trying to avoid!

"Love—which we associate with happiness—can also be tragic. Love is a powerful emotion—giving us great joy and terrible pain. It can make us think crazy thoughts… and lead us to do things we would never dream of." Miss Ivy paused before turning to look out of a window. "Some of us know the feeling all too well."

"Miss Ivy, do all tragedies end terribly?" Jennifer Smith asked without raising her hand.

"What?" Miss Ivy snapped back into reality, then turned her head to look back at her students. "Oh, uh, well… usually yes. The reader sees the potential, or the way the story could have ended *if only* things were different, *if only* the character had chosen the right path."

Miss Ivy wrote on the blackboard, "*Romeo and Juliet.*"

"Who is familiar with the story of Romeo and Juliet? Shakespeare's play is one of the most well-known tragedies about forbidden love."

I had a feeling that Miss Ivy's class would be great this semester, I thought. *Here we are talking about a story of two young lovers who want to be together but are held back by outside forces—much like the story of… Jax and Oliver.*

Anna Rahela Balenovic had to, *just had to* raise her hand—because of course, she knew everything—except the fact that she was totally stupid.

When Miss Ivy called on Three-Name, she answered, "Romeo is a Capulet, and Juliet is a Montague. The two families hate each other, and therefore Romeo and Juliet can never be together. They both die in the end."

I couldn't believe my ears: Had she really just told the ending and ruined the story for everyone else?

Well, that's what she does—ruin other people's lives. If she were sitting next to you right now, she would ruin the ending of this story for you.

The school's intercom sounded. ***Mr. Doyle, please contact the office. Mr. Doyle, please contact the office.***

The sound of Mr. Doyle's name whisked me back to my confiscated pocket watch dilemma and made me uneasy. Miss Ivy looked up at the intercom speakers on the ceiling. She seemed to share my worry at the sound of Doyle's name.

"Let us get acquainted with these tragic characters by opening our literature books to page 57. Begin reading their story silently to yourselves," Miss Ivy instructed.

She turned to gaze out the window.

I opened my book and tried to read the story of Romeo and Juliet. But I started daydreaming of Jax and me, walking home together hand in hand. We talked about the happenings of the school day, and she laughed and giggled at my witty humor. We looked at the clouds in the sky, pointing out the different shapes we found. *Would she drink poison for me like Juliet did for Romeo?* I wondered. *I would drink it for her, no matter what it tasted like.*

My daydream made me look out the window, past one of the stone gargoyles that sat perched on the ledge, and into the small clouds that dotted the deep blue sky. That was when I saw it move—the gargoyle moved its head!

Was I seeing things? I thought.

I had been daydreaming, not focused on anything but the clouds in the distance, when it happened out of the corner of my eye.

Yes, the head was now in a different position, I thought. *Or was it?* I second-guessed myself.

I stared at the stone statue, waiting for it to move again. I stared and stared, but the gargoyle didn't move again. *I must be stressed out—seeing things,* I told myself.

But then I thought about everything that had happened today: the power going out, the whispering in my ear, the figure of a boy I saw as the lights flickered in the gym, and now one of the gargoyles moving. *'Where there's smoke, there's fire,'* I heard Chase's voice in my head say.

Maybe this school really is *haunted.*

I debated whether to jot the sighting down in my journal. Just in case, I opened my journal and readied my pen. However, my thoughts started going down a different path.

Once I document it on paper, it means it really happened. Don't be stupid, Oliver. Statues don't move. You're seeing things. Put the pen down.

I set my pen down and glanced back up at the stone gargoyle.

That's when I caught sight of it moving again! Just at the beginning of my glance, *its head moved back to where it originally was!*

I could feel my heartbeat pulsing through my fingers as I picked back up my pen. I wrote as quickly as I could:

> *Thursday, 1:20 p.m. — literature class: Movement of stone gargoyle seen on the ledge outside the window. Unknown cause or source.*

I stared back at the statue, not blinking for what seemed like hours.

The creature never moved again. *I must have been seeing things,* I thought.

I sighed and looked back at my journal. Now that the sighting was on paper, it looked stupid, and so did I. If it hadn't been written in ink, I would have erased it. Scribbling it out would make my journal look messy, and I couldn't rip out the page because important information was on the opposite side. I'd just have to leave it for now—*documentation of me seeing things.*

Before I knew it, Miss Ivy was calling the class to attention.

Miss Ivy removed her reading glasses. "Class is about over, and before I forget, I'm still in need of a few more volunteers for the school newspaper. Any takers?"

"I'd like to help," Jax said, raising her hand. "I could be a reporter."

"Excellent. Thank you, Jaclyn. Who else?"

Why wasn't I raising my hand? I was the best writer in the school. Jax had volunteered, and I was just sitting there as if my arms didn't work. I could feel sand slipping through the hourglass of opportunity. My brain told my arm to rise, but it wouldn't go up, tied down by my birthmark.

There was a long pause as Miss Ivy looked for any other hands.

"No other volunteers?" she questioned, looking over the class. "We need an editor," she said, her eyes landing directly on me. "Oliver?"

Jax looked over at me and gave a smile that shattered any bonds holding me back.

"Y-ye-yes. Of course, I'll help," I said.

I couldn't get the words out fast enough.

I looked at Miss Ivy with a smile of thanks, and she smiled back in acknowledgment. This *was* the best day of my life.

"I'd like to volunteer also," the stupid voice next to me said. "I could help with the layout."

What? I thought. *Was Ana Rahela Balenovic determined to ruin my life?*

"Very well then. I'll see all three of you after class," Miss Ivy said with a nod.

As the bell rang for the end of class, I felt I had won at least one round today: Jax and I were going to be on the same team. I wouldn't let Ana Rahela Balenovic bring me down now.

The classroom emptied, and I confidently walked to Miss Ivy's desk to find out more about our newspaper. I didn't spare a look at Three-Name when she came up right behind me.

Miss Ivy gave the three of us some handouts, outlining some of the responsibilities for the school's newspaper, and asked if we could meet after school at least twice a week. She said the school paper would be printed every Tuesday morning, giving us the entire week—and weekend, if necessary—to work on stories.

I would be the editor—helping to decide what stories we should print and checking them for grammatical errors and writing style.

Jax would be the field reporter—uncovering stories, and then submitting the written articles to me for review.

Ana Rahela Balenovic would be the nuisance that needed to be covered up.

I left Miss Ivy's class, floating on clouds.

Jax and I would be meeting after school at least twice a week.

It was almost like we were dating.

CHAPTER EIGHT

FABRICATIONS

MRS. HUNTLEY WAS MY sixth-period art teacher. I never met a kid who didn't like her. She was extremely nice and encouraging to everyone—even the kids whose artwork looked like something a trash truck ran over.

Mrs. Huntley wore an apron to class that held paintbrushes, art pencils, and a ruler. And she allowed us to talk while we worked, requiring only that we be silent while she was instructing.

I liked art class even though I wasn't a great artist. Not like Gio, who always won class awards for his projects.

One time, Gio painted a picture that was so awesome that Mrs. Huntley entered it into a statewide competition. Gio didn't win, or even come in third, but he did get in the competition.

Mrs. Huntley never took attendance, at least not that I knew of. Maybe she just somehow knew who was here and who wasn't. I never saw her get upset with any student either, even if someone hadn't completed their homework assignment. She would simply sit down with them, talking gently, asking what the problem was, and how the two could resolve it.

Knowing this made me think about her argument with Mr. Doyle in the hallway this morning. Whatever it was about, they hadn't seemed to resolve it. I wondered what Mr. Doyle could have done that would upset the happy Mrs. Huntley.

I opened my journal and read the notes Chase asked me to write down:

Thursday, 8:55 a.m. — school hallway:

- *Mrs. Huntley seen arguing with Mr. Doyle about some canceled project and money he owes her.*
- *Mrs. Huntley said not to be afraid of something alien, and the Earth will be transformed along with the minds of youth with no toxic effects on the environment.*
- *She threatens Mr. Doyle by saying he'll be dead to her if the project doesn't happen because of him.*
- *Mr. Doyle said it's not his fault.*

Chase was right about one thing: *Mr. Doyle had something going on besides just having my pocket watch.*

I watched the other students find their stools behind the long benches, which had been arranged into one big square. I saved a seat next to me for Gio, the only one of my friends who had this same class. I was eager to hear how his conversation with Mr. Doyle went, and if there was any chance of me pleading for my great-grandfather's pocket watch back.

Ana Rahela Balenovic was here, stalking me. I made sure she saw I was saving a seat for Gio, just in case she got any stupid ideas of making my day more terrible by sitting next to me. I ignored her as she sat on a stool to the right of Gio's empty seat.

I let out a sigh of relief when Gio came into the room and hopped onto the stool next to me.

"So?" I asked, "What happened in Doyle's class? Did you talk with him?"

"Well," he said, hesitating. "Doyle wasn't exactly, uh, in class."

"He wasn't in class… what do you mean?" I asked, completely puzzled.

"I mean, Doyle didn't show up for class! We sat there for fifteen or twenty minutes, wondering if *we* had the wrong schedule, or if *he* had the wrong schedule. Someone finally went to the principal's office. They called his name over the intercom before Principal Sterns came down and babysat our class for the rest of the hour."

"So—Doyle never showed up?" I sputtered.

"Nope. And Sterns spent the whole time talking about how important it was that we all behave when the President comes. B-o-r-i-ng," Gio said, shaking his head.

"Where'd Doyle go, do you think?" I asked.

"Don't know. He has another class to teach today, so maybe he got sick?" Gio said.

"And not tell anyone? But… he's got my watch!" I protested.

Anna Rahela butted into our conversation, asking, "Did you say Mr. Doyle didn't show up for his last class?"

I shook my head *"no"* and tried to ignore her from then on.

"We'll talk more after class," I whispered to Gio as Mrs. Huntley, with her big smile and blue eyes that sparkled, was starting class.

"My friends, it's so good to see all of you! I've missed you over the break," Mrs. Huntley said as she began walking over to a large, intricately carved statue placed on the floor in the middle of the benches. "I'm looking forward to this semester's class."

Mrs. Huntley ran her fingers over the statue and said, "Look at the beauty of this piece, my friends. Notice all the fluent lines that lead your eye around to different parts of this masterpiece, all the wonderful details that demand that you stop and study them." Then she turned and ran her fingers over a coat rack placed next to the statue. "Now look at this coat rack next to it—see its lines and shape? Which one is the greater piece of work?"

The class answered in unison, "The statue!"

"I can't argue with that," she chuckled.

Mrs. Huntley took up a blue sheet from the corner of one of the benches and draped it over the sculpture. "Now, we have taken away all the details, all the distractions of this piece."

She lifted up a red sheet and draped it over the coat rack. "Now, we have taken away the details of both items and broken them down to their simplest shapes."

It seemed simple enough to me: There were two blobs in the middle of the classroom now—red and blue.

"Not only do we now look at each piece differently, but also the environment that surrounds them. Notice how the fabric changes the shape and feel of the objects, and this room," she said.

But I didn't notice anything different. And honestly, I couldn't figure out why someone would want to cover up a statue that they paid a lot of money for. That just seemed dumb.

She dimmed the lights and began a slideshow.

"Today, we shall experience the works of Christo, whose ambitions include wrapping bridges and islands in miles of fabric. He and the late Jeanne-Claude have changed entire environments temporarily through their designs—but their effects last forever in the mind. Nothing is too big for Christo!" she said in a voice dripping with enthusiasm. "And this great artist will be working on a project *right here in Colorado*! He is covering the Arkansas River, and our very own Whispering Falls outside of Raven Ridge, with fabric!"

She turned the lights off, and we watched a slideshow portfolio of photographs of Christo's work: Enormous sheets of colored fabric covered statues, bridges, buildings, and the entire cove of an ocean.

Watching the images made me wonder, *how much fabric would it take to cover up this entire school?*

I wouldn't make that temporary, though. It would be a permanent work of art.

"When we think of covering something up, we tend to associate it with hiding something. But is this what Christo is doing? Is he concealing? Or is he revealing something which one never saw before?" she enthused.

Mrs. Huntley flipped to the next photo of a bridge draped with fabric. "Christo covers the world with fabric. In altering the world's appearance, he is allowing the viewer to experience objects in a different manner—changing the way we feel about our very environment."

The last image on the screen disappeared, and in the temporary silent pause before Mrs. Huntley turned the lights back on, the distant cry of a woman faintly reached my ears. My eyes grew wide in the dark classroom.

"G, did you hear that?" I whispered.

"Hear what?" he whispered back.

I strained to listen over our class, now beginning to chatter without a care. I knew I heard something—a woman wailing, just like the ghost stories told about—but I seemed to be the only one who heard it.

This day has really got to me, I thought. *Seeing things, and now hearing things! What was next—I'd feel something touch me?*

I shook my head to Gio. "Nothing," I sighed.

With the lights back on, Miss Huntley said to the class, "After seeing Christo's work, is this what we sometimes do in life?" Her facial expression became somber as she continued, "We all have things in life that sometimes we want to cover up, don't we? We may think that covering them up—hiding or changing their appearance to others—will change our own environment. But it doesn't. Appearance is temporary, just as Christo's work is temporary. The real substance remains underneath, and it will always be found when it is uncovered. In the end, all things are always shown for what they are."

Mrs. Huntley asked our class to sketch the two draped objects in the middle of the room. She told us to be as simple or as detailed as we wanted. "Simply let the shapes move you. Let the objects speak to you," she said.

By the look of my sketches, the two sheets had told me they were messy blobs.

I was done with my interpretation in about ten seconds, so I doodled on another paper as if I were still working. I didn't understand how some of the kids around me could get into drawing these stupid sheets. Now, if we were drawing something cool, like a giant tank or fighter jet plane, I think I could understand, but honestly, these were probably dirty sheets off someone's bed.

Mrs. Huntley walked by each student, looking at their work and sometimes giving an *"Ooh,"* or an *"Ah,"* while nodding her head in encouragement.

She ignored the tire marks from a trash truck on my paper.

The end-of-class bell rang. It also signaled an end to the school day.

Mrs. Huntley said, "Uncover the world around you, my friends. Look at your environment with a different eye—an artistic eye."

I really didn't care what eye I would use to uncover my great-grandfather's pocket watch. I just grabbed my stuff and rushed out of the classroom with Gio.

In the hallway, we looked in both directions for Chase. We had to figure out our next move.

We spotted him down the hall talking with Nick. Running

to him, we blurted out in panic, "Doyle didn't show up for Gio's fifth-period class!"

"So I heard," Chase replied, sounding calm. "And he didn't show for his sixth-period class either. Nick said there was a substitute by the last hour."

"Two classes in a row?" Gio said, raising his eyebrows. "Doyle must've gone home sick."

"What do we do now?" I said, panicked. "Do we go to Sterns' office like he said? Is he even going to show up?"

Chase smiled. "This just might be the break we need."

"How so?" I asked.

Chase confidently answered. "Because we'll go tell the substitute that you left your pocket watch in the classroom, and you've come back now to pick it up."

"Yes!" I exclaimed, realizing at once what he was suggesting. "And since Doyle's not here, we won't have to go to Sterns' office at all! Brilliant!"

Gio mumbled nervously, "But what if the substitute doesn't believe us?"

Chase lifted his eyebrows. "Then we resort to plan B."

"Steal it?" Gio squeaked.

"No, reclaim it. You can't steal something that is already yours," Chase said matter-of-factly.

I nodded in agreement. His line of thinking was exactly as mine had been when I saw it on Mr. Doyle's desk earlier.

The three of us raced back to Mr. Doyle's classroom, stopping just outside the door. Peering our heads in, we saw a substitute sitting at Mr. Doyle's desk.

The sub was a beautiful young woman who looked as if she had just graduated from modeling college. Her blond hair was pulled back into a ponytail. Her long black eyelashes seemed longer than her small, cute nose. Her full red curvy lips held a pen as she shuffled through some papers.

Without any warning, Chase pushed me through the door, and then Gio.

When she smiled at us, our faces blushed. “Hello, boys. May I help you?”

We all stood quietly for a moment before Chase finally spoke. “Uh… where’s Mr. Doyle?”

She frowned before answering, “He’s not here. I’ve been asked to take his place. Is there something I can help you with?”

“Oliver here lost his pocket watch. We heard Mr. Doyle found it in a later class and left it in his desk,” Chase improvised.

“Well, let me see.” She moved around some books on Doyle’s desk, accidentally spilling a bunch of papers onto the floor. “Oh my, look what a klutz I am.”

We all scrambled to help her pick them up, earning her smile.

The sub pulled out each drawer of Doyle’s desk, moving the inside articles around as she tried to find my watch. “No, I don’t see a watch. Perhaps it was turned in to the main office?” she suggested.

“Yeah, maybe. Thanks anyway,” Chase said with a huge smile. “How long is Mr. Doyle gone for?”

“I don’t know; they didn’t tell me. So perhaps I’ll be back tomorrow,” she said with a big smile.

Her smile caused all of us to smile dreamily before we walked out.

“Wow!” Chase whispered. “I can’t wait for *her* class tomorrow!”

“Yeah,” Gio agreed. “I hope Doyle doesn’t show.”

“He’s *got to show*,” I snapped out in a frustrated and scared tone. “I need my pocket watch back!”

“Oh, right. Of course,” Gio said, nodding his head in agreement.

Right then, an evil sound cut through the air.

“Hey, Freak Face!” Johnny’s donkey voice echoed from down the hall. “Looks like Sterns’ office is a no-go!”

I turned to see Johnny and Miles walking towards the exit.

"What do you mean?" I called.

"Haven't you heard? Doyle's gone for the day; there was a substitute instead. So, if Doyle ain't go'n, then I ain't go'n. So long, losers," Johnny sneered just before he and Miles bolted out the door and onto their skateboards.

"What now?" I whined to Chase.

Chase thought for a moment. He stared at the door to Principal Sterns' office that was just across the hall. "Well, we definitely don't want to go into Sterns' office if Doyle hasn't told him anything. But we also need to get Ollie's watch back. So, the question is, did Doyle tell Sterns about this morning? And if he did, then did he give your watch to the principal?"

"Guess we need to find out what Sterns knows," Gio said.

"Yeah, but how we gonna do that?" I asked.

"We'll go see Sterns for a different reason," Chase said. "If Sterns changes the subject to the watch, then it's obvious he knows. At that point, we tell our side of the story and get your watch back, hopefully without a phone call to your mom. But, if he doesn't know why we're there, then Doyle hasn't told him. And that leaves the real possibility of getting back the watch directly from Doyle later."

"But what other reason would we be seeing Sterns for? We just can't go in there without a reason," I argued.

Chase smiled confidently. "Don't worry, I'll do the talking."

"Okay," I agreed. But it sure sounded complicated.

No sooner had we agreed on our course of action than Jax beamed like a ray of sunlight down the hall and radiated to the principal's doorway.

Our eyes popped as the three of us shouted out in unison, "Jax!"

She stopped and looked behind her. We waved her over.

"What?" she demanded as she approached. "Aren't we supposed to be in the principal's office?"

"There's been a development," Chase said.

A development? I rolled my eyes at his dramatic choice of words.

Chase quickly filled her in, but she did not agree with the plan.

Putting her hands on her hips, Jax said, "Look, why don't we just tell the truth about Johnny and what happened this morning? He's the one who caused this, and he should get in trouble for it. But he always gets away with this kind of stuff."

Chase moved his hands downward, attempting to calm and reassure her. "And we will... *if* Sterns asks. But Johnny's not even going to see Sterns; he took off a minute or two ago. Plus, Mr. Doyle is nowhere to be found. So, if Doyle didn't tell Sterns, then it's probably better to just work it out with Doyle when he gets back. We're not asking you to lie—just not to say anything if not asked."

She stood still for a moment. "Okay," she agreed reluctantly. "But I still want to see Johnny get in trouble."

"Johnny will get what's coming to him, I promise. But for now, let's make sure we stay out of trouble," Chase said, pointing to all of us.

Jax relaxed her arms and asked, "So, what are we going to tell Principal Sterns we've come to see him for?"

"Leave that to me," Chase winked.

CHAPTER NINE

REPORT TO THE PRINCIPAL'S OFFICE

WITH THE SCHOOL day over, kids flew out of the building like pigeons freed at a wedding. They simply couldn't wait to get out of there.

There were only two types of kids who hung around after school; those with after-school activities, and kids in trouble. I fell into the second group this time.

Entering the main office was not fun. When I walked in, the large counter in front reminded me of a wall surrounding a fortress or a castle. It was so high, I could barely see over it.

Behind this barricade sat the office secretary, Miss Hathaway. She was looking down as she typed, but she raised her head when we entered.

Miss Hathaway was older—somebody's grandmother, probably,

with short silver hair which she probably put up in curlers each night. She wore eyeglasses on the end of her nose and puckered her lips each time after speaking.

"Can I help you?" she puckered.

"Yes, please. We're here to see Principal Sterns," Chase said politely.

"Regarding what matter?" she puckered.

"Oh, he's not expecting us?" Chase glanced at the rest of us with a slight smile. "Well, that doesn't surprise me, seeing how busy he is and all. We wanted to talk with him about possible paranormal activity in connection with the power outages, and he told us to see him after school. I guess he forgot with all the other stuff he has to worry about."

Miss Hathaway stared at him with a, *"What the… ?"* look.

A young lady walking in behind us interrupted this exchange. It was Mr. Doyle's beautiful substitute. She was carrying a stack of books and papers that spilled out of her grasp near the counter. Chase, Gio, and I quickly helped her pick them up.

"Oh, what a klutz I am! All these nice papers will be dirty and crinkled now. Thank you, boys." She flipped blond hair out of her eyes and smiled at us before looking at the gatekeeper. "Hello again, Miss… Hathaway, right?"

"Yes. Hello, Miss Lexington. How did the substituting go?" she puckered.

"I really enjoyed it, thanks. I was a little nervous, but I had my inhaler with me in case I was short of breath," Miss Lexington said, holding up a small canister with a mouthpiece attached. "Is Principal Sterns in his office?"

"Yes, he's waiting for you. Please go right in," Miss Hathaway puckered in the direction of our principal's door.

"Thanks," the gorgeous Miss Lexington answered. Like a

supermodel on a runway, she drifted past us, leaving behind an intoxicating smell of perfume.

Mrs. Hathaway cleared her throat. "Have a seat outside his office door, children. When the Principal's done, I'll tell him you're out here."

An old wooden bench awaited us just to the right of Principal Sterns' frosted glass office door. The four of us all sat side-by-side on its uncomfortable seat. Chase was closest to the door, then me and Gio. Jax was on the end.

It was for the best that Jax didn't sit next to me; I could handle only so much at once. And sitting on the bench waiting for Principal Sterns was horrible. I just wanted to get it over with—but then again, I wasn't so sure that I did.

I looked nervously around the room. Hanging on a wall was a framed cover of a magazine called, *The Saturday Evening Post.* The cover had a black-and-white drawing of a woman sitting in front of a mirror. From a distance, the images blended together and looked like a skull. My eyes went back and forth, focusing between the woman and her mirror, and then the skull, and then back to the woman. The artist must have intentionally drawn it like that, but I'm not sure which image the artist wanted to portray more. The subtitle read, *"All Is Vanity."*

Old photographs of the school building also hung on the walls of the office. There were photographs of past principals, teachers, and staff. There also was what appeared to be an old photo of Horace Tanner and his wife Anastasia posing in front of their silver mine.

In it, Anastasia stood to Horace's right in a beautiful gown. Her black hair was done up on top of her head, and her face held a stern look. She was holding what looked to be a mirror in her right hand. Her other hand was wrapped around her husband's arm.

Horace was wearing a black suit with a black top hat. His long silver mustache framed a frown. His right hand was in his pocket, and the other held a pocket watch with a chain—a pocket watch that looked like mine.

But the photo that made me take a second glance, was a photo of Charlie Hackett. It was a memorial photo with small print that read, *"In loving memory of Charles Nathan Hackett, who loved life and deserved more."* His eyes gave me the creeps; they seemed to stare right back at me.

I stared at the dead boy's face for a few moments more before turning my glance to another photo… and that's when the eyes of Charlie Hackett followed me. The hair on the back of my neck stood tall as my eyes darted back to his photograph.

No, his eyes look like they are in the same position as when I first saw them, I thought. *I'm seeing things, like with the gargoyle moving on the ledge outside of literature class.* I didn't know whether to tell Chase.

I finally figured if it happened again, then I would say something. For now, I'd just mark it down to stress.

I turned my focus back to waiting to speak to Sterns. That's when I realized that the principal's door was cracked open. It allowed the conversation inside the office to be somewhat overheard by those of us sitting outside.

"Thank you for filling in," Principal Sterns said. "It was a miracle that you had just stopped by looking for a substituting position. Talk about a happy coincidence!"

"The students were great," Miss Lexington replied. "I love kids, and I love to teach—it's my dream job."

"Well, if you don't mind my asking, why aren't you teaching full time already?"

"I'm looking for a permanent position. I'm just out of college, so I only recently received my teaching certificate. As I'm sure you know, most schools want you to have some experience, so I need to sub for a while to build up my resume. Hopefully, I can find a school with a principal like you; now, that would be great," she said.

"Oh, thank you. Any school would be lucky to have you on their full-time staff. Hmm… you know… there may be a full-time position at this school in the near future."

"Really? Can you tell me more about it?"

"Well, it's not for certain, so perhaps that conversation may be premature. In the meantime, are you free tomorrow? I mean, to substitute."

"Why… of course! I would love to come back!"

"Great, I… we… would love to have you back." Principal Sterns sounded relieved and excited at the same time.

"I'll be here first thing in the morning. Thank you so much."

"Very well, then I'll see you tomorrow morning,"

The office door opened. Principal Sterns stood at his office door, directing a smile at the new substitute. She smiled at him as she walked out, but tripped over her own feet. Luckily, Principal Sterns caught her before she fell to the ground.

"Oh, I'm such a klutz," she said, smiling at him. "Thank you."

"It was my pleasure, really," he said as she walked away, still smiling.

Principal Sterns didn't notice us sitting outside his door waiting for him. He just studied Miss Lexington as she walked out of the office, all the while making that annoying clicking noise with his pen.

Mrs. Hathaway cleared her throat and puckered her lips. "Principal Sterns, these children are here to see you."

"Hmm?" He finally looked over at us. "Oh, yes. Come into my office, students."

Principal Sterns walked behind his massive desk and sat down in his massive leather chair. The four of us sat down in the small, somewhat uncomfortable chairs facing his desk.

The principal's office was neat and tidy. Pens and pencils lined up neatly in a row on the desk, and a pile of papers stacked in an orderly fashion on top. A small nameplate on the desk read, '*Principal Sterns*,' as if you didn't already know who you were talking to.

Large bookcases lined the wall behind the principal. These were filled with large hardcover books, small objects, and a mirror with a silver frame in the shape of a raven wrapping its wings around the glass. Sterns had probably put the mirror there to check out his perfectly combed hair. On the walls hung plaques, framed certificates, and photos of the principal with presumably important people.

"Well, what can I do for you today, students?" he asked, still smiling.

We all looked at each other... *Sterns didn't know. Chase was right! Doyle hadn't told him a thing.*

Chase spoke up. "Well, sir, we were wondering if you might be in need of our services?"

Jax, Gio, and I looked at Chase with the same puzzled look that Principal Sterns gave him. *What was he talking about?*

"Your services?" Principal Sterns asked. "And what might those be?"

"Investigative services... specializing in the paranormal, but not exclusively. Seems you have some mysterious power failures that might need looking into."

Principal Sterns looked like he was trying to suppress a smile. "That's very kind of you, but I think we have it under control."

"What has your investigation into the power failures revealed?" Chase questioned excitedly.

"It has revealed—before you start digging a hole, you must make sure you have enough dirt to fill it back up."

The four of us sat silently. I don't think any of us knew exactly what he meant.

Principal Sterns gave a half-crooked smile and continued. "As

I've mentioned, it looks as if there's been some vandalism to one of the electrical panels for the A/C units. This is causing the older units in this place to work overtime. The added strain on them is knocking out the power throughout the entire building.

"The original building construction doesn't allow for our retrofitted air-conditioning to be effective without a major overhaul. This building is a historic landmark, and by law, we can only modify its design so much. To retrofit this school correctly now, *without* modifying its design, would be cost-prohibitive as well. It's important to do things right the first time and have the proper funding before you start. It should have been done correctly to begin with, but that was before I took over here. So, because of the power outages that went on today, we're just going to have to keep the classrooms a little warmer than we'd like for now."

Chase asked, "What about the rumors of ghosts and spirits haunting this school? Don't you suspect they might be responsible?"

Principal Sterns gave a short laugh. "No, I don't think so. There are no such things as ghosts, and the school is not haunted. But, even if it were, don't you think the ghosts would like it cooler also?" he smirked.

Chase looked around the office, then back to our principal. "What about Mr. Doyle?"

Principal Sterns' face quickly hardened. "What about Mr. Doyle?"

"Is he all right?"

"Why do you ask? Do you know something?"

"No. Just that he wasn't in class," Chase said.

"I'm sure Mr. Doyle is fine and will be back in the classroom soon. Now, all of you have much more important things to worry about, like your studies. Leave the building and teacher problems to me," the principal said.

Chase shrugged. "Well, if you change your mind, please feel free to call on us."

Principal Sterns smiled. "That's quite all right, but thank you."

There was a knock at the door, and Principal Sterns called in a loud voice, "Come in."

The door opened to reveal the dreadful Miss Crabtree. She was not looking very happy. Her frowning lips were pressed tightly together, her forehead was creased with wrinkles, and she had that same look my mother gives me when I've done something wrong. Had Principal Sterns somehow fallen into that category?

"Well, hello, Miss Crabtree," the principal said, his voice slightly hesitant. "To what do I owe this pleasure?"

"May I have a word with you?" There was a hint of anger in her voice.

"Uh… of course. These students were just leaving. Please come in," he said. The principal's smile looked forced now. "Thanks for stopping by, students."

We slipped past Miss Crabtree, who stood unmoving with her arms folded. She forcefully shut the door behind her after we left.

"Looks like you were right, Chase," Gio whispered.

"Yeah," he whispered back. "But something else is going on right now—let's sit back down."

With no warning, Chase pushed me back down on the corner of the bench nearest to Principal Sterns' glass door and then plopped down next to me.

What was he doing? I thought. *Principal Sterns didn't have any idea why we came—Doyle hadn't told him anything, and now Chase wanted to hang around? Was he trying to get us in trouble?*

Gio and Jax hesitated, not knowing what to do, but then sat back down as well. Miss Hathaway peered over her glasses at us with a suspicious look. We all smiled back, shrugging our shoulders. She puckered her lips and went back to typing. Perhaps she thought Principal Sterns wanted to talk to us more after Miss Crabtree left.

Chase leaned over me with his ear towards the door, trying not to be obvious. The rest of us couldn't help but do the same. Their voices were muffled, but we could make out some of their conversation.

Miss Crabtree was saying in an angry tone, "What do you think you're doing?"

"It's just for now until we figure this out," Sterns said.

"It's a bad idea, with everything going on…." At this point, her voice became soft, the sound of it breaking into bits. "Arriving… background… aliens… Doyle… hazardous…."

"Don't worry," he said back. "I'll handle everything."

His voice lowered, and we couldn't hear anything except muffled tones. We leaned farther over the arm of the bench, trying to make out more of their conversation. Chase leaned on me, then Gio on Chase, and Jax on Gio, until suddenly, a loud crack echoed in the room. The arm of the bench broke, and I tumbled onto the ground, with the others falling on top of me. Miss Hathaway stood up from her desk, and the principal's door flew open.

I blinked—a bit dazed from the fall. Principal Sterns and Miss Crabtree towered over me as the other kids picked themselves up.

"Sorry," I mumbled. "I must have been leaning on the arm of the bench. It broke."

"What are you all still doing here?" Principal Sterns' voice had returned to its familiar, mean tone.

Chase quickly answered, "Oh, we forgot to tell you we'd be happy to help with any special projects that might be needed for the President's visit."

Jax, Gio, and I gave him the *what-did-you-just-say?* look. Chase was completely out of his mind! We had never agreed to something that crazy.

"I'll keep that in mind," Principal Sterns said, his voice brisk. "Now, off you go. I've got other matters I need to deal with."

We hurried out of the office under the watchful eye and pursed lips of Miss Hathaway. With a timid smile, I handed the secretary the broken bench arm as we passed the front counter.

Outside Principal Sterns' office, we paused in our tracks. I wasn't sure how I felt. On the one hand, Mr. Doyle had not told Principal Sterns anything. And that might be good news. But on the other hand, I still didn't have my pocket watch, and Mr. Doyle still might tell Principal Sterns everything when he returned—and my mother might discover the pocket watch missing in the meantime.

"Well," Chase said, raising his eyebrows, "we know Doyle didn't say anything. But now we have more questions than answers."

Gio gave a quick nod. "So, now what?"

Jax was quick to reply. "I'll tell you all what! Johnny is going to get away with being a jerk, Oliver's not getting his watch back, and we are all going to be in trouble for lying to Principal Sterns now." Her eyes narrowed as she looked towards Chase.

"Relax! We didn't exactly lie," Chase said. "How could we tell Principal Sterns what Mr. Doyle was supposed to tell him when we don't even know what Doyle was going to tell him to begin with?"

That somehow made sense.

Jax came back with, "What about that story you made up about the power outage, and the whole investigative thing? That was a lie."

Chase looked like he was taken back. "That was one-hundred percent true! We *are* investigating the power outages."

We *are?* Gio and I looked at each other, and then to Chase. *Or was Chase arguing with Jax just to argue?*

Jax put her hands on her hips. "I went along with not telling Principal Sterns about this morning because you convinced me that you and Oliver might be the ones who get in trouble instead of Johnny. But you didn't tell me you were going to lie! Now I'm a part of it, and I might also get in trouble!"

"It's not a lie. We need your help with our investigation," Chase pleaded.

"Uh… how about… *no.* I don't think so. I'm not getting involved. Nope, not getting involved. And if Principal Sterns asks me anything about it at all in the future, I'm telling the truth!" Jax stormed off, leaving us standing there silently looking at Chase.

"She'll come around," he said confidently.

CHAPTER TEN

DEAD COW BRIDGE

"I'M GLAD MR. DOYLE didn't tell Sterns anything yet," I said, rubbing my forehead, "but I don't have my pocket watch to take back home. What am I going to do now?"

"The first thing you're going to do is document what we heard with Sterns," Chase said. "There's more going on with this school than meets the eye, and we're going to get to the bottom of it. We'll come up with some excuse to tell your mother about your watch on the way home. Since you both missed the bus, I'll give you guys a ride home on my bike."

It was good that Chase had ridden his dirt bike to school this morning. Since we had waited around to talk to Principal Sterns, all the buses going home had already left. I could walk, but it was far, and it would seem twice as far in this heat. And missing the bus home was an issue for Gio.

In the morning, Gio's dad dropped him off at school on his way to work at the auto shop. But in the afternoon, Gio's dad was still at work, so Gio needed to take the bus home. It was his leg that was the problem. Walking home with Chase and me for a couple of miles would be too much for him. Gio wouldn't complain about the walk—that much I was sure about—but he would worry about slowing us down and might hurt himself trying to keep up.

We bolted out the exit door, slinging our backpacks and book bags over our shoulders. We headed for Chase's dirt bike. Once we got close, Chase pointed at the bike. "Hey, G, why don't you stand on the back pegs of my dirt bike? Ollie, you can sit on the handlebars."

Gio nodded with a smile. I wasn't so sure how that Chase's solution would work for the three of us; would the bike handle us all? Up close, Chase's bike was a beat-up piece of junk that most likely had been thrown together. The seat was ripped, the handgrips were notched, a lot of spokes were missing, and the pegs that stuck out the rear sprocket were bent. Even the frame itself looked crooked and beat up.

"Are you sure this bike can carry the three of us?" I asked skeptically.

"Of course!" Chase scoffed, undoing his bike lock. "This baby's seen harder action than this, trust me!"

Chase mounted, nodding for Gio to climb aboard. All Gio needed to do was stand on the two short metal pegs that stuck out from the rear tire sprocket and hold on to Chase's shoulders. But I was bigger than Gio, and I didn't quite know how I would fit on the handlebars. Not to mention, if my mom saw me riding without a helmet, she would kill me—if a fall didn't do it first. I would rather Gio, who was smaller in size, sit on the handlebars. But because of his leg, I understood why it wasn't a good idea.

Chase held the bike steady as I wiggled my way onto the handlebars. Sitting there would be difficult once the bike started moving. I knew better than to try to balance the bike—that needed to be left to Chase. Otherwise, the two of us would be working against each other.

But I needed to balance myself and my backpack on the thin handlebars that were going to move every time Chase made a turn. And I had only the bar itself to hold. It was going to be hard.

Chase yelled, "All aboard!"

"Forward!" Gio shouted.

Chase pushed off with a shaky start. He stood on his pedals with all his weight, commanding the dirt bike to move forward. The dirt bike protested, weaving from side-to-side and barely moving. I tried to make myself as small as possible, so Chase could see around me.

The pedals moaned with every push from Chase. The bike did not want to move! Finally, tired from fighting with its master, the dirt bike righted itself and began moving in a straight line.

So far, so good, I thought.

The main road we were on was paved and easy, but I was tense as I thought about the unpaved roads and dirt paths we would eventually take to get home. I knew the heat from the sun would sap Chase of his energy before long. It was hard enough to ride a bike in this heat, let alone one carrying two extra people.

Still standing high on his pedals, Chase dug in. The bike picked up speed. We raced so fast down one hill, my hands practically welded themselves to the bike's handlebars, and Chase stopped pedaling. He sat back as our speed increased and yelled excitedly, "Oh, yes! Here we go!"

Near the bottom of the hill, we veered to the right, onto an unpaved road. It was rough and bumpy. We were going fast, and the bike became unstable on the dirt.

This is it, I thought. *We are going to crash.*

"Hang on, Ollie!" Chase shouted.

But I couldn't. There was not enough bar to grasp onto, and I felt my grip slipping. When we hit a big rut, I flew onto the ground and tumbled, making a cloud of dust. Chase lost control of the bike then, sending him and Gio to the same dusty landing as me.

Hitting the rough dirt road took a large portion of skin off my hands and ripped a hole in the knee of my new blue jeans. My hands hurt as they started bleeding. But I didn't cry. I was too mature and grown up.

Besides, I was thankful that I didn't bang and cut my head. That would give my mother a reason to make me cry.

I looked over at my buddies. Chase and Gio seemed okay. I eyeballed Chase's bike. *It looked okay, but would it still be rideable?*

Chase dusted himself off, picked up his bike, and looked at Gio and me. "Well, that was fun. But maybe we'd be better off walking?"

Both Gio and I shook our heads in agreement. It would take more time on account of Gio's leg, but at least we would live.

We trudged down the hot, dusty road. Both sides of the road were lined with tall grass, thick brush, and towering trees, which helped hide us from the sun's vicious rays.

Along the right side of the road was Miller's Creek. It was a great place to catch frogs and crawfish. It was at its lowest point this time of year, with only a trickle of water running along.

Further south, on the far side of Miller's Creek, were train tracks we'd sometimes walk down. My mother would have a fit if she knew we did that, let alone find out we placed pennies on the tracks for the train to flatten. She hated the train and its horn, which could be heard for miles. Mom told me, *"Every time an evil soul dies, the train sounds its horn, as it carries the soul down to hell."*

I hated the train's horn, too.

We walked for about twenty minutes. It felt like twenty hours in the heat. When we came to a small turn off in the road, Gio blurted out, "Hey, we should take the shortcut."

I knew he was going to say that, and he knows I don't want to take that shortcut because of the bridge.

"Shortcut?" Chase asked.

"Yep, right down that little road there," Gio pointed down the small road that disappeared into trees and bushes as it crossed over Miller's Creek. "But Oliver doesn't want to go down there because he's chicken."

I shook my head. "I'm not chicken," I denied. "If we just keep going this way, the creek becomes low enough to jump over, and we'd make it home even faster."

Chase asked, "And what's down this other road to be afraid of?"

"There's an old wooden train bridge that passes over that road, called Dead Cow Bridge," Gio said. "The story goes that some dead cows were found hanging from the bridge by their hind legs. Old Man Owens, who owns the farm the cows were from, called the sheriff to investigate. When the cow bodies were cut down, they discovered that certain parts of their bodies were missing—a tongue, an eyeball, and even the entire brain of one cow! The sheriff shut down the road that leads to the bridge for months."

"Did anyone ever find out the cause?" Chase asked quickly.

"No," I chimed in. "Some people believe witches live in the wild woods near our school and they perform rituals. Others say it was the work of a mad scientist who needed the body parts for experiments. And some think it was space aliens wanting animal specimens."

"Well, every one of those theories would make sense. We most definitely will go to see this bridge," Chase said enthusiastically.

My heart pounded when he said this. Gio was right; I didn't want to go to that bridge. Even if there weren't cow stories surrounding the place, the area was still scary. The thick wooden trestles that held up the railroad ties and rails spelled out a message: *STAY OUT!* Or that's what I saw anyway.

I had no problem doing just that.

About a year and a half ago, Gio and I had gone exploring there. We had dared each other to stand under the bridge for thirty seconds. I went first, but I got so scared after ten seconds that I ran out from under the bridge, breathing heavily. I don't know why Gio was acting brave now, because he never even tried to do it!

The three of us started down the small dirt road that disappeared into a tunnel of trees. After we had gone around a turn in the road, the camouflage of trees gave way, revealing the old wooden train bridge suspended between two hills—and a surprise for us ahead on the dirt road that traveled beneath it.

We stopped and stared in silence for a moment, then looked at each other.

Gio whispered, "Mr. Doyle's car!"

My heart picked up a beat. "What's it doing here?"

"Maybe he's spying on us?" Gio whispered back.

I shook my head. "Why would he be spying on us?"

We stood in silence on the country road, the sun beating down and the air not moving. It was completely quiet, except for birds chirping and bugs buzzing.

Chase cast a few glances about, then directed his gaze at Mr. Doyle's car. "I don't think he's here. Let's have a look." He started walking his bike towards the classic auto.

Mr. Doyle's car was parked in the middle of the road, about fifty yards from the bridge. Nothing looked out of place, other than the car just sitting there.

We slowly followed Chase, walking up to the rear of the car. We took careful footsteps, with only the sounds of gravel and dirt softly crunching beneath the rubber soles of our shoes.

Chase crept up to the driver's side, followed by Gio and then me. My heart beat faster, urging me to dash off in the other direction. This was the second time that I had a run-in with this vehicle today, and I didn't want to be seen near it. However, Chase's curiosity was rubbing off on me.

Chase cocked his head and slowly peered into the driver-side window. Gio and I cautiously followed his lead.

I expected to see Mr. Doyle napping in the front seat. But the car was empty. I looked around nervously for any sign of Mr. Doyle coming out of the brush.

Chase sighed. "Well, there's no sign of him. Looks like he just parked his vehicle and left it here."

Gio asked, "Where do you think he went?"

Chase moved away, kneeled down to the ground, and dislodged a piece of paper from under the car's back tire. Gio and I moved to peer at it from over his shoulder.

It looked like a rough map of the two roads that led to our school, along with the creek bed, the railroad tracks, and a dotted line that led off from the school. On the side of the drawing were these letters and numbers: **N2O — Xe 1,000 lbs.**

I glanced between the paper and our surroundings. "What is it?"

"Don't know, but we should find out," Chase said in a determined voice. "Let's search for some clues. Look at these footprints around the car," Chase said, pointing to his discovery.

I could see what he was talking about. The prints were bigger than the ones we had made. *Were they Mr. Doyle's?*

"This is weird," Chase said, squatting near the driver's side rear passenger door. "What made these marks?" He motioned to two long straight marks in the dirt. "It looks like something was dragged out of the back seat."

Gio leaned down to pick up something off the dirt road. He held it up. "Hey, check it out! I found a key!"

"Nice eyes, G!" Chase exclaimed. "That could be a vital clue!"

Clue to what? But now I was roped in. I quickly began searching the ground, not to be left out. I saw something. "Look—what's this?"

I picked up a gray button off the ground just outside the driver's door and showed it to Chase. He looked at each side of it while making a few "*Hmm*" noises.

"Looks like a shirt button," he uttered. "Standard."

His remarks caused a corner of my mouth to pull down. *Not as cool as a key, I guess.*

"Do you think this key goes to the trunk?" Gio squeaked. "Maybe Doyle had a body in the back seat of his car and dragged it outta there and threw it in the trunk!"

"Good thinking, G. Let's find out. Give me the key," Chase ordered.

After Gio handed it over, Chase blew the dirt off it and rubbed it with his fingers before examining it.

I shook my head. "No… how 'bout we don't," I said. "I don't think we should be messing around Doyle's car."

Seriously! This whole thing was seriously starting to freak me out! Here we were standing with Mr. Doyle's deserted dented car in the shadows of Dead Cow Bridge, with who-knows-what in the trunk. Was it going to be a dead cow? Or a *dead body*? I didn't want to find out.

Chase paused. "Ollie's right… this isn't a car key anyway," Chase decided with a frown. "I know locks, and this key is for a door. It has markings on it also: *RRA, do not duplicate*." He handed back the key to Gio. "And the marks on the ground lead away from the car to the middle of the road—not the trunk."

I looked out into the field. "Can you tell where Doyle went to?"

Chase kneeled down to examine the faint footprints in the dry dirt. "It looks like his tracks stop here, right in the middle of the road. They just… disappear. I'm not sure which direction he walked in."

Chase pulled a magnifying glass from his back pocket and walked to the front of the car. He examined the hood closely. I don't know what he saw, but what I saw was the dent in the hood from the football I kicked at recess.

Chase ran his finger across the dusty hood, then rubbed his fingers together and looked towards the bridge. He then walked to the rear of the car and did the same thing.

"Interesting," Chase mumbled.

Gio was following him around. "What is it?"

"Dust and gravel," he replied.

So what? I thought. *Did he just discover Mr. Doyle's car needed a wash?*

Chase pointed towards the bridge. "Where does the road from underneath this bridge lead to?"

"Besides through Old Man Owens's ranch?" Gio said, giving a shrug. "Just up to the old abandoned mine."

"Abandoned mine? How awesome is that!" Chase's face lit up. "We've got to see that."

I walked around to the passenger side of the car and, cupping my hands around my face, pressed them to the glass for a look inside the car. I noticed flowers lying on the front passenger seat, along with a few papers.

The door looked unlocked, so I grabbed the handle to test it. To my surprise, it opened. Before I could close it, Gio came up behind me and poked his head inside.

"Chase," he called out, "check this out!"

Pushing his head between us, Chase reached inside. It shocked me when he actually picked up the papers and flowers. I frantically looked around the road for any eyewitnesses. Then I blurted out, "What are you doing? Put those back! Those aren't ours!"

"No, you're right, they're not," Chase sighed. "We're just having a look—that's all. We'll put them right back. Relax."

"*Relax?* We can't be just handling things that aren't ours! Mr. Doyle will kill us!" I screeched.

"What if Doyle's in trouble, and this is a note telling someone where he is, and we didn't look?" Chase waved the paper at me.

"Seems more like *snooping* to me. It's not our business—we could get in serious trouble," I argued.

"And what if your great-grandfather's pocket watch is in here? We could grab it without anyone noticing," Chase countered.

I paused. "Well, it might be okay just to look inside… but *hurry.*"

There was the sound of a vehicle coming down from the main road. We all froze for a moment before frantically looking around for a place to hide.

Acting on instinct, I slammed the door shut. But I did it before Chase could put back the items. With genuine fear, I saw that I had left blood from my scraped hands on the door handle. My blood was also on the window where I had cupped my hands!

So not only had I dented Doyle's car hood, but I had bloodied his car.

I tried to wipe the door handle and the window clean. But that only smeared the blood around. And then it was too late to do anything else.

A white work van flew around the corner. It was the white van with the words *Central Air* on its side that had been at our school earlier today. The same one that had run over Nick's autographed football.

I heard Chase screaming, "Run, Ollie! Run!"

I looked back over my shoulder to see Chase riding off on his bike with Gio on the back. They were going off the road to the west, into Old Man Owens's fields.

Not knowing what to do, I stood shaking back and forth. The van got closer and closer. Finally, my survival instincts kicked in, and my body decided to run towards Chase and Gio. But I hesitated long enough to see, through the van's windshield, the faces of two of the workmen from this morning.

"Hey, kids! What are you doing?" one of them shouted as I turned and made a beeline for my buddies.

I ran as fast as I could into the field, hoping not to fall down. Chase and Gio had ridden out of the range of the van into the bumpy field. I glanced back over my shoulder, trying not to fall.

The two men I saw were walking around Mr. Doyle's car. They were not following me. Even so, I kept up my pace until I caught up with my companions.

Chase, Gio, and I continued to make space between the workmen and us. Finally, we went over a hill and could no longer see or hear the potential witnesses. Here we felt confident enough to stop and catch our breath.

Gio asked in a panic, "Do you think they saw us?"

"Uh… yeah," I snapped back, panting. "I think the, *'Hey, kids!'* was a pretty good sign that they saw us." I shook my head. "I'm *so* busted. They saw *me!* Plus, my blood is on Doyle's car, and it's the same car I dented at lunch."

"I don't think they saw our faces," Chase said, calming his breath. "We could be any kids."

"They'll recognize *me!*" I spat with anger. I was on the verge of tears, too. "They saw my face! They saw my *birthmark!*"

Chase said, "If they report us, we'll just say we were looking for Mr. Doyle. After all, he disappeared from school today."

"But we stole a bunch of stuff out of his car and then ran!" I barked out.

"You're the one who closed the car door before we could put the stuff back," Gio accused.

I sat on the ground with my stomach all torn up inside. "Now what are we gonna do?" I whined. "We're never going to find Doyle, and even if we did, he'd have us suspended for vandalizing his car. We'll be lucky if we aren't arrested by the end of the night."

This day was getting worse by the minute.

How did I get in this spot? I wondered to myself. *It seemed that ever since I met Chase, things had gone the wrong way… except I did get to talk with Jax. That was worth getting in trouble for, I guess.*

"Relax," Chase told me again. "We won't get in any trouble at all. We are going to be heroes once we figure out what happened to Mr. Doyle."

I shook my head in disbelief and made a face. "Chase, I hate to be the one to tell you this, but nothing happened to Doyle—*nothing!*"

I looked around the field. We were on Old Man Owens's property, so we were going to be caught trespassing any minute as well. "Mr. Doyle's probably just out for a stroll, fishing, playing cards, or who knows—*whatever!* But I'm not going to get my pocket watch back, and my mom will be kicking my butt when I get home—that is, if I'm not in jail."

"I doubt he's playing cards out here, Oliver," Gio snorted.

I glared at him through narrow eyes and gave him a short shake of my head.

"Oliver, listen to me." Chase put his hands on my shoulders and looked into my eyes. "Something did happen to Mr. Doyle—I'm sure of it. And I think we can prove it. Look at the evidence we have."

Chase paced back and forth. "We have Mr. Doyle's car parked on a remote dirt road, and a bridge where dead cows have been found hanging with certain body parts removed. Doyle was not in the car, or anywhere to be seen. There are no footprints leading off down the road, or into the field. In fact, the prints stop in the middle of the road. There are the two drag marks near the rear door too that ended unexpectedly, as if Mr. Doyle disappeared, vanishing into thin air.

"The dust and gravel were much heavier on the car's hood than on the trunk. That means something kicked up dirt between Doyle's car and the bridge. It had to be something strong enough to kick up gravel, as there's no wind today. We also have this piece of paper with what looks to be a quick sketch of a map with strange letters—maybe a secret code."

"So?" I cocked my head to Chase and shrugged my shoulders.

Chase continued, "Everything so far—Doyle's disappearance into thin air, the gravel on the hood that was probably blown up by rocket propulsion, the secret code on this map, and the history of this field and bridge with aliens—leads me to think he didn't go anywhere." Chase looked to the sky. "I think he was abducted."

Gio and I looked at each other. Chase had noticed things we hadn't. He had thought of things we hadn't. He had figured out things we hadn't, and he knew more than he had told us. He truly was a detective, and his explanation made sense.

Chase's look was one of confidence and purpose. "But we can't rule anything out. That means we have to look at all the other evidence we've found."

"Other evidence?" Gio squeaked in surprise.

"The key on the ground, the button, and these items we have from his car—looks like flowers… a poem… and a receipt," Chase said. He looked around the field. "We need to open a full-scale investigation on this, which means we need a base of operations; it needs to be somewhere secret and secure—any ideas?"

Gio and I glanced at each other. We knew just the spot.

I spoke up—words coming out faster than my mouth could move. "Down near Miller's Creek, hidden in a bank of trees not too far from here, there's an old treehouse… well, at least it used to be one a long time ago. Now it's in shambles." I caught my breath before continuing. "We found it last year when we were looking for crayfish in the creek. Don't know who built it, but I climbed up inside it back then. Looks like it's been abandoned for years. It might work."

Gio excitedly said, "Yeah, we could rebuild it. I don't think it would take very long. I can borrow some tools from my dad!"

The sound of rocks clicking together came from the west—from the embankment of the railroad tracks. We squatted down in the brush to hide.

Thoughts raced through my mind: *Could the sound be Mr. Doyle returning to his car? Or, the workmen following us?* My heart pounded.

At once, a figure emerged running along the tracks. With each step, the oncoming stranger became increasing familiar....

Gio was the first to recognize him. "Coach Conley! What's he doing out here?"

"Looks like he's jogging along the railroad tracks," I said as I watched through my eyebrows, keeping my head down low. "He's jogging back towards Doyle's car!"

"I wonder if Doyle's running with him?" Gio whispered.

"Doyle, a runner?" Chase huffed. "Doubt it."

"Why's Coach running out here?" Gio tried to keep his squeaky voice low. "Along the tracks on Old Man Owens's property?"

Coach Conley continued his jog east along the railroad tracks, back towards the bridge, Mr. Doyle's car, and the eyewitness workmen. When he was out of sight, we stood back up and glanced at each other.

Gio let out a puff of air. "That was close."

"He's gonna see Doyle's car—and then the workmen will tell him they saw us—saw me!" I was back in panic mode. "We need to get out of here before someone else spots us."

"Then lead the way to our new treehouse!" Chase exclaimed.

Through Old Man Owens's field and then down to Miller's Creek, we raced as fast as Gio could go. We followed the winding outcroppings of trees that grew wildly around the creek bed and back to the west towards our school. The brush became thicker as it met the dense forest of trees and bushes. We finally reached a spot where the canopy of trees completely blocked out the sunlight.

I led the way then, even though there was no discernible path to the abandoned treehouse structure. We had to push through tall grass, sharp bushes, cattails, and tree branches; they often snapped after us, hitting the person behind. When I made a few wrong turns here and there, Gio corrected me, thanks to his photographic memory.

We finally reached a clearing with a large elm tree in the middle. The giant tree stood watching us like a sentry. High in its branches was the structure that Gio and I had found last year; it looked completely unchanged. It was so camouflaged by the tree's leaves that a person would miss it unless they already knew it was there.

We looked at Chase and shrugged. "What do you think?"

"Perfect," he said. "Hard to find, secluded. Perfect."

We grinned at each other. We had found the perfect spot.

Chase walked around the tree, touching the trunk as if introducing himself to the tree. He paused, examining the bark.

What was he going to do now, I thought, *suddenly explain what type of tree this was, the variety, and how many of them are in the world?*

"Looks like whoever built this treehouse was in love," Chase said. Running his finger over the carving in its trunk, he read out loud, *"B + E = true love forever."*

That, of course, gave me an idea: *Oliver + Jax... O + J =... OJ? Orange Juice?* I rolled my eyes. That didn't work quite like I had imagined.

Chase turned his attention to us, rubbing his hands together. "Let's get home and gather supplies. How about we meet back here later this afternoon?"

"I can't," Gio said, shaking his head. "I've got chores to do and homework, too. First day of school and I've got homework already."

I looked at Chase and nodded with a flat expression, indicating I was in the same boat. Chase shrugged his shoulders and said, "Of course we need to take care of that kind of business first. What about afterwards?"

"I could come back after dinner," Gio said. "Should be plenty of sunlight left, and my dad will let me stay out till dark."

Chase looked at me to see if I could make it. I couldn't promise I could, though. "I still don't have my great-grandfather's pocket watch. If my mom sees it's missing—" My voice trailed off.

"You just need to distract her somehow until we can find Mr. Doyle." Chase put a comforting hand on my shoulder. "Do you think you can do that?"

I nodded and cracked a smile. "Yes, I think so… I can do that."

"Awesome," Chase said. "Let's go!"

We headed towards our homes on a mission—a mission not only to save my pocket watch but also save Mr. Doyle at the same time.

CHAPTER ELEVEN

THE COVER-UP

AFTER THE THREE of us had split to go to our homes, I thought about everything that had happened today. This morning, I had borrowed my great-grandfather's pocket watch to show Mr. Doyle, fully expecting he'd be so amazed and eternally grateful that he would give me extra credit even before I had my first class with him this year. Then I'd safely and securely return the watch back to its prominent spot on our bookshelf in the front room, all before my mother got home from her first job as a grocery clerk at Sid's Market. My plan was simple—but stupid Johnny Ricker had screwed it up.

The closer I got to my house, the slower my legs moved. I checked the bottoms of my shoes for molasses or chewed chewing gum, but found none.

Maybe hidden kryptonite was inside my backpack, planted there by Johnny Ricker himself, and it was now sucking away all my strength?

I knew, though, the real reason for this explosion of bodily weakness was that I had not thought of a believable story to tell my mom, so she'd excuse my actions. In fact, I had no excuse at all.

If Chase were with me, he'd be able to come up with some really great, brilliant, and believable story on the spot.

Then again, maybe Jax's advice of just telling the truth was better. After all, could my mother really be so mad at me if I did that? The truth was that I had borrowed the pocket watch to impress Mr. Doyle in order to improve my chances of getting a better grade—but because of Johnny Ricker, the pocket watch was confiscated, and then Mr. Doyle was abducted by aliens from our haunted school, and now Mom's grandfather's pocket watch was somewhere in outer space?

Nah, she won't be able to handle the truth, I thought. *I need to make up a story.*

But I had nothing.

I stared at the two-story brick farmhouse I had always lived in with my mom and my annoying little brother, Adam. It had belonged to Mom's parents before they died.

The house was skinny and tall—all stacked on top of itself. It was old too, built before my mom was born. It didn't have any of the newer features of the newer houses, like newer paint, a newer roof, newer windows, or newer anything.

It didn't have air conditioning either, and in the summer, we used fans to circulate the air. During the winter months, our home was drafty, forcing Mom to lay blankets next to the doorways to keep the cold air out. The furnace still worked, but always threatened to go on strike during the coldest days of the year, when we needed it the most. The floors creaked when you walked on them, the doors squeaked when you opened them, and the roof leaked when it rained.

My mom referred to our old house as *"The Old Man."* She'd

tell Adam and me, *"The Old Man watches over us and keeps us safe from the outside world. He will always be here to welcome us home and see us goodbye."*

I believed her, and I was hoping he would protect me now.

In the back of our house stood a giant oak tree that Adam and I liked to climb. When Mom wasn't looking, we'd try to reach the top. She didn't mind us climbing it—just not so high. Our oak was the tallest tree around, and if you climbed close to the top, you could see everything for miles.

Mom liked the tree because it helped shade the house in the summer. She liked its yellow and orange colors in the fall, and the sound of its leaves rustling when the wind blew. She especially liked to sit underneath it and read.

My mom sure did like that tree, which is probably why she wouldn't let us build a treehouse in it. She did let us hang a tire swing from one of the big branches, and Adam and I often got into trouble for swinging too high on it.

My uncle always told my mom that she needed to trim some branches off; otherwise, they might break and damage the house during a snowstorm or when the wind really kicked up. Mom always refused, saying, *"Like our family, this tree has deep roots and many branches. Who can say which branches are the most important, and which ones are expendable? An arborist can tell you, 'Oh, this is a bad branch,' or, 'This tree doesn't need this branch,' but how can they know how important that one branch is to the tree?*

"It may be true that when a branch is broken or lost, the tree can still survive, but the tree still feels the loss all the same. The tree sees all of its branches as useful, no matter how small, how new, or how old. The tree wants all of its branches—just like I need all of my branches."

Just as I stepped onto the front porch, my annoying little brother Adam came charging out the front door with a big smile. In a sassy tone, he said with a smirk, "You're in big trouble."

If I had a giant flyswatter, I'd use it to smash annoying little Adam, I thought.

After all, that's what he was: an annoying little fly. He never minded his own business. He was always trying to get into my stuff, always following me around, always listening to my conversations, always snooping in my business, and always, always, always being annoying.

Sure, I'd hang out with him if I had nothing better to do, but it didn't matter; he was still annoying. And did I mention he was a tattletale? Only the biggest tattletale on the planet! It didn't matter what it was; he'd make sure I got in trouble for it.

One time, Adam threw *his* Frisbee onto the roof, so I volunteered to climb up and get for him. As soon as I threw it down, he ran and told my mother I was on top of the roof! *Annoying little fly—annoying little brother—annoying little Adam.*

I looked down at Adam and gave him a cutting look. He was, of course, smaller than me, with straight brown hair that draped over his annoying little head. My mom cut our hair, and it looked like she placed a bowl on top of his head as a guide. So, of course, I called him *Bowl Head.*

There was only one good thing about Adam. Although I called him many names, complained to Mom about his annoying habits, and occasionally thumped him in the arm when he really got on my nerves—he never teased me about my birthmark. Maybe it's because he always knew me with it—kinda like how I always knew Gio with one and one-half legs.

I took a deep breath, strode past Adam, opened the front porch door, and walked in.

"Oliver?" I heard my mom yell from another room. "Is that you?"

"Hi, Mom, I'm home!"

I tried to sound as normal as possible.

"You're in big trouble, Mr. Teller! Come in here, Oliver. We need to talk."

I slowly walked into the other room where she was. Mom was standing there, hands on her hips, and frowning at me. I had no story. I had no excuse. I decided to throw myself at the mercy of the court and strike first.

"I'm so sorry, Mom," I said, feeling like I was about to cry.

"Young man, what are we going to do about this?" Her voice was stern.

"It was an accident, I swear."

"An accident? How can you call it 'an accident'?"

"Well, I didn't mean for this to happen," I mumbled.

"How many times do I have to tell you that you need to call me if you're going to be late? It's only your first day of school, and already I'm worried about you. Over an hour late, and no phone call! I've been worried sick."

I stared blankly at her until my mind caught up. I finally stuttered timidly, "I-I-Is… is that why you're so upset? Because I didn't call?"

"Of course! Oliver, we've gone over this before, haven't we? Many times! I don't mind if you stay late after school, if you want to walk home, or hang out with your friends, but you have to *let me know* where you are and what you're doing. You didn't tell me you were going to walk home from school today! I expected you off the bus over an hour ago! Don't make me worry about you!"

She flashed me a smile, but then it quickly faded away. "My goodness, Oliver, what happened to your pants?" She was staring at my ripped jeans. "And your hands; what happened to your hands?"

I looked down at my ripped jeans as I tried to hide the palms of my hands. I couldn't tell her that I was riding on Chase's bike without a helmet; she would freak. "Oh, some of the boys and I were playing football, and I fell down," I lied.

"You are late because you were playing football? Oliver, you know how I feel about you playing contact sports—especially football. You could be hurt! God only gave you one body, so take care of it. And you've only got five pairs of jeans, so you need to take better care of them. Now get yourself upstairs, wash those hands, and take off those pants. I'll have to find the time to mend them."

I smiled. She wasn't upset with me because of the pocket watch; she was upset with me because I was late and hadn't called. "Okay, sorry. I'll do it right now."

I turned to walk out of the room, but stopped. "Mom, I won't let it happen again," I promised. "Oh, and I made a new friend at school today. He's a really cool kid."

"Oh? What's his name?"

"Chase. He rides a dirt bike!"

"Well, you remember that if you ever want to ride a bike, you need to wear a helmet."

"Of course, I remember."

I remembered, but I just didn't do it today.

Suddenly, I froze, looking beyond my mother at the bookshelf behind her. There, on the second shelf from the top, was a spot containing an empty glass display. My great-grandfather's pocket watch had been in it this morning. It was empty now.

"Oliver? Why haven't you gone upstairs to change those pants and wash your hands?"

"Well…." I looked down at the glass of whiskey and ice Mom was shaking in her hand.

She followed my gaze to her glass and then quickly back up to my eyes. "Don't start with me, Oliver. It's been a long day! Don't you think I'm entitled to a drink?"

"Isn't it a little early?" I mumbled.

"It's the end of my day… well, the end of the first part of my day. Now I've to go to my second job."

"But you're drinking before you go to work," I objected.

"I work at a bar, Oliver. Drinking is not only permitted but encouraged. And it's especially necessary if I have to deal with Bob."

During the mornings and daytime, Mom worked as a stockroom clerk at Sid's Market in town. Evenings, for her second job, my mom worked as a waitress at Jam'n Joe's Bar. I don't think she liked either job very well. She complained about her bosses from them all the time.

"Well, it just seems—" I started.

"It's fine, Oliver," my mom interrupted me. "It's just one drink—that's what it is. Now you march yourself right upstairs, take off those pants, and wash those hands before you get a nasty infection. I'm going to need to mend those jeans, so leave them out so I can find them."

Mom took another drink from her glass as I stood there staring at her.

"What are you waiting for?" Mom scolded. "Get upstairs and do what I said!" She bustled out of the front room into the kitchen.

I glanced back at the shelf and the empty glass display case for the pocket watch. Then I walked up the stairs to my room, feeling a bit troubled.

I was worried about my mom. She was a small, slender woman who described herself as "five-foot-nothing." But trust me, she was something—a ball of fire! Half Irish and half Native American, she had feisty blood running through her veins and was downright nasty if you got on her bad side.

Mom said she liked to "drink and fight," and sometimes it seemed she'd argue some point just to argue. She never backed down from her position, even if she was wrong. But she was also fun and outgoing—that is, when she let herself have fun. But it seemed that she was always working so she could make things nice for Adam and me.

I thought she seemed lonely, even though she dated different men from time to time. She was very pretty, with her long, midnight-black hair and blue eyes, but unfortunately, Adam and I seemed to ruin her relationships. Mom had a knack for bringing home losers, and they left every time once the guys found out about us.

I never understood why Mom was attracted to dirtbags in the first place, but she'd been dating that kind of guy ever since Dad left. Was it because they were the only type of men who came to the bar where she worked? Well, whatever the reason, I thought she could do much better.

Mom had a beautiful voice, and so she often sang karaoke at the bar. She sounded like a professional. People told her, "You're wasting your talent!" and, "You should go to Hollywood and become a big star!" I thought the same. My uncle said though, "*People are where they are because they want to be where they are.*"

I didn't agree with him about that because I knew for a fact; I didn't want to be in this predicament I was in right now. I wanted to hang out with Chase and Gio, with no cares about finding a missing pocket watch. Or taking a long walk with Jax hand-in-hand. This *definitely* wasn't where I wanted to be right now.

My mother had not discovered the pocket watch missing from the display case—which was a good and a bad thing.

The good thing: I still had time to recover my great-grandfather's pocket watch and replace it before Mom noticed its disappearance. The bad thing: If Mom discovered the pocket watch missing before I told her about it, my punishment would be ten times worse.

But I was committed to seeing this thing through without telling my mother. It was a calculated risk that I was willing to take. Besides, I was a chicken when it came to telling. Confession was not one of my strengths.

So, what I needed to work on right now was buying myself

more time to ensure that my mother did not notice the watch's disappearance. Placing something in front of the display case to hide the emptiness inside might seem logical—but it also might bring attention to it. I needed a distraction.

That's when it hit me. Remember Mrs. Huntley's art class? *Change the shapes in the room, and break them down into their simplest forms?*

Yes, that's it, I thought—*I'm brilliant!*

I quickly changed out of my jeans, washed my hands, and ran out of my room. "Mom! Mom, where are you?"

"I'm in the kitchen, Oliver. I'm getting ready to leave for work! Where is your brother?"

"Mom, can I use an old bed sheet?" I asked as I skidded into the kitchen beside my mom.

"What are you going to do with a bedsheet? And where's your brother? I need to leave for work."

"Well, my art teacher, Mrs. Huntley, asked us to create an art project inside our own homes. We are studying this guy named, uh, Monte Christo. He covered the Grand Canyon with sheets or something like that. Anyway, she wanted us to create our own art project by covering a piece of furniture inside our house with a sheet and leaving it there for a week or more."

"Cover a piece of furniture for *a week?* For what purpose?"

"She said it's supposed to help break down shapes into their simplest form and change the way we see our environment. It's supposed to make a room feel different." I tilted my head to the side. "She said we would get extra credit if we did. So, may I… ? May I get extra credit?"

"What are you going to cover? I hope not the fridge or television. On second thought, both you and your brother are watching too much TV lately, so that might not be such a bad idea."

"She said it should be something tall, like, uhh… I know—like the bookshelf in the front room. I promise I will take it down as soon as the project is over."

My mother opened the back door and yelled for my brother before turning to me and dismissively nodding *yes*.

"Now, Oliver, we have only a couple of good sheets; I don't want you ruining them by building forts. Use just one for your project and take care with it. I've got to leave now. Go out and bring your little brother inside. You're in charge while I'm gone."

"Okay. Thanks, Mom," I said with a smile. "Oh, after I get my homework and chores done, would it be okay if I met up with my friends for a while?"

"As long as you take care of Adam—understood?" she said, and she grabbed the keys to her car.

I brought Bowl Head inside, did my chores, finished my homework, and prepared to visit the treehouse. I couldn't wait to meet back up with Chase and Gio and get started on fixing up the treehouse.

Gio would bring some tools from his father's workshop, and Chase would carry in some wood to build and make repairs. So, I gathered together the other supplies we might need, like paper and pencils.

I decided to bring along a little surprise too: peanut butter sandwiches. Since we'd be working hard, we might need some nutrition. I made them extra special, with honey.

However, there would be one problem. One that jeopardized everything in our investigation.

CHAPTER TWELVE
HAMMERS AND NAILS

MOM HAD SAID I had to take care of annoying Adam. And that meant I might have to let him tag along with me if I wanted to go to the treehouse. But he just *couldn't* come! Not only was he too young, but he'd also tattletale to whoever would listen. Having to watch Bowl Head would keep me stuck at home.

That's only, though, if I couldn't get Mrs. McMillan to watch him.

Mrs. McMillan was a neighbor who used to watch both Adam and me when Mom was at work. Now that I was older, though, my mother decided it was all right if I watched Adam by myself. But Mrs. McMillan still made sure to look in on us when we were alone, checking to make sure we didn't need anything, and letting us know she was there if we needed her.

Well, today I needed her. I needed Mrs. McMillan to watch Adam while I went to meet up with Chase and Gio.

Mrs. McMillan's house was just down the dirt road from ours. She had lived there before I had been born—probably even before my mother had been born! She lived there alone now; her husband had died years ago, and her children were all grown up and moved out of state. So maybe that's why she took an interest in Adam and me. She was always baking cookies, cakes, and yummy things for us.

Mrs. McMillan was like a grandmother: warm and kind, but very strict on manners. She insisted that both Adam and I learned the proper manners and that we practice them while at her house. She would say, *"Good manners are good habits, and good habits are good to have."*

I liked Mrs. McMillan, and I did not mind learning good manners or practicing them. But I think annoying Adam had a hard time with it. One time, Adam and I were eating dinner at her house when Adam wiped his mouth with his shirt collar. Mrs. McMillan about came out of her seat and landed on the moon. "*That is why we have napkins placed on our laps, not on our shirts,"* she scolded. "*Food is for eating, not for wearing."*

I think my mom liked the fact that Mrs. McMillan taught us manners. I think it also made Mrs. McMillan happy that she could share her knowledge with us.

Today I gathered up some paper, a journal, my best pencils and pens, my water jug, and my special peanut-butter-and-honey sandwiches. I stuffed them all in my backpack. Then I went out to the garage and looked at my bike.

It wasn't exactly a dirt bike. It was more of a city ten-speed bike my mom found at a garage sale a year ago. It was baby blue and a little big for me at the time she bought it, but she got a good deal and said I'd grow into it. It wasn't a popular name brand. It was a brand called *"Unimpressive."* That might be why I hadn't ridden it very much.

After locating my bike, I looked for my helmet. Of course, it wasn't there. Annoying Adam had probably taken it.

I searched the entire garage without finding my helmet, but I did find an old wooden box with a black latch that resembled a small chest. I strapped it onto the back of my bike, then yelled for Adam to tell me where he hid my helmet.

All I got was his annoying little response of, "If you put it in the proper place, then you'll find it staring at your face." It's what our mother always said to us when we couldn't find something! So, I quit looking for my helmet and began looking for a giant flyswatter.

But time was slipping away, and I hadn't found my helmet or a giant flyswatter. So, I had to make a quick decision: *No helmet it was*. Adam, of course, would tattletale on me, but if I just walked my bike beside him, he couldn't say I was riding without a helmet.

After all, I couldn't get in trouble for not wearing a helmet if I was just walking my bike, now could I?

Adam, of course, wanted nothing to do with Mrs. McMillan. He wanted to follow me around, snoop in my business, and tattletale on something—anything. "Where are you going?" he asked in his sassy tone. "What are you doing?"

"None of your business," I snapped back.

"*I* want to go."

"No, it's not for little kids. You need to stay with Mrs. McMillan."

"I don't want to; it's boring over there. And she's going to make me do all kinds of stupid stuff, like sit up straight, comb my hair, and not burp."

"Don't care. Sorry."

"I'll tell Mom that you ran off to somewhere secret, with that chest, and no helmet—"

Sure enough, he was ruining my plans.

"Fine. How 'bout I drop you off at your friend Samuel's house instead? You can hang out there until I come back and pick you up. But you have to promise to keep your big mouth shut."

"On the way to where? And why can't I go with you?"

"I'm hooking up with Gio and Chase, and we are going to ride our bikes."

"Who's Chase? And I want to ride bikes too."

"Chase is my new friend, and you're not invited because you're annoying. So, your choice is Mrs. McMillan, or Samuel's—what's it gonna be? I shouldn't even be giving you a choice to begin with."

Samuel's house it was. The risk existed that my mother would not approve of my pawning Adam off on Samuel's mom. But I took the chance.

After annoying tattletale Adam was out of my hair and sight, I jumped on old blue and rode furiously down the dirt road. There was still plenty of sunlight left, and Chase and Gio would already be at the treehouse.

The treehouse was about halfway between our houses and our school. It took me less time to reach it than I thought.

I dismounted at the thatch of trees and bushes that served as an entrance to our new home base. I pushed my bike through the thicket until both of us disappeared from the sight of the main road. The water in the creek was low, and it took no effort to lift my bike over.

I made my way into the dense foliage until I recognized the sound of pounding hammers in the distance. I sped up, dragging my bike through the brush and ducking under the branches.

When I arrived at the clearing, I discovered Chase and Gio had already made a rope ladder. It dangled down from the platform of the treehouse.

I looked up and saw Gio swinging a hammer. I whistled, and he stopped, and then he waved me up. I secured the small wooden box to my backpack, then threw my bike to the ground. I climbed up the rope ladder with absolutely no grace or style.

When I reached the platform, Gio gave me a hand to steady me. "Welcome aboard," he said.

They had done a lot. The floors and walls were already patched, and Chase was working on the roof. He looked over at me, saying, "So your mom didn't notice the pocket watch missing, huh?"

"How'd you know?" I said, completely confused.

"You're here, aren't ya?" he shot back.

True enough. If Mom had noticed the pocket watch missing, I'd have ended up missing!

"This looks awesome," I said out loud.

Gio looked down at the ground below us. "I don't think anyone will find us up here. Plus, we're safe from zombies."

Chase motioned for me to hand him a board to replace one on the roof. He said, "Looks like this treehouse is pretty old." He grabbed the board and put it in place. "But the tree is a whole lot older." He swung his hammer, driving in a nail. "The branches haven't outgrown the fort."

He was right: The house *was* old. The boards were warped from years of weathering the elements. And the bark on the tree was thick, like scales on a dragon. However, the work Chase and Gio had done so far gave a fresh look to our new fort.

I helped by securing floorboards and patching any holes in the walls or roof. Before I knew it, our base of operations was up and running.

The three of us sat in the middle, admiring our work. It was no longer a rundown treehouse: It was now a sturdy tree-fort.

"What's in the small chest?" Gio asked, pointing to the wooden box I had found in my garage.

"Nothing yet. I kinda thought we could store our evidence in it," I admitted.

"Epic idea!" Chase said. "Let's get started. Did ya bring something to write on Ollie?"

This was the moment I was waiting for. I grabbed my backpack and pulled out my journal and a sharp pencil. I handed out some notepaper and pencils to Gio and Chase, along with the sandwiches I made.

"Nice—I like peanut butter and jelly," Chase said.

"I made them with honey!" I proudly replied.

"Even better," Chase said, as he unwrapped the sandwich and took a bite.

Chase then pulled out the items we found earlier in the day from his backpack.

"Do you really think aliens abducted Doyle?" Gio asked eagerly.

Chase nodded. "We found Mr. Doyle's car abandoned near a bridge where there were reports of dead cows with missing body parts. And Old Man Owens's fields have had reports of alien activity. This evidence alone suggests Doyle was abducted. But let's look at all the evidence we have," Chase said as he spread out the items on the wooden floor. "By his car's back tire, we found this map with initials or symbols… a key with RRA inscribed… a gray shirt button… these flowers on his seat… this looks like a poem he wrote… and this looks like a receipt for something."

I listed each item in my journal, along with a brief description of each. Gio made sketches of every object on the notepaper he held.

"What do these things have to do with aliens?" I asked.

"Well, for starters, we don't know for certain aliens abducted that Doyle. It could be something else paranormal. So, we have to consider all possibilities and eliminate ones that don't make sense," Chase answered.

"You mean something else could have happened to him?" I asked. "Like someone kidnapped or killed him?"

"We go where the clues take us," Chase instructed. "Nothing is off-limits when we start an investigation."

"Like, maybe zombies ate him?" Gio squeaked.

"Nothing is off-limits," Chase declared again.

Gio smiled.

Chase continued, "First, we found marks on the ground by the rear door of Doyle's car. Maybe something heavy was taken out of the back seat—?"

"Like I said before," Gio interrupted, "maybe it was a body Doyle was dragging to the trunk?"

Chase gave a quick, uncertain shake of his head. "I don't think so. His footprints and the two marks on the ground disappear right in the middle of the road!"

"Maybe his footprints were covered by tire tracks from other cars?" I said.

"No one drives on that road, Oliver. It goes nowhere under the bridge, dead-ending at the old abandoned Tanner Silver Mine," Gio pointed out. "Doyle was eaten by zombies—he had to be."

Chase raised his hands. "I didn't have a lot of time to examine the tire tracks. The road was so dry it that was hard to tell if any of the tire tracks were recent or covered his footprints."

Gio raised his eyebrows. "I'm just saying zombies are a possibility."

Chase continued, "The gravel on the car hood was much heavier than on the trunk. This tells me something blew the gravel up in front of Doyle's car in the direction of the bridge. This is a strong indication of rocket propulsion. This evidence, along with Doyle's vanishing into thin air in an area with a history of cattle mutilations, reinforces an alien abduction theory. But let's review the other evidence just in case something else happened to him."

Chase picked up the paper we had found near the car. "This paper we found lodged under the rear tire has a drawing of a map—see these lines?" He traced them on the paper with his finger. "These lines look like the two roads leading to our school right there." He landed his finger on a square. "This line looks like the railroad tracks." His finger traced another line with tic marks. "Then, there is this long-dotted line that leads from the school to the south—to this **X** here." He tapped his finger on the **X**. "This tells me something important is at this spot."

"That leads through Old Man's Owens's Fields to the area of the mine," I said.

"Near where we found Doyle's car—interesting, isn't it?" Chase raised his eyebrows. "See these letters and numbers on the side of the paper? **N2O — Xe 1,000 lbs.** Anyone know what they mean?" Chase looked at us as Gio and I shrugged our shoulders.

"Alien code?" Gio suggested.

Chase nodded. "Probably."

I thought for a moment before saying, "I know who we could ask… Eduard."

"No, not him," Gio said. "He's a know-it-all."

"Exactly," I nodded. "He'll know something."

"You mean the kid I sat next to in science class today?" Chase inserted. "He seemed all right. Let's ask him in a roundabout way tomorrow."

Gio shook his head. "I think it's a bad idea getting him involved. I don't like it."

Chase continued with the evidence.

"Next, we found this key with the inscription *RRA do not duplicate*," Chase said, holding it up. "Like I said, it's not for a car. It's for a door. But the question is—to what door?"

"Maybe Doyle's house?" I threw out.

"Possibly. But two things don't point to that," Chase said, holding up a finger. "First, if it were his house key, it most likely would not be by itself. It would probably be with his other important keys, like his car keys. And we didn't find those with it." He raised another finger. "Second, there are three letters etched on the base, *'RRA.'* They are the same letters that start with the name of our school, Raven Ridge Academy."

Wow, Chase was a genius, I thought. *He had thought of things that I would never have.*

Still, I had to shrug my shoulders. "So, what if Doyle has a key to the school? That doesn't seem strange since he's a teacher there."

"True enough," Chase said as he passed the key around. "But the question is, which door in the school does it open?"

I picked up the gray shirt button I found. "Hey, what about this button?"

Chase looked at it with his magnifying glass. "The few threads attached to this gray button are frayed, but the button looks new. Maybe it was torn off his shirt?"

"While Doyle was defending himself from the aliens?" I suggested.

"Probably," Chase nodded.

I smiled. I was getting the hang of this investigation thing.

"Now, as to the stuff we found inside his car...." Chase picked up the flowers, the poem, and the receipt. "I'm not sure what to make of these, or how they tie into an alien abduction. The flowers are wilting now, but they were fresh when we found them. And there's this poem that looks like Mr. Doyle wrote it—his signature's on it."

Gio started sketching what the flowers looked like.

Chase gave me the poem to read aloud:

My love for her is infinite, my admiration great
Standing on the edge of time and of space
She commands the stars, she commands the moon
She is all I wait for, forever do I swoon

The heavens sing her name
She is stardust, she is forever
My heart forever hers
To her universe, I surrender

How will she ever know my love?
For the stars hold my secret
I will one day sing her my song
For I can no longer keep it

How long can I wait?
Waiting is all I do
Forever is not too long
Waiting for her to say, "I do."

- Charles Othello Doyle

"Ahhh… I know!" I shrieked, thinking I had just solved the mystery! "Doyle was going to meet someone for a secret date near the bridge! But while he was waiting, a spaceship came down looking for cows and took him instead, kicking up dirt while it blasted off into space."

"Or zombies ate him," Gio said.

I rolled my eyes. "Don't you think there would be a lot of blood and guts if that happened? *Seriously.*"

Chase continued with the next piece of evidence. "We also have this receipt that we found in his car—looks like it's from a pawnshop." Chase passed the small piece of paper to us as we looked at the information.

Past & Present Pawnshop

1602 Stoker St.
Denver, Colorado 80202
Date: July 31st
Item Number: 3467
Pd. $300.00 Cash

"What do you think he bought?" Gio asked.

"He was into collecting antiques, so could be anything," I said.

"Could be unrelated to his abduction, but we need to keep it in mind in case someone else is involved," Chase said.

"Do you think someone else had something to do with his disappearance?" I asked.

"Maybe. Could be aliens did not abduct him at all, but maybe someone wants us to think that he was, to throw us off their trail." Chase stroked his chin as if pondering some thought. "Does he have any enemies?"

I huffed, "He was arguing with everyone this morning at school."

"Then we need to start looking at everyone as suspects," Chase demanded.

"Everyone?" Gio squeaked.

"Everyone is a suspect," Chase nodded. "We can rule no one out—even ourselves."

Not everyone was a suspect. I knew Jax wasn't involved. And that was a fact.

Chase rubbed his hands together. "We also need to find witnesses—someone who saw something or has some information."

"What about Coach Conley?" Gio asked. "He was out there running—maybe he witnessed what happened?"

"Or, had something to do with it," Chase corrected. "Remember, everyone is a suspect."

"Speaking of witnesses—what are we going to do about the

workmen in the van?" I spoke in a worried voice. "They saw us… they saw *me.* They probably thought we were breaking into Doyle's car, and you know they'll tell the sheriff…. When he investigates, he'll find Doyle's car broken into, my blood on his window, and Doyle missing. I'll be the main suspect!"

"I still don't think they saw our faces," Chase tried to reassure me. "Besides, once we find Doyle, or what happened to Doyle, the sheriff will thank us—not arrest us." Chase pointed to my journal. "Oliver, start a list of suspects. We need to find out who else knows what else."

I began listing the names of teachers and staff members at our school while Gio worked on his sketches. We were so focused; we barely noticed the sun going down and the sky growing dark.

Finally, we realized it was time for us to quit and go home. We planned on returning tomorrow to pick up the important work we had started, not knowing where it would lead.

Chase and Gio climbed down, but I sat in our tree-fort for a few minutes watching the vibrant sunset. It looked like a beautiful painting, and I swore to myself I would someday bring Jax here with me to watch the sun go down. I wanted to show her the same magnificence that I saw.

No words would be necessary between us. I knew she would appreciate its beauty, like I appreciated hers.

CHAPTER THIRTEEN

WALKING IN SOMEONE ELSE'S SHOE

DAY TWO OF the new school year, and I was eager to get to Raven Ridge Academy. My backpack stood at attention by the front door, ready for action and loaded with the supplies I would need for school. My bike was oiled and greased for speed and efficiency. I had found my helmet with the help of my mom and placed it on the handlebars. After a hearty breakfast of Frosted Flakes and a quick check of my hair in the mirror, I was out the front door. That was, just about out the front door… until my path was blocked by the most annoying little kid in the world—Adam.

Adam's eyes narrowed into thin slits, and his lips curled into an evil little smile. My eyes narrowed back, my jaw clenched tight, and I growled under my breath, "What do you think you're doing?"

"I'm coming with you, of course."

"You most certainly are not," I snapped.

"Oliver!" shouted my mother. "You need to walk your brother to his bus stop."

I scowled. I thought Mom was busy getting ready for work and hadn't heard me jetting out the door like an F-16.

"But Mom, I'm riding my bike to school, remember? I need to leave early, and I don't have time to walk with Adam!" I hollered.

"And you remember I said it was okay for you to ride to school as long as you took care of your little brother?" she shot back.

I rolled my eyes since Mom wasn't in viewing distance, and let out a puff of hot air. "Fine!" I yelled back. I mumbled to the little brat, "Let's go, Bowl Head."

Because we lived in a rural area, we had to walk a ways to the nearest bus stop. The few houses here were scattered far apart on old farms and ranches, and connected by dirt roads. Adam's bus stop was located down a way, just past old Mr. Griswald's house.

Griswald was a mean old man who rarely came out, and when he did, it was usually to yell at someone. Mom told us to stay away from his property, which we never had a problem obeying.

I didn't want to be bothered with the drill of walking with Adam this morning, because I wanted to arrive at school early. Instead, I had to waste time walking Adam down to his precious, annoying bus stop first while he glowed with the satisfaction of knowing that the first thing he did this morning was annoy me.

Maybe I should walk him to a different bus stop, I thought, *one that goes to a different school. That would freak him out.*

However, if my mother found out, she would put me on a different bus too—one to Siberia.

Of course, on the way to his bus stop, Adam made sure to be extra-annoying, by asking annoying questions like, "Why are you riding your bicycle?" and, "How long is it going to take you to ride to school?" and, "What happens if you get a flat tire?" I told him if he didn't stop asking annoying questions, the only thing that would be flat would be his lips from me pressing them shut.

Halfway to Adam's bus stop, Mr. Annoying realized he had left his lunch at home. As it was, I was going to be lucky to make it to school on time because I had to walk him to his bus stop. Now, I was sure to be late.

Quickly, I got on my bike and told Adam to climb on the back. I stood and pedaled us back home as fast as I could. I could've left him at his stop and not come back for his lunch, but I took action. Like Superman would've done. Or Chase.

I rode like a Supercross racer, maybe even faster. I shot off my bike to retrieve his annoying lunch and gave him a ride back to his bus stop in an even faster time, dropping him off with not so much as a "thank you" from him.

I sped off thinking to myself: *This must be what it feels like to be a superhero, saving the day at a moment's notice, acting in a time of crisis when there isn't a second to lose.*

I was a boy of action in a thankless world, putting the undeserving ahead of my own safety and convenience. With superhuman energy flowing through me, I raced off into the sunrise on my trusty sidekick of a bike as fast as it would carry me.

Because of annoying little Adam, I was behind schedule, so I took shortcuts. I had time to make it and not be late if I snuck in through the teacher's parking lot. When I did, I used the opportunity to look for Mr. Doyle's car.

It was nowhere to be found, but I did see the white work van from yesterday. It was parked in the same spot, but something was different. The tires on all four of its wheels were flat.

I stopped my bike next to it for a closer look. Quickly glancing around to make sure that no one was watching me, I dismounted and crouched down for confirmation of what I suspected. Sure enough, the tires had been slashed.

It dawned on me that this vandalism must have happened just this morning, since the van had been near Dead Cow Bridge yesterday afternoon.

Impressed with my apprentice detective skills, I began to get back on my bike when I heard footsteps and a man's low voice coming towards me from the opposite side of the disabled vehicle. "I'm sure I left it in the van. I'll grab it and be right back; I need a smoke anyway," the voice said.

I crouched back down, looked back underneath the vehicle, and saw work boots walking towards the van and me. My first instinct was to get on my bike and ride away, but the pedals were a little long for me, so it would take me a few moments to gain momentum. I looked around for a place to hide—there were none.

I glanced across the parking lot and saw the fence that enclosed the playground. I fixated on the small crack between the post and the building where Nick was able to squeeze through yesterday.

Maybe if I made a run for it, I could make it through the small opening before this guy sees me, I thought, *but I would have to leave my bike.*

I didn't know what to do.

The footsteps got closer. That's when I heard, "*What the?* The tires are flat!"

Panic set in. I jumped on my bike and pedaled towards the opening. I don't know what I was thinking. Being on my bike slowed me down, and the bike was too big to fit through the fence.

"Hey, you! Stop!" the voice behind me screamed.

But I did not stop, I did not turn around, and I did not fall. I just pushed my legs harder until they burned.

The small opening was within a few feet of the skid marks that shot out from beneath my bike as I jumped off. I could hear thundering, racing footsteps getting closer, but I did not look back. I quickly snatched off my backpack and pushed it through the small opening. Then I scooted sideways through, making myself as small as possible.

I had made it all the way through when a tug on the bottom of my pants tripped me to the ground on the other side of the fence.

"Get back here, you brat! I've got you now!"

I latched onto the grass, and with all my might, pulled myself forward, as whoever-it-was-behind-me pulled my foot back. It was a tug of war; something had to give.

It was my shoe, which popped off. But I didn't care.

Free, I scrambled to my feet in a panic and set off on a dead run. I ran around the building, and through the front door of the school. Once inside, I ripped off my helmet and shoved it in my backpack. I melted inconspicuously into the mass of kids drifting through the halls.

I tried to breathe normally as I thought, *Even though I had nothing to do with slashing the van's tires, I was now the main suspect. And for evidence, not only did the dude have my bike, but one of my shoes. He may not have seen my face or my hair—thanks to my helmet—but spotting a kid wearing only one shoe would be fairly easy if Principal Sterns made us line up.*

I calmed my breathing down and wiped the sweat from my forehead. My heart was still racing as both Chase and Gio found me with only minutes before the school bell rang. I barely got out my story when Gio quickly took off one of his shoes—the shoe on his fake leg—and gave it to me.

"What's this?" I asked. "What are you going to wear?"

Gio shrugged. "I don't need it on my artificial foot."

It was a good idea: Gio, and I both wore the same brand of shoes, although his were significantly smaller than mine. I loosened the laces as much as possible and squeezed into it while Chase ran to his locker and retrieved his gym shirt for me. Just as quickly as Superman changed back into Clark Kent, I changed back into an average kid.

I said to Chase, "They're going to think it was me, you know. I'm gonna get blamed for those tires."

"They won't ever find you—don't worry," he reassured me.

"If they find out it was me at Doyle's car yesterday, and then at their van this morning, there's no way I'm not going to do hard time," I fretted. I could barely think straight.

"We'll worry about that if that ever happens," Chase patted me on the back. "Come on, let's get to class. We've got work to do."

We dashed down the hall and took our seats in the middle of dreadful Miss Crabtree's classroom.

Miss Crabtree looked like she was having an unpleasant morning too: Her lips were pursed out, and wrinkles showed on her forehead. She snapped at us students, ordering us to take our seats quickly.

"Homework assignments, please. Pass them to the front. Come on, let's go. You all know the drill; you all know what is expected of you," she snapped.

The bell had just rung for the start of class, and she was giving us no time to catch our breath—no time to prepare for the mental torture that was about to take place.

Everyone scrambled to grab their homework assignments out of their backpacks and book bags under the watchful eye of Miss Crabtree standing there, tapping her foot menacingly.

Maybe she didn't have enough coffee this morning, or maybe she forgot to bring the correct purse, and her purse didn't match her outfit?

Whatever the reason for her crappy attitude, everyone could tell that she was in no mood to play games.

"Thank you," she said crisply when the requested papers arrived. "I'm glad to see everyone took my advice and did their homework last night. I hope your answers are correct, as I will grade them during class. No one's pretty looks will help their grades in here; numbers don't care how you look. Nor will pretty looks get you jobs when you're adults. Studying, putting in time and effort, is the only path to success. Now, everyone, open your book to page forty-three. We will begin today's lesson on fractions."

Turning to walk back to her desk, dreadful Miss Crabtree mumbled in irritation, "It's going to be another hot day. We'll have to see if the air conditioning holds out in this relic of a building." Clearly, still in a bad mood, she flung our homework on her desk. "They promised me that this would be a first-rate school—humph."

Suddenly, as if the school building heard her mumblings and decided to play a cruel joke, the lights flickered and shut off—along with the air conditioning.

"Are you *kidding me?* Perfect, just perfect!" she snarled.

Yesterday, the class had giggled and cheered when the outage happened. Today, the foul mood of Miss Crabtree made for complete silence. Afraid to even glance at her, everyone pretended to read their textbooks in the dim window light.

"I worked all these years to get where I am. Did I flaunt my looks to get a job? No!" she muttered as she marched over to fumble and pull at the first window. "I *worked* to get where I am. I should be in a university, or employed by some big business by now, but no… I am here at a second-rate school. I've made sacrifices, and for what? To be pushed aside? I'm a professional! And how is a professional supposed to work under *these* conditions?!"

"Miss Crabtree?" Chase stood up from his desk and walked to the windows. "Please allow me to open those windows for you."

Miss Crabtree stopped in her tracks, paused, and then turned towards Chase. She tried to crack a smile. "Why, thank you, young man. Obviously, chivalry is not completely dead in this school—at least not among you students."

"Well, I simply had to. You look so pretty today, Miss Crabtree, if you don't mind my saying so, and I wouldn't want you to have to mess up your clothes for your date with Mr. Doyle," Chase said in a casual tone.

My eyes popped out of my skull at his words. So did Miss Crabtree's. So did everyone's.

"What!" she screamed. "A date with *Mr. Doyle?* Why would you say such a thing?"

"Well, it's just that I saw Mr. Doyle all dressed up, and you're all dressed up, and Mr. Doyle has a love note and flowers in his car. It seems like you two might have, uh, plans."

"Absolutely not! I have no relationships with *any* teacher at this school—is that clear, young man?" dreadful Miss Crabtree said in a chilly, make that icy, tone.

A blanket of silence covered the class. Chase stood motionless, staring at her. The awkward silence that followed caused her to straighten her jacket and take a deep breath.

"Now," dreadful Miss Crabtree said, "Mr. Doyle is here, you said? Then why is that substitute in her little skirt back here this morning?"

"Oh, did I say Mr. Doyle? I meant Professor Wetherby—sorry," Chase drawled, opening his eyes wide.

"Unh-huh! You *should be sorry!* I will not tolerate accusations like that. Next time, it will be straight to the principal's office. Now hurry up with those windows and take your seat," Miss Crabtree huffed.

Chase walked to the windows, unlocking and opening the first one with a slight tug. The second one opened with no problem. Then he moved to the third window, the one that would not open yesterday. It would not open today either.

Chase pulled out his magnifying glass from his back pocket and began examining the windowsill. This produced giggles from the students.

Miss Crabtree asked, "Young man, what on earth are you doing?"

"Miss Crabtree, this window is nailed shut!" Chase observed. "Do you know why?"

"Probably because it's broken, I would imagine… and that fits with the rest of this school," she complained.

Suddenly, the lights flickered and came back on. There was a hum of motors, and cool air poured into the room.

Miss Crabtree shook her head at Chase. "Young man, you may now close the windows and return to your seat."

Chase did as he was told, and before he sat back down, whispered to me, "Well, that got her blood going, didn't it?"

"What was that about?" I asked, my tone half-inquisitive, half-angry. "We didn't see Mr. Doyle this morning!"

"I wanted to see her reaction to his name. Make sure to document her response," he whispered back. "And I'm curious why that one window is nailed shut."

I opened my journal and wrote:

Friday, 8:10 a.m. — math class:

- *Power outage.*
- *Miss Crabtree freaked out when asked about Mr. Doyle.*
- *She said she has no relationship with any teachers and is surprised to hear we saw Mr. Doyle.*

Miss Crabtree narrowed her eyes at the clock on the wall, and then back at the class. I quickly closed my journal, opened my book to page forty-three, and began our lesson.

After math class was over, Chase and I started down the hall towards science class. As we walked, he said, "Hey, what about the power shutting down again? There's something to this, Ollie."

"Yeah," I agreed. "You might be—"

Just then, I saw two air conditioning workmen sifting through the sea of kids in the hallway. One of them had my shoe underneath his arm.

Chase and I both turned to go in the opposite direction, but our path was blocked.

CHAPTER FOURTEEN

CHEMICAL REACTIONS

FRANK, THE SCHOOL'S maintenance man, was in our way. He looked down the hallway at the two repairmen, and then back at us. "Either of you missing a shoe by chance?" he questioned.

"Nope," I said quickly—maybe too quickly?

Chase and I both showed Frank our feet. "Why?" I gulped, my heart fluttering inside my chest as I curled up my cramped toes even more inside Gio's shoe.

"Mischief and boys go together like peanut butter and jelly," he answered cryptically.

"I prefer honey with my peanut butter," I said, trying to put on a grin.

"Glad you got shoes on your feet; I wouldn't want you two boys growing up delinquents. You need to stay in school, study, and work hard, and walk the straight and narrow. Otherwise, you'll wind up bums with no jobs, expecting the rest of society to provide for you. Or worse yet—you might work for the government. Our government is the ultimate sponge," Frank blasted.

I felt one of Frank's sidetracked rants coming on. Even though there was little time between classes, Chase encouraged his now distracted thoughts.

"Isn't this school funded in part by the government?" Chase asked. "And doesn't that make you one of the bums, then?"

"I ain't no bum." Frank's eyes narrowed, and his tone became low. "I work for a living—not like those do-nothings in Washington. They're all corrupt, every last one of them! Even worse, their ringleader will be here next week."

"You're not looking forward to the President's visit?" I asked, trying to sound astonished and naïve. It was dawning on me that the longer we kept talking to Frank, the more likely it was that the workmen wouldn't take note of us.

"With all the hoops I've had to jump through for His Majesty? It's bad enough I have to put up with all the whining and complaining from the teachers, but now there are a bunch of special accommodations the school is going to have to observe. We have to deal with the Secret Service and the press, and we have to prepare for any stupid protesters. I can't imagine the cost to the taxpayers for this little three-hour visit. Think about the cost of the President and his entire entourage flying here, and the security—both the Secret Service and all the extra work I'm doing. Who's paying for all that? *We are*—the taxpayers, that's who."

"Are you going to be one of the protesters, then?" Chase asked.

"Are you kidding? Be one of those stupid Earth Warriors idiots? No way," Frank denied. "I may hate the imbeciles that run the government, but I'm not like *that* bunch of idiots! They have their own agenda—earth first, humans last. They think humans are the sole cause of all negative impacts to the earth, and that this country is especially responsible.

"Now, I don't doubt our government is covering up toxic pollution—everyone knows the politicians are in someone's back pocket; that's no secret. But there's bigger problems facing this country other than this group's little cause. They say they are going to make the world pay attention when the President gets here, but I can tell you that holding up signs and shouting doesn't get the attention of the dimwits in our government!"

"What does?" Chase asked, sounding genuinely curious.

Before Frank could answer, the start-of-class bell rang. We were late for Professor Wetherby's class.

We ran off, yelling back at Frank over our shoulders, "Thanks for the advice; we'll stay in school!"

We hurried into the unorganized mess that was Professor Wetherby's classroom. He was so engrossed in writing complicated equations on his blackboard he didn't notice us sneaking in—until Johnny Ricker shouted, "Nerd alert! Nerd alert!"

Professor Wetherby caught sight of us as we slid into our seats. But he was too involved in his equations to scold us and turned back to the blackboard to finish writing them down.

Chase, on his chair next to Eduard, quickly whispered, "Well, this is turning into quite the mystery."

"What mystery?" asked Eduard.

Gio answered snidely, "It's a private mystery."

I nudged him to be quiet.

"The mystery of this piece of paper with these markings and map—any idea what they mean?" Chase asked.

He showed Eduard the piece of paper that contained the map and the marks:

N2O — Xe 1,000 lbs.

"Hmm," Eduard said in an uninterested tone. "Maybe some kind of abbreviation, equation, or code? I don't know. I wouldn't waste my time on it."

"Yeah, Gio said you wouldn't be able to figure it out," Chase said. "Well, thanks for looking anyway."

"Oh, really?" Eduard lifted his chin and flattened his lips before glancing over his shoulder angrily at Gio. "Here—let me copy it into my notebook."

Chase winked at both Gio and me as Eduard quickly copied the note.

Professor Wetherby finished writing on the blackboard and turned his attention to the class. "Ladies and gentlemen, good morning. It's a pleasure to see all of you. Let us waste no time and proceed with today's lecture."

He began his trademark walk, moving back and forth in front of the class with his hands clasped behind his back. "Yesterday, we touched on the properties of the universe—cosmology. Today, we switch to the discipline of chemistry. Please open your chemistry books to page twenty."

There was a rustling sound as we all did as instructed.

"Here we find the periodic table. If we were to bake a cake, we would first need a recipe, and then need the proper ingredients to follow that particular recipe. Thus, it is with chemistry. We must first learn the basics of our ingredients—the periodic table—before we start mixing our recipe. But not all chemicals mix well with each other. Sometimes volatile reactions occur, both explosive and deadly."

Chase saw an opportunity and raised his hand. "What kind of chemistry did you have with Mr. Doyle?"

Professor Wetherby stood still for a moment with a look of bewilderment. "Uh… whatever do you mean?"

"Well, the way I see it, people are made up of different chemicals, and like you said, sometimes certain chemicals don't mix well with others. So, I was wondering how your two different chemicals got along with each other?"

"Chemistry between people is a figurative expression, young man. It is used primarily to describe compatible personalities—which would be more of a social science question."

"Okay... but then, did the two of you get along? I mean, personality-wise?"

Professor Wetherby's expression became troubled before he shook his head back and forth. "Young man, for the benefit of the class, let's stick to our current topic of chemistry. We can talk after school about the relationships and connections between people if you'd like."

Chase nodded in agreement, then looked at me through the corner of his eye and winked. As Professor Wetherby droned on about chemistry, Chase whispered, "Did you see his reaction when I asked about Mr. Doyle? Mark that down, Ollie! I'm definitely going to have more questions for this guy later."

I didn't know what to jot down in my journal except:

Professor Wetherby's chemistry = 100% boring.

Just then, I felt a small wet slap on the side of my face. I looked down to see a spitball on my desk. Across the room, Johnny and Miles started laughing.

"Bull's-eye!" Johnny whooped as he gave a high five to Miles.

"Yeah, that's a big target on your face, Freak," Miles laughed at me.

Professor Wetherby stopped talking for a moment and studied the class. When Johnny and Miles sucked in their laughter and tried to act as if nothing happened, Professor Wetherby continued with his boring lecture.

Was this teacher lost? I thought. *Could he not tell Johnny Ricker and Miles were up to no good?*

"Now, we must first understand that all matter in the universe is made up of elements," Professor Wetherby intoned as he chewed on the end of a pencil. "And all elements are made up of molecules, which are made up of atoms. Atoms are unique building blocks, to which varying combinations create unique elements."

Professor Wetherby continued hypnotizing us to sleep, and my eyelids grew heavy. I fought Wetherby's attempts to put us into a deep sleep, but it was difficult. He kept droning on.

"For example, if we want to change water into something completely different, we need to add additional molecules. For instance, if we added another oxygen atom to our compound of water, we would then have two oxygen atoms and two hydrogen atoms." Professor Wetherby wrote *H2O2* on the only clean space of his blackboard. "What was once water would then be something completely different—hydrogen peroxide."

What would happen if I created a chemical formula that would shrink things? I thought. *If I poured it on Johnny and Miles, it would shrink them down to two inches in height. At that point, I would put them in my fishbowl and let them swim around and around while I tapped irritatingly on the glass.*

I guess science wasn't so bad after all.

CHAPTER FIFTEEN

A SUBSTITUTE FOR HISTORY

WHEN SCIENCE CLASS ended, Chase, Gio, and I scurried down the hall to see if Mr. Doyle had returned to his classroom, or if the substitute from yesterday was in his place.

As we approached history class, I clutched my journal tight with anticipation.

We found the young, super-beautiful substitute from yesterday standing near the doorway and greeting each student with a smile as they entered the classroom.

Gio, Chase, and I nodded to each other in silent acknowledgment at the confirmation of what we had expected to find: *No Mr. Doyle—and that meant no pocket watch on the desk. Both were still missing.*

Gio walked off to math, while Chase took what should have been my seat in the front next to Jax.

If only I'd taken that seat, I thought, *I'd be the one sitting next to her whispering and passing love notes.*

Banished, I made my way to the back—next to Ana Rahela Bale-novic. The start-of-class bell rang, and the substitute smiled widely.

"Good morning, children. My name is Miss Eva Lexington. I am your substitute for Mr. Doyle, and I am so excited to be here. I hope all of you are as well. So, let's begin by getting to know each other with roll call."

She pulled out Mr. Doyle's attendance list and began calling out names.

"Ahbrea Ames?"

"Here," a voice squeaked.

"Kelly Anderson?"

"Here," answered another.

Then, with no pause—no special smile cracking her face—she called out the name, "Ana—Ra—hela—Bale—novic? Did I say it right?"

Ha, I thought, *finally someone who didn't know who Ana Rahela was.*

"Present!" Ana Rahela shouted out.

"Well, aren't you an eager student," Miss Lexington said dryly.

"My essay won the national Presidential essay contest, and the President of the United States is coming to our school now!" Ana shrieked.

I rolled my eyes. *Could she be any more boastful?*

"Oh, is that right? How exciting! I understand he'll be sitting in on our class. I can't wait to meet him," Miss Lexington said.

Ana Rahela furrowed her eyes. "You mean Mr. Doyle won't be here for his visit?" she asked, her voice a bit tight.

"Well, I don't think so! I've been asked to fill in for Mr. Doyle for a while. What's the matter? Don't you enjoy having me here?" Miss Lexington responded brightly, but with an exaggerated frown.

"Well, it's just... Mr. Doyle was so looking forward to meeting the President! I can't imagine he's going to miss it," Ana Rahela whined.

She sounded pitiful.

"Well, sometimes things don't always go the way we plan. But if you give me a chance while I'm here, I'm sure we'll get along just fine," Miss Lexington said before continuing the roll call. "Troy Carter?"

"Here."

"Patrick Duncan?"

"Here."

"Oliver Teller?"

"Here," I said in a low, mature tone.

Our substitute beamed a smile at me.

Maybe she had heard of my awesome writing skills and knows that Ana Rahela Balenovic did not deserve to win that contest. Maybe she could see I was more mature than the rest of my classmates. Maybe she was my ally, on my side, and not Ana Rahela's.

Mr. Doyle's class was getting better and better with each passing minute.

The substitute finished taking roll and flipped open one of her books. "All right, class. Let's begin by opening our history books to Chapter Three—*The Revolutionary War.* Now, after you all read the chapter, I'll hand out a short quiz. But before we begin reading, who knows what America dumped into the Boston harbor?"

Ana Rahela raised her hand. "Excuse me, Miss Lexington?"

"Yes—what is it... uh, I'm sorry. I forgot your name."

"It's Ana Rahela Balenovic, the Presidential essay contest winner? Remember?"

Did she always have to be the center of attention, making sure that the substitute knew who she was, all three of her names, and what she had done?

"Of course. What's your question?" the beautiful Miss Lexington asked.

"I, uh, well... Mr. Doyle was teaching us about the history of the Presidency to prepare for the President's visit," Miss Three-Name said.

"Of course," Miss Lexington said. "That is why we are starting at the beginning, when George Washington discovered America."

"You mean George Washington was our first President?" Ana Rahela corrected.

"Well, of course he was. After discovering America, I'm sure they made him president," Miss Lexington snapped.

Ana Rahela turned to me with a frown, shaking her head in short bursts of disbelief. I smiled, knowing she had no ally in this class anymore.

Before Ana Rahela could ask any more stupid questions, there was a knock at the door. In walked... some of the potential witnesses against me!

The older workman with gray hair, Murdoch, said, "Sorry to disturb your class, but we have a few items we need to check out in this room."

The younger repairman, Finnegan, looked at us students with a suspicious gaze. I sank into my desk, hoping he wouldn't recognize me. When he spotted our substitute, he gave her a long look. He smiled. She returned his smile.

The smile on his face disappeared when he turned his glance back to the students. And their feet.

"One of the students in this school slashed my tires earlier today. He ran off when I approached, but I managed to get one of his shoes. You wouldn't have noticed anyone missing a shoe, would you?" Finnegan asked.

"Oh? Well, it couldn't have been one of these angels," Miss

Lexington purred, waving her hand at us students. "Maybe you're mistaken? Could you have run over something on the road?"

"No, all four tires were deliberately slashed!" he snarled. "And when I get my hands on the little brat, why—"

"That's quite enough," Miss Lexington quickly and sternly interrupted. "You have a job to do, and I suggest you focus on it, while I focus on teaching these young children."

She smiled at him again. It caused him to smile back.

"Of course," Finnegan said, backing off a step.

Relieved, I looked over at the older workman. He was reaching up to one of the air ducts as if feeling for air movement. Pulling his hand back out with a frown, he shook his head at the younger man and started walking back out of the classroom.

Miss Lexington continued with her brilliant teaching by asking, "Now class, who knows what America dumped into Boston Harbor during the Revolution?"

"Tea," answered Kelly Anderson.

"That is correct," Miss Lexington said. "America's first documented act of pollution."

"Miss Lexington," Blake Williams raised his hand. "Just how much tea did they dump in the harbor?"

"Um, well, um…." Miss Lexington opened her book and flipped some pages.

The classroom became silent as Miss Lexington searched for an answer.

"Three hundred and forty-two chests of tea," the gray-haired repairman said on his way to the door. "Give or take."

"Oh?" Miss Lexington said.

"The Sons of Liberty carried it out—an underground resistance organization, formed to protest the abuses of the British government. Their actions helped to escalate the revolutionary war," the gray-haired repairman explained. "I apologize. I don't mean to infringe on your class, but history's a hobby of mine."

"Well, thank you… uh, sir. Sounds like you should be teaching this class."

"No, you're doing a fine job with what you need to do," he winked at her. "Thank you, ma'am, for your time. Keep up the good work."

Miss Lexington nodded back in acknowledgment.

Finnegan followed him out, giving one more look at the class before turning his attention back to Miss Lexington. They smiled and held each other's gaze before he walked away.

I didn't like the way he looked at her. I imagined taking off my shoe and smacking him on his head while saying, *"This is the other shoe that you're looking for—the other shoe you didn't pull off this morning. And by the way, you're lucky I don't flatten your face."*

Lucky for him, I couldn't get my shoe untied before he left.

Near the end of class, Miss Lexington walked around the classroom, handing out the quiz. I didn't hold it against her. I'm sure she really didn't want to give it, but Principal Sterns forced her to.

I looked it over and shook my head. I hadn't been paying attention to what I had read in my textbook, but instead was thinking about: Mr. Doyle and aliens; who else might be involved in the mystery; the ghosts in this school; Principal Sterns' connection to it all; and what Jax was talking about with Chase as they sat cozily in the front of the room.

Ana Rahela Balenovic couldn't contain herself. She turned to me, saying, "I'll help you with the answers if you want."

"No, thanks. I got this one," I murmured back.

I wasn't going to take her help so she could later brag that she knew more than me. I knew some of the answers, but I had to guess on the rest.

I handed the test back to our substitute with a big smile on my face. She was so kind I was sure she would cut me a break for trying so hard.

When the end-of-class bell rang, Miss Lexington stood up from her desk and said, "Thank you for being such great children today. I'll grade these over the weekend and see all of you bright and early on Monday. Remember to recycle and not waste. This is the only planet we have."

"I hope Mr. Doyle's back Monday. I don't like her," Ana Rahela said to me as I walked out.

"I hope he doesn't come back. Miss Lexington's great," I replied in a snide tone.

I started moving away from Ana fast and caught up to Jax and Chase, who were arguing some point. I heard Jax say just before she stalked off, "You guys are stupid. That's what I know."

I looked at Chase. "What was that about?"

"She's still upset about yesterday when we didn't tell Sterns the truth about the watch and Johnny. If she only knew the factual truth about this school and the alien abductions."

"Did you tell her?" I asked.

"Of course not. She's not sworn to secrecy," Chase replied.

"Well, just as we thought, Doyle's not here. What do we do now?" I said.

Chase raised his eyebrows. "We talk with the person who may know the most about what's going on."

CHAPTER SIXTEEN
THE CLIMB

WALKING INTO COACH Conley's gym class with Chase, I noticed Johnny Ricker and Miles were unusually quiet. That was strange for them. They were up to no good; I could just feel it.

Coach Conley seemed out of sorts as well. He had a different tone in his voice as he lined us up for our stretches, and he swung his whistle around nervously. He drifted off into other thoughts, what were usually twenty-to-thirty-second stretches, leaving us stretching for well over a minute each time.

Chase nudged me to look at Coach Conley's leg. It had a bandage on it. I observed some large bruises on the inside of his forearm, too.

"I wonder what that's from?" I asked.

"Let's find out." Chase raised his hand, asking, "Coach, are we going to be doing any running drills today?"

"Running drills?" Coach Conley said in a faraway voice. "Yes, a few laps to warm up. But then we are going to be climbing the wall."

"Well, you probably won't be running with us, seeing as how your leg is hurt," Chase said.

"My leg? Oh, that? My leg is fine to run; it's just a minor scratch." Coach bent down and rubbed at the area surrounding the bandage. "I tripped and fell while I was jogging, that's all."

"Were you running with Mr. Doyle yesterday?" Chase asked.

"Mr. Doyle? No. I wasn't running with Mr. Doyle yesterday," Coach answered.

"You didn't see him at all?" Chase pressed.

"No, I was running alone. Why?" Coach said in a defensive tone.

"My mistake," Chase shrugged. "I thought he was with you because I saw his car parked on the side of the dirt road you were on. Maybe you saw it while you were out running?"

"I wasn't… um… no… no, I didn't see his car." Coach swung his whistle, twisting it around his finger. "Let's get on with class, okay?"

Coach blew his whistle and barked out for the class to jog around the gymnasium to warm up.

Before we started, Chase looked at me and whispered, "He's lying! He might not have seen Doyle, but there's no way that he didn't see his bright yellow car parked on that road—he was running right towards it."

I whispered back, "Why would he lie?"

"To hide something," Chase said before we began jogging around the gym.

Coach noticed I was wincing and favoring my foot that was crammed into Gio's shoe that was too small for me. I told Coach I had a cramp, and I'd be fine. But I really wanted to take Gio's shoe off and run barefoot. When we finished with the laps, Coach lined the class up in front of the climbing wall where Johnny and Miles had pulled their prank yesterday.

There were three sections of the climbing wall, each varying in terms of difficulty. The section on our right was the easiest, the section in the middle more difficult, and the section on the left the hardest.

We all lined up in front of the easy section.

Chase had no problem climbing the first wall, scurrying up it quickly. Coach Conley was impressed and said so. This compliment did not sit well with Johnny Ricker, who was determined to climb the first wall and better Chase's time.

But Johnny tied with Chase for the fastest time to reach the top of the wall. Coach, who always encouraged competition, moved both boys over to the second wall.

It made for an exciting class as the two squared off against each other, one for the cause of good, and the other—for evil. I was Chase's belay, and Miles was Johnny's.

I knew before the race began who would win this climb. Chase was going to beat Johnny. I just knew it.

Coach blew his whistle, and the two climbers jumped onto the wall like grasshoppers and furiously began to climb. They progressed much slower than before, especially as the wall became progressively harder.

At one point, Chase looked like he was stuck when he waited for a moment. Johnny gained the lead. But Chase must have been studying the rock formations and making a plan because when he re-started his climb, he knew where to place his hands and feet every time.

Johnny started struggling after having gained a few feet. He had worked himself into a spot that had no additional grip, and he couldn't climb higher without repositioning himself.

Chase took the lead.

The excitement of impending victory was ready to burst out of me, and the hairs on the back of my neck stood up. Just then, I felt a whoosh of air blow by my ear and spied a flash of white up near the ceiling. A push on my back jolted both the anchor rope and me.

The shove had to have come from Miles. But Coach Conley was watching the two climbers and didn't see it.

Vibrations traveled up the rope and threw Chase off balance. He lost his grip and slipped.

I held the rope tight as Chase dangled high in the air above me.

Johnny passed Chase and reached the top, winning the climb thanks to a shove in my back from Miles. They had won the only way they could: by cheating.

Johnny hung at the top of the climbing wall like King Kong and shouted out his victory.

I lowered Chase to the ground. As he got his footing, I looked at him and shook my head. "Sorry. Miles pushed me. You should have beat Johnny."

"No big deal," Chase smiled. "Everyone knows who really won."

Johnny's victory shouts were replaced with yells of fear. "Ah! Ah! Get me down! Ah! Get me down—now!"

The class looked up at Johnny with confusion: *Was he hurt? Was he suddenly afraid of heights?*

Miles and Coach Conley quickly lowered him to the ground while he scrambled to get out of his harness, as if it was filled with stinging bees.

"He's up there! He's up there!" Johnny shrieked, his voice as high as a girl's.

"What? Slow down," Coach Conley said. "Who's up there? What happened?"

"Charlie Hackett! He's up there—I saw him," Johnny choked out.

"Johnny, what did I tell you and Miles about pulling pranks?" Coach Conley said in a much sterner tone.

"No, Coach! I'm serious. He was up there, showing me his

teeth—and they were all bloody! You've got to believe me. Someone else had to have seen something too, right?" Johnny said.

Everyone in the class remained silent, refusing to be made fools of a second time.

I saw something yesterday, I thought to myself, *but I'm not telling. Go on and look stupid in front of the class, Johnny Crybaby Ricker.*

When no one said anything in support of him seeing the ghost, Johnny said in a panic, "You saw him too, didn't you, Miles?"

Miles looked unsure about how to answer. "Um… yeah… I did. Johnny's telling the truth."

I could tell Miles was lying, and so could Coach. He shook his head and told both boys he would see them after class.

Chase raised his eyebrows at me. "Is he so stupid to think we'd fall for it twice?"

"Yeah, what a dummy," I answered.

I thought to myself about the flash of white I had just seen near the ceiling and the whoosh of air on my neck. And I too had seen a boy in the corner of the gym yesterday, when the lights flickered—someone just like Johnny described.

Should I support Johnny's claims, I wondered, *or was he tricking me into seeing things as well?*

I didn't want to be thought of as being as stupid as Johnny Ricker, so I kept it all to myself.

Coach Conley blew his whistle. "That was a great race. It's too bad that someone had to lose, but in my opinion, both competitors are winners. I want everyone to understand something: losing is a part of winning. No one is undefeated—no one," he said, walking around. "Every elite athlete has faced defeat somewhere in their career, and those defeats have made them better. It's through our losses we appreciate our victories. Our losses teach us how to handle disappointment and make us find out if we have the resolve to try again."

Here, Coach stopped talking and looked around at each one of us.

"Sometimes you learn more from your losses than from your victories. They show us who we are—our limitations," he said as he straightened himself to stand tall. "We must push through those limitations and try again! That is how we win!

"Just because you have a loss, or make a mistake, doesn't brand you a loser for life. It's overcoming the losses or mistakes that determine who you are—learning from your mistakes and not making them again."

The end-of-class bell rang, and we walked out of the gymnasium, leaving Johnny and Miles with Coach Conley. As we headed for the cafeteria, I couldn't stop thinking about what Johnny said he saw, and the things I saw, felt, and heard yesterday, and why no one else had experienced them.

I asked Chase, "So, if there are such things as ghosts, can only certain people see them? I mean, Johnny said he saw something no one else saw. I'm sure he's lying about that, but what about other people?"

"Ghosts can reveal themselves to whomever they want for their own purposes—good or bad," Chase answered.

"So, if there was a ghost in… say, this building, and a person saw it, could the ghost attack them?"

"Depends—most ghosts are harmless. They often are trying to communicate with the living, and some of them don't even know they're dead! But there have been reports of ghosts attacking people."

"So, do you think a ghost might be responsible for Mr. Doyle's disappearance?" I asked.

"It's definitely a possibility, and as paranormal investigators, we can never rule out anything. But I think our current evidence points more towards an alien abduction."

CHAPTER SEVENTEEN

THE PLOT THICKENS

WE STOPPED TALKING when we reached the cafeteria. It was filled with kids ready for yet another chance to be poisoned by the cooks. I had brought my lunch, but Chase and Gio were buying the gross mess here they called "food."

The cooks were back to their usual bad-mood selves, scowling, frowning, and flashing threatening glances at each student who passed through the cafeteria line. Standing at an arms-distance from Chase and Gio in line, I held my lunch sack high, so the cooks could see I had brought my lunch.

As we went through the line, discussing what might be the correct antidote for each kind of food, I saw the head cook flinging his bulging arms about in the back of the kitchen. I could hear him yelling some type of gibberish at someone—wow. It was Principal Sterns.

The principal was standing with his hands in his pocket and not saying a word. The cook sure looked angry, pointing and waving his finger at the head of our school.

"What do you think that's all about?" Gio softly asked.

"Well, that cook doesn't look very happy," Chase whispered back.

"I'll tell you what it's about," I whispered. "Sterns made them cook up Mr. Doyle for lunch."

A loud bang from behind the counter made me jump out of my skin. One of the cooks had struck the counter with his ladle, and he was pointing it at me. He said, "You… you eat?"

"Uh… well, I uh… brought my lunch… see?" I gulped.

I held up my bag containing the peanut-butter-and-honey sandwich, low-fat yogurt, and celery sticks.

Why couldn't I have some nun-chucks or Chinese throwing stars in there instead? I could then say, "No, I'm not eating your gross food. It's disgusting, and what are you going to do about it? Hmm?"

I decided I should say that another day.

Quickly, I moved on down through the line. No sooner had the three of us sat down at our table than Principal Sterns strode out of the kitchen and stalked off down the hall.

"Let's follow him," Chase whispered.

I raised my bag. "What about lunch?"

"Leave it; we'll come back. Let's move!" he said.

"I'll stay here with our food," Gio offered. "You guys go."

I got up half-heartedly; I was hungry. But as Chase hustled off in the direction of Principal Sterns, trying to act as normal as could be, I followed him with the same undercover skills.

Principal Sterns had walked halfway down the hall towards his office when I asked Chase, "Why are we following him?"

It seemed obvious that Sterns was either going back to his office or the teachers' lounge for lunch—where was the mystery in that?

The cooks probably were angry with him because he had brought his lunch like me.

"He just got out of an argument," Chase whispered back. "And that makes him vulnerable to mistakes."

The hallways were empty and quiet, so we kept our distance, hiding behind hall lockers and corners as we followed our principal. When the hallway split, he turned to the right, towards his office. That's when a woman's voice called out from the opposite direction to the left.

"Alec?"

Principal Sterns stopped and turned, looking behind him and almost seeing our bodies as we tried to hide behind a locker. "Oh, there you are," he called back.

He walked to the left, around the corner in the hallway, until he was out of sight. His voice became so soft, we couldn't make out what he was saying.

Chase and I quietly tiptoed closer to the corner, making our bodies razor-thin against the wall. We were able to get within a few feet of where the principal was and eavesdrop on the conversation.

"Well, they weren't happy, but they're just going to have to deal with it," he was saying in a barely audible tone. "We can't take any risks with the Secret Service here checking everything out; it could ruin everything. It's hard enough just keeping them on track with feeding the kids."

"Which is why I don't think it's wise to bring in outsiders at this juncture; that gives more reasons for them to dig deeper," the female voice whispered back.

"Yes, yes, I know—but thanks to that idiot, Doyle, I have to deal with things differently," Sterns whispered back. "Believe me; no one wants all of this to be over more than I do. I hate extortionists."

"Do you think it ever will be over?" the unknown woman's voice asked.

"Yes, my love—yes," Principal Sterns answered. "But for now, we each must play our part in this tragedy."

Gurgle….

My stomach started growling because I was hungry. I tried to suppress the noise, but it was pretty loud. Chase looked at me to do something, but all I could do was cover up my belly. So Chase motioned for me to move back to the cafeteria.

We tiptoed backwards until we reached the lunchroom.

"Wow," Chase said as he plunked back down in his seat. "I think we're really onto something! Did you hear all that?"

"What do you think it means?" I asked, focusing on my lunch.

Gio, with a mouth full of a gross mess, asked, "What does what mean?"

"Principal Sterns has something going on here, and it's not just—" Chase began to explain, but he was interrupted.

"Hello, boys." Jax was standing right behind Chase.

"Whoa… careful about sneaking up on someone like that," Chase snapped. "I could have taken you out by accident, thinking you were some kinda evildoer."

"You mean… don't sneak up on people, like the two of you were just doing to Principal Sterns?" Jax smiled sweetly as we looked at each other guiltily. "What's going on?"

"Umm… well, it's top-secret right now. We can't share," Chase said back.

"Can't, or won't?" Jax said, placing her hands on her hips.

"I seem to remember you didn't want any part of this," Chase said.

"Oh? And I remember you telling me you all needed my help," she smiled. "But if you don't need me anymore, then I guess I'll just tell Principal Sterns you were following him through the halls at lunchtime."

Jax smiled even bigger this time. The sight melted my heart.

How could Chase resist? I would never keep a secret from her. Never.

"Okay, okay," Chase said, giving in. "We're investigating a mystery, but you need to swear to secrecy."

"A mystery? You mean that paranormal junk you fed to Principal Sterns? Come on, you expect me to believe that?" Jax scoffed.

"Yep, and we are in the process of—" Chase stopped mid-sentence, interrupted by the sight of Eduard walking through the cafeteria looking for a seat. He quickly motioned for Eduard to come sit with us.

"Don't tell him to come over here!" Gio snapped. "He's too good for us.... All we'll hear about is how much money he has, or how smart he is."

"He's okay," Chase defended him. "Besides, we need him on our team."

"For what?" Gio quizzed.

"For exactly what you just pointed out," Chase said cryptically.

Eduard walked over to our table. "Hello, fellow students," he said in a snobby tone.

"Hello, Eddie," Gio said, whipping out a snide tone.

"Hello, Giovanni. And it's Ed-dwhard, thank you," Eduard said.

"Sit here," Chase directed, pointing to the open chair.

With his chin in the air, Eduard looked down through his glasses before nodding once and taking the seat. He relaxed a bit, saying, "I was reviewing our chemistry textbook, and came up with a startling discovery."

I heard a hint of excitement in Eduard's voice that I'm not sure I'd heard before.

"The paper you showed me earlier in class—the one with what you thought had codes?" Eduard said as he pulled out his textbook from his book bag. "They're not initials, or codes, or abbreviations at all." He flipped through some pages as we all gathered around.

"I noticed one in particular.... Here—look at that," he said in a proud tone. The page showed the chemical formula *N2O*—the same formula written on the paper by Mr. Doyle's car. "This is a chemical formula for Nitrous Oxide."

Chase looked up. "Awesome job, Eduard. But what does that whole equation mean?"

"I don't know yet. I'll have to do more research. But now that I know these are chemical formulas, I'll be able to find out what they're used for," Eduard promised.

Chase patted him on the back. "Awesome. I knew you could figure it out."

With a smug smile directed at Gio, Eduard asked, "What else can I help you guys with? Homework? Financial affairs? Social networking?"

Chase folded his arms and softly asked, "How about finding a missing person?"

Both Jax and Eduard's eyes flew open as they asked in unison, "Who?"

"Mr. Doyle." Chase leaned back in his chair. "We were walking home yesterday and found Doyle's car parked on a dirt road."

"By the bridge where dead cows were found hanging from," Gio added.

"Those stupid stories never really happened," Jax scoffed. "So what if you saw his car?"

"Doyle was gone without a trace, but we did find these...." Gio said.

He opened his sketchbook, showing Eduard and Jax the drawings he made of the flowers, button, and key. Gio then pulled the key from his pocket and showed it around.

"So what?" Jax shrugged.

"So, Doyle is missing, and we found his car along with a bunch of stuff scattered about—that's what," Chase fired back.

"How do you know he's missing?" Jax shrugged her shoulders. "Maybe he just took the day off, and he was out for a walk that day."

"Hmm…" Eduard said thoughtfully. "Gentlemen, did you report finding his car to the authorities?"

"Not yet," I said, hesitating. "We were, uh, spotted."

"What?" Jax furrowed her eyebrows. "What do you mean, 'spotted'?"

I frowned. "Those repair guys here at the school—they came up the road and caught us looking in his car. Now, when Doyle doesn't show back up, we are going to get blamed—especially me!"

"Relax," Chase interrupted. "They didn't get a good look at you or any of us. But, something happened to Doyle all right… that's for sure."

Eduard adjusted his glasses. "So, what now?"

"The authorities won't believe anything we say without proof, so it's up to us to open a full-scale paranormal investigation on this case," Chase answered in a matter-of-fact voice.

And that's when Gio squeaked, "Guys, I think Oliver might be right—we've got problems."

CHAPTER EIGHTEEN

A GRAVE MATTER

WE ALL TURNED our heads towards Gio, who was gazing out a nearby window. We all moved over and looked out it.

The sheriff's car was parked by the front doors of our school. Its presence was anything but ordinary, and its arrival meant only one thing: trouble.

"He's here because of the flat tires on the work van!" I mumbled nervously. "Those workers recognized me from yesterday… they found my blood on Doyle's car… I knew they'd bust me! I knew it… I'm going to *jail…* I don't *want to go to jail!"*

"No way! Chill out," Chase reassured me. "The sheriff could be here for several reasons!"

"Should we tell him about finding Mr. Doyle's car?" Gio asked.

"Maybe," Chase replied, "but I'm more interested in what he knows. Let's go talk with him."

I followed Chase, but really, I was thinking to myself, *this is such a bad idea. A cow doesn't go searching for the butcher to find out what's for dinner, and yet here we were, about to ask for the menu.*

"I'm coming too," Jax said, following close behind me.

"I don't know if that's a good idea," Chase told her, stopping short. "We're in an investigative mode right now."

"I'm the school's investigative reporter.... But I suppose I could talk with the sheriff on my own," she volleyed back at him.

"Fine! Just let me do the talking," Chase said, continuing to walk.

We found the sheriff talking with Principal Sterns in the hallway outside his office. There would be no running away now. I would have to face what came my way.

I had seen the sheriff many times before while riding his horse and patrolling our town. But I had never seen him up close and in person, like now.

Sheriff Booker Graves was big and burly—taller than Principal Sterns. His shoulders were wide, as if he was wearing shoulder pads. His chin was square, strong, and shaped like an anvil. He held a cowboy hat in one hand, and his cowboy boots shot him up taller than he already was. There was a large revolver on his hip, and his sheriff's star, pinned to his khaki uniform on his broad chest, gleamed in the light.

"Thank you for stopping by, Sheriff," Principal Sterns was saying as he shook the sheriff's hand. "I will let you know if we see anything."

"I'd appreciate it. You have my number," the sheriff said in a deep, rough voice that he rolled out with a twang.

The sheriff was about to walk out of the building until the four of us corralled him.

"Excuse us, Sheriff," Chase asked in a soft voice. "Do you mind if we ask you a few questions?"

"What can I do for y'all?" the sheriff asked, peering down at us through steel-gray eyes.

His intimidating figure was unnerving. I felt like the Cowardly Lion coming to see the great Oz. I was ready to jump out the window and run away at any given moment—but with Jax by my side, that wasn't an option.

Chase gulped and hesitated before speaking. This allowed Jax to step in front of him and ask, "These boys are wondering if you are here investigating the disappearance of Mr. Doyle?"

"What do you mean, *the disappearance of Mr. Doyle?*" the sheriff asked back in a soft voice.

Chase answered, "Mr. Doyle has been missing for two days now, and no one seems to know where he is."

"And you know he's been missing *how?*" the sheriff asked back.

I noticed that the sheriff was using a tricky technique when asking his questions. By simply asking someone to clarify the meaning of their words, he was making them reveal more of what they knew without asking them outright. It was very clever.

"Mr. Doyle went to his car during lunch and never came back. We've had a substitute teacher for the last a day and a half," Chase said.

"And we saw Mr. Doyle's car abandoned on the road down by the bridge near Old Man Owens's ranch," Gio offered.

Stupid Gio, I thought. *Now we definitely were going to get in trouble. Gio had just admitted to the sheriff that we were the ones those repairmen saw.*

"What were you doing on that road?" the sheriff asked in a sharp tone. "That road goes through Mr. Owens's property."

"We were taking a shortcut home," Gio nervously answered.

My uncle had once told me, *"Shortcuts only cut you short."* Now I understood what he meant.

"Listen, I want you kids to stay away from that road, y'all

hear? It runs through private property, and Mr. Owens doesn't want trespassers on his land—y'all need to respect that. But, most importantly, y'all could get hurt. It's dangerous," the sheriff said in a firm voice.

"Dangerous?" Chase questioned, using the sheriff's technique himself. "Why?"

"The old Tanner silver mine lies down that road. It's been abandoned for who knows how long. The mine's tunnels and airshafts run under the ground, sometimes for miles. We don't even know where all of them are! Parts of the ground there aren't stable and are prone to collapse. In fact, Mr. Owens has lost a mess of cattle because of a few of those tunnels collaps'n. I don't want to be on the evening news, pull'n you kids out of some mineshaft," the sheriff lectured.

"And if that's not enough, there's been predators coming out of the hills, killing the livestock there. Y'all need to be more careful no matter where you are—so walk in groups if you can," the sheriff said as he pulled out and handed us a card with his name and phone number on it. "You can call me anytime if you see anything suspicious. Now be careful out there and do not go anywhere near Mr. Owens's property—y'all hear?"

Without waiting for a response, Booker Graves put on his cowboy hat and walked out the front doors.

I realized he had disclosed nothing to us about the whereabouts of Mr. Doyle.

"This gets better by the second," Chase said with a grin.

"Why didn't you show the sheriff the stuff you found, like the key?" Jax asked.

"He might have taken it from us before we could find out what it opens," Chase answered.

Jax put her hands on her hips. "That's because it's *his* job—not yours."

"We'll give it to him *after* we find out where it leads—along with the rest of the stuff," Chase said.

"How are we gonna do that?" Gio squeaked. "Try every door here?"

"The maintenance guy, Frank, might know what it opens," I said.

Chase liked my idea. "Let's find him! There's still time before lunch and recess end."

Jax folded her arms. "I don't think that's a good idea. We're not supposed to be wandering the halls at lunchtime."

"True—it's probably too dangerous for girls," Chase sneered. "You can head back out for recess, and we will catch up with you later."

"You're ridiculous. I'm coming with you," Jax snapped.

Gio, Eduard, and I looked at each other and shrugged before following the two of them. Jax and Chase seemed to be in a race down the hallway now.

We found the door to the maintenance room door closed. Chase knocked a few times, but there was no answer. "No one home, I guess," he mumbled.

Mrs. Huntley walked by and asked us, "Is something wrong?"

Chase smiled. "Nothing much; a clogged toilet in the boy's bathroom. We want to do the responsible thing and report it to Frank immediately. Have you seen him?"

"Oh, what good citizen students you are," she said with a cheerful smile. "I saw him walking towards the gymnasium just a little while ago."

We headed off in that direction as I tried to think of which boy's bathroom had a clogged toilet.

When we reached the gymnasium, Chase popped his head inside. No Frank, no Coach, and no students—just emptiness.

Gio couldn't help himself and yelled to hear his own echo. "Hello!"

Jax punched him in the arm to silence him. Just then, a crash came from inside the equipment room. All of us froze in our tracks.

Somebody, or something, was in there—in the same room we heard a noise from yesterday when the lights had gone out in gym class, and Johnny and Miles had pulled their little prank.

I knew those two troublemakers weren't in there now because I had just seen them in the cafeteria.

"Who do you think's in there?" Gio whispered.

"I don't know who," Chase said, looking at Jax before finishing, "or what... but let's find out."

"Wait," I whispered. "Don't we need something... like, I don't know, a baseball bat, or a machine gun?"

"There's no time," Chase said. "We have to act quickly. Let's go."

He held up his finger to his lips, silencing us, and then began tiptoeing over to the blue double doors. We all followed, not knowing why or what to expect.

The lights in the gymnasium were on. But if they went out, I might be running in the other direction, Jax or no Jax. Looking for ghosts in a haunted school wasn't exactly what I had in mind when I grabbed my backpack in the morning.

What was next? I thought. *A trip down to the basement, where I'm sure all sorts of dead bodies are buried?*

I could feel my heart beat faster. As we inched closer to the doors, we heard shuffling inside. Jax grabbed my arm for support, which caused me to lose all concentration.

It was so odd: Suddenly I was scared and brave at the same time. I wasn't sure which I was more.

Chase reached out his hand to the doorknob of the equipment room, turning the knob slowly. The door creaked.

Suddenly, the door flew open, causing us all to scream in fright. An enormous figure appeared in the doorway—a large, bald figure. A large, bald figure named Frank, the maintenance man whose eyebrows were furrowed, and jaw was clenched tight.

He stared at the three of us. "What are you kids doing here?" he bellowed.

"Uh…." Chase mumbled. "We were… uh… looking for you."

"Me?" Frank said, obviously surprised. "Why?"

"Well," Chase continued, "For several reasons, actually. Jax here," he said as he pointed towards Jax, "is researching a story for the school newspaper. She wanted to ask you some questions about the school since, obviously, you are so knowledgeable and an expert. Would that be okay?"

Jax looked at Chase with a surprised look, which she quickly changed to an angry glare. Chase shrugged and smirked back.

Frank softened his expression. "Well, I suppose I am the most knowledgeable person here about the school, and for most other things, for that matter. Not that anyone here listens to me."

Chase nodded. "Precisely why we came to you first."

Jax caught her breath. She was on stage now, and our star. Fortunately, she knew her role and quickly got into character.

"Now, let me start by asking, how long have you worked at this school?" Jax asked, her tone rather perky.

Chase nodded to me and made a gesture with his hands as if writing with a pen and paper in the air. I nodded back; I understood he wanted me to take notes.

This had become my new role: the note taker/writer/journalist. Probably it had come about because I carried my journal with me wherever I went, and I always had very nice pens and great penmanship—not to mention that I was the best writer in school.

"I've been here fifteen years, and counting; longer than any of the teachers," Frank boasted.

"And why did you decide to become a janitor?" Jax asked with a bat of her lashes.

"I decided to become a *Facilities Maintenance Manager* because I like to work with my hands. I took this job on a part-time basis, thinking it would only be temporary. But it turned into a full-time gig, and here I am, fifteen years later. I could have finished my degree in philosophy and history, and then I'd be teaching classes here instead of one of these bozos. But it's okay; I'd rather do hard work than be a softy like one of those clowns."

Jax nodded and continued with her questions. "So, during your time here, you must have witnessed many changes?"

"I'll say—the teachers, principals, students; all of them have changed over time. The only one still here is me. Heck, even this building has changed, although it was like pulling teeth to get the renovations approved. And now, if Principal Sterns gets his new plans past Mr. Doyle, I'm sure it'll mean more work for me. And do you think they'll approve more full-time help for me? Humph, never.... But I'm sure they'll hire more new teachers," Frank said in a disgruntled tone.

"What do you mean by *'plans past Mr. Doyle?'*" Jax asked.

"Mr. Doyle's the chairman of the Raven Ridge Historical Commission, and all historical building modifications have to be approved by his board. He and Principal Sterns have been at odds over the school's new expansion plans, so who knows if they'll be approved. That's what happens when you give these guys like Mr. Doyle power! They feel the need to use it."

Chase jumped into the questioning. "So, speaking of Mr. Doyle, what about him?"

"Mr. Doyle? What do you mean, 'what about him?'" Frank asked, clearly confused.

"Have you seen him?" Chase clarified.

"What? No—why?" Frank replied.

"Oh, he's not here again today. I just thought you might have come across him during your rounds," Chase said casually.

"His absence is at least one improvement to this school," Frank said in a haughty tone.

"You don't like Mr. Doyle?" Jax jumped back in.

"He's a know-it-all, except he's a know-nothing-at-all about history. He can't tell you what actually happened during the Second World War, but I'm sure he knows what the football scores are. I could run circles around his *supposed* knowledge of historical facts. That's what happens when they put these idiots with their degrees from Ivy League schools in charge of our youth—they teach their own version of history. I don't agree with what they feed you kids here at the school—poisoning your minds!"

Frank must have caught himself ranting because he calmed his tone and finished with, "That's all off the record, of course—*right?*"

Jax nodded yes, and then started to ask, "Have you—"

Chase cut her off. "We heard there had been some vandalism and items missing. Can you tell us what was taken?"

"Some antiques in this building, like a music box, a vase, and one of Anastasia's silver vanity mirrors," Frank said, becoming suspicious. "Why… have you seen any of these items?"

"No, no. But when you say, 'one of Anastasia's silver vanity mirrors'—are there more?" Chase questioned.

"There were three mirrors, but only one was thought to exist still—until there was one recently found in the basement." Frank let out a big yawn and stretched. "I suppose I should start by telling you about the owner of this here building, and the legend of Anastasia's vanity mirrors."

His voice became soft and dramatic, like he was telling a ghost story around a campfire.

"Horace Tanner owned the Endless Mine, once the most profitable silver mine in the country. His wealth was immense, and so was Tanner's ambition. He had married a beautiful young woman named Anastasia Petrov, whose beauty was matched only by her vanity. She was an East Coast socialite who despised the West; she thought it was dirty, and its people uneducated, and at first, she refused to move out here with her husband. Horace promised her that the town of Raven Ridge would soon become the crown jewel of the West, with universities and buildings taller than those in New York City, and that she would be the queen of his silver empire. So, she reluctantly agreed to move out West despite her reservations.

"Horace built up the town, creating a newspaper, an opera house, shops, and this building—it was his crown jewel. He spared no expense on its construction, and people referred to it as *'Redstone Castle.'* None of it, though, would make his Anastasia happy. She was homesick and threatened to return to the East Coast all the time.

"One day, a traveler passed through town selling artifacts from around the world. Anastasia took note of three mirrors he was selling. She could not help but stare endlessly into them, apparently captivated by her reflection in the mirrors. She claimed she had never seen herself so lovely. The traveler told Anastasia the mirrors were magical—made from lightning glass.

"She asked him what lightning glass was, and what was so magical about the mirrors. So, he explained to her that when lightning strikes sand on a beach, it melts the sand into glass. Ancient glassmakers believed the *lightning glass* to have magical powers, and they used the lightning glass to create these mirrors. The traveler then told her that fortunetellers used these magic mirrors to tell a person's past, present, and future.

"Anastasia asked the traveler if he could see her future in these mirrors. The traveler confessed he was only an amateur fortuneteller, but agreed to try, and gazed at her reflection from one of the mirrors. After a few moments, he broke off his stare and told

Anastasia she would appear beautiful forever in these mirrors if she bought them.

"However, he warned her not to look into the mirrors during a lightning storm, for if the mirrors attracted the lightning, the lightning glass would capture her forever. So, if there ever were to be a storm, the mirrors needed to be covered with black cloth.

"Anastasia was more taken with her own reflection than with some silly tale, and she bought the three mirrors. The traveler handed each one over to her, wrapped tightly in black cloth while warning her again not to look into them during a storm.

"Only a short time later, Anastasia used silver from the Endless Mine to frame each mirror with a silver raven that enveloped the glass with its silver wings. She became so obsessed with her reflected image in the mirrors that she gazed into them night and day, and carried one of the mirrors with her wherever she went. This caused the townsfolk of Raven Ridge to say, *'Anastasia is so vain she carries her mirrors of vanity wherever she goes; looking at her reflection, she doesn't even eat or drink.'* This is where the term '*vanity mirrors*' came from.

"One night, a big storm rolled into town. Horace had been out at his mine all day, and he was heading back to Redstone Castle when the lightning flashed across the sky, and the rain fell. It slowed his return.

"Anastasia was in Redstone Castle, still looking at her reflection and not paying any mind to the traveler's warning not to look into the mirrors during a lightning storm. Horace was just about to place a foot on the steps of his castle when he saw lightning strike the room where Anastasia kept her mirrors. A scream followed the strike.

"Horace ran up to rescue his Anastasia, only to find the room empty—except for the silver raven mirrors. When he picked one of them up, he saw his wife's reflection looking back at him. The lightning glass had taken her!

"Horace cried out for Anastasia to come back, but her image faded with the ending of the storm. Horace sat for days looking into the mirrors, but her reflection never returned. Meanwhile, the silver industry came undone, and his Endless Mine went bust. Horace had lost his wife, his fortune—everything. Deeply depressed, Horace took the mirror that had shown him his wife's last reflection and wandered into his Endless Mine, never to be seen again. It is said that her reflection can still be seen in the mirror if one looks long enough.

"An artist for the *Saturday Evening Post* came to Raven Ridge one day to draw the famous silver mines. Hearing the story of Anastasia and her mirrors of vanity inspired the artist to create a now-famous double-image drawing, a copy of which hangs on the wall of the school's office. At close-range, the illustration depicts Anastasia in front of her mirror—but from a distance, it looks like a human skull. The artist entitled it, *'All Is Vanity.'*

"Only one of the three of Anastasia's famous vanity mirrors was thought to exist still, and that one is displayed in the principal's office. Recently, another one, covered with black cloth, was discovered in the school's basement. Mrs. Huntley was going to restore it before we displayed it in the school's foyer."

Suddenly, the building lights started flickering. Even though the power didn't go out, Frank shook his head in disgust. "I swear those A/C guys don't know what they're doing. They should've had this problem fixed already. Good help is hard to find these days. I could have fixed this myself days ago if I wasn't so busy."

He turned around to look up at the ceiling lights, and Chase pointed for us to look at the back of Frank's head. But all I saw was a big, bald spot.

"Did something happen to the back of your head?" Chase asked, sounding concerned. "You've got a red mark on it."

"What?" the janitor said, rubbing the back of his head. "Oh, I must have bumped it on something." His face flushed. "Shouldn't you kids be getting back to the lunchroom now?"

"Yes," Jax said. "That was quite the story! Thank you for this valuable information about the school. I hope we can ask you more questions later?"

Frank nodded yes, and we began to walk away. But Chase stopped and turned back, asking, "Oh, one more question.... What were you doing in that equipment room?"

"What?" Frank stuttered. "W-w-working.... Organizing the equipment, of course."

"Oh? I see. Thanks again," Chase said.

Once out of Frank's sight, Eduard asked, "Why didn't you guys show him the key? I thought that's the reason we wanted to talk to him."

Jax answered for Chase, saying, "Because he thinks something's going on with Frank now, I'm sure."

"Maybe," Chase agreed as the end-of-lunch-recess bell rang. "We need to talk more about this. Everyone meet by my hall locker after school?"

We all nodded our heads and started off to our classes; I had Literature with Jax and Eduard. As we walked down the hall, I made sure Jax was on my left, so that I could hide my birthmark on my right from her.

I gulped when she asked me, "So, Oliver, what do you think is really going on?"

What was really going on? My heart was beating as fast as a hummingbird's wings because I was walking next to her. That's what was going on, I thought.

"I don't know," I softly said back. "But Chase will find out."

"Well, if you ask me, it's all just one big misunderstanding, that's all. There's nothing going on here that's paranormal. Who believes that junk, anyway?" she scoffed.

"I certainly don't," I quickly agreed.

"Mr. Doyle will return on Monday, and Chase will look like an idiot," she said with a crisp nod of her head.

"Yeah, probably," I said.

I would agree with anything she had to say.

CHAPTER NINETEEN

GREAT MINDS THINK ALIKE

WHEN WE ARRIVED in literature class, Jax took her seat next to her popular friends on the far side of the room near the front. Eduard and I took our seats in the middle of the room, next to the not-so-popular nerds like Ana Rahela Balenovic.

Miss Ivy looked exceptionally delicate and fragile, clad in a white linen shirt and lavender skirt. She gazed out the window as the class drifted into their seats, lost in her own thoughts.

Her look was expressionless: neither happy nor sad, worried nor mad. I couldn't guess where her mind was—but it wasn't here. Maybe she was writing a new poem in her head or concluding a novel.

Eduard leaned over to me and said, "I think Chase is right; there must be more to Mr. Doyle's disappearance. Chase has offered to show me some of his findings after school."

I could see Ana Rahela Balenovic trying to listen to our conversation, and I motioned to Eduard to be silent.

The start-of-class bell brought Miss Ivy out of her trance. Turning towards the class, she gave a slight smile. She opened her poetry notebook as we settled down, and silence took hold. She paused and then read:

Look in thy glass and tell the face thou viewest,
Now is the time that face should form another;
Whose fresh repair if now thou not renewest,
Thou dost beguile the world, unbless some mother.
For where is she so fair whose unear'd womb
Disdains the tillage of thy husbandry?
Or who is he so fond will be the tomb
Of his self-love, to stop posterity?
Thou art thy mother's glass, and she in thee
Calls back the lovely April of her prime;
So thou through windows of thine age shalt see
Despite of wrinkles, this thy golden time.
But if thou live, remember'd not to be,
Die single, and thine image dies with thee.

-William Shakespeare, Sonnet III

"Good afternoon, class. Today, we will continue our journey with Shakespeare. We will spend this class reading one of his plays, *Hamlet*."

Jax glanced at me from across the room and pointed towards Miss Ivy's desk. I wasn't sure what she was trying to tell me. But for now, we would have to make do with our long-distance relationship.

True lovers don't need words anyway, I thought. *They just know what the other person is thinking.*

I looked at Miss Ivy's desk and saw nothing out of sorts. As always, her desktop was neatly organized with a few books—never too many—her nice pens lined up neatly in a row, a small stack of nice notepaper—no doubt for writing important poems or her thoughts down—and a vase filled with purple flowers.

Anna Rahela Balenovic saw Jax's glance and tried to butt into our silent conversation by sticking her big, stupid head in my line of sight. She said, "Hello, Oliver. What about getting together after school and discussing the layout for next week's newspaper?"

"I don't have time after school… homework, ya know," I said.

"But you're the editor! You need to edit my layouts and designs," she pointed out.

"Fine. How about showing them to me on Monday?"

"Well, I do need some copy first…. What stories are you working on? The President's visit, no doubt—do you want to interview me? I mean, seeing as how I'm the reason he's coming to the school and all."

"Um… no… I don't think so," I mumbled.

"Really? It's kinda important that people know the background behind his visit, don't you think?"

"Um… no."

Ana Rahela Balenovic drew her stupid head back and raised her eyebrows. "What kind of editor are you, anyway?" she said in a less friendly tone.

"One that makes the school paper interesting," I snapped.

Miss Ivy finally gave out the assignment. "Class, today we will read Shakespeare's story of a prince named Hamlet. His dead father's ghost is asking Hamlet to avenge his death. I want you to think about the characters and their motivations, and to reflect on Hamlet's internal struggle. Is Hamlet really seeing the ghost of his father—or has Hamlet gone mad?"

We all opened our books and began reading. This struck me as odd because Miss Ivy always interacted with the class a lot. But today she was keeping to herself and just telling us to read. Something was bothering her; I could tell. The good thing about it was, I didn't have to talk with Ana—*I can't shut my mouth because I have three names*—Balenovic, and that was nice.

I looked out the window at the stone gargoyle I saw moving yesterday. I stared at it for a while, wondering if it really had moved. I glanced back at my textbook and then looked back up at the gargoyle, hoping to catch it—but nothing had happened. Discouraged, I went back to reading like the rest of my classmates.

It was quiet—almost too quiet for me to concentrate on the words in front of me. And that's when I heard the clicking noise in the hallway. *Principal Sterns must be roaming the halls clicking his stupid pen,* I thought. I looked around at everyone else, but they were all intent on their reading. I looked back out the window—the ear of the gargoyle had moved! It was now in a different position, perked up and turned towards our class.

The class continued reading, unaware of what was going on. I sat staring out the window while the clicking noise slowly disappeared. *I know what I saw,* I told myself. *I have to document this and tell Chase.* I wrote down what I witnessed while keeping an eye on the gargoyle out the window. It never moved again—and I never read anything in my textbook.

At the end of class, Jax waited near the door for me. I tried to act like I didn't notice her while trying to shield the right side of my face.

"Oliver, did you see what I saw?" she said with excitement as we strolled out into the hallway just like a real couple—a dating couple!

She had seen the gargoyle moving, I thought to myself in excitement. *I wasn't the only one. It's another sign that we are meant to be together....*

"You saw it too? Thank goodness; I thought I was seeing things!

I couldn't believe my eyes. I kept staring out the window, but at first, it didn't—"

"The window?" Jax looked at me funny as she interrupted me. "What are you talking about? I was talking about Miss Ivy's desk. Didn't you notice what was on it?"

"Yes… of course I did!"

I quieted myself quickly. *How had those words jumped out of my mouth?*

"What do you think?" she prodded.

"I… I… well, I… don't know. I like the type of pens she uses, but her paper stock is a bit thin for important writing," I said.

"No… the flowers. They are the same kind that Gio drew in his notebook!" Jax said, her face flushed red with excitement.

"Right! Of course, they are… yes—that was the first thing I noticed too!" I babbled.

"That was a little coincidental, right? We'll talk more after school, okay?" Jax smiled at me before she left for her next class.

Of course, we will, my love, I thought.

I walked off to my art class on clouds of air.

Forget about the gargoyle and the flowers. The school day couldn't end soon enough for me.

CHAPTER TWENTY

KEEPING AN EYE OPEN

BEFORE ART CLASS started, I showed Mrs. Huntley the sketches I had made of my Monte Christo project. I had sketched the sheet draped over the display case, and while I was at it, made it look as if I had covered the entire room with sheets.

So far, the project at home had concealed from my mother the fact that my great-grandfather's pocket watch was missing from the display case on the bookshelf. Now I was about to find out if the same project would provide me with some success in Mrs. Huntley's art class. After all, I had told my mother that the wrapped bookshelf was for extra credit—something which had never been said. But if Mrs. Huntley could be persuaded from viewing my sketches to give extra credit to me—that would basically nullify my lies to my mother.

How proud Mrs. Huntley should be of me, I thought, *to take it upon myself to create my own Monte Christo art project at my house.*

I said to my teacher proudly, "I hope you appreciate my *extra* effort. I created this at my house."

"You did all this?" she exclaimed, giving me a huge smile. "Wonderful, Oliver! Simply wonderful!"

"Well, I have to say it was your inspiration that motivated me to take the risk to do this," I said. "I wanted to put forth *extra* effort this year."

I was laying it on *extra*-thick; after all, I had come this far—why not see how much further I could go?

"I simply love your sketches of it as well. This, my boy, is definitely worthy of extra credit."

Genius! That's what I was, genius! Success never felt so good.

For the first time, I felt I was in control of my destiny, and everything was working out. And my sketches looked fairly decent as well. I really wasn't that bad of an artist after all.

Heck, maybe my next art project would be to wrap Johnny Ricker and Miles together and drop them into a manhole.

Ana-*Nosey*-Balenovic came behind me trying to see. I shielded my sketches from her view.

"May I see your drawings?" she asked.

On the one hand, I didn't want to show her. But on the other hand, how could I miss an opportunity to brag about extra points to *Miss Braggy* herself?

"Of course—see?" I turned my notepad, practically sticking it in her face.

"Very nice; nice clean lines. Congratulations," Ana Rahela Balenovic said with a half-smile on her face. "Although it would be great if you had a photograph depicting the final results, just like Christo."

Mrs. Huntley gushed, "Oh, that would be wonderful, simply wonderful. What a fabulous idea, Ana. Oliver, do you think you can take a photograph and bring it in on Monday?"

"Gee, I would, but… we don't have a camera, except the old film kind… and I don't think it even works—sorry," I said.

"Oh, not a problem. Here—you may borrow my classroom digital camera," Mrs. Huntley offered. "Please bring it back on Monday."

"Uh… sure, I guess," I hesitantly replied as I reached out and took the camera she was holding out to me.

I stumbled forward and sank into my chair. Gio, who was sitting beside me, leaned over, glanced at my sketch, and asked, "Did you really do all that at your house?"

"Of course not!" I angrily whispered.

Stupid—stupid—stupid Ana Rahela Balenovic.

Mrs. Huntley floated around the room. "Let's begin class with a discussion on form and shape—"

The lights flickered, and I eagerly anticipated what was to follow next: The power went out, and the room became dark. The windows provided some light—although not as much as Miss Crabtree's classroom. That meant that drawing anything would be a problem.

Mrs. Huntley smiled widely, almost illuminating the room. "The spirits of this school must be upset today. No matter. We don't need our eyes to draw."

Chatter began through the room: *What was she talking about? Of course, we need our eyes to draw; how else would we see what was on our papers? Had our teacher lost a screw?*

"Yes, you heard me correctly. We don't need our eyes to draw; we can use our mind's eye."

Mrs. Huntley drifted into the center of the dim classroom, holding up a sheet of drawing paper and a pencil. Placing the paper on an easel, she turned her head away from the easel and began to draw. We all watched, expecting a mess of scribbles, but instead were surprised to spot—even in the dim light—the remarkable sketch of a man.

"You see, my friends, what you can imagine in your mind, you can trace onto paper. Now all of you take out a sheet of drawing paper and your pencils, and let's begin. Close your eyes and imagine something—whatever comes into your mind. Then, once you see every detail, imagine it on your paper, and begin to trace the lines of what your mind sees."

I obediently closed my eyes and began the impossible task of drawing something other than scribbles on my paper. I didn't know what to think of, though. My mind was drawing a blank.

The room became quiet as all the other students started their assignment with their heads up, eyes shut.

A clicking noise came from the hallway, followed by a soft knock on the door.

"Mrs. Huntley? May I have a word?"

Principal Sterns was leaning in through the doorway. *Maybe he was speaking softly because he thought we were all sleeping…?*

"Oh, but of course!" Mrs. Huntley lightly walked towards the hallway while instructing the class, "Continue on, my friends. I'll be but a moment. Let your spirit move you."

As she walked out to Principal Sterns, I heard him whisper, "Is it done yet?"

"Oh… well, not quite…." she whispered back as they moved further outside the door. This made me unable to hear what else they were whispering about, so I shut my eyes and tried to focus on the assignment.

Suddenly, an image came into my mind—that of a large, grotesque alien monster. I squinted at my paper and quickly drew out the image of a monster attacking a man. It wasn't the greatest work of art, but I did it better than if I would have if my eyes were completely shut.

As I drew, I heard a faint cry of a woman in the distance: *Was someone in trouble?* I raised my head and peered around the room, but it seemed no one else had heard the cries. The rest of the class was continuing to draw quietly.

I need to have my hearing checked, I thought.

Mrs. Huntley walked back into the classroom. "How are we coming along, my friends?"

I shut my eyes again and pretended to continue work on my drawing.

"Wonderful," she said, probably as she was walking by three-name Ana Rahela Balenovic. "Very impressive," she said next.

I peeked; she was walking by Gio. Then, she walked by me.

"Wow—Oliver, I'm not sure what to say."

I smiled while still keeping my eyes shut. *I'm really getting this art thing down,* I thought.

"It looks a little disturbing," Mrs. Huntley said in a worried tone.

My smile faded.

A low rumble shot through the air as the power returned, along with the lights and air conditioning. Mrs. Huntley said to the class, "What perfect timing! All right, friends, let us open our eyes and see what our minds have drawn."

Chatter and laughs filled the air as we all looked at each other's drawings. Faces with eyes and noses off to the side, buildings that looked more like the Leaning Tower of Pisa, and animals that didn't belong on this planet.

Gio leaned in to see mine. "You did that? Awesome!"

I shrugged. "Yeah, thanks."

I looked at Gio's drawing, which would be incredible even for someone who had their eyes open. It was a drawing of a young boy riding a dirt bike—with two good legs.

Mrs. Huntley gave another enormous smile. "What did we all

learn from this? Some of you were perhaps a little afraid of drawing blindly, but you probably became surprised at your results! This is a great exercise in keeping you in alignment with yourself, exploring your mind, and letting your spirit guide you. Our imaginations can create visions, characters, and objects so real; it's as if we could reach out and touch them."

I looked over at Ana—three times stupid—Balenovic's drawing—which, of course, she had left out for me to see.

It looked like a boy giving a girl a flower… and it was drawn very well… better than mine.

She must have opened her eyes, I thought.

Cheater.

CHAPTER TWENTY-ONE

THE INTERROGATION

WHEN ART CLASS ended, Gio and I ran out the door to find our team. The school day was finished, and kids from every corner of the school were grabbing their belongings from lockers and rushing to the exits.

Gio and I met Eduard and Chase by Chase's locker, just as Chase was pulling out a book about paranormal encounters to show him.

Jax walked over and teased, "So now what's the mystery, boys? Ghosts taking kids' homework?"

Chase replied, "You know something weird is happening—otherwise, your curiosity wouldn't have dragged you over here."

"Something *weird* like *you*—yes," she sassed. "But I'm more curious about what you're up to than anything else."

I drew in a breath; I felt the tension building between Chase and Jax.

"She's, uh, a great addition to the group," I said awkwardly. I wanted to change how the conversation was going.

Everyone looked at me like I had just spoken out of turn or something in assuming Jax was a part of our group. But it made sense to me: She was too intertwined *not* to be a member now. And Chase was right: She wouldn't have come over if she didn't want to be here.

I turned my head when Chase said, "Now, there's the guy we need to talk to!" He was nodding his head towards Principal Sterns, who was heading towards his office.

"He's involved with Mr. Doyle's disappearance; I'm sure of it. We need to interrogate him and find out more," Chase whispered heatedly.

"You really are crazy," Jax chuckled. "Now you want to interrogate Principal Sterns?"

"Not me—you," Chase corrected her.

"What? No thanks," she objected with a swift shake of her head.

"You're the one who said she's the school investigative reporter, so investigate… or is this story too much for you?" Chase challenged. "I suppose we *could* interview him without you."

"First of all, there is no story," Jax responded, "and second, *Oliver and I* work for the school's newspaper. The rest of you don't have any such credentials."

"Why do we need credit?" Gio asked in a confused tone. "We're too young to have credit cards."

"I meant qualifications—you're not qualified or authorized to ask questions on the school's behalf," Jax explained. "But Oliver and I are."

"Which is why you'll be asking the questions," Chase instructed. "But don't forget, we are part of a paranormal investigative unit—so we are more than qualified to be present at the interview. Come on," he said as he hurried towards Principal Sterns. "Let's catch him before he gets into his office."

Without time to really think about what we were doing, we all raced after him.

Chase yelled, "Excuse us, Principal Sterns. May we have a moment of your time?"

"Yes, of course. What can I do for you students?" the principal smiled as he clicked his annoying pen.

Click-click-click.

"Jaclyn and Oliver are writing an article for the school newspaper and need an interview with you," Chase said.

Principal Sterns looked confused for a moment before he said, "Of course. I always have time for the, uh, press."

"The rest of us would like to join in if that's all right," Chase said smoothly.

Gio folded his arms and said, "We are members of the paranormal investigation unit, and we have plenty of credit."

Principal Sterns smiled and said, "I suppose so. Please come into my office."

We walked in, past Miss Hathaway's end-of-nose glances and the wooden bench with the broken arm. *What questions were we going to ask him?* I wondered. *And what if he becomes suspicious and starts asking us questions back? We hadn't got our stories straight.*

"Have a seat, students, and tell me what you'd like to know: my history? Where I was born? What university I attended? My favorite TV shows? How I keep in shape?" Principal Sterns said all this in a booming voice as he sank into his high leather throne behind his massive desk.

Jax, Gio, Eduard, and I sat down in the only four chairs. Chase stood behind us.

Chase began with a doozie of a question: "For starters, how many dead bodies are underneath this school?"

Principal Sterns stared at Chase. It wasn't too gentle of a stare. "Is that a serious question?" he asked.

"Yes, of course," Chase answered without breaking eye contact.

"None that I'm aware of," Principal Sterns answered in a dry tone. "Now, I'm busy with important school affairs, so if this interview—"

Jax quickly spoke up. "Let me ask a few questions on behalf of the school newspaper." After a quick glare at Chase, she asked, "Principal Sterns, is this your first time meeting such a high-ranking official as the President of the United States? And what does the President's visit to our school mean to you and Raven Ridge Academy?"

Principal Sterns looked refreshed by her questions as he contemplated his answer. "I have met many highly important people in my career, but this is quite an honor for both the academy and me," he began. "I think the President's visit shows the quality of our programs and curriculum we have here at our school. Of course, it was no easy task bringing together, and managing, such a talented teaching staff such as ours," he drawled before leaning back in his chair and linking his hands behind his head. "But it's extremely rewarding to see the fruits of my labor sowing the seeds of tomorrow."

I jotted all this down in my journal as fast as I could, trying to keep my handwriting as neat as possible in case Jax wanted to look at my notes later. I was trying to think of something smart to ask, but Jax was on a roll and continued her questioning.

"You must be very proud of your student Ana Rahela Balenovic," she observed.

The principal's eyes lit up. "Of course! What a bright young girl, and what a great story too! She is an immigrant child whose parents came to this country in search of a better life. She is an example of my vision—helping students to succeed in their lives."

"Did you check her essay for plagiarism?" I asked.

Gulp. I hadn't meant to ask that out loud.

Principal Sterns stared at me and raised his eyebrows. "Why?"

There was a pause; everyone looked at me.

"Uh, well... because it was so good, I can't imagine that she wrote that all by herself," I improvised.

Saying those words made me feel like I was going to throw up. But it was the best I could do, given what I had just said.

The principal looked at me steadily. "No. I'm sure she wrote that on her own."

Jax straightened in her chair. "How long have you been the principal of Raven Ridge Academy?"

"Oh, three years now, I believe. I came from a large company in Chicago before moving out here to Colorado," Principal Sterns answered.

"Do you miss Chicago?" Jax asked.

"Occasionally. It's a slower pace here, but I enjoy it," the principal said.

"And why did you leave?" she asked.

"To make an impact on the minds of the future. I wanted to create an environment to help young minds grow," Principal Sterns said.

"Speaking of the future, what are your future plans for Raven Ridge Academy?" Jax questioned.

"I hope to expand this campus with state-of-the-art equipment, making it a crown jewel of the West." Principal Sterns spread his hands and looked up into the air like he was watching something. "I would like to see Raven Ridge Academy become the model school for the rest of the nation; the school everyone looks up to! In fact, I plan to write a book about how to build a successful school program."

"Principal Sterns, do you believe that the power outage problems will be solved in time for the President's visit?" Chase asked.

"Absolutely! We've had only minor problems today, and next week will go smoothly, I'm sure. We've had technicians working to solve this problem, and they assure me that everything is going according to plan. We are right on schedule," Principal Sterns said.

Jax jumped back in to regain the principal's attention. "Who is your favorite teacher here at Raven Ridge Academy?"

"I like our teaching staff equally," Principal Sterns said smoothly. "They are all excellent teachers with the highest standards."

"How about Mr. Doyle?" Chase asked in a suspicious tone. "Is he one of your favorites as well?"

"Like I said, I have no favorites. And yes, I do appreciate Mr. Doyle as well as any of the other teachers on staff here," Principal Sterns said.

"Where is Mr. Doyle?" Chase asked bluntly.

Principal Sterns paused. "He's unavailable to teach at the moment, but we hope to have him back soon. In the meantime, we have a very capable substitute to continue his fine curriculum."

"When do you expect him back?" Chase asked, seemingly unable to let this line of questioning go.

"We don't have a timeframe for his return, but I suggest you worry about your studies rather than Mr. Doyle," the principal instructed.

Chase pressed on. "Has anyone seen him or heard from him?"

"No," Principal Sterns clipped out in a short, business-like tone.

"Was Mr. Doyle in favor of the school expansion?" Chase probed.

"Excuse me, young man… why do you ask such questions?" the principal asked.

"Let me rephrase. Did you and Mr. Doyle argue about the school expansion?" Chase questioned.

"I have no idea what you're talking about. Mr. Doyle has nothing to do with the expansion. Who put these questions in your minds?" the principal asked in a surprised tone.

Jax followed up with, "Mr. Doyle is chairman of the Raven Ridge Historical Commission, isn't he? And he has a lot of pull with the other board members."

"Ahh—I see. Well, I'm sure Mr. Doyle is in favor of plans that do not disturb the original architecture of this building—to which I am not. However, the current expansion project doesn't alter the original building, but adds space to the area outside, much like the gymnasium did."

Chase pointed to the bookshelf behind him and observed, "I couldn't help but notice the mirror on your shelf. Its frame is a silver raven."

Principal Sterns looked at the shelf on which it sat. "Yes, it is one of the antiques of this building—one of only three that were made."

"Is it my bad eyesight, or is it chipped?" Chase questioned.

"What?" Principal Sterns asked. He spun his chair about and got up to examine the mirror closely.

Chase quickly pulled a piece of paper off Principal Sterns' desk and placed it under his shirt. Jax gasped, and the rest of us sat in utter terror, not moving a muscle.

What was he doing? He had just stolen something right in front of our principal!

Principal Sterns sat down and turned his chair back to face us, apparently unaware that anything had gone on. "No, it's just a little dusty, that's all."

Chase paused and thought for a moment before asking, "Sure you haven't found any dead bodies in the basement?"

"Young man, I don't enjoy this joke you are making," Principal Sterns said in a fierce tone, his eyes lighting up with a bit of fire.

Jax stood up. It was time to go.

"Okay, thank you so much for your time today, Principal Sterns. We hope to ask you some more questions in the future." Jax smiled and batted her long eyelashes at him.

Principal Sterns took a deep breath before smiling again. "Anytime, students. It was my pleasure."

I thought the principal sounded a bit relieved.

We hurried out of the office and gathered in a circle in the hallway. Jax grabbed Chase by the arm and demanded, "What do you think you're doing?"

"Uncovering the truth," Chase said, shrugging her arm off his.

"No, you were committing crimes! Stealing!" Jax insisted.

"I didn't steal this," Chase said as he pulled the piece of paper out from under his shirt. "I just relocated it."

"Taking something from someone is stealing, and now we all are accomplices!" Jax's voice shook with anger.

"Relax, we aren't stealing it," Chase coolly said. "This paper still belongs to Sterns, and we aren't going to keep it. We'll give it back after we finish with it."

"What does it say?" Gio asked.

Just then, Principal Sterns walked out of his office and gave us a look before he headed off down the hall.

Chase quickly tucked the paper back under his shirt and whispered, "It's not safe to talk around here… let's meet at the tree-fort. Eduard, you remember where I told you? We'll meet there in, say—two hours?"

"Where's the fort?" asked Jax.

"It's a secret location," answered Gio.

"Close to here," I spoke up. "Just past County Road 7, over by Miller's Creek."

Gio and Chase gave me a dirty look.

Eduard sighed. "My parents would rather I didn't ride a bicycle, but I suppose I can borrow one from a neighbor to get there."

Jax slung her book bag over her shoulder. "So, I need a bike to be in this club?"

"You don't *need* a bike; if you want to walk there, that's up to you," Chase said. "But this isn't a club."

"Yeah, it's not a club," Gio said as he puffed up his chest. "We're more like… like a bike gang."

"No, we're not a gang," I quickly corrected, horrified at the possibility of being a part of a gang. "Jaclyn, meet me at County Road 7 and Grisham Road in about two hours. I'll show you where it is from there."

Wow, I actually asked her to meet me! It was like asking her out on a date!

Jax nodded her head before she and Eduard ran to catch the second bus back into town. The rest of our, uh, gang walked out to where Gio's bike was chained next to Chase's dirt bike—which was chained next to the empty spot where my bike *should* be.

I felt sick. *What was I going to tell my mom about my bike?* I wondered to myself. *That my bike was stolen, perhaps? No, no, that wasn't a good idea. She'd call the sheriff—who probably by now had it in his possession and was waiting to arrest its owner.*

Gio saw my look, and as if he knew what I was thinking, asked, "Do you want to borrow my bike for a while? I mean… until we get yours back."

"What are you gonna ride?" I asked.

"I can ride home on the back of Chase's bike. Besides, my dad doesn't like me riding it to school anyway; he'd rather drive me. It'll be fine."

Gio was able to ride a bike, but he had a hard time with it because of his leg. That's why his dad preferred that he not ride it.

I agreed immediately, even though Gio's bike was much shorter than mine. I got scrunched up when I sat down—my knees came all the way up to my chest. Nevertheless, Gio's small bike was better than no bike at all.

As the three of us began riding home, Chase looked over at me. "We should go see what's happened to Doyle's car."

"No! If we go back and somebody sees us, we'll be in trouble for sure," I said. The thought of returning to Mr. Doyle's dented car with my blood on the window made my stomach turn.

"Nothing's gonna happen. That was yesterday; today, we are just passing through. I promise we won't go that near it."

What could I say to that? If I said I wouldn't go, I'd sound like a sissy. I knew Chase was going to go with or without me, so I followed him and Gio down the split in the road, through the tunnel of trees, and around the turn, until we saw the old black wooden Dead Cow Bridge in the distance.

What we didn't see—was Mr. Doyle's car. It was gone.

I stopped Gio's bike next to Chase's. "Did he move his car, or did it get towed?" I asked.

Chase looked around the area and shook his head. "I don't know. But if it were towed, the sheriff would know."

I nervously looked around. "I hear a car coming! Let's get out of here!"

I started riding back to the main road. Chase hesitated and then turned his bike to follow me.

It was a lie. I had never heard a thing. But I said I did just to get out of there.

CHAPTER TWENTY-TWO

AN ANNOYING PROBLEM

WHEN I ARRIVED home, I leaned Gio's bike up against the house and walked up the steps where the ambassador of annoyance was waiting to greet me.

"Whose bike is that? Where's your bicycle?"

Annoying questions were buzzing out of Adam's mouth like flies around a dead cow.

"None of your business, Bowl Head," I sneered.

"Was it stolen?"

"No."

"Did you wreck it?"

"No."

"Are you going to get it back?"

"Listen—I got a flat tire. Gio's dad is going to fix it, and then I'll get it back," I lied. Again.

"I knew you were going to get a flat tire. I knew it! Told you so."

Full of smug satisfaction, Adam jumped off the front porch and ran off. He was lucky I didn't have a giant flyswatter.

But I didn't have time to deal with his annoyance. I had to quickly complete my homework and chores because then I could meet my true love at the tree-fort. However, when I walked through the front door, I forgot about everything—even Jax.

The sheet that had been covering the shelf had been moved! It was now strung with a thin rope to our couch, creating a makeshift tent. Adam had taken apart my art project—and exposed the shelf that once had displayed Mom's grandfather's pocket watch.

I could hear my mother's footsteps coming down the stairs.

"Oliver? Oliver, is that you?" my mother was calling.

My mother had been upstairs; perhaps she hadn't noticed the empty spot yet!

Sweating, I scrambled to untie the knots in the rope. Then I tossed the sheet back on top of the shelf.

I was frantically smoothing the sheet in place when my mother walked into the room.

"Hi, uh, Mom," I said as I straightened out some wrinkles.

"What's going on here?" she asked.

"Adam! Adam destroyed my art project. Mrs. Huntley gave me her camera to take photographs of it, and… and now Adam's messed it all up!" I screeched.

"I'm sorry, Oliver. I should've told him not to touch this. Here, let me help you," Mom said as she moved closer to help me.

"No! No, I'm sorry, Mom, but it's my art project. I should do it."

"Okay. I'll tell Adam not to touch, or even look at, your art project. Now, how long does this need to be up for again?" she asked.

"Well, I'm not sure, but I think a little while longer. Mrs. Huntley was really proud I was doing this, you know," I boasted.

"Well, I'm very proud of you too, Oliver. Now, I have to run some errands before I go to work tonight. I'll be back in a bit, but make sure you keep an eye on Adam while I'm gone."

"Uh… well, I was hoping, after I finished my homework and chores, that I might be able to meet Gio, Eduard, and Chase. I would, of course, make sure it was okay for Adam to stay over at Samuel's house."

"That's fine, but I don't want to be taking advantage of Samuel's mother. If she's not okay with him being over there, then you need to watch him—understood?" my mother said.

"Okay. Thanks, Mom."

Mom turned to leave the room. That's when I noticed that while I had been covering up the empty shelf, Mom had been covering up an empty glass of whiskey.

I shook my head and set about taking care of my chores and homework. When I was done, I was out the door to meet Jax… that is, just about out the door.

Adam stood on the porch, wanting to go with me.

"You're not going anywhere with me, Bowl Head," I said.

"Why can't I come with you?" he whined.

"Because it's not for nerdy, annoying, little snot-nosed kids."

"I'll tell Mom you got a flat tire on your bike," he threatened.

"She already knows I got a flat tire. So, I'm dropping you off at Samuel's house."

"But Samuel's not home today," Adam said. "His mom took him into town for swimming lessons." Adam then smirked. "Looks like I'm coming with you."

This was turning into a crisis, and I had to act. "No. I'll call Mom and ask if you can stay with Mrs. McMillan."

"What? No! I don't want to!"

"Look, I know you destroyed my art project in the front room. If you don't want me to tell Mom," I threatened, "then I suggest you start to like Mrs. McMillan's house. Besides, you have no choice."

He thought for a minute, then nodded with a frown. I called Mom at Jam'n Joe's Bar and received her permission to ask Mrs. McMillan if she would watch Adam. We started down the road towards her farm.

Mrs. McMillan's brick farmhouse was larger and older than ours. It sat on several acres of land that Mrs. McMillan and her husband used to farm. After Mr. McMillan had died, Mrs. McMillan ended up selling some of her land to help pay the bills. She still has quite a bit of land and animals, but not like before.

Mrs. McMillan just keeps a few cows, horses, chickens, and a mean rooster named Barney, who bit Adam so hard that it made him bleed. Barney keeps all the other chickens in line, bossing them around. He doesn't let any other animals come in the back near his chicken house either, chasing away any dogs and cats who come sniffing. I heard one time Barney even chased a bear off that farm.

If I didn't know better, I'd think Barney ran the farm.

When we arrived on Mrs. McMillan's front porch, Barney had already sounded the alarm that someone had arrived. Mrs. McMillan greeted us at the door with a huge smile.

"Hello, boys, have you come to visit?" she asked.

Adam looked down at his shoes while I said, "Sorry to bother you, Mrs. McMillan, but I was wondering if you might be able to keep an eye on Adam for a while? I've got some important work to do, and my mom's out."

"Well, of course. Adam, come in," she invited, her grin spreading from ear to ear. "I just made some apple butter; would you like some, Oliver?"

"Oh, no, thank you. I have to run," I said.

"Just a bite?" she asked with a twinkle in her eyes.

I didn't want to disappoint her, so I nodded yes and walked in.

It was like stepping back in time. Mrs. McMillan had changed nothing in her house for fifty years, I swear! The hardwood floors showed their age, and her furniture was antique stuff. She had a liking for the color green, so her drapes were green, her furniture was green, her rugs were green, and even her wall paint was green. Plus, Mrs. McMillan's house always smelled like mothballs—unless she was baking something really delicious.

Today, her house smelled of her delicious baking, as Adam and I followed her into the kitchen, where she spread her homemade apple butter on bread and gave each of us a piece. I wanted to stuff the entire piece in my mouth so I could leave and meet Jax right away, but I knew that Mrs. McMillan would watch to see if I minded my manners. So I ate slowly, making sure to wipe the corners of my mouth after each bite.

Adam just shoved the bread in his mouth, leaving traces of apple butter in a mess around his face. Mrs. McMillan gave him a disappointed glance.

"That was so delicious, Mrs. McMillan! Thank you so much—and thanks for keeping an eye on Adam. I'll be back in a few hours to pick him up."

"It's not a problem at all. Adam can help me with a few chores around here."

Adam about choked on his bread. "Not clean the chicken coops! I hate Barney!" he whined.

"No-no, my dearest, you can stay clear of Barney. There are many other things to do, and have *fun* with here," she smiled.

I walked out of the kitchen while Adam pouted.

As I walked out to meet Jax, I momentarily stopped in front of a silver mirror displayed on a shelf in Mrs. McMillan's house to check my hair, and then practically ran out the front door to get started on my way to meet my true love.

I jumped on Gio's bike but carried my bike helmet with one arm, so I wouldn't mess up my hair. I got to the spot where I was to meet up with Jax fifteen or twenty minutes early. I was so nervous;

my stomach felt like a churning popcorn popper full of grasshoppers. I thought of the things I would say on the way to the fort that would impress her, like how many books I've read, or how I could do some amazing trick, or how skilled I was at kung fu.

The waiting was horrible.

Where was she? I wondered. *Maybe she got lost. Or maybe she couldn't come. Or worse yet—maybe I was being stood up.*

My fears were put to rest when I saw her—the beauty of the world.

As Jax rode her bike towards me, adrenaline cranked up my body heat ten degrees. But I had my best-smelling deodorant on, so I wasn't worried.

"Hi, Oliver," she greeted me in the most beautiful voice.

I almost fainted upon hearing her say my name. *This was the first time she and I were alone together!* I gathered myself and tried to remain calm. "H-h-hello, Jaclyn," I stuttered.

"Jax," she smiled. "You can call me Jax."

"Uh… yeah—okay." I could feel my face blushing. "Nice bike."

Her bike was a pink street bike with a white seat and handgrips. A small pink-and-yellow basket was strapped to the front handlebars. But the best part was—she wore the same type of helmet I had. It was a sign—I was certain of it.

I quickly strapped on mine.

"Thanks. Yours too," she said. "But it looks a little small for you."

"Oh, this is Gio's bike….. I have a dirt bike; you know—a racing type? But it was stolen. So Gio lent me his until I get mine back."

"So, which way?" she asked.

"Follow me," I said, nodding to the woods in the direction of the fort.

I know the other guys were a little apprehensive about bringing a girl to our secret tree-fort because it was widely known that girls could not keep secrets. And what was the point of having a secret tree-fort if it would not be kept secret? I didn't have an answer if they were to ask me that, so instead, I thought of reasons why we needed her in our group.

Hmm... She was so smart, but then again, so was Eduard. She was witty and likable, but then again, so was Gio—and so was I, for that matter. She was creative and imaginative, but then again, so was Chase.

I had it: she was *beautiful.* And that was a fact no one could dispute or compete with.

CHAPTER TWENTY-THREE

PLEDGE OF ALLEGIANCE

INSIDE THE FORT, Jax looked around but said nothing. We guys all looked at her while not saying anything either.

She eyed the drawings hanging on the walls: maps of the school, our neighborhood, and surrounding area, along with a crude cartoon of Johnny Ricker. Her eyes moved to a few empty milk crates we used for sitting around, the writing supplies for writing, and the cattails we had pulled from the creek.

Does she think the fort is stupid? I thought. *Or maybe the fort is so awesome she's speechless?*

I broke the silence. "What do you think?"

"It's nice," she answered back.

Nice? No one expected that. This fort was solid and rugged; it looked like boys, smelled like boys, and was anything but *nice.* But I figured since she was a girl, maybe she was trying to give us the first girl compliment that came to her girl mind.

"Who drew the maps?" she asked.

"I did—and the cartoon of Ricker," Gio proudly responded.

She walked over to the pile of cattails and picked one up. "And these? What are they for?"

"They're grenades," Chase answered. "Well, kinda like grenades… for throwing at intruders who might attack the fort."

Yes—that was the original plan, but since the cattails were ripe and full, we just liked to throw them at each other and watch them explode.

She pointed to the old-wooden-chest-looking box with the black iron latch I had found in my garage. "What's in there?" Jax asked.

"That's an evidence box I brought from home," I answered in a proud tone. "We put all the evidence we find into it for safekeeping."

"Hmm…." Jax folded her arms while jutting her lip out and nodding. "Okay, so what now?"

Chase clapped his hands. "First things first. We all need to swear oaths of loyalty and secrecy. Raise your hand, cover your heart with your other, and then repeat these words after me:

"We pledge allegiance and loyalty to each other in good times and bad. We swear secrecy of all secrets large and small. We promise to defend each other from threats of great danger and fight the forces of darkness wherever they may be found. We promise to investigate and explore the unexplained, pursue every paranormal lead, and commit ourselves to truth, justice, and the American way. We so solemnly swear by penalty of gruesome death, the manner yet to be determined."

We all repeated the words, but Jax hesitated before repeating the last sentence. She even rolled her eyes and shook her head. Nevertheless, she repeated the vow, as we all did.

It was official! We were all sworn to secrecy—and to each other now. Jax and I were tied together for life.

"So, now what do we do?" Eduard asked.

Chase began walking back and forth like Professor Wetherby. "The crisis of Oliver's missing pocket watch needs to be solved, but in order to get his pocket watch back, we need to first figure out what happened to Mr. Doyle. If we find Mr. Doyle… we find Oliver's pocket watch, and in the process, we find out what's going on at our school. Let's begin by looking at all the evidence and try to come up with some theories.

"First off, what do we know? We know Mr. Doyle has been missing for a day and a half; he was last seen at lunchtime in the teacher's parking lot arguing with Principal Sterns. We encountered his car after school on an abandoned road, but Mr. Doyle was nowhere to be found. Outside his vehicle were footprints, along with two lines or drag marks in the dirt coming from the rear passenger door—as if something was dragged out of the backseat, and then all but disappeared into the middle of the road.

"There was heavy dirt and gravel on the hood of the car, but not on the trunk, indicating something kicked up dirt onto the hood from the direction of the bridge—the same bridge that has cattle mutilation stories associated with it."

Chase brought the evidence box to the center of the tree-fort, and we gathered around in a circle. "Then, we found this evidence around the outside and inside of Doyle's car." He opened the box and pulled out an item. "First, there is this key. I noticed the same type of keys on Frank's keychain hanging from his belt with this inscription: *RRA*. Assuming it stands for 'Raven Ridge Academy,' it could belong to Frank or Mr. Doyle. But whoever it belongs to, it still should be a key to one of the school doors."

Eduard scratched his chin. "Why you didn't ask Frank about it today?"

"Because we should find out which door it opens first before Frank confiscates it," Chase said.

"Maybe it opens the door to the bell tower stairs?" Eduard suggested. "That door is always locked."

Gio nodded his head in agreement. "Yes. And there are stories of the mysterious flickering light up there, and the face that sometimes people see at night."

"Good thinking. We should try it out there," Chase agreed.

"But not actually go up in the tower, of course," Jax spoke quickly in a worried tone. "We just see if the key fits—right?"

"Of course," Chase said, giving her a slight smirk before he pulled another piece of evidence out of the box and held it up for everyone to see. "Oliver found this button outside Mr. Doyle's car. It was probably torn off from Doyle's shirt—since the threads look frayed."

He passed the button around.

"It's not his," Jax declared before handing it back to Chase. "Mr. Doyle was wearing a white shirt yesterday, and this button is gray. Gray buttons aren't on white dress shirts."

Chase raised his eyebrows. "I was going to say the same thing."

"I'm sure you were," she said back—smartly, I thought.

"Moving to the other items, we found this inside his car." Chase picked up the receipt. "Looks like he was at this place, *'Past and Present Pawn Shop,'* not too long ago. It reads:

Past & Present Pawnshop
1602 Stoker St.
Denver, Colorado 80202
Date: July 31st
Item Number: 3467
Pd $300.00 Cash."

"We've concluded that he bought something there for three hundred dollars," I said.

"No, not bought—sold," Eduard corrected me. "This is a claim ticket for something he sold to this pawnshop. So, this says they paid him three hundred dollars for an item."

Gio stretched out his fake half-leg and scratched his head. "Pawning your stuff usually means you need money."

"Well, he was accused of being in debt by: Frank, Mrs. Huntley, Coach Conley, and Principal Sterns," Chase pointed out.

"Maybe he pawned my pocket watch?" I suggested as a tinge of fear coursed through my body.

"Maybe… but Mr. Doyle is into all kinds of antiques, as he's a lover of history," Jax reminded me. "He could have pawned anything."

"Nevertheless, we should check it out," Chase said.

My mind began thinking about this new possibility: *Maybe we didn't need to find Mr. Doyle at all, but instead, just go in the pawnshop, buy back my pocket watch for $300.00, and then bring it home before my mom noticed it gone! Then again, it might be easier finding Mr. Doyle than having to come up with three hundred dollars….*

My thinking on the subject was interrupted when Chase said, "We also found this poem in his car, which talks about the universe and stars. It's signed by him—*Charles Othello Doyle*. We found it along with these flowers, which are now wilted." Chase passed the latest evidence around. "It would seem he intended on giving them to someone."

Jax shrieked. "Miss Ivy has the same type of flowers on her desk!"

"Yes," I agreed before I loyally added, "but Miss Ivy had nothing to do with Doyle's disappearance."

"I didn't say they were the same flowers, just the same *type,*" Jax corrected me.

"Sounds a little too coincidental if you ask me," Chase pondered. "We need to keep tabs on her."

I tugged my mouth to the side in a bit of a grimace while I thought *I know Miss Ivy had nothing to do with Mr. Doyle's disappearance.*

Chase picked up the map. "Next, we found this paper wedged by Doyle's car tire. It looks like a drawing of the roads around here, the railroad tracks, the creek, and our school. And we believe this dotted line leads from our school into Old Man Owens' fields, near where we found his car."

"Could it be a map to the school?" Jax asked.

"He knows where the school is! Mr. Doyle wouldn't need a map," Gio pointed out.

Chase adjusted his glasses. "More puzzling are these markings on the side of the map: **N2O — Xe 1,000 lbs.** Eduard, were you able to find anything out?"

Eduard cleared his throat, raised his chin, and gave a slightly smug smile in the direction of Gio. "I was able to do some research," he declared as he reached into his pocket and pulled out a paper, unfolded it, and read the words on it aloud. "N2O is the formula for the chemical compound Nitrous Oxide. It's a common gas used for a variety of things, but mostly in rocket engines—it's sometimes added to the fuel of racing cars to give them an extra boost. It also can be used in cooling units—which apparently our school could use more of—and also as anesthesia to knock out a patient when a doctor operates, kind of like a knockout gas."

"Used in rocket engines? Maybe like… a space rocket?" Chase looked at Gio and me with wide eyes. "Hmm… what about Xe?"

"Xe is the chemical element symbol for Xenon; it's a colorless, heavy, odorless gas. It's used in many things, like plasma televisions and cooling units, and sometimes as anesthesia to make people unconscious—just like Nitrous Oxide. It's also used in lasers, and in ion thrusters for spacecraft," Eduard answered.

Gio's eyes grew wide. "Nitrous Oxide and Xenon gas are both used to knock people out for operations, or… to perform experiments on them?"

My excitement boiled over. "And Xenon gas is also used for lasers, and in thrusters for spacecraft!"

Chase summed up what the three of us were thinking: "Space rocket engines, gas to knock people out to perform experiments, and lasers? It all makes sense that what happened to Mr. Doyle was an alien abduction!"

"Aliens?" Eduard straightened his back and opened his eyes wide as he comprehended what Chase had said. "You guys think aliens abducted Mr. Doyle? That's awesome!"

Jax shook her head as if to clear her hearing. "Aliens? What? You can't be serious. That's… that's ridiculous!"

Chase jumped up and glared down at Jax, who was sitting with the rest of us in a kind of circle on the floor of the fort. "His disappearing into thin air—near an area known for UFO activity and cattle mutilations? Rocket propulsion, which would have kicked up the gravel onto the hood of his car? Don't you see? The evidence all points to a classic alien abduction!"

Jax rolled her eyes. "Why would aliens want Mr. Doyle?"

"It's obvious," Chase said. "He's a history and political science teacher! If anybody knows anything about the history of the earth or the way our political process works, it's Mr. Doyle. Obviously, the aliens would want him in order to extract information from his brain."

"I agree," said Eduard. "Doyle would be a likely target."

Jax looked up at Chase through raised eyebrows. "So, this is the theory you've come up with—*aliens?!* Seriously, guys!"

"It's just one of the theories we've been working on," Chase corrected her. "A good investigator never rules out any possibility. And there is a possibility more people know about this."

"What about the possibility that you're crazy?" Jax scoffed.

"The theory totally fits with this piece of evidence," Chase said as he pulled a piece of paper out from under his shirt.

Jax folded her arms. "Is that the paper you stole off of Principal Sterns' Desk?"

"Stole? No, I told you, I just relocated it… from there to here. It still belongs to him," Chase said.

Gio couldn't contain his squeak. "So why did you take it? Uh, I mean, relocate it? What does it say?"

We gathered around the handwritten note that Chase relocated from Principal Sterns' desk and silently read:

> Principal Sterns- Your attempts to alienate certain members of the faculty and create a toxic environment have not worked. There's no change in my opinion. However, this must not affect the plans for my star. Time is short, and there is still much to do. We must meet ASAP to discuss the arrangements for the President – COD

"Why did you take this note?" Jax demanded.

"Because, if you'll notice… this note mentions—aliens." Chase smugly pointed to the note.

"It says '*alienate,*' you idiot!" Jax snapped. "*Alienate* means to keep someone out, or to make unfriendly—not make into spacemen."

"Well… it could mean—" Chase began.

"It *could mean* that the only crimes that have been committed so far are by you guys!" Jax interrupted. "There, I've solved the mystery. I'll report you all to the sheriff, and this little game will be over."

"And Mr. Doyle will still be missing—waiting to be rescued by some investigative reporter who really wanted to uncover a big story, but only followed obvious and conventional clues that went nowhere, and who turned her friends in to the authorities—thereby ending the investigation," Chase replied.

"Plus, you swore secrecy—remember?" Gio added.

At this reminder, Jax looked as if she were ready to pull her hair out.

Eduard adjusted his glasses. "I must say—the evidence indicating an alien abduction is quite compelling. But what about other paranormal causes?"

"I'm glad you asked," Chase nodded. "We need to consider *every* paranormal possibility."

Jax closed her eyes. "I can't believe you guys are actually talking like this. You *can't* be serious."

Chase reassured her. "This *is* serious! With all the evidence we've collected so far, it looks like a classic paranormal case. And as paranormal investigators, we can't accept normal explanations for abnormal circumstances. That is where ordinary investigators fail—and we succeed." Chase looked at me. "Oliver, read what else we have documented."

Since Jax clearly wasn't into believing anything paranormal was in play here, I decided to skip over my documentations of the gargoyle moving, the whisper I heard, and the image of the boy I saw in the gym corner. I opened my leather-bound journal and read aloud:

"Thursday, 8:15 a.m. — math class: Power outage.

Thursday, 11:20 a.m. — gym class: Power outage.

Friday, 8:10 a.m. — math class: Power outage.

Friday, 2:05 p.m. — art class: Power outage."

"See!" Chase said. "It's a pattern… a pattern of power outages—classic paranormal activity."

"No," Jax said. "Vandalism caused the power outages to the electrical panels in the basement. Principal Sterns said so."

"No," Chase bounced back. "That is what Principal Sterns *wants* everyone to think—so, of course he said that. But electromagnetic disturbances from alien spacecraft could have disrupted the power. Ghosts in the building could also be responsible."

Eduard asked, "Could it be possible ghosts kidnapped that Mr. Doyle in the school?"

Chase gave a quick shake of his head. "Highly unlikely. Even though the school probably is haunted, I don't think ghosts kidnap people. But there is a first time for everything, so we won't rule it out."

Gio shrugged. "Mr. Doyle had talked about losing a bet. What if he made a bet with the gambling ghost and lost? The stories say that the loser must spend eternity inside the mine. That might explain why he's missing."

"And his car was on the road that leads to the mine," Eduard pointed out.

"Yes, of course," Chase said as he raised his eyebrows in delight. "Now we are talking! That's a real possibility. Great deducing, Eduard and Gio."

"Oh, good heavens… this is too much," Jax said as she shook her head, and then covered her eyes.

"We haven't even talked about zombies yet," Gio pointed out.

Jax waved her hand to shush him. "Okay, okay! Enough talk about aliens, ghosts, and zombies. What about something else… some kind of *non*-paranormal explanation. We need to consider every possibility, right? Don't you have anything else?"

"Of course," Chase reluctantly nodded. "There's the possibility that someone else is involved with his disappearance. Mr. Doyle was seen arguing with multiple faculty members. It's classic for people to have confrontations with would-be kidnappers or killers before they go missing!"

"Now, who would want to kidnap or kill Mr. Doyle?" Jax asked. "And why?"

"Good question," Chase applauded her. "Would it be due to revenge, jealousy, or money? Oliver, show Jax our list of suspects."

I handed Jax our list, and she read it aloud.

"Frank, the maintenance guy?" she questioned.

"He definitely isn't a fan of Mr. Doyle," Chase explained. "He accused Mr. Doyle of vandalism and taking something from the basement. Mr. Doyle then accused Frank of working with Principal Sterns to set him up. When we asked Frank today about Mr. Doyle, he said he was glad Doyle was gone. Frank said he's the one who should be teaching history, not Mr. Doyle."

Jax read the next name. "Miss Crabtree?"

Chase elaborated. "She freaked out when I asked her if she was dating Mr. Doyle. She seemed curious when I said we saw Mr. Doyle in the morning, and she asked, *'Then why is that substitute back?'* It was like she… she *expected* Doyle not to be there! When I told her I had made a mistake about seeing Doyle, she had nothing nice to say about Doyle."

"Professor Wetherby?" Jax read.

"They were seen arguing yesterday morning," I said. "Mr. Doyle blamed him for some bad equation, and Professor Wetherby said he '*didn't have a remedy.*' Mr. Doyle then told the professor *'he only had the poison.'*"

Jax read the next name. "Mrs. Huntley?"

Chase raised his eyebrows. "She was arguing with Mr. Doyle yesterday morning about some project that was '*going to transform the Earth and the minds of students*,' and that Doyle had tried to stop the project. She asked him if he had done so '*because he was afraid of something alien.*' She told him he owed her money, but not to worry about paying it back because '*he would be dead to her*' if some project didn't happen. I think Mrs. Huntley might know something more about the aliens."

Jax raised her eyebrows as she read the next name. "Miss Ivy?"

Chase let out a puff of air and said, "Nothing on her… yet, other than she has the same type of flowers on her desk that we also found in Mr. Doyle's car."

She read off the next name. "Coach Conley?"

"They were also arguing that morning," I said. "Mr. Doyle accused Coach of giving him bad information that caused Mr. Doyle to lose something, which sounded like a bet. Coach said, '*it was Doyle's own fault,*' and, '*not to drag him into his problems.*' Doyle wanted Coach to '*talk to his people and buy him some time*,' or else he threatened to expose Coach's past. Coach didn't seem to take that very well."

Chase continued. "We also saw Coach jogging along the railroad tracks after school the day that Doyle disappeared in the direction of Mr. Doyle's car, but today when we asked him if he saw the car, he said '*no*.' Also, he had bruises on his arm and a bandage on his leg. There's no way he could have missed Mr. Doyle's bright yellow classic car—so he had to be lying."

Jax huffed out the next name. "Principal Sterns?"

"Without a doubt, the main suspect," Chase declared. "He was arguing with Mr. Doyle in the teachers' parking lot just before Doyle went missing. He was trying to convince Doyle to '*come on board and make history*.' Doyle said he '*wanted to preserve history instead,*' and '*they are monsters that will destroy everything.*' Sterns said he would '*do whatever it took to get his plan in place.*' Doyle threatened to leak something to the press, saying, '*This cover-up will haunt you.*' Then, Sterns said he would get rid of Doyle if he had to."

I furthered the allegations. "We followed Sterns in the hallway after he argued with the cooks during lunch, and he met some woman who whispered that there was some '*danger of being exposed by the Secret Service digging around and not to bring on anyone new.*' Sterns said he '*had to deal with things differently because of Doyle, but not to worry.'* And let's not forget Sterns' plans for the school expansion that Mr. Doyle needed to approve."

With a tinge of disgust, Jax read off the next name. "Johnny Ricker?"

"Obvious suspect," Chase said. "Guilty of something, but probably not the kidnapping or murder of Mr. Doyle."

"And the cooks?" Jax read. "What are they up to?"

There was a pause as we all thought for a moment. Then I said, "They look like they just got out of prison."

Gio thought for a moment. "They talk funny and act weird."

Eduard spoke up, "They could be aliens, disguising themselves as cooks."

"Yes!" Chase blurted with excitement.

We all nodded with enthusiasm at this new revelation—except Jax, who stared at us with her mouth open in disbelief.

"If they *are* aliens," Chase asked, "and we have every reason to believe they are, given the way they look and talk in gibberish, then what are they doing posing as cooks serving food to children?"

Eduard suggested the answer. "Trying to get us to eat their food—food designed to brainwash us!"

"Yes," I agreed. "Everyone's tasted their food. It's disgusting—obviously not real."

Chase was quick to mention, "Remember what Frank said? *'I don't agree with what they feed you kids here at the school—poisoning your minds.'* He must have been talking about the alien cooks and their brainwashing food!"

Jax crinkled up her cute nose. "But why would they be trying to brainwash us?"

Gio came up with the answer. "To create an army of zombie children, so at a time of their choosing, they can command us to carry out their orders."

"Brilliant!" Chase yelled.

"Dumbest thing I've ever heard," Jax said as she rolled her eyes again.

Chase hung a piece of paper on the wall and said, "Okay, now let's write all our theories on this paper." He took a marker and began listing them out:

- *Mr. Doyle lost a bet with the gambling ghost and is now imprisoned for eternity inside the old silver mine.*
- *Mr. Doyle has been abducted by space aliens who are extracting information from his mind to overtake the planet.*
- *Teacher / Principal kidnapped or killed Mr. Doyle for revenge or other possible motives.*
- *The cooks are aliens in disguise and are feeding the students mind-controlling food, while Principal Sterns and other faculty members help aliens abduct Mr. Doyle (see #2).*
- *A werewolf.*

"Werewolf?" Jax asked, surprised. "What does a werewolf have to do with this?"

"Because," Chase replied, "werewolves are *cool.*"

"What about a zombie-alien werewolf?" Gio asked.

"I like it," Chase said, "but let's try to keep it real."

"You guys have lost your minds," Jax said. "I should have known this wasn't something serious. You guys are just playing around."

"Well, do you have any theories?" Chase countered.

"How about he's not missing—just sick?" Jax suggested.

"Then why was his car all abandoned on that road?" Gio pressed.

"I don't know," Jax gave a quick shrug. "Maybe he went for a hike and got lost—or was attacked by a predator, like a bear?"

We looked at each other, shaking our heads, before Chase said, "I don't think so."

"But you said we can't rule out any possibility—and that's more of a possibility than aliens or a ghost."

"But it doesn't fit with our evidence or list of suspects," Chase said.

"It doesn't have to," Jax answered him. "But even so, let's suppose someone on your list is involved in his disappearance. You said you heard Mr. Doyle mention a '*cover-up*,' right? Maybe someone doesn't want him around because they're trying to cover up something. That's what we should be investigating—not some kind of paranormal alien abduction."

"Of course we should, and we will—along with all the paranormal leads we have," Chase said.

Jax threw her hands up. "Whatever… you guys are going to do whatever you're going to do, no matter what I say."

Gio asked the group, "So, what *are* we going to do?"

Chase took a deep breath. "If anything's gonna happen, it'll happen tonight."

"Tonight?" I asked, somewhat taken aback by this news. "Why tonight?"

"Because it's Friday the thirteenth, and there'll be a full moon," Chase said. "Double chance for trouble. This calls for—nighttime surveillance."

"Where?" Gio squeaked. "At the school?"

"Yep. We need to see what's going on at the source," Chase said.

"How are we going to do that?" I asked back. "Our moms won't let us stay out all night, or even out at night."

Chase acted like he already had a solution. "I'll have a sleepover at my house. I'm sure my mom will agree. It's Friday night, and we'll say we want to go to the movies. My sister Aspyn can give us a ride. And for the right price, she'll drop us near the school instead of the movies.

Gio nodded his head eagerly. "I'm in! My dad will let me come over."

"I won't be able to because my parents and I have a prior engagement," Eduard said stiffly.

I huffed, "I'm sure I'll have to watch my little brother until my mom gets home from her second job, and that's not until like two in the morning."

The words came out of my mouth like a balloon deflating.

"But maybe I can get Adam a babysitter?" I wondered aloud.

"Well," Jax said flatly, "not to state the obvious, but count me out. I think it's a stupid idea. What if you get caught?"

Chase answered confidently, "Not gonna happen. Oliver and G, meet at my house before it gets dark—okay? All of us will meet back here tomorrow morning for a debriefing on what we find."

Suddenly, we heard a snap of a branch outside the tree-fort. We all froze.

"Somebody's out there!" Gio whispered.

Scrambling to peer through open cracks of the plank walls, we caught a glimpse of something, or someone, trying to conceal themselves in the rustling bushes.

"Grab the ammo," Chase whispered. "Battle stations, everyone."

There were no battle stations, but Gio and I rushed to grab the cattails from the milk crate and moved toward the open windows.

"Maybe it's an animal?" Jax whispered.

"Yeah, maybe a mountain lion—or a bear?" I whispered back, breathing heavily.

"Or zombies?" Gio whispered.

"It's daytime, Giovanni," Eduard corrected.

"So what? They can attack at any time," Gio shot back.

The bushes rustled again; this time, we could see a hint of red.

"Fire at will!" Chase commanded.

Cattails rained down onto the concealed intruder as we all hurled our missiles down from our lofty perch. They exploded into fluffy fuzz as they hit the ground, creating a small cloud of haze. A few hit their mark, causing a loud cry, and then—a young boy emerged. An *annoying* young boy.

As Adam stood up, one of the cattails struck him in the face, causing an even bigger yelp.

We all stopped throwing as I yelled, "Adam! Adam, what are you doing here?"

Tears were running down his face as he caught his breath to answer. "I overheard you talking on the phone, and I wanted to see your fort."

"Does Mrs. McMillan know you followed me?"

"No."

"Seriously? Do you know how much trouble both you and I will be in if Mom finds out?"

"I don't care!" Adam whined. "I hate Mrs. McMillan's house."

"And I don't care if you hate her house; you're not supposed to be here. Now turn your butt around and get back there before she realizes you're missing," I ordered.

"I'm telling Mom you hit me in the face with a cattail!" he wailed.

"Go right ahead, and I'll tell her you snuck out of Mrs. McMillan's house and followed me here. In fact, I might tell her anyway," I threatened.

"Okay, okay, I'll go back to Mrs. McMillan's house. But why can't I stay?" Adam asked.

"Because you're too young and too annoying," I snarled at him.

Dropping his head, Adam turned and began to walk back toward Mrs. McMillan's house.

Jax looked over at me and said, "Oliver, is that your little brother?"

"Unfortunately—yes," I answered, completely mortified.

"How cute is he, following his big brother like that? What's the harm in letting him stay?" Jax asked me.

I blinked my eyes in surprise. "Well, first of all, he's not cute—he's annoying. Second, if I let him stay, then he'll want to come every day, and that would be too annoying for everyone to handle. How would we get any work done? Besides, once Mrs. McMillan notices he's missing, she'll call Sheriff Graves to look for him if she hasn't already."

I hated to admit it—but I felt a little bad about what I had just said. After all, Adam was curious, and just wanted to hang out with me. But he was simply too annoying to have around.

"Speaking of the sheriff," Jax said in a concerned voice, "he warned us about predators—not to walk alone, remember?"

"That would solve a lot of my problems," I sarcastically replied before I looked down below at Adam's drooping figure. "Well, maybe I should make sure he gets home okay," I admitted with a heavy sigh. "Sorry, guys, I should go."

Stupid, annoying Adam, I thought. *Just like him to ruin my day with Jax. Adam was such a—*

"I'll go with you," Jax quickly said. "I need to get home anyway."

I suddenly had a change of heart: *Adam was a genius*, I thought. *I'm going to walk Jax home with Adam! I'll be the protector of both of them!*

"Adam, wait up, I'm coming with you," I hollered.

Adam turned about, and his face lit up.

Before I could even make a move, Chase said, "Yeah, we all should get home anyway. We've done good work here. G, call my house, and we'll make plans. Ollie, call me if you can make it."

I nodded. But even though everybody was now heading home together, I imagined it was just—Jax and me.

I'm sure she was thinking the same thing.

CHAPTER TWENTY-FOUR

THE SLEEPOVER

I PACKED MY backpack for the planned overnight at Chase's house with essential items: a writing pad with nice pens, energy candy bars, deodorant, and a toothbrush, along with some toothpaste. I decided to leave my Superman pajamas at home, even though we were on a mission to perhaps save the world, and they might be appropriate attire.

I placed Mrs. Huntley's camera in the front pocket of the backpack so I could document any supernatural encounters. I also made sure that the batteries in my flashlight worked before placing it in my pack. Being able to see in the dark was crucial for tonight's mission. I would have felt better if I had packed some nun-chucks and Chinese throwing stars too, but there was no room in my bag.

Grabbing up my completely full backpack, I hustled down the stairs.

Annoying Adam stood in front of the front door with his arms folded. He whined, "Where are you going?"

"Somewhere you're not," I said before I dropped my backpack and turned to look in the hall closet for my jacket.

"I want to go," he whined again.

"I've already told you, you're not invited," I threw back over my shoulder as I hunted around the mess in the closet. "Besides, you're lucky I managed to persuade Mom to let you stay the night at your friend Samuel's house—it could've been Mrs. McMillan's."

I found my jacket, then backed out of the closet to put it on.

"And don't get any ideas of following me," I told Adam. "Mom's already talked with Samuel's mother, and she'll be checking in on you often."

"Come on—please?" he begged.

"Tonight is for the good of humankind—not for watching over you," I said crisply, as I picked up my backpack and slung it over my shoulder.

Just then, Mom came around the corner, hands on her hips. "Oliver, where do you think you're going without finishing your chores for tomorrow?"

"Tomorrow's chores? Why can't I do them tomorrow? I've got to get over to Chase's house in time for the movie," I said in some surprise.

"You know you won't be here until tomorrow afternoon—so get them done today," Mom ordered before taking a sip from her whiskey-filled glass. "Or you'll stay home for the night."

I nodded my head in agreement—leaving my backpack and evil Adam's little satisfied smile by the front door.

"Oh, by the way," Mom turned to me, saying, "I talked with your friend Chase's mom on the phone about your sleepover. You failed to mention she was going out for dinner—and that Chase's older sister will take you to the movies."

"I didn't think it was a big deal 'cause his mom will be home when we get back from the movie," I said, shifting my feet guiltily.

"Next time, the full details, please. No funny business tonight, either—otherwise, you won't be sleeping over at anyone else's house until you're twenty-five," Mom said.

I paused for a second. *Did someone leak the details of our stake-out? It was almost like Mom knew about our secret plans....*

But I really didn't have any time to think about that possibility. Instead, I completed my chores as fast as I could, then kissed my mom, grabbed my backpack, glared at Adam, and bolted out the front door and onto Gio's bike. Now it was on to the work of saving the world.

I arrived at Chase's house, not sure what to expect—but his house was by no means extraordinary. In fact, it looked very similar to mine—and by that; I meant ordinary.

It was an old, red-brick farmhouse set off from the dirt road and surrounded by trees of different types, but none of them as tall as the tree in my backyard. It was further to the north of my house and closer to the town, but still in the rural area where we lived. There were chickens and a rooster. I dismounted Gio's bike, then rang Chase's doorbell.

A dog's low bark announced my arrival.

The door opened, and I was greeted by a large, dark Rottweiler, who barked and wagged his short-cropped tail. I liked dogs, and I wasn't afraid.

Coming up behind the Rottweiler and smacking the dog on its rear to be quiet was a beautiful young woman dressed in jeans and a t-shirt. Stylish eyeglasses framed her green eyes. A mix of chestnut and blond hair fell around her face, and she had an athletic body.

Chase and his sister must have been born years apart because she looked a lot older.

"Hello there, and who are you?" she asked.

"My name's Oliver. I'm here to see Chase—is he here?" I said.

"Oh, of course! He's told me all about you," she said with a smile as she held the door open. "Please come in." She pushed the dog back with her leg. "Don't worry, he won't hurt you."

The monster-of-a-dog sniffed me while wildly wagging his stubby tail. I patted the dog on his massive head while he licked my face.

Wow, I thought. *He told his sister everything about me! I wonder if he was trying to set me up with her?*

"His name's German—I think he likes you," she smiled. "Chase?" she called out. "Chase, your friend Oliver's here."

I heard Chase in the distance answer, "Okay, Mom."

"Mom?" I said aloud, causing the girl to glance at me. "Uh… I'm sorry; I thought you were his sister?"

"Oh, I'm so sorry! Where are my manners? I'm Chase's mom—Jessie Adams. But you go right on thinking I'm his sister! Such a bright boy—I love you already," she enthused.

I felt somewhat embarrassed and felt I needed to explain. "Well, I was confused for a moment because I didn't think Chase's sister was that old."

Her smile disappeared, replaced with a look as if she just stepped in something.

Realizing it was me who just stepped into something, I tried to recover. "I didn't mean that you're old—it's just you look… well, you don't look old either." I tried to change the subject. "Uhh… German? Is that his name because he's a German dog?"

"No." She gave me a soft smile. "Chase's sister Aspyn wanted to name him *Jermaine*, but when Chase was younger, he could only pronounce it as *German,* and the name stuck."

Chase appeared and waved me down the hallway. "Hey, Ollie. G's already here—come on back."

"It was nice to meet you, ma'am," I said before I scrambled off in Chase's direction. German followed close behind me.

I entered Chase's bedroom. Gio was sitting on a twin bed pushed up against the wall and flipping through a comic book. I looked at the walls covered with different types of magazine articles, cut-out newspaper clippings, and photos. My eyes raced across the headlines as I tried to take in as much as I could: *UFO Spotted over Phoenix—UFO Crash Site Found—Ghost Haunting Young Couple's House—Bigfoot Evidence Found—Spirits Haunt Downtown Building—Real Werewolf Shot.*

The evidence was clear: Chase was a nerd.

German jumped up onto Chase's bed as we began planning our stakeout on Chase's floor. That's when a young girl poked her head in the doorway and asked, "So, is this your crew?"

"Yep," Chase answered, opening his arms wide. "Oliver and Gio—this is my sister Aspyn."

This looked more like the girl Chase had described as his sister. Sure, she was older than us—old enough that she could drive—but not too much older.

Aspyn had bright red lips, soft brown eyes, and Chase's nose—straight and thin. Her blond hair was pulled back and up and held together with some kind of sticks. Aspyn was slightly taller than us, and she wore tight blue jeans with heels and a t-shirt that had some rock band's image on it. She was beautiful—and I now wondered what Chase had told her about me.

"What are you dorks up to?" she asked.

"Planning," Chase replied, looking back at our drawings. "What about you?"

"Trying to figure out how you talked Mom into making me and Spencer take you and your dork friends to the movies tonight."

"We are in pursuit of something really important, that's why," Chase said.

"Something important, like trying to ruin my night. Well, I hope you're not planning on having any fun, because I'm not going to now," she said.

Just then, a series of loud bangs came from outside, followed by a revving car engine. German's ears popped forward.

The doorbell rang, and German jumped off the bed and gave a series of loud barks. Aspyn slung a giant purse over her shoulder and turned to walk off, saying, "We'll be back later, dorks."

"Who's here?" I asked Chase as my eyes followed Aspyn out his door.

"Our ride for later," he said in a careless tone. "Spencer—Aspyn's boyfriend."

Gio and I stuck our heads out the door of Chase's room and watched as Chase's mom answered the front door.

A tall, lanky kid with a varsity jacket walked in. His hair was a thick, black mess. He looked like he needed to shave—a bunch of black stubble covered his face.

"Hello, Miss Adams," he said to Chase's mom. "You look really nice today."

"Why, thank you, Spencer. That's the second compliment I've gotten today. It must be my outfit; maybe it makes me look like Aspyn's sister?" she hinted.

"Uh, no.... Aspyn doesn't have a sister," Spencer said un-surely, "does she?"

"No, she doesn't," Chase's mom said. "But if she did—well, you know, don't you think I might look like her?"

"Oh, no—I would never think that—of course not. I'm sure she'd be a lot younger than you," Spencer answered.

Chase's mom gave a toss of her head before she walked off into a nearby room. Gio and I watched while German sniffed at Spencer's clothes.

"Spencer, you're late!" Aspyn yelled as she stomped toward him down the hall. "You were supposed to be here fifteen minutes ago! Now you've cut into our shopping mall time. We'll barely have any time before we have to come home and pick up these dorks for the movies!"

"Sorry, but I couldn't find my car keys," he said.

"How about keeping them in the same spot every time?" Aspyn huffed. As she got close to her boyfriend, she brushed against German, who drooled some slobber on the leg of her pants. "Gross, Germ! Mom!!! Come here! Germ slobbered all over me again!"

Chase's mom reappeared to help her wipe it off. "Oh, you'll be okay, honey. You can't even see it," she reassured her.

Aspyn let out a big sigh, "Worst day of my life, I swear. Now let's go, Spencer! Love you, Mom. Bye."

"Love you too. Remember, I'm leaving for dinner in one hour, and you need to be here to pick up the boys for their movie."

The two left, and we could hear the backfire—and roar—of what must be Spencer's car as it sped off.

Now that Aspyn was gone and Chase's Mom was getting ready for her dinner out, the three of us got down to the business of serious planning. "Okay… G, did you get a thermometer?" Chase asked.

"Yep." Gio pulled it from his bag. "Right here."

Right then, German nosed open Chase's door and jumped back up on the bed.

"This is a thermometer that you stick in your mouth to take your temperature!" Chase said in a surprised tone.

"Yeah, that's what you told me to bring—a small thermometer," Gio said.

"We need a thermometer to take the *outside* temperature," Chase said in a tone that now sounded—annoyed.

"You didn't say that. Why do we need a thermometer anyway? I can tell you it's hot outside," Gio said.

"Because ghost hunters use thermometers to see the difference in air temperature; there are cold spots where ghosts are present. This one does us no good," Chase answered.

Not wanting Gio to feel stupid, I said, "We still should bring it anyway since we have it. It might come in useful at some point."

"Ollie, did you bring the camera and a flashlight?" Chase asked, turning his attention to me.

"Of course." I pulled out Mrs. Huntley's digital camera and showed it to both of them. "The flashlight's in my pack, and I even checked the batteries before I left."

"I've got a small pen flashlight," Chase said, pulling it out of his pocket. "And my magnifying glass."

We got sidetracked during our planning and talked about different subjects as they came up: TV shows, music, and the other kids in our school. Before we knew it, the sun had gone down, and German jumped from Chase's bed to dash, barking towards the front door.

We gathered up our things and hurried to the front room where Aspyn and Spencer were waiting.

"Ready to go, dorks?" Aspyn asked in the most annoyed tone. One would have thought that we ruined her entire life.

"We are, but how safe is it going to be with your hairy boyfriend driving? I mean—are we going to get there in one piece?" Chase said.

"Probably not, so you should walk," she sassed back.

"All right, all right; we'll take our chances—let's go. Oh, I need to get my bike," Chase said.

"You're not taking your bike," Aspyn said flatly.

"We need it in case you forget to pick us up. I'll put it in the trunk," her brother said.

"What's the backpack for?" Spencer asked, nodding his head at it.

Chase replied as if it was obvious. "Investigations of the paranormal."

"What would you need to be investigating at the movies?" Aspyn asked.

Right then, Chase's mom came to the front room covering the mouthpiece of a telephone with her hand and pleading, "Aspyn, please be careful. And make sure you watch the boys, okay?"

"I will, Mom; don't worry. We'll have them back right after the movie's over—then I can go back out, right?" Aspyn asked.

"That'll be fine, just as long as I'm home." Chase's mom gave Spencer a long, hard look. "And Spencer, no speeding with these kids in the car—you hear?"

Spencer raised his eyebrows and replied in a sincere tone, "No, of course not. I'll be extra careful tonight, ma'am."

She continued to give him a look through her eyebrows as she went back to her conversation on the phone.

Chase, Gio, and I ran out the door, put Chase's dirt bike in the trunk, then piled into Spencer's back seat. It was a Mustang convertible.

"Careful of the paint!" Spencer shouted.

Careful of the paint? More like be careful of the primer, I thought to myself.

Spencer's car was a work in progress. The interior was in good shape, with newer carpet that I found out Spencer had installed himself. The dashboard had a few minor nicks, but was polished and clean. The car's body had been worked on in several stages, and it was covered in primer—it seemed painting would be the final touch. However, one thing in the car *was* complete: Spencer's car stereo. He must've put more money into that stereo than the rest of the entire car, and it sounded louder than the roar of the engine when he turned it up. It was *awesome.*

The engine revved, the tires squealed—and as we got started,

Aspyn accepted Chase's offer of our movie money if they would just drop us off at a spot close to the school.

As we rode in the back seat, Gio was staring at Spencer. "How often do you shave?" he asked.

"Oh, I don't know—two, sometimes three times a day," Spencer said proudly.

"Three times? No way! How come?" Gio yelped.

"Once in the morning, and later to take care of the five-o'clock shadow. And I do it again if I want to go out at night.... Yep, that's what you do when you get to be my age," Spencer drawled.

"Isn't that a little stretch?" Aspyn interjected. "I mean, you're not that hairy."

"He's abnormally hairy," Chase jumped in, "and that makes me wonder—why." Chase leaned forward from the back seat and began staring closely at the side of Spencer's face. "Have you been bitten by any strange animals lately?"

"No... no, of course not," Spencer said uncomfortably, squirming a bit in his seat.

"There's a full moon tonight; do you feel any different? Itchy, like you can't be in your own skin?" Chase probed.

"Shut your face, dork!" Aspyn turned and spat from the front seat. "I've had *enough* of you and your para-*stupid* ideas."

"Just say'n," Chase said, giving Gio and me a significant look.

We were at the drop-off spot before the end of the fourth song on Spencer's car stereo. It was completely dark outside.

"So, what are you guys up to? Gonna throw toilet paper on someone's house? Graffiti a wall? Throw eggs at the school?" Spencer chuckled.

"None of the above," Chase said as he crawled out of the back seat. "Our intentions are good."

Spencer popped the trunk so Chase could haul out his bike and backpack.

"Remember," Aspyn said out of the window, "if you get caught—I know nothing about this. As far as I know, you got dropped at the movies and snuck out without us knowing."

"And don't you forget to pick us back up here in two hours," Chase said.

"Okay. Love you, dork," she lightheartedly said, right before the Mustang and its music raced off back down the road.

We stood alone on the dark empty road, silently staring into the silent, pitch-black darkness. Chase finally said, "Let's move."

CHAPTER TWENTY-FIVE

THE STAKEOUT

AS WE CREPT down the dark, tree-lined road towards school, I kept hearing Jax's voice in my head telling me what a bad idea this was. After all, we didn't tell anyone where we were going, so if we turned up missing in the morning, the school would be the last place that anyone would look.

In the distance, we could see the pointed silver roof of our school's enormous bell tower glinting in the moonlight. Our school creeped me out during the day, but during the night—times ten!

Chase took the lead, inching us towards the red menace. We were moving at a snail's pace, and it wasn't because of Gio's leg either. All around the perimeter of the building, ground spotlights shot upward, illuminating the red walls of the massive structure with a monstrous glow. I just knew the gargoyles were watching us from their perches high above, ready to swoop down and snatch one of us—probably Gio, because he was the smallest.

"Guys," Chase whispered, "do you see that?"

Gio and I didn't want to, but we strained to see what he was looking at. I really hoped we wouldn't see anything. Since Chase was looking towards the bell tower, that most certainly meant a gargoyle was coming to life.

"What… what do you see?" whispered Gio.

"There… in the bell tower window…. Do you see that flickering light?" Chase barely breathed.

I didn't want to look; I didn't want to know—but I couldn't help looking up at the window. And there it was: a faint light flickering in the bell tower window, hardly noticeable, but confirming the stories I'd heard.

I hoped the same stories of a face—maybe Charlie Hackett's—looking out the bell tower window at night were still false.

Then, not watching where I was walking, I tripped. I went over a small log and crashed into some dry brush.

"Are you okay?" Gio asked as he helped me up.

My face was scratched; I could feel blood on my cheek. "Yeah, I'm fine… stupid log," I snarled. "We need the flashlight."

"Not yet," Chase whispered. "We need to maintain our cover."

When we were only about a hundred yards from the school, we hunkered down in the wild brush, behind bushes and tall grass that outlined the outskirts of the nicely kept school grounds.

"Ollie, take a photo of the school," Chase commanded.

I pulled out the digital camera, then snapped a few photos of the building and surrounding area while Chase and Gio kept a watchful eye. I made sure to get as many shots as possible.

"We need to be closer. Let's move," Chase whispered.

We made our way over the freshly cut grass of the school grounds to the south side, and then to the back of the building, which was less illuminated than the front of the school or the teacher's parking lot. An outcropping of finely manicured bushes next to the school provided some cover so that it could conceal us while only a few feet from the back of the building.

"What now?" Gio asked.

"We need to get inside," Chase whispered back.

"Are you crazy?" I objected, forgetting to whisper.

"Shhh... something's going on in the bell tower, and we need to find out what it is," Chase said.

Chase was serious—and I knew we were in for serious trouble if we were caught.

"I'm going to climb up the side of the school to that window," Chase said, pointing to a window that belonged to Miss Crabtree's classroom. "Once I get inside, I'll come down and let you guys in."

"How are you going to get in?" I whispered. "That's three stories up, and the window's locked!"

"It's not locked; I unlocked it this morning when I opened the windows for Miss Crabtree," Chase told us as he leaned his dirt bike against the school.

"But... you're going up... by yourself?" Gio asked in a squeaky whisper.

Chase looked at me first before he declared to Gio, "It'll be easy. I've done this before. But I need some lookouts. You guys go back into the brush on the outskirts so you can see the road. If someone comes down the road, warn me by flashing your flashlight three times. If anything goes wrong, and we become separated, then we'll meet back where Spencer dropped us off. Now give me a boost."

I knew why Chase was going in by himself: Chase knew Gio couldn't climb the wall, and we couldn't leave Gio alone because of his leg. Someone needed to stay with him.

Gio and I pushed Chase up on the wall until he could grab onto an edge to pull himself up. Finding another crack, Chase began to scale the red stones. Chase made climbing the wall look easy—just like he had with the rock wall in gym class. Getting down, however, would not be. I wondered what would happen if Chase got up there and found the window locked.

Gio and I made sure that Chase had made it to a ledge on the second story before we started back to the road to be lookouts.

There was a loud *thud!* that shook the ground below our feet. Gio and I stopped in our tracks, thinking it might have been our imagination or a train passing by in the distance, shaking the ground. But then it happened again.

"What's that?" Gio whispered in a half-panic.

There was a scratching—maybe a scraping—noise from directly beneath our feet. It was followed by a low grumble and the ground shaking below us again.

I looked around. "Something's trying to come out of the ground!"

"Zombies!" Gio trembled. "Let's get out of here!"

"Run," I whispered, my feet already moving as my mouth struggled to keep up. "Run to the road!"

Gio and I ran as fast as we could. We went so fast, I could have sworn that Gio had two good legs!

We made it to the wild bushes located outside of the border of the neatly kept school grounds. Then we turned to look back for Chase, who had disappeared in the shadows up the side of the building. He most likely would have been safe from whatever it was in the ground—it was Gio and me who had to get out of there.

We strained our eyes for any movement but saw only darkness. As we looked, my mind worked on what had just happened.

Could it have been my imagination? No, both Gio and I had felt the ground beneath our feet shake. Something was trying to get out of the ground—and that could only mean one thing—the undead.

As if the night could get any worse, headlights from a car shone from far off down the road.

"Someone's coming; flash your flashlight at Chase!" Gio gasped.

I rummaged through my pack, feeling for my flashlight that I had placed in there before I left home. But I was finding nothing but energy bars, pens, a toothbrush, and toothpaste.

What could have happened to it? I know I packed it, I thought to myself. But then it hit me: *Adam! I had left my pack by the door when I did my chores, and stupid annoying little ruin-my-life Adam must've taken it out.*

Chase couldn't see the approaching vehicle as it was on the opposite side of the building, and now I had no way of warning him—a big problem… if the zombies didn't get to him first.

Gio blurted, "Where's your flashlight? Come on! There's a car; we have to warn Chase! And the zombies are still coming out of the ground!"

"I… I… I don't have it!" I admitted, feeling sick. Saying those words made it real—sickeningly real.

"What? How are we going to warn him?" Gio said, sounding as flustered as I felt.

The car came around the bend, its headlights passing over the bushes that concealed us, like a spotlight searching for escaped inmates. Gio and I made ourselves as small as possible.

"Who *is* that?" Gio whispered.

"I don't know," I said before popping my head up and down quickly enough to see the marking on the side of the car; it was the sheriff's!

I immediately breathed a sigh of relief: The good guys had arrived, and so Gio, Chase, and I would not be the main course on the zombies' one-course meal.

But then it hit me how much trouble we were going to be in if Sheriff Graves caught us. It would be so much trouble that we might have wished to be eaten by zombies!

"Gio, it's Sheriff Graves's car! We need to get to Chase before the sheriff spots him," I said in pure panic.

"And how are we going to do that? We don't have a flashlight or a walkie-talkie," Gio said, stating the completely obvious.

"I'm going to make a run for it. When the sheriff pulls his car to the side of the teachers' parking lot, I can make it to Chase without him spotting me," I said.

"And then what? Chase is probably inside the school already. And what about the zombies clawing their way out of the ground? They're probably to the surface by now!" Gio squeaked.

"I've got to warn Chase somehow—" I whispered desperately.

The sheriff's car pulled in front of the school and shined its spotlight on the building as it slowly passed by. It was headed for the teachers' parking lot, just as I had guessed it would be.

"This is it!" I looked at Gio as if it was the last time I'd ever see him again. "I'm going!"

"Not without me, you're not," Gio said in a steady voice.

I smiled and nodded okay. Then, as if pulled up by some imaginary giant rubber band, Gio and I sprang to our feet and raced back towards the trouble spot we had just fled.

We flew there, hyper-aware enough to realize that the ground had stopped rumbling. So either the zombies had stopped digging out from the ground, or they were already out searching for us.

Gio looked around at the grounds as I looked up the building, shouting, "Chase! We've got company!"

But Chase was nowhere to be seen—he had disappeared into the shadows of the building. And by now, the sheriff's car was pulling out of the teacher's parking lot and starting to make its way around to the south side.

"Hey, where are you?" I called again, out my voice desperate. "We have to get out of here! *THE SHERIFF'S HERE!*"

I saw the dirt bike still propped up against the school building. But there was no sign of Chase. Gio and I paused and looked all around us. *Had Chase fallen? Did zombies eat him?*

The hesitation cost us: The lights from the sheriff's car exposed us like two grass stains on a white shirt.

We sank to the ground as if we were moles disappearing into our holes—except there were no holes, and the sheriff was the hammer, ready to whack us. His car stopped; his spotlight fixated on us. Red and blue lights on top of his vehicle sprang to life, illuminating the entire area.

We were caught.

A deep voice came through the sheriff's loudspeaker: ***Stand up and walk to the vehicle!***

Neither of us moved, I guess, because we were still hoping he was talking to someone else.

The voice from behind the blinding light called out again: ***Stand up and walk to the vehicle, now!***

I looked at the sheriff's car where it was parked on the road. It was a good distance from where we were crouched on the manicured lawn. Then I looked at the wild brush and wild woods on the opposite side of the school grounds.

The sheriff wouldn't drive over the nice and tidy lawns, would he? I thought to myself.

I don't know what got into me, but I shouted to Gio, "Come on! Run for it!"

Together at once, we ran as fast as we could towards the thick foliage and dense, wild woods that surrounded our school. We did not look back.

Stop! the loudspeaker voice commanded.

We just made it to the thick brush on the outskirt of the school grounds when we heard the patrol car's door slam shut and its engine rev.

"Come on!" I yelled as Gio and I tore through the brush. "Keep running! This way!"

The patrol car must have quickly delivered the sheriff to our escape route because it gave him time to jump out and pursue us on foot. He had a flashlight—something I wish I had.

It was all stupid, annoying little Adam's fault. Had he not taken the flashlight out of my pack, I would have been able to warn Chase in time, and none of us would have been caught. Now Gio and I were fleeing for our lives from both the sheriff and zombies.

I'm going to feed Adam to the zombies if I get out of here alive, I thought. *Or eat him myself if I'm turned into a zombie.*

We weren't hard to follow: Gio and I made a ton of noise, breaking every branch, tripping over every rock, and not to mention shouting at one another. Luckily, the full moon provided just enough light for us to spot the barbed wire fence in our path and bring us to a halt.

Breathing hard and looking for another alternative, we stood motionless. But the footsteps and flashlight of the sheriff prompted me to grab the barbed wire and pull it up so Gio could get through. He held it for me, but my backpack caught on the wire—and I was trapped. The harder I tried to push through, the deeper the barbs embedded into my pack. In a panic, I thrust the pack off my shoulders and scrambled to my feet—the sheriff only footsteps behind.

The sheriff was close, and no doubt he knew it. *Could we outrun him in the dark? How far would he chase us?* My bet was he would chase us to the ends of the earth.

The adrenaline in our bodies kept us moving, but it was definitely harder for Gio than for me. We had to slow down—or stop.

Gio and I stood looking around for a moment before jumping behind a large log. We laid down flat on the ground.

The sheriff came to where we were standing only moments before, shining his light on the ground. Gio and I stopped breathing altogether as his beam of light passed over the log.

This is it, I thought. *The game's over—we are caught.*

Suddenly, a low growl emerged in the distance. The sheriff's light swung away from the log we were hiding under. Something was out here with us, and the sheriff heard it too. I didn't know how much more frightened I could become: ghosts in the school, zombies in the ground, the sheriff arresting us, and now who knows what.

Sheriff Graves walked slowly away from us, right in the direction of the growling noise. Gio and I knew it might be zombies or some other creature of the night, but it was too late to warn the sheriff. We lifted our heads to see the sheriff moving into thicker brush with both his shotgun and flashlight leading the way.

"What should we do?" Gio whispered in a panic.

"We need to go back to the spot where Spencer dropped us off," I said, trying to clear my head of my own panic and become focused.

"But Chase… what if he gets caught?" Gio worried.

"He won't!" I reassured, although I wasn't so sure. "C'mon, it's time to start back."

We crept on the ground for a while, trying to keep quiet and far from where the sheriff had headed. The full moon allowed us to navigate; we spotted some recognizable landmarks for a while and got close to the road where Spencer had dropped us off. Just as we emerged from the wild woods into thick brush near the road, we spotted the sheriff's car blazing with blue and red lights in the far distance. We hurried up the road, staying close to the wild brush.

It seemed like we walked ten miles. We finally made it back to the spot where Spencer had dropped us off earlier in the night. There was no sign of Chase or Spencer's car, so Gio and I hunkered down into the bushes on the side of the road to wait.

I hugged my legs, sinking my head down while Gio sat next to me looking back and forth in the darkness. Then he asked in a quiet voice, "Do you think Chase got caught?"

"No," I said.

"When's Spencer going to pick us up?" he asked.

"Anytime now."

"What was the sheriff going after?" Gio asked.

"Don't know."

I was short with Gio. I didn't want to talk—I wanted to cry. The truth was, I had no clue what time Spencer would be back, and I thought there was a real possibility Chase had been caught.

Bang-bang-bang!

The sound of gunfire ringing through the air made both of us jump.

"Oh, what have we done?" Gio's voice was shaking; he too was on the verge of tears. "Chase… he's probably dead!"

"No, no! The sheriff wouldn't shoot Chase," I wheezed, my entire body full of despair.

Bang-bang-bang echoed in the distance again.

"It's the zombies… the sheriff's shooting zombies then!" Gio hollered.

"Where's Spencer?!" Now I was in a full-blown panic. "Maybe we should run!"

No sooner had the words shot from my mouth than we heard the distinct grumble of Spencer's car. We raced to the middle of the road, meeting the Mustang's headlights with waves of panic and gaping mouths. Spencer brought the muscle car screeching to a halt in front of us before revving the engine—*bang!* The car backfired as we scampered to the passenger side door and climbed in the back.

"Where's Chase?" Aspyn angrily demanded.

"I don't know…. We lost him," I tearfully admitted, slamming the door closed behind me.

"Lost him?" Aspyn furrowed her eyebrows. "What are you talking about? What's wrong?" Aspyn's questioning tone became heated.

Breathing hard, I tried to talk. "We lost him—in the brush—running from the sheriff."

"And zombies!" gasped Gio.

"You're running from Sheriff Graves?" Spencer blurted out, whirling about in the front seat. "I *hate* that guy—he gave me three tickets. What'd you guys do?"

"Who *cares!* Where's Chase?!" Aspyn demanded, sounding worried.

"I don't know," I answered. "He told us to meet him here, and we came, but he's not here!"

"And we even heard gunshots!" Gio added while putting on his seat belt.

"What! *Gun*shots?" Aspyn shouted. "We need to find my little brother—now Spencer!"

Spencer looked over at Aspyn and said, "But, what about the sheriff? He's still around here, right? He'll—"

"Now, Spencer, *now!*" Aspyn shrieked.

Spencer revved the engine and engaged the gears, squealing the tires as we tore off in the school's direction, when… the figure of Chase running up the road popped up in the headlights. Spencer slammed on the brakes.

"Chase!" we all screamed once the car stopped. "Get in!"

Chase ran and jumped into the open door of the Mustang. Even before the door was fully shut, Spencer smoked the tires as the engine roared. He spun the beast around in dramatic fashion. He finally straightened it out and sped away from the red-and-blue lights burning in the distance.

Aspyn was leaning over the seat in an angry, aggressive fashion. "Chase, what happened? What were you guys doing *running from the sheriff?*"

Chase stared back at her with a glassy look in his eyes, like he had just seen a ghost.

"What happened?" I asked in a much softer tone. "And where's your bike?"

"Was the sheriff shooting at you?" Gio whimpered.

"It was epic…." Chase finally whispered. "Epic."

"Chase is alive—so it probably was Spencer's car backfiring, and not gunshots, you dorks! *No one* was shooting at you," Aspyn snapped. "But if Mom finds out that we dropped you off here instead of at the movies, she'll be the one shooting at us, not the sheriff." Aspyn flipped back around in her seat in a disgusted huff. "I swear you better not get me in trouble."

"Don't worry about it, Sis," Chase tried to say calmly. "We did nothing wrong, and the sheriff never saw us anyway. Let's get home."

He looked at Gio and me and whispered, "Epic development… you'll never believe what happened."

Spencer and Aspyn dropped us off in front of Chase's house. Miss Adams opened the front door to greet us—and with a roar, the Mustang tore off again.

She smiled. "How was the movie?"

"Unbelievable," Chase said. "Epic."

I bent down to pet German, who started sniffing my cheek.

"Oliver! What happened to your cheek? It's scratched and bleeding." Miss Adams looked at all of us, and our dirty clothes—which were clean when we left. "What happened to you all?"

"Uh…." Chase looked down at his clothes while saying, "Nothing… we just were wrestling in the parking lot, that's all."

"Boys, you should know better!" Miss Adams scolded. "Why don't you go get cleaned up and ready for bed, okay?"

As we filed by her, Chase said softly, "Thanks for everything, Mom. It's good to be home."

"Chase?" She stopped him with a hand on his shoulder. "Are you all right?"

"Yeah. It's just been a long night. Love you," Chase said before he squirmed away.

We headed into Chase's room under his mother's suspicious

eye. We shut his door, and all of us—German included—plopped onto Chase's bed and gave out the same deep sigh.

Gio and I started peppering Chase with questions.

"What happened?" Gio asked. "Did you see any zombies?"

"How did you avoid the sheriff?" I asked. "Was he shooting at you?"

There was a long pause as Chase looked at us. "Gentlemen," he said, "what I'm about to tell you can never leave your mouths."

Our night out may have been at an end—but what Gio and I were about to find out meant the adventure had just begun.

CHAPTER TWENTY-SIX

ODYSSEY

THE FOLLOWING IS a recounting of what Chase told Gio and me. I was not present during the affair, and therefore I cannot give a first-hand eyewitness account. However, I can vouch that Chase's retelling had an intense and convincing tone that only someone telling the truth is able to use.

The large red stone blocks of the school building were well suited for climbing, and Chase's foot and handholds got him to the third-floor window ledge in quick time. He glanced back down at the ground and spied his two friends running off. He thought about how smart they were to conceal themselves so quickly.

He slid open the window he had left unlocked earlier in the day, then brought his body into the empty classroom. Now he was inside the building—a haunted building with only the full moon's light shining through the window he had just come through to lead his way.

Chase's ears perked with a heightened sense, scanning for any sound. His eyes grew wider, peering into the dark corners of the classroom. He looked at the empty rows of chairs that faced the empty desk of Miss Crabtree. The silence gripped him for a moment, not allowing him to move. But he had not come this far just to go back; he had a job to do.

His first step was silent, then followed by another one just like it. Moving towards the dreadful Miss Crabtree's desk inch by inch, Chase hastened his pace. Shadows on the walls moved with the moonlight, causing his eyes to dart from side to side. A creak from the floor beneath his shoes stopped him for the briefest moment before he resumed course. He could hear the sound of his own nervous breathing, and he tried to calm himself.

He thought of the path he needed to take: He would go down three flights of stairs, down the hallway, past the entryway, and to the gymnasium before opening the school's back door to let in his accomplices. There would be several dark spots he would need to navigate, and he would need the small flashlight he now gripped in his hand.

Not yet, he told himself; in order to keep his presence a secret, he must wait to turn it on until it was *completely* necessary.

He reached the door of Miss Crabtree's classroom, and he looked back at the window he had come through, then to the empty seats once again, before peering down the hallway. It was darker than he had thought it would be. In the distance, he could just make out by the moonlit hall windows, the edge of the stone staircase leading down.

One foot in front of the other, he told himself. *There was no turning back now.*

Halfway down the hall, he heard some sort of whisper from behind. The hair on the back of his neck rose as thoughts of Charlie Hackett's ghost entered his mind.

Surely, the ghost couldn't harm me, he reassured himself—*that is, unless it manifested in some material form.*

He hesitantly looked over his shoulder down the dark corridor. He spotted a faint flickering of light under the crack of a door.

The light from the tower? He wondered.

Curiosity mixed with fear held him paralyzed. *Was someone, or something, here with him?*

His thumb readied the on switch of his flashlight as he stepped back—onto something that wasn't there before.

Looking down, Chase saw he was on what appeared to be a black boot. He turned, pressing the flashlight on, but he was instantly pulled into a classroom. His flashlight clattered to the ground.

A hand covered his mouth, and the cold steel of a knife's blade pressed against his cheek. A wave of terror shot through his body, causing him to become as rigid as a statue.

Charlie Hackett's ghost is going to cut me to pieces, he thought, *and the entire school will find my body parts scattered across the building.*

He tried to remember an anti-ghost remedy—any one he could think of—but his mind could not operate.

Suddenly, he was spun around like a rag doll—to come face-to-face with his oppressor.

In the dim light, intense green eyes stared back into his. Chase realized it was no ghost of a dead boy at all, but a woman staring back at him. She was holding a black-gloved finger to her lips while still covering his mouth with her other hand. She nodded to Chase for silence.

He nodded back in understanding, and she then relaxed her grip on his mouth.

Chase stood motionless. His captor was unnervingly beautiful. Blond hair fell around a sharp face. Her brilliant green eyes pierced the dark; her red lipstick glistened in the moonlight. She was athletically built with long legs and fully dressed in tight black leather. Strapped to each of her thighs were holsters holding guns. A belt with many compartments banded around her waist.

She spun her knife through her fingers, sheathed it on her belt, and then placed her hands on her hips before speaking in a soft and smoky voice. "Mind telling me what after-school activity you're here for?"

Chase swallowed hard. He wasn't sure what to do.

Scream for help—that might get his throat slit.

Try to run—she had guns, and he couldn't outrun a bullet.

He was at her mercy, and he didn't know what her intentions might be. *Was she a thief? An assassin? A secret agent?*

The fact that she hadn't killed him, or hurt him, reassured him—and helped him calm down. Maybe he could talk his way out of this.

"Are… are you a… security guard?" he mumbled.

"Hmm… well, I guess you could say that, but I'm the one asking the questions. Now tell me, what are you doing up here?" she asked.

"We—" Chase caught himself before continuing. "I… I was trying to get the answers for a test on Monday."

"Breaking and entering to cheat on a test? Sounds like studying would have been easier—and legal," she shot back. "You're lucky the gargoyles didn't grab you."

Chase straightened himself, studying his captor more. "It's a hard test, and Miss Crabtree is a hard teacher."

"So I've heard. Why don't you take her out then?"

"What? Are you serious?" Chase breathed in shock.

"Don't I look serious?" She bent down and stared him in the eye. "Now, why don't you tell me the real reason you're here while I still have an ounce of patience?"

Chase looked around the room again, as if there was an answer sitting out there, waiting for him to spot, but he found none. "I must warn you, I have training not to talk," he hedged.

"Training?"

"You know—not to talk with strangers—and you are clearly the strangest stranger I've ever come across," Chase said truthfully.

"Humph. Well then, things could get very interesting," she said as she began walking back and forth, feeling her knife.

"Well," he gulped, "I'm not say'n I wouldn't be willing to talk to you; I just don't know who you are. My name is Chase."

She stopped and turned, looking at him through her eyebrows before she cocked her head and whispered, "Odyssey."

"That's your name? *Odyssey—really?*"

"Really," she sarcastically mimicked.

"Who do you work for?"

"Santa Claus, and if you're lucky, I won't report you awake past your bedtime." She bent down and narrowed her cat-like eyes. "So, kid… now that we aren't strangers, mind telling me what you're doing up here?"

"Investigating paranormal activity," he admitted.

"I see—another ghost hunter," she smirked. "Stay in school and study math, kid. It will take you farther."

"I'd be willing to guess you're doing something along the same lines?" he asked.

"You're free to guess all you want, kid. It's classified information," she said.

"Okay, it's just that—suppose I have some information about Mr. Doyle and aliens. I'm sure that wouldn't interest you—or would it?"

She stopped and slowly turned her head back to Chase. "What kind of information?" she said in a smoky whisper.

"Well, it's classified information," Chase retorted, folding his own arms.

"Touché," replied Odyssey.

"Now, we could share information," Chase said in a more confident tone. "But then we'd have to be on the same team."

"Yes, I suppose we would. But the problem is I work alone, and my work is dangerous."

"My work is dangerous too."

Odyssey's eyes narrowed. Chase opened his mouth to talk—but instantly, she was behind him with her hand over his mouth.

Is this it? he thought. *Is she going to end the interrogation right here and now? Kill me before I could identify her—and with no witnesses?*

"Quiet," she whispered.

Chase realized she had heard something. He strained to listen, but he heard nothing except his own fierce breathing against her leather glove.

"We've got company," she muttered.

She moved both of them to the window before releasing his mouth once again. She was looking down into the parking lot. Blue and red lights began flashing against the wall from the opposite window.

"The sheriff?" Chase asked.

"Yes—but he's not what I'm concerned with." Odyssey moved to another window and glanced down. "They've blocked my escape route."

Chase looked down the window to see a yellow Ford Pinto parked in the lot. A black sedan blocked it in.

"That's your car? A Pinto?"

She shrugged. "I'm undercover." She looked out another window before walking towards the hall, asking, "Is that your bike down there?"

"Yes, of course."

"You're one to talk—care if I borrow it for a while?" she asked.

"I suppose, but what about me?"

She moved to the classroom door and peered down both directions of the hallway. She then looked back at Chase and said, "You'll be fine. It's me they want. Just stay here until—"

Odyssey quieted, stood tall, and looked back down the hallway into the dark.

Chase couldn't see or hear anything.

"Change of plans. How good are you riding that bike of yours with an extra passenger?"

"Awesome," Chase grinned.

"Good, 'cause you're taking us for a ride."

She ran back into the classroom, opened the window, and threw down the end of a rope. She then attached the rope's other end with a small hook, securing it to the window's stone frame corner, and gave it a tug. "Come on, climb on my back!" she invited, just before she hauled her body out the window.

Chase raced over, gripped onto her shoulders, and tossed the rest of his body out the window. Odyssey skimmed down the rope with lightning speed, Chase hanging on her back.

When they reached the ground, Chase ran to his bike as Odyssey whipped up her rope—releasing it from the window's corner and pulling it to the ground. He glanced up and spotted shadowy faces at the window from which they had just escaped.

A car's engine sprang to life, and car headlights from across the grass illuminated Chase and Odyssey like actors on a stage. Chase mounted his bike, and Odyssey jumped up on the rear pegs.

"Ride as fast as you can, and if you make any comments that I'm too heavy, I'll kill you myself. Now go!" she commanded.

"But where?" Chase blurted out.

"That's your job. Anywhere but here."

Chase pedaled as hard and fast as he could. Surprisingly, Odyssey did not seem to weigh much of anything. Maybe it was his adrenaline, maybe it was pure strength, or maybe she was as light as a feather. But whatever the reason, he could move the bike forward with great speed.

A car's engine roared behind them. Chase heard tires spinning and gravel kicking up. He knew they were being pursued.

He concentrated on keeping his balance, feeling Odyssey's grip on his shoulders. Then, gunshots rang out behind them: *Bang-bang-bang!*

Chase hunched his shoulders and ducked his head to keep from being shot. He felt Odyssey let go of his shoulders as she yelled, "Keep going!"

In an amazing feat of acrobatics, she spun around on the back of the bike to face her oncoming opponents. Drawing both of her 9mm, she fired back.

Bang-bang-bang-bang-bang-bang!

Bullets whizzed by them as Chase maneuvered the dirt bike in zigzagging patterns. It amazed him that Odyssey managed to stay balanced on the bike.

Out of the corner of his eye, Chase spied another car approaching from his right at high speed while the vehicle, in pursuit from behind, continued gaining ground on them.

"Odyssey!" Chase yelled in warning.

He felt her head and hair flip back as she extended her guns toward the new threat.

"Steady," she mumbled.

Bang!

Blood splattered the windshield of the adjacent car as Odyssey's bullet found its mark. The car went into a tailspin and slammed into a tree.

Another car took its place to hunt them down. Odyssey continued firing and reloading as the occupants of the car shot at them. Bullets peppered the ground. Suddenly, oncoming headlights shined on them from the road ahead.

Chase held his breath. They were on a collision course with the other vehicle!

"Odyssey! In front of us!" Chase yelled.

Her weapons fired over his head: *Bang! Bang! Bang!*

The car's oncoming headlights shattered, and one of the front tires burst from the penetration of Odyssey's bullets. The vehicle skidded sideways.

"Get us off this road now!" she yelped.

Chase looked off the road, spotting the creek on their right. *If he could jump it,* he thought, *the pursuers wouldn't be able to follow in their cars.*

Chase had never jumped a creek with another person standing on the back of his bike. In fact, he had never jumped a creek on his bike before.

There's a first time for everything, he thought. *Why not two firsts at once?*

He yelled, "Hang on!"

His dirt bike veered off the road into the brush, heading straight for the creek. The black sedans followed, furiously spitting dirt.

Chase closed in on the embankment, and he tightened his grip on the handlebars. With all his might, all his weight, he pushed on the pedals.

There was no time to think what would happen if he did not make it across; no time to wonder if his friends had been caught; no time to contemplate the woman on the back of his dirt bike firing guns at cars that were chasing them through the dark.

*He thought only one thing—**jump.***

At the moment his bike was about to launch, Chase felt the weight come off the back tire. Odyssey had already jumped up, while still firing her guns at their unrelenting pursuers.

Chase coiled his legs before releasing them, springing his bike into the air. Time stood still as bullets whisked by—his body standing tall on the pedals, sticking its neck out like a ski jumper soaring and getting every last inch out of a jump.

A thud greeted his tires as his bike landed, followed by another thump, as Odyssey somehow managed to land on his bike.

They had not wrecked.

Chase resumed pedaling his bike furiously forward through the brush, when a loud crash from behind them made him look over his shoulder. He saw both cars nose-first in the creek. His plan had worked! The cars had wrecked!

This success did not stop him from continuing to pedal. Chase continued to move the bike forward, riding with the same vigor that helped them escape.

Finally, Odyssey said, "You can stop now; we've lost them."

Breathing heavily, Chase stopped the bike and gasped, "What was that all about?"

Odyssey hopped off the back of the bike and holstered her 9 mm. "That was the enemy."

"The enemy? Who's the enemy?"

"Agents from the other world," she said, taking a few huge gasps of air herself.

"What do they want?"

"Me dead—among other things."

"The *other world*? Uh, what do you mean, *the other world*?"

"Listen, kid," she said, pausing, "there are things you can see, and things you cannot see." She walked around him, brushing off the dirt on his clothes. "You asked if I was a security guard. Well, I'm kinda like a safety valve between this world and a hidden one that must be kept in check."

"You mean, a paranormal world—like space aliens? Vampires or zombies?" Chase asked.

"I suppose you could say that," Odyssey said in a muted tone.

"Does this have anything to do with the disappearance of Mr. Doyle?" Chase asked.

"I'm not sure, but I'm going to find out," Odyssey said.

"You mean *we* are going to find out—we're on the same team now."

"No, we are not."

"B-b-but I saved your life," Chase sputtered.

"I saved yours first."

"When?" Chase demanded.

She turned to him and smiled. "When I decided not to kill you."

Chase couldn't think of a response to that. After a short period of time, Odyssey shrugged her shoulders. "I suppose I could use a little help," she said, "but I must warn you: Once you start down this path, there is no going back."

Chase nodded in understanding.

She narrowed her eyes. "I'm going to need you to be on the inside of the school, finding out what's going on there. Get me more on this, 'Mr. Doyle,' and who else is involved with his disappearance. Watch yourself, trust no one, and tell no one about me—deal?"

Chase stuck out his hand to shake hers. "Deal," he said.

She reached into her shirt. "Here's my card."

Chase looked at it. It was a playing card. "The queen of hearts?"

"Feel fortunate it wasn't the queen of spades," she said as she dusted her behind off. "Nice driving tonight, kid; your bike was a real lifesaver."

Chase looked at his bike. The handlebars were out of whack, the rim was bent, and more spokes were broken. "Yeah, it might need some repairs."

Odyssey took the bike from him and mounted it. "Repairs? I'll have it repaired all right—with a few modifications."

"But—"

"You said I could borrow it—remember?"

"Uh, I guess I did.... When will I see you—and it—again?" Chase asked.

"You'll see me when you need to see me," she answered.

And just like that, she disappeared into the shadows.

When the sun rose the next morning, it found our eyes open. What happened the night before, and the story Chase had told us, ensured insomnia for the rest of our lives.

We didn't know what to do with the information.

As we lay in our sleeping bags discussing what had gone down for the gadzibillionth time, Chase's mom called out that breakfast was ready.

Our minds were numb as we drifted into the kitchen. We all felt like the zombies we had run from the night before.

"I had a feeling you boys would be up all night. Here, eat some pancakes and eggs—juice, anyone?"

Chase's mom had no idea what we had been through, but she was right about one thing—well, two things: We hadn't slept a wink, and we were hungry.

The breakfast she made was delicious. Gio and I took seconds and doused our pancakes with maple syrup. The food replenished our brains, brought us back to life, and allowed us to talk again.

When his mom was out of earshot, Chase, with his mouth completely full of food, said, "We need to assemble the team at the fort and figure this out today."

Gio and I nodded enthusiastically.

"G, make the phone calls to let everyone know. Ollie, prepare our notes. We'll meet there in two hours, and we'll debrief Eduard and Jax."

Gio and I left Chase's house that morning with a purpose. We were now involved with some super-secret something, and the fate of humanity might depend on us! We hurried back to our houses to prep and ready ourselves to meet back at the fort with the rest of our team.

I found Mom at home, reading underneath her tree in the backyard in a pair of dark sunglasses. I scurried about the inside of the house, noting that my Monte Christo project was still intact, and Adam was still over Samuel's house. Nothing stood in my way.

So, I changed my clothes and kissed my mother, hello and goodbye.

My mother pulled her sunglasses down and eyeballed me. "And where do you think you're going without doing your chores?"

I stopped in my tracks and looked back at her. "I did them already, last night—remember?"

She stared at me, picked up a couple of aspirin out of the bottle sitting on the table next to her, and said, "They better have been done. And speaking of projects, when are you going to take down that sheet from my shelf? It's been two weeks, hasn't it?"

"Two days, Mom," I corrected quietly. "I'll take it down soon—I hope. Mrs. Huntley sure likes it and is giving me extra credit for doing it."

"Schools and their projects, activities, homework, extra credit; whatever happened to just plain *learning?* Don't these teachers know parents have to work? Sometimes I think they expect us parents to teach our kids." She shook her head, tossed the aspirin in her mouth, and gulped them down with a large swallow of water. "Maybe if they didn't spend so much time in my bar, they might actually have time to do their jobs."

I looked at her. "What did you say? *My* teachers hang out in *your* bar?"

"Yeah, yeah… and they don't tip very well either, cheap bastards," Mom said with a grimace.

"Which teachers?" I asked, curious.

Her answer threw me.

"Oh, I don't know. Some tall guy with a comb-over; he said he was a teacher at Raven Ridge—as if we're all supposed to be impressed. Well, I can tell you his tip wasn't impressive. Charlie… yeah, that was his name."

Charlie… Charles Doyle???

"When was he there?" I breathed.

"Oh—who knows… last week sometime… maybe Monday? Yeah. That's right. That Charlie couldn't leave the chips and salsa alone. He ate them all night while watching the Monday night football game, but he wouldn't order any food. When his team lost, he threw a fit and tossed the chips on the floor. That's when Bob threw him out."

"Did my teacher come back any more after that?" I asked excitedly.

"Nope—never saw him again. Funny you ask that, though. Just the other night, some guy wearing a suit came in looking for him. He waited around for him all night. Charlie, the teacher, never showed up, though, and the guy in the suit left after only ordering water all night. No tip from him, either."

"And what did that guy in the suit look like?"

"Mmm, I never really saw his face… he stayed in the shadows of the bar, mostly. You'd think with that expensive suit, he could afford a decent tip. I hope neither of 'em ever comes back. I need customers who drink a lot and tip even more. Now, if your chores are done, young man, you may leave, but be home before dark. We have church tomorrow."

There wasn't time to time to record my findings in my journal; I had a meeting to get to. I made a mental note to tell my colleagues and then raced off to our secret tree-fort.

I was the last to get there; everyone was already gathered. Chase looked over at our group, who sat silently, waiting for him to tell us his tale. His eyes landed upon Jax.

"What I'm about to tell you is *beyond* top-secret. In fact, it brings you great danger just by hearing it. But we must undertake such dangers in the fight against the forces of darkness," he said.

I thought Chase was being a little over-dramatic, but it was a dramatic experience after all, so I forgave him.

"Secrecy is not optional," Chase concluded. "Do you all still want me to continue?"

Jax and Eduard nodded in agreement. Chase then retold his encounter with Odyssey. My heart started pounding as I listened to his story again. I thought about how Jax was hearing it for the first time, and I imagined her feelings of excitement.

When Chase had finished, Eduard let out a breath as if he'd been holding it the entire time. "Awesome," he said

Jax sat silently, staring at Chase with her mouth open. I knew she was astonished, but I wondered if she was now afraid. No doubt she was wondering what she had gotten herself into. But it was too late for her to turn back; she had heard the story, and she was a part of our team. She had said the oath, so there was no turning back now.

After a long moment of silence, Jax blurted out, "Are you kidding me? That's the most ridiculous story I've ever heard! Ha-ha-ha-ha," she scoffed. "Great imagination."

Chase narrowed his eyes. "It's not a joke… it's real."

"Yeah, and Superman flew into my room last night and asked if I could help him save the world too, but I told him I had plans to work with a secret agent who just so happens to look like a supermodel. Ha-ha-ha." Jax stood up and brushed off her sundress while shaking her head. "You are all out of your minds. No wonder you asked me to join your nerd club; you needed me to bring some sanity here!"

Chase leaned his head forward. "We didn't invite you, remember? You invited yourself—and it's not a club."

Feeling the tension—and fearing Jax might leave—I said, "We're all on the same team, so let's focus on solving the mystery." I looked at Jax and Chase. "Something did happen to Mr. Doyle and my pocket watch; we all can agree on that—right?"

There was a moment of strained silence in the tree-fort as Jax hesitated.

"Okay," Jax said, nodding her head before she sat back down. "Let's figure this out."

"Agreed," Chase nodded back.

"So, what does this *Odyssey* want us to do?" Jax smirked.

"Find out more about Mr. Doyle, and try to figure out what's going on inside the school and who else might be involved. She'll take care of things on her end," Chase said.

"Well, I just found out some new info on Mr. Doyle," I proudly offered, getting everyone's attention. "He was in Jam'n Joe's Bar last Monday night, watching a football game."

"So?" Gio said. "What does that have to do with anything?"

I explained, "Well, my mom also said that a few nights after, a man dressed in a suit came in looking for Mr. Doyle. I asked her what the man looked like, and she told me she didn't get a good look at him because his face was always in the shadows."

"An agent of the other world?" Eduard speculated. "Do you think Mr. Doyle was involved with them somehow?"

"I don't know," Chase said. "We need to find out more about where he's been and who he's been involved with."

Eduard asked, "Where do we start?"

Chase picked up the claim ticket to the pawnshop. "With this piece of paper."

"You mean go into the city?" I asked. "To the pawnshop?"

"Yep," Chase nodded. "We need to talk with the owner; find out what he knows. Maybe we'll even find your pocket watch there."

"Yes!" I said, getting excited.

Jax flattened her lips. "How are we going to get to downtown Denver? And what about our parents? They won't let us go."

"I think I can arrange us a ride," Chase said with a bit of a smirk. "And we won't be gone that long, so our parents won't even know we've been down there." He looked around. "Who's in?"

"I am," both Gio and I said simultaneously.

"I have a prior engagement," Eduard sighed. "However, this is much more important—so consider me in."

"Well," Jax said as she folded her arms. "I guess I'll have to go too, just to make sure we hear no more wild and crazy stories."

CHAPTER TWENTY-SEVEN

ONE MAN'S JUNK IS ANOTHER MAN'S TREASURE

ASPYN POPPED A bubble with her chewing gum. "All right, dorks. But no funny business this time. No splitting up, running off on your own, or getting in trouble with the law—understood?"

"Yes, Mommy," Chase nodded.

"Chase, if you don't like it, you can stay home," Aspyn hissed.

"Yeah, you can stay home," Spencer echoed.

"Sis, we aren't gonna do anything stupid! We just need to go to the pawnshop—that's it," Chase said.

"We aren't waiting around all day, either. I've got things to do that involve a lot of shopping, so you guys need to be quick," Aspyn ordered.

"You can pick us up after you're done shopping," Chase said.

Aspyn looked at Jax. "So, who's your new girlfriend?"

“She’s not my girlfriend; she goes to our school. Jaclyn, this is my sister, Aspyn,” Chase introduced.

“Hi, Jaclyn. This is my boyfriend, Spencer,” Aspyn said.

Spencer gave Jax a half-wave, like he was half-asleep.

“Nice to meet you, Aspyn,” Jax said sweetly. “You can call me Jax. And thank you so much for the ride to the city.”

“So, Jax, what are you doing with these dorks?” Aspyn asked with a toss of her head.

“I just try to keep them on track, that’s all,” Jax beamed.

“Impossible, if you ask me. Let’s go,” Aspyn said.

Spencer’s car fired up with a roar and several backfires as we piled into the back seat. Jax sat between Gio and me, and Eduard was on my right, next to my birthmark. Chase sat in the front seat with Aspyn and Spencer.

It made me nervous to be sitting next to Jax, and I was thankful for the nice-smelling deodorant I was wearing.

“Ready for takeoff?” Spencer smirked.

“Let’s see if you can just keep it on the ground, Captain,” Chase sarcastically laughed.

“Shut your face, dork,” Aspyn snapped as she popped her gum again.

Music blared as the Mustang tore down the road, spinning its tires with a cloud of dust towards the city.

The traffic thickened as we approached Denver’s city limits. People and cars were everywhere. If we got lost, I wouldn’t know where to go or what to do. This was foreign territory for me.

Before I knew it, Spencer stopped the Mustang, to drop us on the corner of Sixteenth and Wazee.

Chase peered out the window first. “This isn’t where the pawnshop is.”

Spencer cocked his head. “It’s a one-way street that direction—I’d have to go all the way up three blocks, then circle around another three blocks to come down this street. Besides, there's no parking anywhere. So, you should get out here."

Aspyn blew another bubble. "It's only a few blocks from here; you guys can walk. We'll be back in an hour, so you had better be done and ready to be picked back up *right here on this corner.* Okay?"

"Yeah, yeah, we'll be here," Chase promised. "But you don't be late either."

We jumped out of the back seat and shut the car door just as Aspyn held her hand out the window. "Um... are you forgetting something, little brother?"

Chase reached into his pocket and pulled out some cash, which he handed over. "Okay...."

"Love you, dork," Aspyn said as she took the money and waved. "Be careful!"

The Mustang squealed off, backfiring a goodbye.

We looked around. A few blocks away, we could just see a large sign reading, *'Past & Present Pawnshop.'* Chase led us towards it through the smattering of oncoming pedestrians.

On one street corner, a bunch of people were holding up signs that read, *"Down with the pollution of man—up with the Earth!"* and, *"The United States will pay!"* and, *"We are the warriors of the earth. We will not back down!"* and, *"The President will taste the waste, and the world will hear our message!"* and, *"Desperate times call for desperate actions!"*

These must be the protesters Frank had talked to me about, I thought.

Their protest signs reminded me of something my uncle once told me: *"Desperation begets desperation."* He told me desperate people would take advantage of me, steal from me, or hurt me if they had the chance.

Too, my uncle had always told me the city—Denver—was a

dangerous place because it had so many desperate people. He said the people in the big cities didn't care for one another, unlike the townsfolk in our small town.

I couldn't understand why anyone would want to live in a city, anyhow. I'd take a cow pasture and rural, open lands over a skyscraper, crowds, and traffic any day.

Jax looked up at the tall buildings and a smile crossed her face. "I love coming downtown," she breathed. "The city has such a romantic quality to it."

"I think so too!" I quickly agreed. After all, I was sure I could get used to it.

Passing by restaurants that smelled absolutely delicious reminded me we hadn't eaten lunch yet. If I had the money, I would treat Jax to a delightful meal down here, perhaps on one of the verandas. The two of us could watch the people walk by as we sipped our soda and discussed something interesting. Afterward, we could take a horse-and-carriage ride through the city as we snuggled together.

I guess the city did have a certain romance to it.

Curious looks from many of the passers-by also brought feelings of apprehension: *Are they all looking at my birthmark? Or are they just puzzled why a group of kids is walking down the sidewalk alone?*

We passed a man standing in the shadows of a building and playing a guitar. I dressed him in black, with all sorts of jewelry hanging around his neck. A silver bracelet with charms and tiny mirrors hung from his wrist. A large brimmed black hat was pulled low over his eyes. An open guitar case lay in front of him; it contained several dollars and coins from passing contributors. He did not look up as we slowly walked by.

Jax paused to listen to the beautiful notes that came from his instrument. His music was rhythmic, almost hypnotizing.

Our group kept walking—Jax did not. This caused us to stop and look back.

"Jax," I urged.

She stood looking at the musician as if she didn't hear me. With his head down and his hat concealing his eyes, the musician continued to play. It was at this point that I worried we were going to have to pay him for playing—as I had only a few dollars in my pocket.

He ceased his playing with a beautiful and dramatic stroke of his fingers. Without looking up, he asked Jax in a low and soft tone laced with an accent, "What did you think?"

"It was absolutely beautiful—I loved it," she breathed.

He raised his head slowly, revealing electric blue eyes and a thin, black, well-kept goatee. His face broke into a smile. Looking intently at Jax, he said, "It was for you—I thought you'd like it."

"What was it?" she asked. "It sounded familiar, but I couldn't remember where I've heard it."

He answered, "It's an old tune from my people; it has deep meaning. The notes cry my people's story."

"Where do you come from?" Chase asked.

"Far, far away," the musician said. "My motherland was torn apart from many years of war, leaving my people to wander without a home."

"You're homeless?" Gio asked.

"No, no. My home is here in my chest, and therefore I can never be homeless. I am a traveler, on a journey wherever life takes me," the man breathed.

"Why did you come here?" Eduard asked.

"In search of… well, it would be difficult to say, but… I'm here because the stars led me," the man said softly.

"You traveled from far away because the stars told you to?" Gio asked.

The musician smiled. "We all follow our own star, my boy—the question is whether or not we stay on course. Now, children, what star leads you here?"

Jax smiled. "We are heading to the pawnshop down—"

"Jax," I interrupted. "We shouldn't be talking to strangers."

"O-o-h… uh-h…." she stuttered, realizing I was right.

"Your friend is wise. You should not talk with strangers, my child… now off you go. I hope you find what you are looking for. The past can show us many things about the future," the man said as he gave a strum on his guitar.

Jax pulled a few dollars from her small pocketbook, but the musician stopped her with a wave of his hand. "No, no, my child, that tune was my gift to you," he said. "But thank you for your act of kindness."

She smiled. "Thank you for the beautiful melody."

Thank goodness, I thought as our group moved forward again. *I didn't want to pay for that song. I'd rather buy a soda or ice cream.*

Now, off to the pawnshop.

Christmas sleigh bells hanging on the door announced our arrival in the shop. I looked about: Unusual items filled the store, with seemingly no rhyme or reason as to their placement. A suit of armor stood next to a television, which stood next to a chainsaw, which stood near a stuffed moose head up on a wall. The group of us spread out to examine the eclectic items for sale.

A dirt bike resting in a corner caught my attention. I walked over and inspected the bike up close, feeling the grips, squeezing the seat, and running my fingers over the frame. It was used, but still in much better shape than my bike—well, my bike that was taken by the repairmen at our school.

Unlike my bike, this was a true dirt bike. It reminded me of Chase's and sent visions into my mind of me riding next to him over dirt trails and jumping over all kinds of things.

Yes, if only I had the proper bike, I thought, *it would allow my skills to develop properly.*

I looked at the price tag with a frown. The cost was far too much for my wallet.

"Do ya like it?" a low voice startled me from behind. "Ya can sit on it," a large man gruffed.

I glanced up. The man was grossly overweight, with an enormous belly hanging out over his belt. His face displayed black and gray stubble on plump white cheeks, accented by bushy gray and black eyebrows. His thin hair circled his head, leaving an island of white flesh on top. He chomped on an unlit cigar.

"I… I can't afford it," I said.

"I see… I'll tell ya what; this bike's been here fer a while. So, I can reduce the price by ten percent. How's that sound?"

The shopkeeper moved his cigar from one side of his mouth to the other with his tongue.

"Still too much, but thank you," I said, even though the truth was I couldn't figure what ten percent off the price was. "You have a lot of different stuff in here."

"Ya'd be surprised at the things people bring in," the man said as he took out his cigar with his fingers. "It amazes me still, and I've been doing this forever."

The man's breath was so bad it caused me to take a step back.

"So, what are you looking fer then?" he asked.

"I… err… we—" I said, pointing to my friends, "are looking for a pocket watch. Do you have any?"

"Come to the counter; I have a bunch."

My friends gathered around as we moved up through the store and peered into the glass counter. The man had several pocket watches on display, but none that looked like my great-grandfather's. I sighed in disappointment.

"Still not what you're look'n fer?" he asked.

"No," I sighed.

Chase pulled the claim ticket from his pocket. "Oh, and we have this ticket from Mr. Doyle. He asked us to come here and claim this item for him."

"Charles? Umm… let me see that," the shopkeeper said.

Chase handed it to him, and he placed glasses on his nose and held the claim ticket at a distance to read it.

"Oh…. Well, I'm sorry, but I sold this. I had a lot of interested people waiting fer it to go on sale," the man said.

Chase took back the ticket. "But I thought you got your stuff back with this claim ticket?"

"The pawn process works like this, young man," the owner said kindly. "When ya bring in an item, we give ya a loan for it, and if ya don't pay back that loan within a specified time, it then becomes our property, and we sell it. Now, sometimes ya might just want to sell an item outright with no loan—fer which I give top dollar—and then we resell it here in our shop. Charles brought this in to me, all dusty from the basement, and used it as collateral for a loan, but he never repaid the amount in the appropriate time—so I cleaned it up, and it went on the market."

"So, did he tell you he wanted this item back?" Chase asked. "I mean, tell you he was going to repay the loan?"

"Yeah, he said he needed it back, and he'd repay it quickly. But like I told ya's—he didn't repay the loan quickly enough, and I had to sell it. Charles knows the rules." The shopkeeper sounded annoyed. "Is that why he sent ya's in here instead of coming in himself—to see if I'd sold it?"

"No, no, of course not. But can you tell us what the item on this claim ticket was?" Chase asked—a bit eagerly, I thought.

The man drew back and looked at Chase with suddenly suspicious eyes. "Wait a minute… I thought ya said Charles sent ya here?" he questioned.

"Oh… um… well," Chase stammered, saved by the ringing of the front doorbell and new customers.

The shopkeeper looked in their direction, then back at our group. "Kids, I take pride in keeping others' privacy, so I don't think we should be having this conversation. Bring Charles that receipt back and tell him to deal directly with me next time. Now, I've got another customer. Is there anything else I can do fer ya's?"

"No, no. Thanks for your help," Chase said as he placed the receipt back into his pocket, and we hustled out.

As we walked back to meet up with Aspyn and Spencer at the corner where they had dropped us off, we discussed what we had just learned.

"Looks like Mr. Doyle didn't pawn Oliver's pocket watch," Eduard said.

"Maybe not," Chase said. "But did you catch what the shopkeeper said—that Doyle brought something in *all dusty from the basement* for a loan? And remember, Frank said one of Anastasia's vanity mirrors was missing from the basement?"

I nodded my head in agreement. "Yeah, Frank did accuse Mr. Doyle of taking something from down there—it makes sense it was the antique mirror."

"Unless the shopkeeper was talking about something dusty from Mr. Doyle's *own* basement, and not the school's," Jax pointed out. "Which means it could be anything."

"Yeah, like Anastasia's magic vanity mirror," Gio quipped.

Gio's remark drew an irritated look from Jax.

Carefully, we walked back the same way we had come, passing the same shops and alleyways. Except—no musician was standing against the building strumming a guitar. No one said anything, but I noticed Jax looking around for him.

Just as well, I thought. *He was a stranger, and we shouldn't be talking with him.*

Just then, Jax bent down and picked up something off the sidewalk. She held it up to the light.

"What is it?" I asked curiously.

"Looks like a small mirror charm. It must have dropped off the charm bracelet of that man playing the guitar," she answered.

"Finders keepers," Gio said.

Jax looked around for the man before placing it in her pocket.

We continued to stroll down the block, peering into various shop windows, until we stood on the corner where Spencer's Mustang had dropped us off earlier.

We were on time, but his car was nowhere to be found, and after a while, I began to wonder if Spencer and Aspyn had forgotten us. My fears were put to rest when I heard the now-familiar backfire of our ride coming down the street.

Spencer was in the far lane—but he did not slow down! As he passed by, we all yelled at him and waved. But the Mustang turned down the next one-way street, and we looked at each other, shocked. *How could he have missed us?* We wondered.

"Great," Gio whined. "Spencer forgot us, and we are stuck here!"

Chase hollered at us, "Stay here! I'll catch him through the alley." And he began running after Spencer's car.

Jax threw her hands up. "Stupid idea. He'll never catch up to them."

"He's pretty fast," I said, not really knowing whether or not it was true. "Besides, maybe Spencer's just going around the block?"

We waited for what seemed to be fifteen minutes—and by now, I agreed with Jax and Gio: *We were truly stuck downtown.*

Sure, I could call my mom, but this was her day off, and she would be upset about having to come all the way downtown to pick us up. Not to mention, I didn't tell her we were coming to the city;

that would make her even more upset. I'd probably be better off if we spent two days walking home.

Gio paced back and forth on the corner, while Eduard, Jax, and I sat on a nearby brick half wall. "Chase must have caught them, don't ya think?" Gio said, sounding completely unconvinced of his own words.

Eduard stuck out his chin. "You're correct, Giovanni. He should have been able to cut through that alleyway and catch them. He's probably in their car right now, and they're navigating to our location."

Jax crossed her legs. "You're assuming he didn't get mugged in the alley."

The entire city stopped moving, frozen in horror at the words she had just said. Fortunately, it got moving again with the roar of Spencer's engine, followed by a backfire.

The Mustang pulled up along the curb, and Aspyn flung open a door. "Where's Chase? Why isn't he here?" she asked.

"He took off after you guys down that alley when you drove by us before. We thought you forgot where you dropped us off," I said as we climbed into the back seat.

"We didn't forget—well, I didn't. Spencer was in the wrong lane and couldn't get over. We had to go all the way around because it's all one-way streets here," Aspyn said.

"Yeah," Spencer grumbled. "Stupid one-way streets and lights—I hit every one of them."

"Which is why you should've listened to me," Aspyn sassed, and then looked back at us. "Now, where did Chase go?"

"He ran down that alleyway there," I pointed. "Should we drive around and look for him?"

"No, we need to stay here," Aspyn snapped. "Otherwise he'll come back and miss us, and then we'll be driving in circles for hours. Seriously, I wish my mom would just get him a cell phone."

"I can't just stay parked here," Spencer whined. "I'll get a ticket!"

"Fine, but then just drive really, really slow," Aspyn ordered.

We pulled around the corner at a snail's pace, then by the alleyway Chase had gone down. Suddenly, out of the shadows, Chase came walking. He looked upset, as if he'd seen a ghost or something.

Aspyn threw open her door. "Idiot! Get in the car!" she screeched.

Chase looked back behind him into the alley first, then slid into the front seat with Aspyn and Spencer.

Aspyn lectured, "You should have stayed on the corner—you shouldn't have split up. Something bad could have happened to you."

"I'll say," Chase mumbled as he looked back at us with a worried look.

I mouthed the words, *"What happened?"* to him—to which he gave a short shake of his head in silent response.

Something had happened, we all could tell. The talk on the walk to our fort sure was going to be interesting.

CHAPTER TWENTY-EIGHT

THE SHADOW

THE FOLLOWING EYEWITNESS account you are about to read was told to us by Chase as we walked to the tree-fort. It's about his experience in the alleyway.

Chase's nose warned him not to go any further. The foul stench from some of the restaurant's dumpsters could make even the most iron of stomachs puke in the heat. *The smell will pass if I just hold my breath,* he told himself.

The alleyway was long and seemed to narrow the farther he traveled down it. His pace slowed as the shadows grew with the tall skyscrapers; dark pockets hidden from the sun were all around him. *Maybe I shouldn't have run down here alone*, he thought. *But too late now. Just keep alert and try not to breathe.*

At that moment, he heard the sound of metal on metal behind him. Turning around, he caught only a faint glimpse of what he thought was a passing shadow; his breath escaped him. It could have been his mind playing tricks on him—*but then again, could it be… Odyssey?*

He took a small breath of the rank air and refocused on the task of catching up to Spencer's Mustang. He turned back to continue forward when he was confronted by an enormous shadow of a man emerging from between two dumpsters.

The shadow spoke. "Hello, young man." The figure moved into the light just enough so that Chase could see the dark suit and tie he was wearing; the man's face remained in the shadows. "I don't believe we've met."

"Who are you?" Chase's eyes darted between the shadowy figure and down the alleyway for any other sign of trouble or a passerby he could yell for if there was trouble. "What do you want?"

"I'm a friend, and I want to help set you on the right path."

"I don't know who you are, but I've got all the friends I need," Chase said. "Excuse me."

Chase made a move to walk away, but the figure moved into his path, causing him to stop.

"Of course you do," the shadowed face said. "But tell me: have you made friends with any tall blondes lately—tall blondes with pistols?"

"No," Chase said, "but, even if I did, I wouldn't tell you."

"Loyal—I like that—and trustworthy, no doubt." The faceless figure placed his hands in his pockets while scraping the alley with his foot. "But you trust much too quickly. People aren't always who they seem. Tell me… why is it you trust *her?* What makes you think she's not playing you for a fool?"

"I don't know what you're talking about," Chase answered, unnerved by the surroundings and the darkness of the figure before him. "I'm late, so I've got to go."

"By all means, don't let me hold you up," was the response Chase got. But the shadow continued to stand in his path.

Chase decided it would be better just to go back in the direction of his friends. He turned and hurried away.

"I'd hate to see you get hurt," the faceless man shouted after him. "I suggest you find new friends."

Chase emerged into full sunlight, thrilled to spot Spencer's Mustang—and not at all unhappy about hearing Aspyn shout, "Idiot! Get in the car!"

He gave a quick look back into the alleyway, saw only empty shadows, and slid into the front seat with Aspyn and Spencer.

After Chase had told his story, none of us knew what to say—except Jax.

"Wow, this gets better by the second," Jax said. "I knew I should have gone down that alley with you, because who knows where your imagination will take you next."

"My imagination didn't make that up," Chase said defensively.

Eduard adjusted his glasses while sticking out his chin. "What do you think the faceless guy wants?"

"Yeah, and why didn't he kidnap you?" Gio asked. "Or kill you?"

Jax answered for Chase. "What fun would that be? Then, he wouldn't be able to tell his little made-up stories."

Chase shrugged her comments off. "I don't know, Gio, but I'm sure Odyssey's gonna want to hear about it."

Jax let out a short laugh. "Tell one imaginary character about another—now that's great."

Chase smiled at Jax and said, "Jax, sounds like you're jealous."

His words, which I didn't really get, caused Jax to frown. "You're ridiculous. You expect us to believe—"

Jax cut her words short as we all noticed something that wasn't right: huge splinters of wood littered the pathway that led to our fort. Realizing what they had to be from, we broke into a run.

We reached the clearing and found our once-mighty fort, built to withstand hurricane-force winds, now in pieces on the ground. No storm had caused this. A deliberate act of destruction had.

Our evidence box lay on the ground, open. The dried flowers were ripped to shreds, and the map torn to pieces. The gray button couldn't be found—but luckily, Gio had the key in his pocket.

"Somebody is on to us," Gio gasped.

"Somebody… or something," Chase whispered back.

Pulling his magnifying glass from his back pocket, Chase began examining the ground and the wood that had once been the walls, roof, and floor of our secret gathering spot.

I couldn't believe his mind was already working on solving this crime; my mind was still in shock that someone did this to our fort: *Who would want to do such a thing? Who even knew where our secret location was? None of us would have told—*

It was at that moment that the creeping realization hit me; the possibility that Jax had somehow let our secret out. I, of course, ruled out this possibility immediately, but I could see by the other silent stares in her direction. Everyone else had not.

"Why… are you all looking at *me*?" Jax asked quietly.

Gio's mouth tugged sideways, and he answered in a monotone, "Because you're a girl."

"So what!" she scoffed. "Why does that matter?"

"Girls can't keep secrets, that's why," Gio flatly said back.

I waved my hand. "Just because she's a girl doesn't mean she told anyone."

"Pretty coincidental, I'd say," Gio challenged.

"Even if she told someone else," Eduard interjected, "who would want to destroy our fort?"

"A rival gang, that's who!" Gio huffed.

"We aren't a gang!" I looked at Chase, who was still examining the wood with his magnifying glass. "Maybe it was something else? An animal?"

"What do you think, Chase?" Eduard asked with his chin in the air. "Could it be something else?"

"Not sure," he said. "Look at the way this debris is scattered around. I'd say someone or something was mad when destroying our fort. The branches are broken, and the wood is smashed. Something blunt—something powerful—came through here. Over there are two wide scrape marks on that piece of wood—clawing, maybe? The maps and the drawing of Ricker are torn apart."

"Agents of the other world?" I asked.

"Maybe zombies!" Gio chimed in.

"Let's not forget aliens," Eduard added.

"There's no such thing as zombies, or aliens, or werewolves," Jax said.

"Werewolf? Yes, of course—let's not forget a werewolf," Chase nodded. "Whoever, or… whatever it was—is definitely after us. We need to solve this mystery now more than ever."

Jax shook her head and announced, "We need to report this to the sheriff. That's what we need to do!"

"Are you kidding?" Gio threw up his hands. "We'd probably be the ones getting in trouble if we did that."

I quickly nodded my head. "I totally agree with Gio. We should not tell the sheriff anything."

"I suppose… the thing to do now… is rebuild," Eduard sighed as he cleaned his glasses off with his shirt. "The question is—where? This spot's been discovered by someone unfriendly to us."

"I know just the spot," Jax said with a big smile on her face.

"Where?" I asked.

"Right here," she said, sounding quite smug.

Gio's eyes popped out of his head as he squeaked, "Are you *crazy*? We're lucky we weren't here when this disaster happened."

"Giovanni's right," Eduard agreed. "This location's secrecy has been compromised."

Chase nodded in agreement. "We need somewhere else—secret and safe."

"Yeah," I said, trying to sound reasonable. "Rebuilding it just so it can be destroyed again…?"

Jax walked over to the base of the tree and stood there with her hands on her hips. She said, "We can either be intimidated and run, or we can make a stand and fight back." She looked around into the forest. "Besides, whoever's after us will find us again anyway."

The four of us looked at each other, united in not wanting to agree with her. She was the girl—acting brave and challenging us, the boys, to stand our ground against this unknown threat.

Chase looked up into the branches of the tree. "I guess… the floor and one of the walls still look okay. And… well… it might be easier rebuilding here."

With a quick look at each other, we all nodded in excitement and agreed.

"We're gonna need tools and more wood," Chase said. "And we need to design some traps this time to catch intruders."

"I'll be in charge of that," Eduard said. "I'll need some paint, fishing line, lots of rope, a slingshot, and some balloons—oh, and some fireworks."

Chase circled his hand in the air. "Let's split up to get supplies and quickly meet back here to start our work."

We divided up the list of items we needed before we all raced off. Within no time at all, we had all assembled back at our fort, and the work of rebuilding commenced. Learning from the mistakes we had made before, and with the help of Eduard and Jax, more thought went into the design this time. The roof suffered with a few gaps, as we were low on lumber, but we could patch it later.

It was hard work, but we worked as a team, knowing our fort had to be completed as soon as possible. Something or someone didn't want us to have a fort, and none of us knew why, but it gave an extra sense of urgency to its completion. And next time, we could defend it, thanks to Eduard.

Eduard's elaborate trap designs were absolutely awesome! Eduard had thought out *everything,* for almost every situation imaginable.

If someone tried to sneak up from the west, Eduard had strung fishing line across the way—so anyone tripping the line pulled out a pin in a nearby tree, releasing a slingshot loaded with a big water balloon filled with lime-green primer paint from Gio's dad's auto shop. The balloon would strike the would-be intruder, covering them in the sticky paint. When the invader stumbled forward from the surprise and the impact, a second tripwire would trigger a catapult of branches that would release a barrage of ripe cattails. These would hit their target with not only stinging pain but also an explosion of fluffy white fuzz that would stick to the paint on the intruder. If, at that point, our uninvited guest decided to run away, they would be very noticeable and unable to hide their identity. But if they pressed forward, then a third tripwire would release a pin holding down a bent branch, which was tied to a rope with a lasso on the ground. The released branch would spring up, the lasso would pull and tighten around any feet in the area, and the rope would hoist the intruder upside down in the air.

Eduard's trap to the north was more of a deterrent than an entrapment. He had strung a tripwire between trees that, when tripped, would release a pin which pulled the trigger of a lighter—igniting pop-bottle rockets. The missiles would shoot out, hitting anyone in their path. In the event that someone saw this tripwire and stepped over it, Eduard had placed a second wire just beyond the first. Tripping the second line, released a pin holding down a thatch of thorn bushes that would whip up and whack anything in their path. Someone was going to have some *serious* thorns in their side.

To the east, Eduard had positioned a tripwire that would release a bent branch; when it sprang around, it would whack a beehive. Angry bees would chase off any would-be trespasser.

To the south, Eduard's tripwire would pull on a pin that held a rope tied to a large log in the trees. When the pin released, the rope slackened, and the log would fall. In turn, the log would quickly pull a different rope along the ground, trip the intruder from behind, and land them flat on their back. The log then would hit a seesaw that had a bucket of the green paint on one end—sending the bucket flying through the air, and the sticky primer onto the intruder on the ground.

Eduard also had designed a booby-trap wooden ladder leading up to the tree-fort. We slightly cut the wooden rungs that were halfway to the top of the ladder so they would break when someone tried to climb them, tossing the climber to the ground. We hid our original untouched rope ladder in the branches, while the other booby-trapped ladder leaned against the tree in plain view.

The trap door to get into our fort through the floor was booby-trapped with a wire that would dump a bucket of paint onto unknowing heads—unless the person first unhooked the line.

Jax insisted on placing signs around the perimeter of the fort that read, *"WARNING! Trespassers, Proceed at Risk of Pain and Suffering! Turn Back Now!"* If someone decided to ignore our warnings, they would be sorry.

For now, the tree-fort was finished, complete with a secure perimeter, and ready for action once again. As the day was almost over, we agreed to meet back at our rebuilt tree-fort tomorrow afternoon at two p.m. to get back to the business of solving the mystery of the school and Odyssey, the absence of Mr. Doyle, and the disappearance of my pocket watch.

CHAPTER TWENTY-NINE

A DANGEROUS DETOUR

SUNDAY MORNING, I had a hard time paying attention in church. My mind kept drifting to aliens, secret agents, ghosts, and the missing pocket watch. It looked more and more like I would never get the pocket watch back, and I'd have to 'fess up to my mom.

I decided I'd wait to do so until after my buddies and I saved the world—my punishment might not be so severe.

Mom was home on Sundays, so I didn't have to watch annoying little Adam. In addition, she didn't make either Adam or me do chores on Sundays, so I could ride off to our fort on Gio's bike with no delays.

That afternoon, everyone had made it to the tree-fort except for Chase. We sat, talking about music and different TV shows while we waited. Fifteen minutes went by; then, a half-hour—with still no sign of him. The longer we waited, the shorter our breaths became, as anxiety began to choke out the oxygen in the fort.

Eduard finally asked the question we were all thinking. "Where's Chase? I can't believe he'd be late."

Gio was quick to share his paranoid thoughts. "Maybe he was kidnapped?"

"No, he's probably doing house chores," I said in a reassuring voice that was more for me than the others.

Jax doodled in her notebook, bored with the waiting game. "Well, if he doesn't get here soon, I'm going to leave. I've got homework I still need to do for tomorrow."

I looked out through the slits between the planks of one wall, searching the ground below. "He'll be here any minute now. I'm sure of it."

Gio also looked through the cracks. "Do you think he forgot about the traps and is caught in one of them?"

Jax continued to doodle, and without looking up, said, "If he's so stupid to forget where the traps are, then he deserves to be caught."

My eyes grew wide along with my smile when I saw the bushes move, and Chase's blond hair as he pushed his dirt bike into the clearing. "He's here! And he got his dirt bike back!"

Eduard stuck his head out the window while holding his glasses as if they were binoculars and yelling, "You must have gotten it back from Odyssey—did you see her?"

Chase nodded his head yes and pointed to a column of smoke in the far distance.

Gio squeaked, "What happened?"

"I'll come up and tell you," Chase said in a heavy tone.

"Oh brother," Jax rolled her eyes. "Here we go again."

The following story was told to us by Chase—and detailed vividly here by me through my writing.

The dry dirt on the road puffed up underneath Chase's sneakers. Running an errand for his mom meant he had to take the long way to the secret tree-fort, and his sneakers felt the distance as they cried out for his dirt bike. As he ran, Chase wondered if he would ever see Odyssey again, and what it all had meant.

Without warning, an old yellow-and-green station wagon pulled up beside him on the empty road. It was covered in rust, oxidized, and dented all the way around. A cloud of dust arising from the tires caused him to hold his breath.

Chase squinted as he tried to look through the dark-tinted windows shielding the inside of the vehicle. The engine sputtered, shaking the car as it came to a halt. The driver-side window rolled down to reveal the blond hair of a woman wearing large mirror sunglasses and cherry-red lipstick.

Odyssey turned her head, pulled down her sunglasses, and winked at Chase. "Get in, we've got work to do," she ordered.

Chase ran to the passenger door and climbed inside, sitting on a torn seat while looking at the tattered surroundings of the vehicle.

Odyssey saw his looks and shrugged. "I'm undercover—okay? I'm a soccer mom. Now buckle up."

Chase looked at her outfit. Odyssey was not in the black leather attire she wore at their last meeting. Today she was wearing a tight black miniskirt and a low-cut black shirt. Gone, too, were the holsters with guns strapped to her thighs, and the belt that housed many compartments. A small chain necklace around her neck and large bracelets had replaced them on her arm. Chase could make out a tattoo on her left inside bicep—it looked like a playing card of the Queen of Diamonds.

"You don't look like any soccer mom I know," Chase said,

pulling the frayed seatbelt over his shoulder and waist. The car tore off. "Odyssey, where have you been?"

"Busy—you know, all the soccer practices," she sighed.

"What's going on?" Chase asked in a worried tone.

"There is a lot of activity in the other world right now," she said, her tone suddenly solemn. "I believe something big is about to happen."

The station wagon sputtered down the dirt road, causing Chase to glance at the car's gauges. *Would it break down at any moment?*

"What have you found out?" she asked.

"Still no sign of Doyle, but we followed a lead to a pawnshop. Apparently, Mr. Doyle had been pawning items for money. We have his claim ticket."

"What was he pawning?"

"The item on the claim ticket was already sold, and the shopkeeper wouldn't tell us what it was. We wondered if it was an antique mirror that was taken from the school's basement."

Odyssey's eyes narrowed as she asked, "An antique mirror?"

"Yes. Frank, the school's maintenance man, said it was one of Anastasia's antique vanity mirrors. He said that it was recently discovered wrapped in black cloth in the basement. Frank also said someone tampered with the wiring of the electrical panels housed down there." Chase looked inquisitively at Odyssey. "Why? is that important?"

"Maybe," she said before she paused for a moment. "Did the shopkeeper tell you *who* bought the item that Mr. Doyle pawned?"

"No," Chase said with a sigh. "He clammed up when he figured out we weren't there on Mr. Doyle's behalf."

"What else?"

"Oliver's mom encountered a man dressed in a suit looking for Mr. Doyle in her bar last week, but his face was in the shadows,"

Chase said. "Do you think he's connected? Maybe an agent of the other world?"

"At this point, anything's possible," she said. "Do you have any other leads?"

"Well, Jax has come up with her own theories that Doyle's just lost or been attacked by an animal. And, that maybe something is being covered-up by one of the other teachers. But nothing paranormal."

"And what do you think?" Odyssey asked.

"Her theories are too simple. We believe the cooks are giving brainwashing food to the kids to—"

"To create an army of zombie kids that space aliens will control?" Odyssey finished for him.

"Exactly!" Chase said enthusiastically.

Odyssey raised her eyebrows. "Sounds more likely to me. This is a critical stage right now. I need you to lie low and find out more about what Principal Sterns is planning and which teachers are involved."

Construction signs ahead, along with workers flagging them to decrease the car's speed, caused Odyssey to slow the station wagon to a shaking crawl.

She glanced over at Chase. "The closer the enemy gets to their goal, the more desperate they'll be to ensure their plans are carried out."

The car moved slowly through the construction zone as Chase looked out the window at the workers who were enduring the heat of the day. Some of them were wearing short sleeves with brightly colored safety vests. He wondered if they had put sunscreen on; otherwise, the scorching sun would burn their pasty-white skin brighter than the blaze-orange vests they wore. He sure was glad the junk car had air conditioning.

"Odyssey, there's one other thing. When I was walking through a downtown alley, I—"

Chase looked again at some of the workers they were passing. That's when it hit him: *The workers wearing short sleeves and safety vests had pasty white skin—so they were not accustomed to being in the sun. They were not construction workers at all!*

"Odyssey! This is a trap!" Chase yelled.

Her eyes darted to Chase, then to the rear-view mirror. Then Odyssey yelled, "Hang on!"

Her foot smashed the gas pedal, commanding the hunk of metal to spring forward. As the car shot forward towards a construction barrier, men who appeared to be construction workers only moments before threw down their picks and shovels and picked up machine guns. They began peppering the station wagon with bullets.

The car did not stop, as ordered by the sign in front of it. Instead, it rammed through the barrier with ferocious anger and careened forward. However, the road beyond the sign did not lead where Odyssey had hoped, and a dead-end cul-de-sac, surrounded by trees, forced her to pull the car to a stop.

Odyssey looked in the rearview mirror at their assailants, who were pursuing them on foot and running down the dirt road. She gave a half-smile and said, "Keep your head down!" Chase complied as she put the car in reverse and stepped on the gas pedal.

The tires smoked, kicking up dust as the vehicle tore backwards over its tracks. Bullets riddled the trunk and shattered the rear window. Odyssey did not take her foot off the gas, as the attackers now looked to get out of her path. But the car was surprisingly fast, and one by one, bodies slammed into the back of the car—some flying over, others sliding under.

Odyssey pushed on the brake pedal, and the car spun around. She meshed the gears forward and floored it. Dirt and rocks spit from the tires, and bullets continued to riddle the side of the car as it raced forward.

Unfortunately, the detour boxed the station wagon in. Concrete barriers on either side of the road forced the car to travel down a single path where, in the distance, a large tanker truck blocked the road. Getting out safely this time would be difficult.

Seeing a small opening between the concrete barriers and knowing their pursuers were behind them on foot at a bit of a distance, Odyssey slammed the car to a halt and popped the rear hatch of the car. "Your dirt bike's in the back! Get it and go… you can make it through that small opening right there."

"What about you?" Chase said as he jumped out.

"Don't worry about me! I can take care of myself, but not little boys. Now ride, and don't look back!"

Chase yanked out his dirt bike, leaped on, and began pedaling towards the opening Odyssey had pointed out. It was hard for him to think ahead with all the bullets being shot behind him.

Just when Chase wiggled his bike through the opening, he heard a loud roar of the car's engine. He looked back to see a bright flash, and the large *BOOM!* of an explosion. It knocked him to the ground.

Fire and debris flew towards him; Chase turned towards the ground and covered his head with his hands.

"Odyssey!" he screamed into the earth, right before he scrambled back up and onto his feet. He wanted to run back, find her in the wreckage, and pull her to safety. But it was too late—the area was destroyed. No one could have survived that deadly explosion—Odyssey was gone.

Alone all at once, he didn't know what to do. He wasn't sure if he had escaped undetected, or if his pursuers were still alive and searching for him. One thing he knew for certain—he had to leave the area!

With his ears still ringing from the explosion, he gave one last look at the wreckage of what had been the car and then turned to ride away. But a firm grip on his hair held him back and caused him to wince in pain.

Chase reached up to relieve the pressure, but the giant hand of a man dressed in construction attire shook him into submission. He gave Chase another fierce tug on the hair as Chase spied a figure lurking in the nearby shadows of the trees and brush.

"Well, what do we have here?" the shadow's voice said. "Little boys shouldn't be playing around construction sites—it's dangerous, and they might get hurt."

Chase recognized the voice as that from the alleyway. "Let me go!" Chase struggled not to think about his stinging scalp. "What do you want?"

"Me?" The figure moved closer to the light, revealing that the man was wearing a suit and tie. The face remained in the shadows. "I want peace and prosperity for all mankind, but we don't always get what we want, do we? Now, tell me, what are you up to?"

Chase bit his tongue. These were the same guys who had just killed Odyssey, and he wasn't about to tell them *anything*.

The shadow walked back and forth; glimmers of light brushed his figure, but his face and features were still concealed.

Chase yelled, "You killed Odyssey!"

"I did nothing of the sort—she did in her own self in. But tell me: Why were you involved with her anyway? What did she tell you?"

"Why would I tell you anything?" Chase growled.

"Because I'm on the right side of things… and you want to be on the right side—don't you?"

"I'm on Odyssey's side."

"And what makes you think she's on *yours*?"

"I just know—that's how," Chase mumbled defiantly.

"Well, I hate to be the one to tell you this, but—"

Click.

The sound of a gun's hammer cocking back caught everyone's attention.

"Let the boy go," said a woman in a familiar smoky tone.

"Odyssey," the man in the shadows said. "I'm so glad you made it. I was beginning to worry."

"I'm not in the best of moods right now. Because of you, I broke a nail. Now let the boy go," Odyssey snarled, giving a nod of her gun, which was aimed at the shadowed suit.

The shadow-faced figure nodded to the man, who was now holding a gun to Chase's head. He released his grasp on Chase's hair but followed Chase with his gun as Chase quickly ran over to be by a dirty and disheveled Odyssey.

"Gentlemen," she nodded, dismissing them. "It was a pleasure."

"One of these days, Odyssey, you're gonna find yourself on the wrong side of a bullet," the faceless man said.

"It's always better to be wanted than to be had," Odyssey said with a smile before she indicated Chase should walk with her back to his bike.

Chase swiftly mounted, and Odyssey stood on the bike's rear pegs, all the while aiming her gun at the two men. Then they were riding off again, into the woods and brush.

After a short while, Chase asked, "Agents of the other world?"

"You're a quick learner."

"I still don't know what they want."

"I told you—me dead." Odyssey's blonde hair flipped on Chase's face as she turned her head to look back behind them. "Which is why we are going to stop here, and you're going to ride on alone."

"But—" Chase protested as he slowed his bike.

"Listen, we'll meet again in a safe place when we have more time to talk." Odyssey stepped off the rear pegs and slipped her high heels back on. "Until then, keep up with your investigation, find out who else might be involved, and lie low. I'll give you a signal when it's time to act."

"How are you going to get out of here safely?"

"I'll be fine, kid; don't worry about me." Odyssey gave a look over her shoulder and then said to him, "Oh, I didn't have time to tell you, but I had some modifications done to your bike. I'll have to tell you about them later."

Before Chase could say anything back, Odyssey disappeared into the brush and trees.

Chase gave a look back at the smoke behind him and then rode for the secret tree-fort.

CHAPTER THIRTY

TEACHER OF THE YEAR

WHEN CHASE FINISHED telling his tale, Jax wiped her forehead and said, "Whew… for a moment there I thought you were going to make up some story about flying unicorns coming to your rescue… Oh, wait; excuse me—I meant flying *zombie alien* unicorns. Thank goodness it was the fictional character of Odyssey instead."

Chase gave her a flat expression in return.

Eduard asked, "So what did Odyssey say about you meeting the faceless guy in the alley earlier?"

"I didn't have time to tell her about that," Chase said.

Gio gave him a suspicious look. "Didn't have time or didn't want to?"

"That dude's obviously a problem," Chase said, waving his hands in the air to change the subject. "But right now, we need to concentrate on what Odyssey wants us to do, and that's to find out what and why all this is going on at our school, and the teachers who are involved." He pointed to me, asking, "What do our notes on the school tell us?"

I flipped open my journal and shrugged my shoulders. "It's haunted, has unreasonable teachers, has a mean principal who is in alliance with aliens disguised as cooks who are poisoning the kids and has grounds infested with zombies. What else do you need to know?"

Jax sighed. "I want practical explanations, and to not sit here and talk about zombies or zombie-chemical food. There are *no such things* as zombies."

Gio looked taken aback. "Then how do you explain the ground underneath our feet shaking?" he challenged. "Something was trying to claw its way to the surface!"

Eduard cleared his throat. "Could it have been an earthquake, a train, or an animal digging a burrow?"

"No, Eddie," Gio steadily answered in an annoyed tone. "It was the undead trying to get to the surface."

"It's *Eduard*—thank you very much, Giovanni. I'm not some dirty mechanic in your father's garage," Eduard huffed, clearly annoyed at Gio's choice of nickname.

"So, what about my dad's garage?" Gio bristled. "You got a problem with it?"

"What about Sheriff Graves?" I butted in, trying to keep our group focused. "He shot at something that night. What was it?"

Chase walked back and forth, nodding. "He might know more than he's letting on. If there is an alien-zombie infestation going on, he would likely want to keep it a secret. Otherwise, people might panic."

Jax showed her frustration once again. "What about coming up with some real reasons? Can we talk about some *real* possibilities instead?"

Chase looked at her briefly. "That's precisely what we're doing. We're trying to find out who else is involved." Chase walked with his hands behind his back, looking like Professor Wetherby. "Okay, the pawnshop tells us that Doyle was pawning items for money—why?"

I answered, "Seems to me he was collecting items to keep, rather than sell."

Eduard stuck his chin into the air. "Maybe he needed the money to invest, or to buy a new car, or—"

"Or because he owed somebody money," I interrupted. "We heard he lost a bet gambling, right? Maybe he lost to the Mafia, and he needed the money from the pawnshop to pay them off. I saw a Mafia movie, and they all wore suits—just like the guy in my mom's bar looking for Mr. Doyle!"

"I think Mr. Doyle losing a bet with the gambling ghost makes more sense," Gio answered. "It explains why he's missing. The ghost gets him in the mine as payment!"

"But it doesn't explain why Doyle needed money in the first place," I argued back.

Jax blinked quickly, as if to wake up. "This conversation can't really be happening, can it? Please stop talking like this."

Eduard cleared his throat. "The shopkeeper implied Mr. Doyle's pawned item had been collecting dust in *the basement*."

Jax raised her head before saying, "But we don't know if he meant Mr. Doyle's basement, or the school's."

"How we gonna find that out?" Gio threw his hands up in the air. "The shopkeeper won't tell us anything."

Chase nodded. "Good question. But we do have the mystery key we found near Doyle's car. If it opens the school's basement door instead of the bell tower door, it will confirm that Mr. Doyle was in the basement. It makes sense for Mr. Doyle to steal the antique mirror since he would know its value. And Doyle might have been trying to delay the expansion plans by messing with the electrical panels so that the historical nature of the building isn't compromised."

I picked up the mystery key and put it in my pocket. "I'll bring the key to school tomorrow, and we'll see if it fits the basement door. I wonder what else might be down there?"

"Zombies," Gio answered with a decisive nod of his head.

Jax regained her interest in our conversation. "Maybe Mr. Doyle needed money to buy a gift for his girlfriend—the one for whom he wrote a poem and intended to give flowers to?"

Chase nodded. "They were fresh when we found them—he intended to give them to someone that day."

Gio wasn't buying it. "Does he even *have* a girlfriend? Isn't he too old for that kind of thing?"

Jax said in a soft voice, "Love doesn't care about age."

I silently agreed with her poetic answer. She probably was referring to the two of us.

"And his flowers must have been for someone who likes… lilies?" Jax said, looking over at me. She knew I knew what she meant by that.

I interjected, "Miss Ivy does have lilies on her desk, but she couldn't be a part of this."

Gio cocked his head. "Unless she's eating the school's mind-controlling food," he suggested.

Chase followed this thought up with, "G's right. If Miss Ivy's been eating the school's food, she's probably been brainwashed. In fact, we need to find out everyone who's been eating the school's mind-controlling food. That way, we can classify them as brainwashed or not."

"What about the gray button?" I asked, trying to divert the attention away from the potential involvement of Miss Ivy, my favorite teacher. "We know it wasn't Doyle's, since he was wearing a white shirt that day."

"It's too common, and doesn't provide us with any leads," Chase said. "We'd have to know who was wearing a gray shirt that day. And we don't."

"What about the piece of paper with the map?" I asked. "It's like a pirate's map to buried treasure. And the formulas for the chemicals?"

Eduard straightened his shirt collar. "Why would someone want to bury or hide chemicals?"

Jax slammed down a pencil, eyes wide. "Yes! That's it—to cover up toxic waste! Of course… that's what's going on! Maybe Mr. Doyle knows something about a toxic waste cover-up, and the map leads to where it's located!"

"Or, Principal Sterns drew Mr. Doyle a map to set a trap for him, so aliens could abduct him," Gio quickly suggested.

"No, I'm serious! This is a real possibility we should look into," Jax insisted.

"Gio's right," Chase said. "The map seems to lead to Old Man Owens's fields, where cattle mutilations took place. Doyle may have stumbled onto their plans, and was taken by the aliens himself,"

"Why am I even here?" Jax said, clearly frustrated. I watched as she went back to doodling in her notebook.

"We need to find out who else knows something about the aliens," Chase said.

"You mean, find out who else knows about toxic waste," Jax corrected.

Chase walked around the fort, looking up at the holes in the roof. "We know Principal Sterns is involved somehow. Now we've got to find a way to interrogate the teachers without them suspecting we know something. We also need to find out from them who else doesn't like Mr. Doyle, and who else is brainwashed from school food."

Gio waved a cattail in the air like he was going to throw it. "They're not going to talk to us. We're just kids."

Jax looked up from her doodling. "But they might talk to the press!"

Eduard adjusted his glasses. "What do you mean? Are you suggesting we go to the press about this?"

"You could say that," Jax smirked. "It just so happens we have members of the press right here. Tomorrow, Oliver and I can interview some of the teachers for the school newspaper, like we did with Principal Sterns and Frank. If there is a toxic waste cover-up going on—"

"I love it!" Chase interrupted in a strong, matter-of-fact tone. "We'll find out what they know, what they'll confess to, and how they feel about Mr. Doyle. We also can ask if they are eating the school's food, so that later, we can classify them as brainwashed, or not brainwashed. It's a great idea."

Jax scoffed. "It's not a great idea to ask about aliens or brainwashed food. We need a *good* reason to conduct the interviews, like a toxic waste cover-up, and not your stupid paranormal questions. You're not a reporter anyway."

"You make a good point," Chase said, not taking offense. "We don't want them suspecting we know about Mr. Doyle's abduction and the alien invasion, so we'll have to interview them about something off-topic. Like, how about Mr. Doyle being nominated for *Teacher of the Year?* That will allow us to ask all the teachers questions about how they feel about Mr. Doyle, and then somehow ask whether or not they eat the school's food."

Jax folded her arms and scowled. "But there's no such award! That's deceptive! It goes against the ethics of journalism."

"Sure there is," Chase said as he opened his hands. "We just created it… and I nominate Mr. Doyle."

Jax shook her head. "But—"

Chase waved her off before she could say anything else; he was on a roll. "They don't know what we know—so by acting like we don't know; they won't know we're finding out what they know."

Eduard scratched his head. "But what happens if Mr. Doyle comes back?"

Chase shrugged and resumed pacing. "Then he wins *Teacher of the Year*—he'd deserve it anyway, after escaping from aliens."

Jax sighed. "How about asking some questions about the history of the school—it could be a way to find out from the teachers if they know about any toxic chemicals in the school's past?" She drew a line under her doodles and made a few bullet points. "I'll create a list of questions for the interviews about the history of the school and toxic waste. I'll also use the school's library to do some research on the school itself. Maybe I can find something out."

Eduard stuck his neck forward to offer his idea. "And I can use the library's computers to research the faculty member's history and do background checks on them. I can find out if any of them have criminal records."

"Perfect! We'll begin spreading the word about Mr. Doyle's nomination and start asking questions." Chase placed his hands on his head. "Oliver, bring the mystery key tomorrow, and we'll find out if it fits the basement door. That will confirm if Mr. Doyle was stealing from the basement."

I patted my pocket with the key. "I've got it."

"Don't forget it," Gio followed with a high-pitched squeak.

CHAPTER THIRTY-ONE

BLOOD AND MUD

I WOKE UP that next morning not knowing what to expect. The world had changed for me, and I was changing with it. A world I couldn't see but knew was out there. A world filled with danger, evil, and good. My uncle had once told me, *"When adversity finds you, you find yourself."* I think adversity might have found—a superhero.

I had a mission today. It might involve saving the world, my neighborhood, my school, or maybe just my grades—I wasn't sure which. So, I made sure to eat a hearty breakfast to provide me with sustenance for the day. Then I checked my front pants pocket once again, to make sure that I hadn't forgotten the mystery key.

I was wearing my best shirt and pants. I would be seeing Jax, and I was eagerly anticipating our many conversations throughout the day. Despite my birthmark's attempts to thwart our blooming relationship, things were going better than expected, and I wanted to make sure they continued on course. Jax would notice my attire rather than my birthmark; I'm sure of it.

After my annoying, boring walk with Adam to his bus stop, I jumped onto Gio's bike and began my commute to school. I could feel myself changed somehow. I knew I was different—more grown up. I'd probably have to start shaving soon, and I began wondering what kind of razors and shaving cream I'd need—and aftershave lotion, of course.

The dirt road gave way to the paved main road. I picked up speed and relaxed. I was on time this morning, which allowed me to enjoy my ride and think about Jax and our new adventure together.

Nothing could bring me down. That was, until I saw the three skateboards by the side of the road—complete with riders full of bad intentions.

I coasted like I hadn't a care in the world—as if I didn't see Johnny Ricker, Miles, and stupid Albert Gonzales all fixated on me. As I passed them, I found the evil smile of Johnny with a corner of my eye. Involuntarily, I picked up my pace.

They started following me—and gaining ground quickly. I pedaled hard—then frantically. A hill was slowing me down.

Johnny was fast on his board, and I could hear his wheels on the pavement behind me getting louder.

"Where do you think you're go'n, Freak Face?" he yelled.

I was still a far distance from the school. I knew they would catch up with me. I had to think of a plan.

If only there was an open manhole around, I thought. *I could jump over it at the last moment while they fell in and then cover it back up until next summer.*

But there was none to be found.

I looked to the side of the road, seeing the creek embankment. *Ahh, I could jump the creek like Chase did when escaping the agents of the other world*, I thought.

It was the perfect plan: they would wreck in the creek, and I would proceed on my way to school—victorious.

I steered Gio's bike off the paved road into the brush. I looked back: Johnny and his friends were slowing to dismount their boards and pursue me on foot. The creek was in my sight, and so I picked up speed. Like Chase, I had never jumped over a creek before—or anything, for that matter. But I knew I could do it... I *had* to.

As I approached the embankment, my muscles flexed, my grip tightened, my knees bent, and the muscles in my legs coiled. The creek's edge arrived at once, and I tried to see how far to the other side it was, but there was no time.

I leaped up, extending my body and neck out, soaring... for all of a half-second before descending towards the earth. Gio's bike smashed into the opposite side of the embankment, throwing me forward face-first into the dirt and mud.

"Wha—hoo-hoo! Ha-ha-ha! Freak Face dumped it hard!" Johnny whooped.

"Look what a mess! Ah-ha-ha!" Miles laughed.

"You're a loser, Freak Face! Ah-ha-ha!" screeched Albert.

This was a complete disaster, and I was a complete wreck. The mud had ruined the nice attire I had worn for Jax. My pants were soaked all around my butt, looking as if I had wet them.

"We'd help ya out of there, but we gotta go. Can't be late. See ya at school, Freak Face. Ha-ha-ha," Johnny laughed before he and his cronies strode away.

I pulled myself, and Gio's bike, out of the deep muddy embankment. I sighed heavily: Instead of saving my life, crossing the embankment had almost taken it.

I looked over Gio's bike, and grimaced: The front forks were completely bent, making the bike unrideable. I would have to walk the rest of the way, push the bike along, and be late for school.

My confidence was lost—flowing somewhere down the creek. Next time, I'd look for an open manhole.

I almost turned around and went home, but I was needed in school today for a much bigger purpose. So, I sucked it up and continued on. I felt the gargoyles watching me as I approached the school. A part of me wanted them to spring to life and snatch me away so I didn't have to deal with the humiliation.

I chained Gio's bent bike to the rack as I looked around the empty school grounds. It was quiet, as all the students and teachers were in class. I looked to the teacher's parking lot: the white work van was there, but not the repairmen. I walked up the stone steps, and then through the massive oak doors that were now closed for the start of school.

What can I tell Miss Crabtree? I wondered. *Surely, she'd understand that I was being chased and fell into the creek, and that's why I'm late—wouldn't she?*

I opened the door to her classroom about ten minutes after the start of class. Heads popped up as students looked up from reading their books.

"Oliver?" Miss Crabtree looked over her fashion glasses from her desk. "Why are you tardy?"

"Sorry… I… um…" I mumbled, at a loss for words.

"My goodness, young man! Your forehead, your clothes—what on earth happened to you?"

I reached up and felt blood on my forehead. I must have been cut and not realized it. "Uh… well… I had an accident on my bike on the way to school," I said, not knowing how to answer.

"Off to the nurse's office with you! That cut needs to be taken care of right away," Miss Crabtree ordered.

Chase shot me a concerned look from his seat. I shrugged and turned to walk down the hallway to the nurse.

I turned a corner and almost collided with one of the cooks.

His arms were completely full of sacks. I must have startled him too, because he gave me a look of surprise before his usual frown returned, and he hurried past me to the kitchen. In the distance, I saw that the basement door was slightly cracked open; had he just come from there?

I stared at the door for a few moments, knowing I had the key that we suspected fit the lock. *Could I just walk over to the door and stick the key in?* I wouldn't be opening it, because it was already cracked open. I would just be seeing if the key fit.

I strolled to the basement door and reached in my pocket for the key. I noticed there was no light coming from the slight crack of the opening—it was pitch black behind the door. I was only a few feet from the opening when a breeze behind my back flicked my hair. My eyes darted side to side—and that's when I saw it.

A flash of white passed by me and went right into the dark black slit of the cracked doorway. *Did I just see what I saw?* I wondered.

Then, a soft whisper or moan rose from the basement, and the door slammed shut before my eyes. I became so scared; it was as if electricity had shot through my body!

A low voice from behind made me jump.

"Hey! What ya do'n?"

I turned to see two of the repairmen standing behind me. The tall younger man, Finnegan—the one who had run over Nick's football and chased me through the parking lot before grabbing my shoe—gave me a suspicious look. *Was he trying to recognize me from somewhere?* He was pushing a two-wheel hand truck that was carrying two green metal tanks.

"You supposed to be wandering around here?" Finnegan asked.

I kept my head down, gulped hard, and said, "I'm a new kid here, and looking for the nurse's office."

"Are you?" He looked at my face, then at my shoes.

Lucky for me, I was wearing my old pair of sneakers since he had one of my new sneakers.

"Yes, they told me it was down this way," I said, shifting my face to conceal my birthmark.

Finnegan looked over at the basement door. "You're not trying to steal anything from the basement, are you?"

The dark-skinned repairman named Santos, carrying an electrical cord over his shoulder, looked at me and asked softly, in an accented voice, "What happened to you, child? You're a mess."

"I fell—I need to go to the nurse's office," I answered, my voice shaking for real. I was more afraid they were about to recognize me from the road with Mr. Doyle's car than from getting hurt on Gio's bike.

"It's down that way, kid. Wandering the halls will only get you in trouble," Finnegan growled. He grabbed the handle to the basement and shook it. "Great! The door's locked!" He glared at me. "Did you shut this door?" he accused.

With my head down, I quickly shook my head no.

As I walked for the office, I heard Finnegan continue to grumble. "I left a wedge in this door so we could get in and out. Now, we've got to find Frank to open it, and who knows where he is!"

"Relax, we will find him," Santos said, his voice still gentle.

I looked back to see them watching me. I turned my head away quickly.

Drat! By my turning around, they just got a good look at my face and probably recognized me. Can my morning get any worse? Now, if anything from the basement is found missing, I'm going to be blamed.

When I arrived at the main office, Miss Hathaway looked up over her glasses, which were perched on the end of her nose. "What happened here, young man?"

"I… I was riding my bike to school, and I fell down and cut my head, and I ruined my clothes."

"Oh, heavens! Go right in and see Nurse Jenny," she puckered.

Nurse Jenny's office was near Principal Sterns' office, and his door was half-open. I strolled by and glanced in. I saw Sterns talking with Frank, and I overheard a bit of their conversation.

"Everything's ready?" the principal asked. "Are you sure?"

"Yes," answered Frank. "I'll have someone on the premises to deal with any problems, but we are one-hundred percent ready to go."

"We can't afford any failures—this needs to go smoothly," Principal Sterns said.

"It will," Frank answered as he turned to walk out.

I quickly went into Nurse Jenny's office so he wouldn't see me.

"Oh my, what have we here?" Nurse Jenny said, then stood from her chair. "Looks like we have a boy who fell from his bicycle, maybe?"

"Yes, and I hit my head," I said, my voice continuing to shake. My eyes welled with tears. It had been a tough morning. "Do you think I need to go home?"

"Well, let's have a look," she said softly.

Nurse Jenny was nice. She sat me down and looked into my eyes while asking me questions like, "How many fingers am I holding up?" and "What's your address?" Easy enough questions.

At that point, Nurse Jenny wiped and cleaned my forehead, then gave me a smile. "Looks like you're gonna live. Now go to the boy's bathroom and get cleaned up. Off you go now."

I thanked her, and then cautiously made my way back down the hall to the boy's bathroom. There were no repairmen around anymore, and I sighed with relief.

In the bathroom, there wasn't much I could do with my clothes except wipe the mud off my shirt and pants, which were almost dry by now. Stupid Johnny Ricker would get what's coming to him—I knew he would—but I wanted it to be today. Still, I told myself, *just forget about what happened and go on with my day of saving the world.*

I was combing my hair in the mirror when I saw the face of a boy behind me—staring at me. I spun around, but there was no one there.

I looked back into the mirror and saw nothing. *Was I crazy?* I thought. *There had been a boy there looking, looking directly at me with weird-looking eyes… Charlie Hackett?*

Fear tore through me, and I ran out of the boy's bathroom like I had just seen a ghost—which I had.

When I raced out, I almost ran into the same cook as a little earlier; this time, he was empty-handed, with no sacks in his arms. He looked at me with a frown, so I put my head down and skirted around him. I entered Miss Crabtree's math class, breathing hard.

Miss Crabtree looked up from her silver compact mirror. "Everything all right, Oliver?"

"Yes, I… I just wanted to get back as soon as I could! I didn't want to miss any more math."

I couldn't believe that actually came out of my mouth.

"Now that's what I want to hear! Oliver, go open your book to page sixty-four and get started reading. We are about to discuss these problems."

I took the empty seat next to Chase, who looked at me sideways and whispered, "What happened?"

"Long story, but I've got new info—"

"Oliver?" Miss Crabtree interrupted our conversation and clapped her hands. "Why aren't you opening your book? Let's go; you're already behind."

"Yes, Miss Crabtree. Sorry."

I opened my torture book to the page of pain as instructed, but my mind drifted off some place else—someplace where Jax and I were sitting, discussing our theories on Mr. Doyle's disappearance and Odyssey, and what we were going to do next. Then I thought about the face I had seen in the mirror, the whisper near the school's basement doorway, and the door slamming shut.

Everyone might think I was crazy, but I saw what I saw, and I heard what I heard.

Miss Crabtree walked around the room, handing out a set of papers. "Now, I know all of you have been studying over the weekend, so I expect you all to do well on this surprise test. The results will be black-and-white in terms of revealing if you understand this material or not, and where any deficiencies lie."

Looking down at equations that looked like hieroglyphics to me, I knew I was in trouble. I had not studied this past weekend for this test—how could I while saving the world? I'm sure Miss Crabtree wouldn't give extra credit for that either, and I could hear her now, *"Numbers don't care about your saving the world."* So, I tried to save as many answers as I could—but there was only so much of me to go around.

Time was up with the end-of-class bell. Chase and I walked up to Miss Crabtree's desk together to turn in our tests.

"Miss Crabtree, could we speak to you for a moment?" Chase asked unexpectedly.

She was placing a stack of papers in her briefcase and did not look up at us. "If you're looking for any leniency on your test today, it's not up to me. The numbers will be grading your test," she responded in a sharp tone.

"No… it's about Mr. Doyle," Chase said.

"Mr. Doyle? What now?" she said in an annoyed tone.

"The school newspaper has nominated him for *Teacher of the Year*, and we—"

Miss Crabtree stopped what she was doing and looked up. "Teacher of the Year?" she said, cutting Chase off. With sarcasm dripping from her lips, she continued, "You mean the same

Mr. Doyle, who is *not in class today?* Well, by all means, why not? Why would you ever nominate a teacher who actually teaches something useful, like math?!"

"You don't like Mr. Doyle?" Chase prompted.

"He's a perfect choice for this school. Fits perfectly with everything else," she snarled, shoving some papers into her briefcase. "I guess one needs to bring the President here to get recognized—although I'm not sure if even that would do me any good." She slammed her briefcase shut. "Maybe I'll work my magic to bring him here next time."

"Is the President going to be sitting in on any of your classes—like he is Miss Lexington's?"

"Miss Lexington? Who's that?" she questioned, arching her eyebrows.

"Our history and political science teacher... you know—Mr. Doyle's substitute. She's very excited to meet him."

"Mm-hmm... I'm sure she is." Miss Crabtree pressed her lips together. "A substitute is just that—a *substitute,* and not the real thing. If someone wants a substitute to meet the head of our country, then...." She paused, shook her head, and took a deep breath. "We are *all* going to meet the President, I am told, while attending the assembly in the gymnasium for him. But no, he won't be sitting in on this class—not that math is any less important."

The next class straggled into the classroom, so Chase cut right to the point. "When was the last time you saw Mr. Doyle?"

"I don't pay attention to the other teachers in this school. I'm focused on my teaching of math and my students. Anything else?"

Chase looked at me, and I swallowed before I asked, "Um... ah... well, do you eat the school's food, or do you bring your lunch?"

"Do you have to ask?" she spit out.

Her icy glare stifled my desire to ask any other questions. Clearly, it was time to leave.

Chase and I ran through the hall, then hurried down the stone steps to Professor Wetherby's science classroom. Right outside the room, we recapped what we had just heard.

"She wasn't too happy about Doyle's nomination for *Teacher of the Year*, was she?" I said.

"Nope," Chase shook his head. "I'd say she's definitely a Doyle hater."

"But does she have anything to do with the aliens?" I asked.

"She's not eating the school food, is she? Mark her down as an *alien ally*."

CHAPTER THIRTY-TWO

PUTTING THE PROFESSOR UNDER THE MICROSCOPE

WITH HIS BACK to the class, Professor Wetherby was writing an equation on the blackboard while holding a pen in his mouth. He was wearing a long white lab coat over a dress shirt and his trademark bow tie.

Chase and I headed towards the back of the classroom, where Gio and Eduard sat waiting for us.

Johnny Ricker and Miles aimed spitball straws at my face, but this time I was ready. I quickly held up my notebook, blocking the slimy wads of tissue they spat at me. *Ha,* I thought, *I'm really getting this superhero thing down, blocking their stupid goon attacks with my quick reflexes.*

I pulled down my notebook and gave a smug grin in their direction, only to be hit directly in the forehead with the largest spitball of all. It made my head snap back, and my eyes blink. The classroom erupted with laughter. Professor Wetherby continued writing on the blackboard, oblivious to the atrocities going on in his classroom.

I took my seat next to Gio, who too was trying not to laugh. I knew he hated Johnny and Miles as much as I did, but I must have looked pretty silly after being hit. He gave me a reassuring nod and said, "Stupid Ricker. He'll get what's coming to him." Gio's look turned concerned as he noticed my mud-stained clothes, and he asked, "What happened to you?"

"Oh…" I looked down. "Well, um, I had a little accident on your bike, um, but I think it's fixable," I apologetically said.

"Small deal," Gio said with a shrug. "We can take a look at it during recess."

With just a few moments before the start-of-class bell, Chase and I quickly told Gio and Eduard what Miss Crabtree said. When the professor finished his thoughts on the blackboard, he turned to the class and removed the pen from his mouth so he could talk.

"Good morning, ladies and gentlemen. So good of you to come."

As if we had a choice.

"Today, we will study the intricacies of biology—unlocking the codes of life!"

Chase raised his hand and asked, "Professor, what would alien life be made of?"

"Aliens? Uh… well, protoplasm most likely—the living colorless substance surrounding the nucleus of a cell. All living things are made of at least one cell—and that, young man, gives me the perfect lead-in into today's topic!" The professor began pacing the floor in front of the class. "*Cells* are microscopic units that come together to carry out specific functions—from the simplest singular cell life forms to the most complex."

Johnny Ricker was a simple, single-cell life form, I thought. *One mean, vile, single cell.*

Professor Wetherby excitedly drew diagrams on his blackboard and seemed to speak an unfamiliar language.

"Here we have the nucleus of a cell, surrounded by the nuclear membrane… and endoplasmic reticulum and ribosomes used to build proteins. Lysosomes filled with enzymes, mitochondria—"

The cells in my body drifted off. It was hard to concentrate on any subject other than saving the world at this point. My mind stepped back and forth—into class, and then out again. Finally, the end-of-class bell rang.

Professor Wetherby stopped speaking his foreign language and said, "So ends our lecture today on biology. Physics and cosmology tomorrow, ladies and gentlemen—be prepared!"

As the classroom emptied of students, Chase, Eduard, Gio, and I walked over to Professor Wetherby. He was already writing on his beloved blackboard and had his back to us.

Chase interrupted the professor's writing. "Excuse us, Professor. Would you mind if we ask you a few questions?"

"Of course not!" Professor Wetherby turned to us with his pen sticking from his mouth. "We must always ask questions… questions lead to answers."

"Great," I said, taking my lead from Chase. "I'm the editor of the school's newspaper, and the staff on the paper have nominated Mr. Doyle for *Teacher of the Year*. Could you give us your thoughts?"

"Oh? I had no idea he had been nominated! Wonderful. He deserves it." Professor Wetherby began chewing on the end of his pen. "Mr. Doyle is quite competent when it comes to history. His students achieve high grades, which speaks to his teaching abilities. I believe he is a suitable candidate for this award."

"Would you say there are any negatives to our choice of Mr. Doyle?" I probed.

"His propensity for risk, perhaps," the professor answered.

"Why? Is he a risky person?" I asked.

"Well… let's just say he has a certain deficit of judgment that often leads to ruinous results," the professor hedged.

"Do you know his whereabouts?" I asked.

"Whoabouts?" the professor questioned, clearly confused.

"Mr. Doyle—do you know where he is?" I clarified.

"No, I can't say that I do," Professor Wetherby said.

"When was the last time you saw him?" I asked.

"I would say… last Friday—yes, last Friday," the professor said.

Chase jumped in here. "The same day you were seen arguing with him?"

Professor Wetherby looked a bit puzzled by Chase's words. "That discussion is of no concern of yours."

"It *is* a concern, seeing he's been missing for several days now," Chase quickly shot back.

"I… I would not have been arguing with him if it were not for his gross negligence in using my equations," the professor answered, seeming somewhat unsettled.

"What equations?" Eduard asked curiously.

"One can formulate an equation based on a known set of variables, and the pattern experience of such, thereby giving a high degree of probability of predicting an outcome. I told Mr. Doyle such an equation would give him the best chance of doing so, but by no means would it predict the future, given the uncertainties of his variables."

I looked surprised. "He was trying to predict the future?"

"Aren't we all? But is it the future or the past? That is the real question," the professor said.

His answer made my head spin.

"Now, if you'll excuse me, I have a class to teach." Wetherby turned and began writing on his blackboard once again.

"How did you get that burn on your arm?" Gio asked, a little loudly.

"Oh, that?" Professor Wetherby looked down at a red mark on his arm and rolled down his sleeve. "From an experiment—it's a nasty chemical burn. I should have been wearing protective clothing on my arms."

Chase asked, "One more question: do you eat the school's food, or do you bring your lunch?"

"I don't eat lunch."

The professor stuck the end of his pen in his mouth and returned to his blackboard. We all left for our next classes with new questions after I marked down in my journal:

Professor Wetherby — alien ally.

CHAPTER THIRTY-THREE

A BAD APPLE

JAX WAS WAITING for us just outside of Mr. Doyle's classroom. She looked curiously at my soiled clothing from this morning.

I winced inside, but met her glance with a casual shrug. "I was jumping the creek this morning on a bike, but I jumped too high. No big deal."

Chase, Jax, and I walked into the room together. Chase took his seat while Jax gave me a concerned smile and asked in a barely audible voice, "Did you interview any of the teachers this morning and find out anything about toxic waste? Please tell me Chase didn't ask about aliens or ghosts."

I pulled my mouth to the side and answered vaguely, "We tried to ask as much as we could, but we didn't find out anything concrete yet on toxic waste. How 'bout you—did you find out anything?"

"I researched the topic in the school's library this morning before the start of school and was able to look a few things up. But I'm gonna need more time," she said.

The bell rang, and Jax took a seat next to Chase—which should have been mine—in the front of the classroom. So, I made my way back to the peanut gallery to sit next to Miss *Three-Name.*

Something was different in the classroom today. By the chalkboard, there was a mannequin dressed in army fatigues and wearing a gas mask. A sign around its neck read, *First World War.*

The class was abuzz about the display: *Is our sub going to give us a hands-on lecture about the First World War? Are we going to get a chance to try on that mask? Maybe she'll bring in a tank next, or have a field trip to see a fighter jet? This class is going to be awesome. Boring Mr. Doyle would never have held such an interesting and engaging class!*

As I sat down, I thought about our substitute, Miss Lexington. Not only didn't she have the long, dry tone of Mr. Doyle, but she was cheerful, beautiful, and most of all, *she didn't know who Ana Rahela was.* Miss Lexington was quickly becoming my favorite teacher. And if only she had found my pocket watch, she would already be.

Ana Rahela Balenovic, however, didn't like her at all: "Oliver, do you think our substitute teacher is a little weird?"

"Not a bit. In fact, I think she's the best teacher in this school," I said back with a slight smirk.

"It's just... it's like she's not an expert on historical affairs—like Mr. Doyle."

"Uh—yeah, she is... I'll bet you she knows ten times more than Mr. Doyle."

At that moment, Miss Lexington walked around the room, calling attendance while handing back the quiz she gave us last week. When she called my name, she handed me mine with a smile.

"Good job, Oliver. But I think you could do even better next time," she said, winking at me.

I smiled back and then looked down at the results of my quiz. I could barely make out that I had received a "C" because my quiz was covered in black smudges.

What had she done with my paper—run it through the dirt cycle in her grading machine? Or maybe Miss Lexington was eating a chocolate bar while grading—after all, who doesn't like chocolate? Nevertheless, getting a "C" wasn't bad for guessing on half the quiz, I thought.

Ana Rahela turned to me and asked, "May I see your paper?"

"No," I said, trying to ignore her.

"Look at mine," she said, showing me her quiz displaying her A+.

"So what? I got a B+," I said back, hiding my paper from her view. "I could have gotten an A, but I accidentally marked a few wrong."

"No… does your paper have these black marks?" she said, pointing to the marks on her paper.

"Yes, it's like her chocolate bar stuck to everything, but…."

Then it hit me: *These weren't chocolate marks—these were smudge marks from my pocket watch! Maybe Miss Lexington has found my watch!* I knew I'd have to tell Chase about this after class.

After Miss Lexington had finished handing back Friday's tests, she asked the class, "How was everyone's weekend? Did anyone do anything spectacular? Are you all prepared for the President's visit tomorrow?"

Ana Rahela raised her hand. "Excuse me, Miss Lexington. Speaking of preparing for the President's visit, would you like me to read my essay that won the national contest—the reason the President is visiting this school?"

"Why, what a wonderful idea," Miss Lexington smiled, waving Ana Rahela Balenovic to the front of the classroom.

Was there no end to Ana Rahela Balenovic's attention-seeking? Wasn't it enough that her name was all over the school, the newspapers, and the television? Could anyone really forget the President was visiting because of her? Was I the only one on the planet who didn't think her essay was that good?

Full of fake bashfulness, Ana Rahela Balenovic went to the front of the classroom. She acted as though she didn't want to read her essay but was being forced to.

The entire class sat quietly, ready to hear the toxic waste that would come from her paper. I gave a swift look into my backpack to check for earplugs, but found none.

Softly clearing her throat, she began with a smile. "*I'm Thankful to be an American*—by Ana Rahela Balenovic—that's me."

I about fell out of my chair. *Yes, we all know you wrote that stupid essay, and we all know your three names. What else are you going to reveal to us? That you live in the United States?*

I felt ill.

"I thank God every day to be an American. I am thankful to live in a country so beautiful, for its spacious skies, where freedom rings from every purple mountainside to the prairies, and to the oceans white with foam. I couldn't say that years ago, nor would I have been allowed to. You see, the country I came from didn't allow anyone to worship anything except the government. My parents escaped to America from war and oppressors who jailed and tortured people.

"I'm thankful to now live in the land of the free and home of the brave; a country that stands up and protects me. A country where sleep is taken for granted. The country where I came from, I never knew if I would wake up in the morning, or what the next day would bring.

"I'm thankful to now live in a country which God crowned with brotherhood. Where people with different beliefs get along with one another, where no bombs are exploding, guns firing, or people screaming and dying in the streets.

"I'm thankful to now live in a country whose broad stripes and bright stars stand above all people and hold them accountable with blind justice; a nation of laws—not of men or political affiliation.

"I'm thankful I now live where opportunity for every person stretches from sea to shining sea, no matter their background, social status, skin color, or religious belief. The sweet land of liberty, where prosperity is restricted only by a person's desire and work ethic.

"I'm thankful for the fruited plains and amber waves of grain; the land of plenty, instead of a land where food is scarce and medicine only for the privileged.

"Someday, the world will change to be more like The United States of America, and I hope I can help it change. I love this country, the greatest nation on earth, and I'm blessed to be a citizen of the U.S.A.—may God continue to shed his grace on thee. God Bless America—now my home sweet home."

Ana Rahela Balenovic gave a curtsy as the class gave its obligatory claps. I kept my hands on my desk, eagerly waiting for the fake applause to subside.

Miss Lexington interrupted the applause. "That's the essay that won you the contest, little girl?"

"Yes," Ana Rahela answered, sounding unsure.

"Hmm. I don't mean to be critical, but your essay is way off-base," Miss Lexington critiqued.

"What?" Ana Rahela Balenovic looked as if a trash truck had just driven over her. "But… but it won."

"Yes. Yes, it did, which is what's wrong with this country," the substitute said.

"But… but… I don't understand." Ana Rahela now looked as if she was going to cry.

"First off, your paper is not only poorly written and lacks creativity, but it is factually wrong. The United States is not the greatest nation on earth… unless you mean the greatest polluter. The reality is, it's the most greedy and self-serving nation on the earth. But the greatest in terms of being magnificent? No, not at all. Every nation that believes itself above others will fail."

Miss Lexington walked up to Ana Rahela and placed a hand on her shoulder. "Now, little girl, you can still change the world, but you need to quit this nonsense of believing that this nation is better than all others—because it's not. It's time to take your seat."

Ana Rahela walked down the row of chairs to her seat with her head down.

Ha-ha-ha. All her showboating finally backfired in her face.

Miss Lexington was officially my favorite teacher now… well, tied with Miss Ivy, anyway.

Ana Rahela whispered to me, "This lady's crazy, Oliver! My father warned me there were teachers like her. He said they'd try to fill my head with all kinds of nonsense."

"Oh, I don't know. I think she had some good points. And she's right; your writing wasn't that good," I said as loftily as Eduard might.

"Oliver! I'm serious," she scolded.

"So am I."

Ana Rahela folded her arms, furrowed her brow, and with a big frown, finally shut her big mouth and allowed me to listen to our wonderful instructor.

"Class, let's talk about what's going on in the world right now." Miss Lexington took up some chalk and drew on the blackboard. "Americans constitute 5% of the world's population but consume 24% of the world's energy. Quite a wasteful nation, aren't we? The earth right now desperately needs our help, and desperate times call for desperate action. We need to be the solution and not the problem."

Ana Rahela Balenovic decided to stop our lovely substitute's brilliant teaching to ask a stupid question: "Miss Lexington, I thought we were going to be studying history—the presidency, and how this country came into itself?"

"Yes, of course we need to discuss how we got into this mess we're in now—good point." Miss Lexington answered. "You all noticed this mannequin here, dressed in a uniform and wearing this gas mask? The gas mask is from one of our world wars—wars that used chemical weapons, and those toxins still pollute the earth *to this day.* It's a bit of shameful history you won't learn from reading in your textbooks, but it's true: this country used chemical weapons indiscriminately on this earth. Not something we should be proud of. Can any of you imagine a world where we all would have to wear a mask like this all day, every day? I hope not. But we all will need help breathing if we don't help change this Earth and this nation's oppressive government."

She walked over to her desk and picked up her small inhaler, saying, "Some of us already need help breathing, with all the toxic pollution spilling into the air."

Miss Lexington placed the inhaler on her mouth and took a deep breath.

Ana Rahela raised her hand and spoke up. "But my father and mother came from a country that was oppressed. We moved here, to the United States of America, for freedom."

Miss Lexington pulled the canister away from her mouth, and with a surprised look, said, "You mean freedom to destroy the Earth? This country has much to learn from countries like the one your parents must have come from," Miss Lexington said as she walked towards Ana Rahela. "Now, I know this is a hard truth to hear, but we can't just learn about all the great things about our nation's history. We also must learn the bad, sometimes uncomfortable truths of our past. I hope you take the time to learn the accurate history of this country. If you don't, well, there's a saying,

'Those who fail to learn history… fail… this class and have to repeat it.' Or something like that," she said, sending a frown in Ana Rahela's direction.

Miss Lexington smiled at the rest of the class as the end-of-class bell rang.

Well said, Miss Lexington, I thought to myself. *Well said.*

As class let out, I quickly made my way by the dejected Ana Rahela Balenovic. I caught up to Jax and Chase, who were arguing some point as they walked out of the room.

Chase was saying to Jax, "These interviews prove what we've been suspecting about the school's food—they're not eating it, and they all have problems with Mr. Doyle."

Jax shook her head. "So stupid, Chase. I gave you some questions to ask about the history of this school and toxic waste, and this is what you guys do? Even our substitute is talking about toxic waste, and she's only been here since Mr. Doyle's been missing. Oh, do what you want!" she sputtered, clearly frustrated. "I've got my own research I'm doing."

"Did you two look at your quiz?" I interrupted.

"Yes. And I'm not happy I didn't get an A," Jax huffed. "I'm gonna go to the office and talk with Miss Hathaway now. I'll catch up with you guys at lunch."

Jax hurried off down the hall.

"Don't eat the cook's food!" Chase yelled after her.

Jax flung a glance back over her shoulder at him and rolled her eyes.

"Chase!" I shoved my quiz paper in his face. "Look!"

"I see, I see," he said. "You got a 'C'—good job."

"No, no. The smudge marks! The smudge marks from my pocket watch—they're on everyone's papers," I explained quickly. "*The sub* must have found my pocket watch!"

He looked at his own quiz, then back to mine. "Yes, yes, they are," he agreed. Chase pulled out his magnifying glass and examined my paper more closely. "Yes, these are definitely smudge marks! And the fingerprints that made them are completely visible. You're right—she must have found your pocket watch!"

His confirmation of my discovery made me smile.

Chase and I spun about and charged back into class, where the substitute teacher was sitting at her desk.

Chase asked politely, "Miss Lexington, did anyone turn in Oliver's pocket watch, or did you happen to find it?"

"No, I'm sorry," she frowned. "I haven't seen a pocket watch. But I'll keep an eye out for it."

"Oh..." Chase said, before giving me a sympathetic look. "Well, thanks, and please let us know if you do come across it."

My shoulders dropped with my frown. I felt helpless once again.

So much for my apprentice detective skills.

Chase gave me a quick pat on my back as we walked back out. "Sorry, Ollie. For a minute there, I thought she found it too."

"But she has to have it," I whined. "The smudge marks are from my watch!"

"Are you sure? Maybe the smudges are from something else?"

"No, I'm sure they're from my watch," I whined again. "She has to be lying."

"Unless..." Chase paused as an idea came into his head. "Ollie, do you have an apple in your pack?"

"Yeah, why?" I said, wondering if he was hungry.

"Awesome. Let me have it," he said, smiling.

I reached into my pack and pulled out my apple, then gave it to Chase. He wiped it off with his shirttail and then walked back into the classroom.

Why did he wipe it off? I didn't have cooties.

"Miss Lexington," Chase said as he tried to pull the apple from his shirt, looking like he was trying not to touch it. "Please accept this apple in appreciation of the great job you're doing here at the school."

As Chase handled the apple with his shirttail, the apple fumbled onto, and then off, her desk. Miss Lexington quickly snatched it out of the air with cat-like reflexes before it fell to the ground.

"Thank you. What a kind gesture," she said, smiling.

"Oh-no!" Chase exclaimed, scooping the apple back up from her with his shirttail. "It has a worm in it!"

Miss Lexington looked surprised as Chase quickly but carefully tucked the apple back in his shirt.

Chase gave her a shrug. "I'm so sorry—I'll bring you another tomorrow."

"That's quite all right," she chuckled. "It was a nice thought. Thank you."

Chase and I raced out of her sight before I asked him, "What was that about? My apple doesn't have a worm in it."

"I wanted to get her fingerprints on this apple," he said.

"Why?"

"She says she doesn't have your pocket watch, but if her prints on this apple match the ones on our papers, then she's lying—she has your pocket watch."

"But what if her prints don't match?"

"Then she's telling the truth—she doesn't have it, and whoever handled these papers not only has your pocket watch, but also knows what happened to Mr. Doyle!"

"Can you get her prints off my apple?" I asked.

"Of course," he said casually. "I'll bring my fingerprint analysis tools to the tree-fort after school."

I smiled once again. He really was a detective, and I was his apprentice.

CHAPTER THIRTY-FOUR

A SMACK IN THE FACE

OUR GYM CLASS was being held outside because the gymnasium was being transformed into an auditorium for the President's visit the next day.

Coach let us play kickball in the scorching sun. Kickball is played just like baseball, only with no bats. A pitcher rolls a big rubber ball to a kicker, who kicks it into the outfield, and rather than touching the runners as they round the bases, the outfielders throw the ball at the runners to tag them out.

We divided into two teams, with Chase and me on the same side, along with a few other girls and boys. Johnny Ricker and Miles were on the other team. I would have rather played a position way out in the outfield, but Chase dragged me along with him to the infield, where he played second base, and I was the shortstop.

The game went back and forth, with neither side doing much

scoring going into the final inning. Finally, thanks to a great kick by Chase, we scored another and took the lead 4 to 1.

When Johnny Ricker's team came back up to kick, our team readied its defense. The other side needed four more runs to win, and this was the last inning. If we held them off, the game was ours.

Pitcher Cammie Davis rolled the ball to Alex Carter, who kicked it right to our first baseman Jason Miller, who got us the first out. We all let out a collective cheer and waited for the next roll from Cammie to Jennifer Collins, who kicked the ball over my head into left field and got on base. Clayton Wilson kicked another base hit, followed by stupid Miles, who loaded the bases. Amanda Levine nervously kicked the ball right to Chase on second base, giving our team two outs. One more out, and we would win. But Johnny Ricker was up to kick with the bases loaded.

That's when I noticed a black sedan on the other side of the fence, parked alone near the entrance of the school. *Was it the Secret Service, or maybe someone more sinister, like agents of the other world searching for us?*

The thought made me a little uneasy until Sheriff Booker Graves pulled up his patrol car beside the black sedan. Knowing that he was here to protect us from any trouble that might break out made me feel relieved.

But my heart stopped and dropped into my stomach when I saw the sheriff get out of his patrol car carrying my backpack—the one that I caught on the barbed wire fence the other night when Gio and I ran from him.

I tried to reassure myself: *The backpack wasn't marked with my name, and there's nothing else inside the pack with my name on it. My journals weren't in there, just some candy and energy bars in the front zipper pocket, and they could belong to anyone. The pack didn't even contain my flashlight—thanks to annoying Adam.*

Then it dawned on me: Mrs. Huntley's camera was in there—the camera with photos of the Monte Christo project in my house. That linked the backpack to me—which linked me to Friday night's encounter with the sheriff. It was only a matter of time before Booker Graves talked with all the teachers, and Mrs. Huntley identified her camera, and my Monte Christo project, and me.

Stupid Ana Rahela Balenovic suggesting I need a photo, I thought. *I'm going to prison now because of her.*

Smack!

I was hit on the side of my face; the blow knocked me to the ground. I grabbed my cheek as stinging pain crackled along my face. Then I saw the rubber ball.

I shook my head and looked around. The opposing team was laughing as runners, including Johnny Ricker, ran around the bases. My team yelled encouragement as I scrambled for the ball that had struck me, but it was rolling away.

Johnny circled third base, heading for home plate just as I grabbed the ball. I threw it with all my might… but it slipped from my grasp and drove straight into the ground, bouncing wildly away from home plate. Johnny was safe with a home-run grand slam.

He stood at home, laughing with his team. My team kicked at the dirt and didn't otherwise move.

We had lost.

I hated sports, and I hated Johnny Ricker.

Chase finally came over to give me a reassuring pat on the back as the end-of-class bell rang.

Johnny Ricker would get what's coming to him, but not today. Today, I had bigger problems, as my race intensified to solve the mysteries surrounding my pocket watch and Mr. Doyle—before Sheriff Graves arrested me, or aliens invaded the earth.

While the other kids wandered back into the building and off to lunch, Chase and I ran over to Coach Conley. Bent over and tying the laces on his running shoes, Coach was getting ready for an afternoon run.

"Coach? Coach?" Chase leaned forward. "Uh… Oliver here is the editor of the school's newspaper, and would like to ask you a few questions if that'd be okay?"

"School newspaper?" Coach Conley looked up from his shoes. "About what?"

Chase gave a carefree tug on his mouth and cocked his head. "We just want to get to know some of the teachers here at the school," he said, sounding upbeat.

"I'm heading out for a good sweat, boys," the coach advised us. "How long will it take?"

"Just a few minutes," I quickly said, while rubbing the side of my face, which was still stinging. "That's all, and then you can get on with your run."

"Well…" Coach looked at his watch and smiled. "Why not? I haven't done an interview since I was in college, playing football."

"Let's start there." I was missing my journal, but I still managed to improvise some good questions. "You say you played football in college—what position?"

"Quarterback, and I was pretty good. I was heading into the pros after my senior year," he answered.

Chase looked surprised. "What happened?"

"I… it's a long story. I was injured during my senior year and couldn't compete. So, when the draft came around, the teams didn't want me," our coach sadly said, looking at the ground.

"So, is that why you're a coach here at this school?"

"Yep—it's great. I love my job, and you snot-nosed kids." Coach Conley smiled, then reached down to mess my hair up.

"That's really interesting," I said sincerely. But having his attention and knowing we had only a limited amount of time, I changed the subject. "Did you know Mr. Doyle is nominated for *Teacher of the Year*?"

"Uh, I think so… yeah, I did. I hope he wins," the coach said in a surprised tone.

"Wow," Chase said brightly. "That's really nice of you, seeing Mr. Doyle doesn't like you."

Coach Conley frowned. "Why would you say such a thing?"

Chase looked like he hesitated to tell all. "Um… We overheard a teacher and Mr. Doyle talking, and Mr. Doyle didn't have nice things to say about you. To be honest, we didn't hear everything he said, but it was something like, '*He's a dumb jock and a has-been.*'"

"Dumb jock? *Has-been?*" Coach Conley's face became beet-red. "*He's* the dumb one! He didn't listen to me, and he got what *he* deserved!"

Chase pounced. "What you mean, '*he got what he deserved?*'"

"What?" Coach shook his head and took a step away from us. "No, what I meant was—he doesn't know what he's talking about, and I hope he gets the *award* he deserves!"

Chase answered, "Oh, okay. Hey, when did you see Mr. Doyle last?"

"Last Thursday morning, I think. He came by the gym to talk about the setup for the President's visit."

Chase raised his chin. "Is that why the two of you got into an argument?"

"Argument? Sometimes teachers have misunderstandings between each other, and that was just a misunderstanding," Coach Conley responded.

I followed up by asking, "Was it an argument over money? I mean, was he short on cash—and did Mr. Doyle ever ask you for a loan?"

Coach Conley arched his eyebrows in surprise. "Listen, kids, I won't discuss any teacher's financial situation with you, okay? Rich or poor, it's their business, not yours or mine." Clearly, Coach was irritated. "Now, what does this have to do with this interview about me?"

"Oh, sorry." Knowing we had pressed him as far as we could, I needed to wrap this interview up. "One more question: Do you eat the food here at the school, or do you bring your lunch?"

"That sounds like a trick question! I bring my lunch. I need my protein shakes and tofu salads; I have to stay fit, ya know. But, I'm not say'n the food here's unhealthy. You kids should be eating it every day and getting your nutrition."

Coach winked at us right before he ran off.

I looked at Chase. "Alien ally?"

"Absolutely," he nodded.

CHAPTER THIRTY-FIVE

KEY FINDINGS

THE LUNCH LINE was missing us today, as we had all brought our lunches to avoid the mind-controlling food. Trying to act as normal as possible, Jax, Gio, Chase, Eduard, and I found an open table far from the reaches of Johnny Ricker and began our meeting.

Jax placed her lunch bag on the table. "So, what did you find out?" she asked as she maneuvered onto a chair. "Everyone in this school is an alien or a zombie?"

"Not everyone," Gio answered.

"We've got some new intel," I said.

I figured using words like "intel" were appropriate, given the type of work we were doing.

"Please tell me you at least asked some of the questions about toxic waste I gave you," Jax said, staring at Chase.

"We didn't have time for long interviews, so we had to cut right to the heart of the matter," Chase replied in a crisp tone. "We'll discuss our findings at the fort after school. We also have some fingerprints of Miss Lexington to analyze."

"Fingerprints?" Eduard said, lifting his head.

"Why from Miss Lexington?" Gio asked in a confused tone.

Chase took a deep breath. "She's told us over and over she doesn't have Oliver's pocket watch, but our test papers that she graded over the weekend have smudge marks from the watch's tarnish on them. If the fingerprints we obtained from her today match the fingerprints on our tests, then she's lying—she has Ollie's pocket watch. But if the prints don't match, then someone else graded our papers."

"But who else would grade our papers, and why?" Jax asked.

"We don't know yet," Chase said. "But whoever it was, has Oliver's pocket watch and knows what happened to Mr. Doyle."

"How are you going to analyze fingerprints?" asked Jax.

"I'll bring my fingerprint analyzing tools from home to the tree-fort this afternoon," Chase said.

"Oh brother, that should be good," Jax sarcastically replied.

"What about you, Jax?" Chase said before taking a bite of his sandwich. "What did you find?"

Jax wiped her cute mouth with her cute napkin. "I talked with the office secretary, Miss Hathaway, who wouldn't tell me anything about the history of the school. She also knew nothing about Mr. Doyle or how we might get ahold of him. But in the school's library this morning, I found some interesting articles. I need to get back in there during recess."

As we focused on eating our lunches from home, we noticed the cooks in the back of the kitchen preparing the toxic mind-controlling food.

"It's sad to think about," Chase said. "All these kids are thinking they're eating a nutritious meal, only to find out it has turned them into zombies one day."

"Yep," Gio agreed with a mouthful of food. "And we're going to have to exterminate them all."

"I'll take out Johnny first," I half-joked.

"Still on this *zombie-mind-controlling-alien-food-thing?*" Jax took a sip of bottled water. "I still say you guys are crazy; we should be looking at *real* possibilities."

Chase arched his eyebrows, and without missing a beat, said, "I noticed *you're* not eating the school's food."

"My own lunch tastes better," Jax said after taking another bite of her sandwich. "Besides, I think there might be a real toxic chemical problem here at the school. I'm uncovering more evidence of it every moment. So, better safe than sorry."

"Toxic mind-controlling zombie chemicals," Gio huffed between bites of his sandwich. "We need to stop this."

In the back of the kitchen, I could see one of the cooks mixing ingredients in a giant bowl. That's when another cook tapped him on the shoulder and pointed out into the cafeteria.

I sank my head down, worried that since we weren't eating their food, they would come out to force-feed it to us. However, both cooks put down what they were doing and hurried out the back door of the kitchen.

At the same time, Principal Sterns and two tall men dressed in dark suits walked into the cafeteria. The noisy chatter in the cafeteria subsided, and all the kids watched as Principal Sterns showed the men around. One man took notes on a small notepad.

"Who are they?" Gio asked in a worried voice. "Agents of the other world looking for us?"

"Could be," Chase narrowed his eyes. "But I doubt they'd be in plain sight. Maybe they're Secret Service agents scoping the place out for the President tomorrow."

I looked back to the kitchen and thought about how two of

the cooks were no longer in sight. *Hmm… were the aliens hiding from the Secret Service?*

"Should we use this opportunity to tell the Secret Service what we think is happening?" I said.

"They're with Sterns—we'll have to wait," Chase said.

"That reminds me," I said. "When I was in the nurse's office, I overheard Sterns ask Frank if '*everything was ready*,' and then he told Frank, '*we can't afford any failures—this needs to go smoothly.*' Frank reassured Sterns everything was ready, and he would have '*someone on the premises to handle any problems if they come up*.'"

"Sounds like they're planning something alright," Chase said.

"I wonder who Frank was referring to being on the premises," Eduard said. "Agents of the Other World?"

Chase nodded. "We have to assume so."

With one or two more bites, Jax finished her lunch. "I'm going to the library to do more research before recess is over," she said. She stood up.

"Right—I'll join you," Eduard said, carefully wiping the corners of his mouth. "I'll use the computers there to do some research on our suspects."

Chase chomped down on a pickle. "Okay… so we'll meet at my locker after school?"

We all nodded in unison, then broke away from the table like a football huddle. We all threw our lunch bags away in a trashcan, and Eduard and Jax strode out of the cafeteria, heading for the library.

Chase leaned over to me. "You've got the key still, right?"

I nodded. I knew what he was asking—that we sneak down the hall and see what's in the basement. I hadn't told him or anyone else about the shadow near the door, and I wasn't sure if now was a good time to tell him there was something down there waiting for us. That might make Chase want to go down into the basement even more.

Chase, Gio, and I walked down the hallway until we got in sight of the basement door. We stood still for a moment and looked around for any teachers, but found the hallway empty. So, we hurried to the entrance.

Chase gave the handle of the door a twist and found it locked. He looked at me and whispered, "Give me the key."

A voice in my head said, *don't give him the key—that key opens the door to death.*

I stared at the locked door, and a chill ran through me. *I had seen something in that doorway earlier; I was certain of it.*

"Come on, Ollie… the key!" Chase demanded. "You brought it, right?"

I reached into my pocket, feeling for the key. *Should I give it to him?*

If it fit, then Chase would surely want to go down there, and I wasn't sure if I was able to do that.

Just tell him you forgot the key, Oliver, the voice in my head said.

"Yeah, don't tell us you forgot it," Gio said in a way that was kind of snide.

That tone made me find the key in my pocket and draw it out. I handed it to Chase.

Chase placed it in the lock.

The key fit.

He turned the handle.

"What doing?" shouted a man with a low, heavily accented voice.

We looked over our shoulder… to see one of the cooks! His heavy footsteps seemed to shake the floor as he raced towards us.

Chase quickly pulled the key out of the lock and shoved it in his pocket.

"Uh... looking for the boy's bathroom," Chase answered.

"You no be there—no be there!" the man hollered at us.

"Oh... sorry, new kid," Chase apologized with a smile.

We quickly walked back in the other direction, back into the cafeteria. We sat down at our empty table.

Gio was the first one to say anything. "Now we know that the key fits the basement door!"

"Since we found the key next to Doyle's car," Chase said, "it confirms he was the one going down in the basement. Looks like Frank is right: Doyle was the one who took the antique mirror and caused the vandalism."

"This is starting to fit together," I said. "Mr. Doyle was short on cash, took the antique mirror to pawn for money, and tampered with the electrical panels to cause a delay to the school expansion project."

"Unless Frank was setting up Doyle, and Frank is the one responsible," Gio speculated.

"It still doesn't explain what happened to Mr. Doyle," Chase pointed out. "We need to sort this out at the fort, but for now, we need to act normal to avoid any suspicion that we're on to something."

We went outside for a brief recess. While we were outside, the three of us were able to bend the forks on Gio's bike back into a rideable shape.

When the end-of-recess bell rang, we headed back inside to our next classes, as normal students would.

CHAPTER THIRTY-SIX

READING MISS IVY

EDUARD HAD ALREADY arrived and taken his seat in literature class, while I waited for Jax outside Miss Ivy's classroom. She waved once she saw me and approached eagerly, brimming over with love.

She said, "Oliver, I think I've found out some pretty important information."

Ana—nosey—Rahela—ruin everything—Balenovic was walking behind her, so I shot her an obvious glance with my eyes so that Jax would keep quiet. When smart, beautiful Jax saw this, she knew my intent; no words were necessary between us.

Jax whispered to me as she got close, "We'll talk after we interview Miss Ivy after class, okay?"

I nodded as we walked into the classroom together. I walked my love to her seat, before going to my seat back by Three Name.

As the start-of-class bell rang, Miss Ivy stood up from her desk and walked to the front of the classroom. She opened her poetry book and began reading:

Shall I compare thee to a summer's day?
Thou are more lovely and more temperate:
Rough winds do shake the darling buds of May,
And summer's lease hath all too short a date:
Sometime too hot the eye of heaven shines,
And often is his gold complexion dimmed,
And every fair from fair sometime declines,
By chance, or nature's changing course untrimmed:
But thy eternal summer shall not fade,
Nor lose possession of that fair thou ow'st;
Nor shall Death brag thou wander'st in his shade,
When in eternal lines to time thou grow'st:
So long as men can breathe, or eyes can see,
So long lives this, and this gives life to thee.

—William Shakespeare, Sonnet 18

"Let us continue our discussion on Shakespeare and his tragedies," Miss Ivy said. "I want you all to read the first thirty pages of 'King Lear' from your literature book. I will give a short quiz at the end of class."

We all opened our textbooks and began our reading. I had a hard time concentrating today, drifting off into thoughts of Jax and me solving this mystery together. Jax and I were going to be working side by side as we uncovered the truth about Mr. Doyle.

I looked out the window at the stone gargoyle that had moved last week. It was now as still as the statue it was. But something was different.

The wings look like they are in a different position than last week, I thought. *Had the gargoyles flown off the building to snatch a student, or fend off an evil spirit? Or were the gargoyles themselves evil?*

I was confused as ever. I decided not to document my sighting in my journal this time. I could always add it in later.

By the end of class, I had finished my quiz with no idea of whether my answers were correct. For the first time ever, I wanted this class to be over; Jax and I were on a mission together.

When the bell rang, Jax and I sprang from our chairs and darted up to Miss Ivy's desk. The rest of the class emptied their chairs, except for *Ana—stupid balloon head—Balenovic,* who followed me to ask, "Are you going to discuss the school newspaper?"

I dramatically shook my head, no. "We've got nothing for the paper yet," I said. "I've got some private issues to discuss with Miss Ivy right now. I'll, uh, get with you later—after school, okay?"

Balloon Head hesitated, but finally nodded, and walked out of the classroom with her big head.

Jax started the questioning. "Miss Ivy? Oliver and I have been working on story ideas for the newspaper. We are thinking of writing an article on the history of this school. Would you mind if we ask you a few questions?"

"Me? Ooh," Miss Ivy hedged, sounding embarrassed. "I've only been teaching at Raven Ridge Academy a few years, and I'm ashamed to say I don't know its history very well."

I quickly asked, "Do you eat the food here at the school?"

Miss Ivy looked surprised at the question, but answered, "Occasionally, when the mood strikes me."

"Did you really just ask that?" Jax said, as she scowled at me. "Sorry, Miss Ivy. If you could just tell us if you know anything that has to do with… the renovation, expansion plans, leaks, or… maybe health hazards, like toxic waste?"

"Ah… no, I know nothing about any of that. Perhaps you should talk with someone who knows a little more about this building than I do—like Frank, the maintenance man?" Miss Ivy said brightly.

"Yes, we've talked to him, and he gave us some good information," Jax said politely. "He also told us that Mr. Doyle is chairman of the Raven Ridge Historical Commission. We'd like to interview him, but he doesn't seem to be around. Have you seen or heard from him?"

Miss Ivy paused and gave us a blank stare for a moment. "Why no, I haven't," she finally answered. She looked uncomfortable suddenly.

Trying to keep the conversation light, I inserted, "We've—I mean, the school newspaper—has nominated him for *Teacher of the Year.*"

Jax elbowed me. "Well… that's still in the works," she said, narrowing her eyes at me.

Miss Ivy began fiddling with some papers on her desk. "Well, that is not surprising. Mr. Doyle is a wonderful teacher, and partially responsible for bringing the President of the United States to this school. That's quite an accomplishment."

"What's your relationship with Mr. Doyle like?" Jax asked.

Miss Ivy was in the process of reaching across her desk for a paper, but she froze like a statue upon hearing this question. "Whatever do you mean?"

Jax continued, "From our interviews, we got the impression Mr. Doyle isn't liked very well here at the school—at least not with most of the staff. So, we were wondering about your relationship with him?"

"I have no relationship with Mr. Doyle!" Miss Ivy stridently said before she corrected herself. "I mean to say, as a colleague, I like him very much. I think he is a fine man, full of passion, especially for history. He is a kind human being and didn't deserve—" Here she stopped herself and looked out the window before she returned her gaze to us and said with a sincere smile, “I think Mr. Doyle is very deserving of *Teacher of the Year.*”

At this point, Miss Ivy shuffled some papers together and said in a business-like tone, “I’m so sorry, but I’m late for another engagement. I have to leave you now.”

“Thank you so much for your time,” Jax said. “We’ll let you know how this turns out.”

We had just turned around to go when Jax turned back to Miss Ivy and asked, “I must say, those are lovely flowers on your desk—they’re lilies, aren’t they?”

Miss Ivy smiled. “Yes—my favorite.”

“And where did you get them from?” Jax asked in a curious and gentle tone.

Looking out the window again, Miss Ivy hesitated, and then softly replied, “From a dear friend.”

Jax grabbed my arm as we walked out of the room. My knees became weak; I thought I might stumble.

Jax began to whisper words of love in my ear. “I’ve got to tell you about what I found in—”

She cut herself off when she saw someone standing just outside the classroom.

Ana—*I can’t mind my own business*—Rahela—*Spy*—Balenovic.

CHAPTER THIRTY-SEVEN

ARTISTIC INTERPRETATIONS

BALLOON HEAD WAS tapping her foot. "I thought you said you weren't discussing stuff to do with the school's newspaper," she accused.

"We weren't," I said. "We just had some ideas to run by Miss Ivy and didn't want to bore you with them until we decide what we are writing about."

"Like nominating Mr. Doyle for *Teacher of the Year?* I think I should know about that!" she huffed.

"Well… I wanted it to be a surprise when he won, you know," I gulped, flashing her a weak smile.

"Humph. Well, I should be in the loop from now on," she snapped.

"Of course, of course! And I'm very interested in your ideas for layouts—" I began.

The bell signaling a start to our next class rang, saving me from explaining any more. Since this meant we were late, Jax only had time to yell, "Ollie, I'll catch up with you after school!" before she hot-footed it down the hall.

I ran down the opposite hall to Mrs. Huntley's class—unfortunately joined by Spy.

As I sped along, I panted. I was all torn up inside: Jax had something to tell me that was important, and I wasn't sure what it could be. Waiting for the end of the day for her to tell me would be torturous.

When Ana Rahela Balenovic and I entered art class, Mrs. Huntley was standing in the middle of the benches. The sight of me erased the big smile on her face.

"Oliver, what happened to you? Your shirt's all mud-stained, and your forehead—it's cut!" Mrs. Huntley worried.

"I had an accident this morning on my bike, but I'm okay," I said reassuringly.

I scooted onto the stool next to Gio's. Mrs. Huntley's reaction to the sight of me, made me to realize that Miss Ivy had never said a word to me about my appearance. Something had distracted Miss Ivy not to notice how disheveled and scratched her favorite student was.

"Oh, my dear boy, I'm glad you're not hurt. Please be more careful in the future." Mrs. Huntley's smile returned to her face. "By the way, did you bring in my camera with photos of your project?"

"Um… no, I think I might have lost it when I wrecked my bike this morning… I'm so sorry," I mumbled, my face flushing.

"That's quite all right. The important thing is you're okay." Miss Huntley gave me another concerned look. "Perhaps someone will find the camera and turn it in."

Someone like Sheriff Graves, who will throw me in jail once he talks with you, I thought to myself.

Mrs. Huntley walked up to her easel, which held a large canvas.

She took a few paintbrushes from her apron pocket, and with her other hand, picked up a small palette with different color smears of paint. "Class, today we get to experiment with color. We will use the primary colors to create paintings. Choose whatever colors you like, but just make sure they complement each other," she instructed.

Mrs. Huntley pulled out a stool. "Giovanni, would you mind helping me for a moment by sitting here?"

Gio moved up to sit on the stool in the center of the room, in front of another easel with a canvas.

"And let's see… how about you, Andrea? Would you mind sitting here?" Mrs. Huntley asked.

Andrea Hinsdale walked up to sit in front of another easel with a canvas, opposite from Gio. Both were awesome artists—the best in the school—so I thought this might be some kind of painting competition.

"Now, I want the two of you to paint the other person; your interpretation of the other," Mrs. Huntley said. "Use any colors you like. Just remember, you're trying to capture the feeling—the very essence of your subject—how you see them."

This was going to be good, I thought.

Gio and Andrea picked up their brushes and began dipping them in the colors on their pallets. They then brushed their canvases with strong strokes.

"Does everyone see what they're doing? Andrea is painting Giovanni the way she sees him—her interpretation—and Giovanni is doing the same," Mrs. Huntley said, beaming as her two protégées dueled it out.

Silently in my mind, I yelled to Gio, *Come on, G! Beat her! Finish first! I know you can do it!*

Just as the competition was heating up, Mrs. Huntley decided to drop a bomb on the rest of us. "Now, I want everyone in the class to do the same. Take your brushes, and paint the person next to you… and they likewise will paint you. This is not a competition; there are no winners or losers—no right or wrong way to do this. This is your artistic vision—your interpretation of the subject—the person in front of you."

I looked at the paints and brushes at my bench, then stared at the canvas in front of me. This was going to be interesting.

On my left side, Alex Green was painting Wendy Carlson. To my right, Gio's stool was empty—leaving only one person looking directly at me: *Three Name*.

Balloon Head closed her eyes and chuckled. "I have to warn you that I'm not the best artist, and if I knew I was going to have my portrait painted today, I would have worn something nicer."

I looked around for another classmate who didn't have a partner, but everyone was paired up; I was stuck with her. I gazed at my subject, wondering if I should paint her with three heads. I gave a little smirk and picked up my brushes.

Mrs. Huntley weaved her way around the class. "My students, try to reveal the true essence of your subject! Uncover who they are, and capture it. Then place your vision on the canvas. Remember, people can hide behind a false image—so find out who they *really* are. Discover their inner being."

Oh, I will, I thought. *I will.*

Just before the end of class, Mrs. Huntley asked us to show our work to the rest of the class. One by one, my classmates showed their paintings—some to the admiration of the rest of the students, and others to giggles. Gio's and Andrea's paintings were amazing; each looked like the other person.

When it came time for Ana Rahela's turn, she showed her painting of me. There were no laughs or giggles; the classroom was quiet, with a few "wow!" compliments. I looked at the painting—it was actually pretty good. It looked like me—except for one thing: She didn't paint my birthmark.

Mrs. Huntley called on me to show my painting, and suddenly, I didn't want to show my rendition of Ana Rahela.

I slowly turned it around for everyone to see.

My painting of her head looked like a balloon—big and bobbling, with a giant mouth. Her teeth were pointed, like fangs, and her eyes were bright red. The class laughed, and when Ana Rahela saw it, she pursed her lips.

"I'm a terrible artist," I apologized to her. "It didn't turn out the way I planned… sorry."

It really did come out the way I planned; I just didn't plan on her painting me nice.

I sat uncomfortably while the other students finished showing their paintings until class was over.

As the students all left Mrs. Huntley's classroom, Ana Rahela asked me, "May I keep your painting of me?"

"Why? It's terrible," I replied.

"It's not that bad. I know you tried to capture my portrait, and that's hard to do because all great subjects are difficult—just like the Mona Lisa, which many people thought was a terrible painting. Beauty is interpreted in many different ways."

"Sure… okay. Here you go."

As I gave her the stupid painting, I was thinking, *she really didn't know what a big head she has!*

Ana Rahela thanked me and then asked, "Now that school is over, would you like to see my layout ideas for the newspaper?"

"Uh…" I didn't have time for this nonsense she was about to bore me with, but I still felt bad about my painting of her. "Yeah, of course."

"Keep in mind, these are just a few. I have many more, and can design around any story you come up with." She opened a notebook, revealing several different layouts of text for the school's newspaper. She pointed to one in particular. "This one I like the best," she said, then whispered, "It will look great for Mr. Doyle's *Teacher of the Year* announcement—what do you think?"

"Okay… they all look great," I said, barely looking at them. I needed to interview Mrs. Huntley before she left for the day, so I was getting antsy.

Ana Rahela did not let me get away that easily. "Don't forget, the President's going to be here tomorrow, and I told you I'd be willing to do an interview to give some background on why he's here if you need another story."

"We've got it under control," I said.

"It's just—" she began to whine.

"Listen, this story we are working on is huge," I interrupted, "but I can't tell you anything more until it's ready to go."

"But I *should* know—I'm a part of the paper!" she objected.

"Yes, I know—believe me, I know. You'll be the first person to find out about it when it's ready to go. You already know the *top-secret* story about Mr. Doyle being Teacher of the Year. Now, I've got to go… we'll meet about this again soon—okay?"

She didn't like my answer, but agreed and walked out, leaving Gio and me alone in the classroom to talk with Mrs. Huntley before she left.

I took a deep breath, shook off Ana Rahela, and cleared my throat. "Mrs. Huntley, I'm the editor of the school's newspaper. May we have an interview with you?"

"How exciting! I've never been interviewed before. By all means, yes."

"Great," I said. "Now then, how long have you been here at Raven Ridge Academy?"

"Three years and counting, but I feel like I've always been here," she gushed.

I followed up with, "And where did you teach before this job?"

"A small school you probably never heard of it before, called,

'*Charles Dixon Academy for the Gifted and Talented.*' But this is my home now, and I love it here."

"What is your favorite thing here at Raven Ridge Academy?" I asked.

"The students, of course! And the other faculty as well," Mrs. Huntley said, flashing her big smile again.

"Speaking of the faculty, Mr. Doyle has been nominated for *Teacher of the Year*—what do you think of that?" I said.

"Mr. Doyle? I see...." Her facial expression became somber. "Well, one of his students is responsible for bringing the President of the United States to our school, so that does make sense."

"You don't seem very happy about his nomination," I observed.

"Oh, not true," she said, forcing a smile. "Even though I strongly disagree with his stance on the pending Christo Project, he's a brilliant teacher, and I sincerely hope he wins."

"What do you mean by, '*his stance on the pending Christo Project*?" I asked.

"Mr. Doyle and I don't quite see eye-to-eye on Christo's latest ambition: to cover the Arkansas River and our very own Whispering Falls with fabric. Mr. Doyle is an environmental purist who doesn't think Whispering Falls or the river should be touched. He said he was going to try to stop it, even though I tried to explain to him it's just temporary and that Christo will remove the fabric after completion. Oh, what a tragedy it would be not to have the great Christo here in our own backyard working on Whispering Falls! It would be one of my life's greatest accomplishments if I could work as a volunteer on that project," she enthused.

"Have you seen or spoken with Mr. Doyle lately? So, uh, you could, uh, talk about the project again?" I asked.

"I saw him this morning, walking in a hurry down the hall. I didn't have a chance to stop him and talk about the project though," Mrs. Huntley said.

"This morning?" I questioned, trying to keep my eyes from popping out of their sockets. "Are you sure?"

"Well, Oliver, it may have been my mind playing tricks on me. I see many strange things that turn out to be figments of my overactive imagination," Mrs. Huntley confessed.

"What do you mean, '*strange things*'—have you seen ghosts around here?" I said.

"Spirits from the past are all around us," Mrs. Huntley affirmed as she looked around the room into the air. "They are energy from the life we all possess. The stronger the energy in one's life while living leaves a stronger energy about after one's death. Sometimes the spirits still have unfinished business here on earth—but that's nothing to be afraid of."

"Do they speak to you?" I asked.

"They speak to all of us in their own way," she said, and then waved her hand. "We just have to be willing to listen."

"So, when you *thought* you saw Mr. Doyle this morning, what was he wearing?" I asked.

"Um… a brown tweed blazer. Why are you so interested?" she questioned me back.

"We would like to talk with him about his nomination. But I thought his class still has a substitute. If he's back, do you have any ideas where we could find him?" I pestered.

"I haven't a clue," she shrugged. "Maybe he's preparing for the President's visit?"

"Yes, maybe… oh, one more question," I said. "Do you eat the food from the cafeteria, or do you bring your lunch?"

"The food here is fabulous. I love it," she said with an other-worldly grin.

"Thanks for your time, Mrs. Huntley," I said with a smile.

Gio whispered to me as we walked out, "Wow! She thinks she saw Mr. Doyle *this morning!*"

"Yeah, but she's always been a little funny in the head," I answered. "So it's hard to tell what she really saw. Plus, she eats the school's food."

"Brainwashed?" Gio asked me.

"Yep," I nodded. "Let's get to Chase's locker."

The school day was over, and just as quickly as the hallways had filled with kids, they emptied with the exception of a few stragglers and our group gathering by Chase's locker.

Jax walked up with a superior smirk on her face. "Okay, we can all finally quit this nonsense of ghosts, goblins, zombies, aliens, and… secret agents. I've been to the library and uncovered the actual story here."

CHAPTER THIRTY-EIGHT

ACCIDENTS DON'T HAPPEN BY ACCIDENT

"HERE," JAX SAID, opening up today's *Raven Ridge Reporter*. "Look at the front-page headline."

Jax pointed to the bold lettering of the newspaper's headline and read:

"EXPLOSION ROCKS RAVEN RIDGE!"

A Griffin Construction employee was killed Sunday afternoon when an explosion occurred in a tanker truck containing an unknown chemical and fuel mixture. The accident occurred around 2 p.m. Sunday on County Road 5 and Miller's Crossing.

Randy Salazar, 45, of Fort Collins, died in the accident. Sheriff Booker Graves said Salazar was pronounced dead at the scene by Life Flight Ambulance Services emergency medical technicians.

Mr. Salazar's body was sent to the Medical Examiner's Office in Denver for an autopsy to determine the exact cause of death. According to the sheriff's office, there was no contamination threat to the surrounding area. No other injuries were reported.

"It was a giant explosion. The column of smoke could be seen for miles," Sheriff Booker Graves said. "There must have been several thousand gallons of fuel mixed with an unknown chemical. We think the explosion blew itself out and feel fortunate the fire didn't spread through the dry landscape, thanks to our brave firefighting crew."

Sheriff Graves said the responding crew of two firefighters noticed hazardous material signs on the side of the truck, prompting them to notify other agencies, including the Denver Fire Department Hazmat Team.

Officials have not yet determined what chemicals were inside the tanker; however, representatives from the Environmental Protection Agency ascertained the surrounding area to be safe from contaminates. The State Fire Marshall's Office and OSHA are still investigating the cause of the explosion, but at this point, it is believed to be an accident and that no foul play was involved. Sheriff Graves said the full investigation could take months.

The radical group, *The Earth Warriors*, was initially considered suspects as a result of their comments, vowing to get the world's attention on their cause just ahead of the Presidential visit tomorrow. They claim no responsibility for the explosion, issuing this statement: "We are a peaceful organization, sworn to defend the Earth from all enemies, both foreign and domestic. This tanker explosion resulted from the toxic sins perpetrated by this government. This nation has covered so many of its toxic lies; we may never really know what was in that tanker."

The Earth Warriors organization is planning a peaceful protest and demonstration tomorrow along Main Street. They will also hold informational seminars on how to heal the Earth through meditation and thought; the cost is $10.

Representatives of the company, Griffin Construction, were unavailable for comment.

"Wow," Gio gasped. "That's the explosion that Odyssey and Chase were a part of!"

"You mean the *accident*?" she snapped. "Look there." Jax pointed to the print. "It says '*accident*.'" She folded her arms and looked at Chase. "Notice how there is no mention of *bullets*? You may have seen the fire or even the explosion. But it was caused by an *accident,* not by Agents of the Other World."

Chase stood tall and crossed his arms, too. "Jax, accidents don't happen *by accident*."

"And bullets and secret agents just don't appear and disappear without a trace," she snapped.

"I was there, and I know what I saw," Chase answered.

"Maybe it was a mirage, like the heat of the day got to you, or the smoke played tricks on your eyes. I don't know what it was, but whatever you saw or heard, no one else saw or heard," Jax said in a much gentler tone.

Eduard looked confused. "So, you're saying… all that was Chase's imagination?"

"Not entirely. That tanker did explode, but not from Agents of the Other World—it was because there was something else in it that shouldn't have been in there, and I think it is part of a bigger picture I've been uncovering. I mean, with this environmental group here protesting and all the talk about toxic waste, don't you think the accident's entirely *too* coincidental? And I have got it all figured out." Jax smiled in satisfaction.

"That's great, but we—"

Chase stopped in mid-sentence as we spied Principal Sterns

down the hallway. The principal looked up and down the hall before ducking sneakily into Professor Wetherby's classroom.

Chase quickly closed his locker. "Come on, let's follow him. Be quiet!"

There wasn't time to ask why. We all hustled after Chase, who was tiptoe-running to just outside Professor Wetherby's classroom door. Once there, we sucked our bodies up against the wall, while leaning our heads forward as we strained to listen. Then we peered around the edge of the door.

We saw Professor Wetherby writing on the blackboard with Principal Sterns standing right behind him.

"Professor, how are things proceeding?" the principal was asking in a clipped tone.

"Ah...." Professor Wetherby chewed on the end of his pencil. "All things in due time, Principal Sterns."

"Time is something we don't have a lot of." Principal Sterns' tone was terse.

"Time is endless—a factor you must consider," Professor Wetherby advised.

"Let me remind you, good Professor, that I brought you here for a reason. When no one else would take you, I gave you this opportunity. You said you could deliver—now I expect you to fulfill your end of our agreement."

"I fully intend to. It's just—"

The pencil cracked in two in Wetherby's mouth, and the professor carefully extracted it.

"It's just what? You need more time, less of a workload? These are children, not college students; you should be doing this with your eyes closed. We can't let this leak out. If the press starts digging around here, then everything will be over."

"I'll continue my efforts," the professor said.

Principal Sterns walked out of the room while still looking at Professor Wetherby. "I'm sure you will. Good day, Professor."

We quickly turned and gathered around each other, as if we were talking in a huddle when Principal Sterns walked out of the classroom.

Spying us, he paused, and then asked, "Aren't you students going to miss the buses?"

Chase popped his head up. "Oh, thanks… we're just discussing a meeting time for a study group."

"I'm glad to see students taking the initiative," the principal said.

He turned and walked towards his office, clicking his pen. *Click-click-click.* Once inside, he poked his head back out and watched us talking down the hall.

Chase whispered, "We can't talk around here. Let's meet at the fort this afternoon in a few hours. Everyone in?"

We all agreed and started off. That's when Jax grabbed my hand, stopped me, and whispered, "Oliver—wait."

I nodded for the boys to go on without me while I stood fast, held in her grasp.

"Come with me. I've got to show you something."

Still grasping my hand, she led me down the hall. My palms started sweating, but honestly, I didn't know where she was taking me, nor did I care. I was holding her hand, and it was *awesome.*

"In here," she said, leading me into the school's library.

She let go of my hand, but I kept hold of her hand for a moment longer, causing her to glance back at me before I let go.

"Over here, in this section…."

Jax walked between two large bookshelves, where she began peering back and forth at the titles.

"What are you looking for?" I asked.

"I just had the book out—I know I put it back right here," she mumbled.

"Tell me the name; perhaps I've read it." I began to think she was looking for a romance novel that might relate to us. *Was she trying to tell me something?* "These are all reference books," I said. "The fiction section is on the other side of the room."

"Yes, I know that," she whispered. "We are looking for *The History of Raven Ridge*. I was just looking at it during recess, and I placed it right back here. I *know* I did!"

"Why are you looking for *The History of Raven Ridge*?" I asked.

"*Shush*… not so loud," she whipped back.

"Sorry," I apologized. "I forgot we're in a library."

"No, we don't want anyone to know what we're looking for," she answered while still glancing around. "Ah, there it is—second shelf. Funny, that's not where I placed it. Someone must have moved it. Can you grab it?"

"Of course," I said, reaching for it.

"Bring it over here," Jax said, motioning to a reading table with two chairs on opposite sides.

She sat down, and I handed her the book while taking the open seat. Jax flipped through the pages until she found what she was looking for. She then spun the book around for me to read.

"See?" she whispered, glancing around the room.

She was pointing to a reproduction of an old newspaper clipping dated 1897.

I started reading:

"FLOOD KILLS THREE PEOPLE
AT REDSTONE CASTLE."

On Thursday, June 14th, a flash flood raced through the town of Raven Ridge, destroying houses and farms. The waters raced through Redstone Castle, filling the basement with water and killing three workers.

Jax then flipped to the next page. The article, dated 1935, had a headline of:

"EXPLOSIVE GAS KILLS FIVE PEOPLE IN REDSTONE CASTLE FIRE."

I tried to read the article, but Jax was already flipping the page forward. She stopped on a page with an article dated May $15^{th,}$ 1965; it read:

"MAN ELECTROCUTED TO DEATH WHILE WIRING OLD CASTLE BUILDING."

Billy Myers of Raven Ridge, Colorado, was updating the electrical wiring of the old castle building on Wednesday when the ladder he was standing on fell. Mr. Meyers grabbed onto an exposed live electrical wire while falling into standing water, electrocuting him to death. He was 43 and is survived by a wife and two children.

"A lot of people have been killed in this building; Chase was right—it's haunted!" I hissed.

"No, no! Keep reading," Jax told me.

The next article was this one:

"LOST SILVER IN MINE STILL A MYSTERY TO THIS DAY."

The Endless Mine was once the largest producer of silver in the West until the mine suddenly went bust. Records show Horace Tanner had a large fortune of silver, but it was never found after his death. Some people speculate he returned the silver back to the mine because of his grief when his wife and lifelong love Anastasia disappeared. People heard him say, *"If were not for this silver, my Anastasia would still be with me."* Horace Tanner was said to have gone mad, due to blaming himself for her disappearance. However, others believe he hid his fortune inside Redstone Castle, where a curse will fall upon any who seek it out.

That's when a revelation hit me.

"Horace Tanner had a stash of silver from his mine, which disappeared after he died," I started whispering to Jax. "Principal Sterns is looking for that secret stash, but if we find it together first, we'll be rich!"

"No! That's not what I'm getting at," Jax quipped back. "Read the article next to it—on the water testing."

The next article read:

"UNDERGROUND WATER TABLES TESTED FOR TOXINS FROM TANNER MINE."

Environmental rights activists claim hazardous waste from the Endless Mine has contaminated the water table and well water of the nearby communities. Raven Ridge Academy is among the areas affected and is home to more than 150 students.

Water testing has produced no evidence of toxins in the water table; however, one group of activists is convinced there is a government cover-up. *"People from our town have been getting mysteriously ill, and it's from that mine,"* said Jacob Nichols, a long-time Raven Ridge resident and environmental activist. *"We must care about our children and their safety—they come first!"*

Officials from the mine have continuously stated that the runoff from the mine is not contaminated and does not affect any of the creeks or streams of the community. The school itself is located near the mine.

Jax unfolded some newspapers from her backpack and spread them out on our table.

"Then I looked up some articles from the local newspaper, and came up with this," she said to me. She pointed to the first article, which read:

"PRINCIPAL NETTER OF RAVEN RIDGE ACADEMY DIES: CAUSE UNKNOWN."

Mr. Edward Netter, the Principal of Raven Ridge Academy, died last Wednesday afternoon while in his office. The exact cause of his death is unknown. He was 64 and is survived by his wife, Emma.

She pointed to another article, which read:

"PRINCIPAL RANDALL OF RAVEN RIDGE ACADEMY DIES HIKING IN CANYON."

Mr. Richard Randall, Principal of Raven Ridge Academy, was found dead in Devil's Thumb Canyon on Saturday. The cause of death was determined to be from a fall. Authorities believe Mr. Randall lost his footing hiking along the *Foot Rock Trail* in Devil's Thumb Canyon and fell nearly 90 feet to his death below. Mr. Randall was 52 and was not survived by any relatives.

Jax pointed to the next article:

"ALEC STERNS NAMED NEW PRINCIPAL
OF RAVEN RIDGE ACADEMY."

And then, she pointed to another:

"WATER NEAR RAVEN RIDGE
ACADEMY DECLARED SAFE."

Then, pointed to another:

"PROPERTY VALUES RISE ON WORD OF
MINE WATER NOT CONTAMINATED."

Jax looked at me. "There's probably hazardous waste here at the school. Principal Sterns is covering it up in order to keep going on with his expansion. That's why he doesn't want the Secret Service or the press snooping around."

"Hazardous waste? From where?" I questioned.

"The old silver mine, most likely—it's probably leaked chemicals into the waters underground around the school. There is a history of the school's basement being flooded and a history of explosive gas fires… Ring any bells of chemical gas equations on a map, or a tanker exploding with unknown chemicals inside?" Jax raised her eyebrows. "Principal Sterns sure seemed impatient with Professor Wetherby's progress on completing some project, didn't he? Some project like—changing the chemical makeup of toxic waste into something undetectable?"

She's right, I thought to myself, remembering something of Professor Wetherby's lecture on changing the molecules of a chemical mixture to form a new chemical. *There really is a toxic waste cover-up going on here.*

"Principal Sterns obviously doesn't want anyone finding out; otherwise, the school will be shut down," she whispered.

"Shut the school *down?* Well, what are we waiting for? We must tell someone!" I urged.

"And we will. Reporters from all over the country will be here tomorrow to cover the President's visit, so that's when we can reveal this front-page story," Jax said with a sparkle in her eyes. "But we're going to need proof. The national press isn't just going to believe what we say."

"We have to tell the guys at the tree-fort after school," I said.

"I don't think they'll listen to me."

Jax had hesitation in her voice.

"Of course they will, especially once you show them all this evidence you've uncovered," I reassured her.

As Jax and I walked out of the library, I noticed the young repairman Finnegan standing in the hallway talking with Miss Lexington. They were standing close—too close, for my taste. She was innocent, and he was… well, he was a tattletale. He had seen me by Mr. Doyle's car near Dead Cow Bridge, and in the parking lot by their van with flat tires. Plus, he had my shoe and my bike. If he recognized me, he'd tell Miss Lexington, and then she'd be my ally no more.

Finnegan glanced in my direction. He started doing a double-take, as if… as if… he recognized me. I spun about and walked off in the other direction.

"Where are you going?" Jax asked, scurrying to catch up. "Our bikes are this way, and I thought we were going home?"

"Change of plans," I gasped out.

Jax hurled a glance at the repairman and Miss Lexington. "Are you running from them?"

"It's a long story. Come on, let's go," I urged.

Jax followed me to the opposite end of the school. From there, we walked the long way around the outside of the building to our bikes. Gio's bike was in bad shape from my wreck this morning, but our repairs during recess made it rideable. The bike's tire wobbled, but I could still ride next to Jax on the way home.

The repairman's face was a reminder to me that ours was a race against the clock. It was only a matter of time before he recognized me and turned me in. But if we could solve this mystery before that happened, it wouldn't matter. Everything would be explained, and we would be heroes—that is, *if* we solved it before he caught me.

Somewhere, my great-grandfather's pocket watch was ticking.

CHAPTER THIRTY-NINE

PUTTING OUR HEADS TOGETHER

THAT AFTERNOON AT the tree-fort, Chase called everyone to attention.

"Okay, Eduard has done some research on our suspects, and we've also interrogated the faculty and collected some forensic evidence we need to analyze." Chase began. "We can now classify who's an alien ally, and who's brainwashed. Give us your report of what you've found with your research, Eduard."

Eduard cleared his throat. "Ah-hmm."

Jax interrupted. "I've done some research of my own and uncovered some incredible evidence as well. I think I can explain this whole thing!"

Chase waved her off. "Okay, okay, we'll hear your theory in just a minute. But Eduard is first with his report on the background checks of the teachers, and then Oliver with our report of our interrogations so we can classify them."

"Ugh!" Jax let out a puff of hot air. "Fine, but please be quick, and no more talk of alien-zombie ghosts."

Eduard cleared his throat again. "Ah-hmm. Now then, I was able to do some research on the teachers."

Eduard pulled a few papers from his pack, and with his chin sticking in the air, read aloud from them.

"Professor Wetherby? Once very well-respected in the science community. He published several papers on the theory of gravity, the theory of space-time, and the theory of causality. His most recent work, *The Code of the Universe,* was not well received. His peers gave him terrible reviews, and Wetherby became enraged, refusing to work with anyone who hadn't supported his opinions. So he's worked alone for years in pursuing his theories."

Chase was quick to expand on Eduard's findings. "Obviously, Wetherby would be connected to aliens with his background of the universe. He argued with Doyle and told us Doyle was misusing his equations in trying to predict the future."

"And how did Wetherby get that burn on his arm?" Gio asked. "He said it was from a chemical experiment."

"He doesn't eat the school's lunches," I added.

"His official classification? Alien ally," Chase proclaimed.

Jax rested her chin in her hands. "Oh brother, this could take all day."

Eduard continued. "Miss Crabtree? Born in Salem, Massachusetts. She was educated on the East Coast at Salem State University, where she majored in mathematics. But that's all the background I could find on her."

Chase shook his head. "She's not a fan of Mr. Doyle, that's for sure."

Gio nodded. "She was in the principal's office when we heard talk of aliens—so she probably knows something about the invasion."

"She doesn't eat the school's food," I noted.

"Miss Crabtree: Classification—alien ally," Chase concluded.

Jax threw her head back. "This is so stupid."

Eduard read the next name. "Mr. Doyle—born in Dayton, Ohio. He attended Ohio State University and majored in chemistry with a minor in history and political science. He has been with Raven Ridge Academy for twelve years now. He also serves as chairman of the Raven Ridge Historical Commission."

Chase let out a sigh. "Still missing," he observed. "Doyle is either working directly with the aliens or was kidnapped by them."

"Or, currently a zombie," Gio said.

I shrugged my shoulders. "We don't know whether or not he eats the school's food."

"Mr. Doyle: Classification—unknown," Chase declared.

"Is this really happening?" Jax asked in a helpless tone.

Eduard cleared his throat again. "Miss Ivy—born in Fresno, California. Attended the University of California, Berkeley, where she majored in literary arts. She has taught at Raven Ridge Academy for four years now. No criminal record on file."

Chase tapped his pencil on his head. "Not much to work with here either. She had lilies on her desk—the same type of flowers Mr. Doyle had in his car. The poem Doyle wrote was probably for her, too—seems like they were dating."

"She eats the school's food only occasionally, so she is probably not a suspect," I murmured.

"If she eats the school's food, she's brainwashed," Gio said.

"Miss Ivy: Classification—brainwashed," Chase proclaimed.

Jax shook her head. "You guys are killing me here—hurry up."

Eduard sighed, "Mrs. Huntley—no records found, either criminal or otherwise."

Gio raised his eyebrows. "She talked about the spirits of the school—I find that interesting."

"She disagreed with Mr. Doyle's opinion of Monte Christo, and accused him of being frightened of something *alien,*" I said. "And she eats the school's food."

"Mrs. Huntley: Classification—brainwashed," Chase said.

"Stupid!" Jax said.

Eduard moved to the next name on the list. "Franklin Dixon, better known as Frank, our school's maintenance man—no records on him yet."

Chase nodded. "Interesting suspect. He seems to know everything about the school, and it's no secret he doesn't like Mr. Doyle. He said Mr. Doyle's absence was an improvement to the school."

"Yes," Eduard agreed. "Frank said he's the one who should be teaching history class because he knows more about history than Mr. Doyle does. Maybe Frank wanted to get rid of Mr. Doyle so that Frank could take his job?"

"Frank also accused Mr. Doyle of vandalizing the electrical panels in the basement and taking the antique mirror," Chase said.

"And why was he inside the equipment room with the doors closed in the gym?" Gio asked. "Very suspicious."

"Frank wears a gray uniform—the shirt button I found near Doyle's car was gray!" I exclaimed.

"He also has keys to every lock, right?" Gio said. "The key we found near Doyle's car might be from him."

Chase nodded in agreement, and then said, "It all adds up. Just one more question—does he eat the school's food?"

"Doesn't sound like it. Remember when he said he *didn't agree with what they are feeding us at the school, poisoning our minds*," Eduard pointed out.

"Frank: Classification—alien ally," Chase said.

"Ugh!" Jax said, slapping the side of her head with her hand.

Eduard's tone became light, and he lifted up his chin. "Coach Conley—he was a star quarterback at the University of Colorado and was expected to go pro until he was caught up in a gambling scandal. It ruined his future in athletics. He has been a coach here at Raven Ridge Academy for three years now. He does have a criminal record related to gambling."

Chase rubbed at his chin. "Well, that explains why he's not playing football, but it doesn't explain why he lied about seeing Mr. Doyle's car, which we know he must have seen while jogging. Possible he was covering up for the aliens."

Eduard added his own speculation, saying, "Maybe he pushed Mr. Doyle down a mineshaft? The sheriff said there are shafts all around Old Man's Owens's fields."

Chase agreed. "If Doyle struggled with him, that would explain the bruises on Coach's arm and the cut on his leg, and why he would lie about seeing Doyle's car."

"But why? Why would Coach get rid of Mr. Doyle?" I asked.

"Maybe he's in with Principal Sterns? Maybe Sterns wanted Doyle roughed up to get him to agree with the building renovations, and he had Coach do it for him?" Gio suggested.

"Coach doesn't eat the school's food either," Chase said. "Coach Conley: Classification—alien ally."

Jax put her head in her hands and muttered, "I can't take much more of this. Can I be replaced by a substitute?"

"Speaking of substitutes," Chase said. He paused before asking, "Eduard, did you investigate Miss Lexington?"

Eduard nodded his head, yes. "No information on her. Besides, she came after Mr. Doyle went missing."

I raised my finger in the air. "What about the smudge marks on our quiz she gave back? They had to be from my pocket watch—she had to have found it." I looked eagerly to Chase. "Can we examine the fingerprints now?"

"Yep," Chase said, patting a small, brown handbag next to him. "I brought my fingerprint analysis kit, so let's get to work."

He reached into the handbag and carefully drew out, and held up by its corner, a small, clear plastic bag containing the apple with Miss Lexington's fingerprints on it.

We all watched in silence as Chase spread a small cloth on the floor, and then placed his magnifying glass on it. He then carefully pulled the apple out of the small plastic bag by its stem, cautious not to touch its sides. He placed the apple on top of the cloth on the floor, next to the magnifying glass.

He then pulled out another small, clear plastic bag containing blue chalky powder from his brown handbag. He opened the plastic bag and sprinkled the blue powder over the entire apple. Next, he pulled out a small, puffy brush from his handbag and began to delicately dust off the powder.

Jax broke the silence. "Fingerprint analysis kit? That looks more like a make-up brush and crushed chalk to me."

Chase paused. "I may have relocated this brush from my sister." He shot a glance at Jax before going back to his task. "And, finely crushed chalk from Professor Wetherby's classroom works just fine, too."

After a few more whisks from his brush, the chalky dust on the apple revealed small fingerprints!

Chase then pulled a small roll of clear tape from his handbag. After tearing off a strip of tape, he stuck its sticky side to the chalky dust on the apple, and then carefully peeled it away, lifting the chalky fingerprints from the apple—onto the tape! Chase pressed the tape with the prints onto a piece of paper and then peeled it away again. The chalky fingerprints from the apple were now imprinted on the paper.

Chase picked up his magnifying glass and began comparing the prints on our quiz to the prints from the apple. My heart pounded with anticipation, although I wasn't sure what either outcome would mean.

After a few *hum* noises, Chase looked up and said, "The prints don't match."

"What?" I said, thinking I heard him wrong. "What does that mean?"

"It means Miss Lexington is telling the truth. She doesn't have your pocket watch," Chase said. "Someone else handled our quiz papers."

"But who else would grade our papers?" Eduard asked.

"Well, whoever it was, knows about history and the whereabouts of Mr. Doyle," Chase said in a confident manner.

"Maybe they are Mr. Doyle's fingerprints, since he was the last one who had my watch?" I asked. My tone was hopeful.

Eduard thought for a moment. "How would smudges get on our papers then, since Doyle went missing before the weekend, and we got the papers back on a Monday?"

Gio thought of an answer. "Maybe he really did make a wager with the gambling ghost and lost, and it's his ghost's fingerprints?"

This sounded plausible, and it all started to come together for me. "Mrs. Huntley thought she saw Doyle walking down the hallway, so maybe what she saw was his ghost?"

"Yes!" Chase agreed eagerly, as he stretched out his neck. "Gio may be right about this gambling ghost. We've heard Doyle lost a bet, and if his bet was with the gambling ghost, Doyle might be trying to send us a message from the dead."

Jax looked at us with a blank stare. "So, let me get this right—Mr. Doyle, who you guys first said was kidnapped by aliens, is now dead inside the abandoned silver mine because of a bet with a ghost, and now Mr. Doyle's ghost somehow got ahold of our test papers, putting his ghost smudge marks on them—because Doyle's ghost wants us to figure out somehow that it's a secret message from him about an alien invasion of brainwashed zombie kids?"

Somehow, when Jax said the whole thing aloud, it didn't sound as cool as what we had imagined.

Chase tried to salvage our theory. "Sometimes, ghosts continue doing everyday tasks because they think they are still alive."

Jax pulled a piece of paper from her notebook and then dropped it to the ground. "Maybe it's not smudge marks from Oliver's pocket watch at all," she suggested. "Maybe Mr. Doyle's substitute—Miss Lexington—dropped the papers in the dirt or grease? We all saw what a klutz she is." Jax then picked up the paper. "And someone else helped her pick them off the ground." She showed us the dirty marks on it and sighed, "Mystery solved."

"I know what smudge marks from the watch look like," I started to protest, "and—"

Jax had had enough. "Can't we all agree that your theory is *stupid?* We've got much more evidence in support of a cover-up. Who handled our test papers doesn't have anything to do with any of this, and this isn't paranormal—so let's move on."

I frowned, and we all gave a silent pause in response to Jax's scolding tone.

Eduard cleared his throat, and said briskly, "Principal Sterns—born in Chicago, Illinois. Educated at the University of Illinois, where he majored in business. Was employed by Dumont Chemicals before coming to be Raven Ridge Academy's principal. No criminal records on file."

Chase softened his voice. "We all know he's involved in this somehow, but the question is, what exactly is Sterns up to, and why?"

I nodded. "He says the food here is great, but he won't admit to eating it."

"Principal Sterns: Classification—alien ally," Chase said.

Jax waved her hands in an animated fashion. "He was the CEO

of a *chemical company?* That's a dead giveaway! Why would he come to Raven Ridge to be a principal of education after having a job like that? This is what I'm getting at!"

"Jax is right; we've got to be overlooking something with him," Chase said. "What about that handwritten note I relocated from Sterns' desk… the one that mentions *alienate*?"

I grabbed up the note and read it out loud again:

> Principal Sterns- Your attempts to alienate certain members of the faculty and create a toxic environment have not worked. There's no change in my opinion. However, this must not affect the plans for my star. Time is short, and there is still much to do. We must meet ASAP to discuss the arrangements for the President —COD

Jax opened her hands up as if pleading with us. "Even this note Chase took talks about creating a toxic environment, not about aliens or ghosts. Does it need to be spelled out more clearly?"

Gio squinted his eyes as he asked, "What does C-O-D mean?"

Chase answered in a confident tone. "Cod is a type of fish—it's probably a secret code name."

"No." Eduard raised his chin before continuing. "C-O-D stands for *Cash on Delivery*—which means expecting something to be delivered before payment is made."

I thought out loud. "What would Principal Sterns be selling, or delivering? The way it's written, it almost sounds like he's making arrangements for the President's delivery."

Chase lit up like a light bulb. "Something like—make arrangements to deliver the President to someone for cash!"

Gio understood where Chase was going, and with the same amount of enthusiasm, said, "That's what is going to happen!

Principal Sterns is working with the agents of the other world; he's planning on kidnapping the President and selling him to the aliens! Cash on delivery!"

Jax closed her eyes. "Please stop this nonsense, *please!*"

Chase walked back and forth with his hands behind his back as he summarized his theory. "Principal Sterns is planning to capture the President using his students, whom he's turning into a mindless zombie army by feeding them brainwashing chemicals created by Professor Wetherby. These chemicals are being put in the school's lunch food by alien cooks, while Coach Conley, Mrs. Huntley, Frank, and Miss Crabtree help our principal cover his tracks. Then the aliens will pay Principal Sterns in cash when the President is delivered—*C-O-D.* The note is from one of the alien cooks, who met with Principal Sterns and argued with him about the plans for the abduction.

"Mr. Doyle uncovered the plans of the alien invasion and confronted the faculty and Principal Sterns, which is why he was arguing with everyone that morning. When Mr. Doyle would not agree to join the rest of the faculty in assisting the principal in turning the President of the United States over to aliens, Principal Sterns drew a map for Mr. Doyle, sending him into a trap near Dead Cow Bridge, where Frank was waiting to attack. The two fought, and Frank lost one of his shirt buttons and a key to the school during their struggle. Frank then helped the aliens abduct him—which is why Doyle's missing."

Chase's words made complete sense. "This all makes sense now," I agreed with a nod of my head.

Eduard agreed with us, too. "Everything fits perfectly."

Unfortunately, Jax differed.

"Or," Jax interjected, "maybe Mr. Doyle uncovered something—something like toxic waste at the school—and he was going to release the information to the press, and that's why Principal

Sterns wanted him gone?" In a desperate-sounding voice, Jax begged, "Work with me here, boys!"

We all looked at her as Gio asked, "But how does that fit with aliens and zombies?"

Jax threw her arms up in the air. "You guys are impossible!" She unfolded a newspaper clipping. "Look at this! It was in yesterday's paper. It talks about a protest planned during the President's visit."

We all looked at the article she spread out on the floor. It read:

"THE EARTH WARRIORS PLAN DEMONSTRATION IN SMALL TOWN, VOWS WORLD WILL FINALLY LISTEN."

When he arrives on Tuesday, the President of the United States will be greeted with more than cheers from the small town of Raven Ridge, as the environmental group The Earth Warriors will be demonstrating outside the school grounds. Local officials have banned the demonstration on school property, citing disruptive activities during school hours. The group is vowing to fight the ruling in court, but it has contingency plans to hold a rally in the center of town where the President's motorcade will drive through.

The activist group claims that the United States government is to blame for countless atrocities around the world, including covering up toxic waste in well water and streams while this nation continues drilling for oil and gas. The group promises that the world will know who they are after their demonstration.

The small town of Raven Ridge is home to farms and ranchers but is not deaf to protests. The Tanner mine was one such subject when activists believed the mine contained toxins that were leaking into nearby water tables,

> causing residents to become ill. The federal government investigated the charges, but they found no evidence of water contamination.

Chase puffed his cheeks out and looked at Jax. "Okay, so what?"

"*So what?*" Jax echoed, clearly taken aback. "This is probably what's going on here—chemicals in the water—and this is the group that knows about it." She pounded her finger on the article. "Listen… this information about toxic waste at the school could be monumental."

Chase looked at Jax while adjusting his glasses. "Yeah, but that still doesn't explain why Frank would attack Doyle."

Eduard agreed. "Or, help the aliens."

"You idiots! There is no such thing as aliens—get that idea out of your heads. My theory is a real possibility—one that reporters wait a lifetime to expose—and we're still talking about *aliens?*" Jax hooted.

"Well, not just aliens," Gio objected. "Zombies too."

"Unbelievable!" Jax screamed.

I wanted Jax to know I supported her, so I said, "Okay, everyone, it's Jax's turn… Jax, why don't you tell them what you found with your research, and explain everything you think happened?"

Everyone quieted down to listen.

"Here's what happened," she said as she paced the floor like Chase. "During my research on the history of our school, I found there has been chemical contamination in the past from the old silver mine. I believe the toxins are leaking into the basement of the school, and Principal Sterns was hired to cover up this problem in order to keep the school open and property values high.

"Mr. Doyle, who is chairman of the Raven Ridge Historical Commission, discovered the existence of the toxic waste when reviewing expansion plans for the school. He drew a map of where he thought the toxic waste was coming from and listed the symbols of the chemicals on the side.

"Since the President is coming, there will be reporters looking around the school, and they might discover the school's toxic waste problem. Principal Sterns used the cooks to help cover-up the existence of the toxic waste by pumping the hazardous material into a tanker truck. And, Principal Sterns was arguing with the cooks because they didn't want to have to do extra work. The shaking Oliver and Gio felt that night was the toxic waste being pumped out of the basement at night by the cooks. In the morning, Sterns had the tanker truck moved to a nearby country road. But the chemicals became unstable in the heat of the day, and the tanker exploded—the same tanker truck Chase saw explode.

"Principal Sterns had hired Professor Wetherby to develop an equation to change the molecules of the toxic waste into something undetectable, but the professor ran out of time. When Oliver and Chase overheard Mr. Doyle confront Professor Wetherby in the hallway, saying, *this was all his fault with his equations*—Mr. Doyle was talking about equations to change the molecules of the toxic waste! Then, when the professor said he *didn't have a remedy*, Mr. Doyle said to him, *you only have the* poison—meaning the *toxic waste, poison* of course!

"When Mrs. Huntley tried to convince Mr. Doyle that there was *no threat to the environment*—she was referring to the *toxic waste* from the mine. And when she told him that she wanted the plans to go through, it was probably because she wanted her property values to go up.

"Mr. Doyle tried to get Coach to help him. He wanted Coach to talk with his people—meaning Frank and Principal Sterns. But Coach didn't want to get involved. Coach tried to warn Mr. Doyle not to interfere with our principal and Frank, but Mr. Doyle wouldn't listen.

"Mr. Doyle threatened Principal Sterns that he would leak his findings to the press. However, Sterns continued to try to convince Mr. Doyle to get onboard and not say anything. Sterns offered to make Mr. Doyle rich in the process and pay off some of Mr. Doyle's debts. But Mr. Doyle wouldn't agree. That is what Doyle and Sterns were arguing about during recess when Mr. Doyle said, *'this cover-up will haunt you.'*

"Mr. Doyle was pawning *his own* items from *his own* basement to cover his debts. That's why the pawnshop ticket was in his car.

"Frank, who never liked Mr. Doyle, was in cahoots with Principal Sterns all along. Frank stole the antique mirror from the basement in order to frame Mr. Doyle as a thief and a vandal, thereby ruining Mr. Doyle's credibility. There never was any vandalism in the basement; that was just a story to cover up the toxic waste damaging the electrical panels and to get workers down into the basement. The workers are the *visitors* Mr. Doyle told principal Sterns *he knew about*. They are helping to cover-up the toxic waste before the President arrives.

"When their intimidation tactics didn't work on Mr. Doyle, Principal Sterns decided to have Frank *take care of* Mr. Doyle, by either kidnapping or killing him!

"Mr. Doyle was driving to the abandoned silver mine to get more evidence, when Frank attacked him on the side of the road. In the struggle, Frank's gray button was ripped off his gray work uniform, and Mr. Doyle dropped the basement key and his map of the mine's underground toxic water that seeps into the basement of the school. Frank then dragged Mr. Doyle's body, then threw him onto his shoulder, which is why the drag marks disappear. He tossed gravel on the road to cover his tracks, carelessly spraying the car's hood, and then carried Mr. Doyle's body along the railroad tracks so he would leave no footprints. He then flung Mr. Doyle into a mineshaft.

"Coach knew about Principal Sterns and Frank's plan and tried to save Mr. Doyle after school. He looked along the railroad tracks, but never found Mr. Doyle. Principal Sterns probably intimidated Coach into keeping silent—that's why Coach Conley lied about seeing his car."

Jax smiled, spreading her arms wide. "Ta-da…."

We all sat in silence.

We all stared at Jax.

There was more and more silence.

Finally, Gio managed to speak. "But… how does all that fit in with alien zombies?"

"Seriously?" Jax yelled, flinging her arms up. "I give *up!* Believe what you believe, but I, for one, think it's a cover-up." Jax folded her arms and crossed her feet. "Since we seem to disagree, we need hard evidence to get to the bottom of this. We must get into the basement and find out what's down there. We have the key, right?"

Eduard blinked quickly. "There is no chance of getting down there without being spotted these days. The Secret Service will have everything buttoned up."

"But," Jax whined, "we've got to uncover what's going on before it's too, late and Principal Sterns gets away with it!"

Chase shook his head no. "Odyssey told us to be ready, and that she'll be the one to give us the signal."

"To do what?" Gio asked.

Chase pounded his fist into his hand. "Fight the alien/zombie invasion—"

"No!" Jax hollered. "We must uncover the toxic waste cover-up!"

One of them was right, and I was right in the middle; I had to choose a side. My heart wanted me to believe Jax, but my reason told me to believe Chase. I didn't know whom to choose—so I chose both.

"Yes—of course, you're both right!" I exclaimed as everyone

looked at me. “It makes perfect sense! It is a cover-up of toxic chemicals at this school by Principal Sterns. The aliens are using the chemicals to poison the school lunches and turn all the students into zombies so they can capture the President, and Sterns will be rich due to keeping property values high! Frank knows what’s going on, but doesn’t agree with it, but he has to do what Principal Sterns orders him to do.”

Everyone began thinking about what I just said.

“Now that we know what’s going to happen, shouldn’t we warn the sheriff so he can tell the Secret Service?” I urged.

“He might blow our cover,” Chase said in a concerned voice. “Odyssey told us to lie low.”

“Or he might blow our big expose about the toxic waste,” Jax said.

I was quick with my response. “lie low from the aliens, the zombies, and Principal Sterns. But not from the sheriff—what if Odyssey needs backup, or the toxic waste is being guarded?”

Eduard agreed with me. “It wouldn’t hurt to have reinforcements.”

Chase thought for a moment. “I suppose we could put the sheriff on standby. Let’s go find Sheriff Graves.”

Jax sighed. “He’s not going to believe your ridiculous story—that’s for sure—but he might listen to my toxic waste theory, and I still might get credit for uncovering this cover-up.”

CHAPTER FORTY

REINFORCEMENTS

WE MOUNTED OUR bikes—Gio stood on the back of Chase's—and rode in force to find Sheriff Graves. We knew we were risking arrest in revealing what we knew about the contents of Mr. Doyle's car, but it was a chance we had to take. We had information vital to the safety of the United States President and our school.

When we arrived in town, we saw the sheriff's patrol car parked in front of his office, and his horse tied to a rail. No sooner had we dismounted than the sheriff came out of his office and began walking to his horse.

There was no turning back.

Chase shouted out, "Sheriff Graves? May we have a word with you?"

As we approached, the sheriff looked down at us from underneath his cowboy hat. "What can I do fer y'all?"

Chase was the first to speak. "We have some information

—information about the disappearance of Mr. Doyle, and the safety of the President of the United States and the school."

The sheriff's jaw clenched a bit, and in a low tone, he said, "Go on. I'm listening."

"Now, this may sound a little crazy, but we believe Mr. Doyle has been abducted by aliens—the same aliens that are posing as cooks in the school cafeteria, feeding the students mind-controlling food with the help of Principal Sterns. They are attempting to create a mindless army of zombie kids to capture the President of the United States."

Booker Graves stood silent and motionless, as if waiting for the punch line—which never came.

"I see.... well, I appreciate your information," he drawled. "I'll look into it."

Jax desperately added, "Or, it could be there's a toxic chemical cover-up by Principal Sterns to keep the school open and property values high. This involves the kidnapping or murder of Mr. Doyle... instead of aliens?"

"Listen, it's good y'all are keep'n an eye out, but I have no time to play games right now," the sheriff said. Then he pulled on the brim of his cowboy hat and turned, obviously preparing to mount his horse.

Chase wasn't giving up.

"Mr. Doyle's been missing for days, and his car was parked on the road leading to the old silver mine, near the train bridge and fields where dead cows have been found!" Chase said. "Sheriff Graves, Principal Sterns has been acting suspiciously since Mr. Doyle's disappearance, and so have the cooks—it all makes sense, don't you think?"

"Mr. Doyle's car was not on that road. I was out there Friday afternoon, and didn't see it," the sheriff said.

"But *we* saw it there then! And how do *you* explain Mr. Doyle's disappearance? And the cooks and Principal Sterns acting so weird?" Chase shot back.

"I don't explain it, and y'all shouldn't try to either. Y'all focus on your studies and let me focus on the disappearance of Mr. Doyle. Okay? It's my job," the sheriff said in a tone that sounded somewhat stiff.

"So then you *are* investigating the disappearance of Mr. Doyle, huh?" Chase said, jumping on the tidbit of information the sheriff had given us.

Sheriff Graves grabbed the saddle of his large horse, then shook his head.

"Let me tell you kids something. While it's good to be vigilant and watchful, even suspicious of people—especially strangers—it doesn't always mean someone's guilty of a crime. Don't let your suspicions and biases shape your judgment in an investigation. Otherwise, your theories will shape the facts, rather than the facts shape your theories," he lectured.

"But something has to be done—the President might be in danger!" Gio said with a squeak.

The sheriff was quiet as he mounted his horse. Once both of his feet were in the stirrups, he looked down at us.

"I'll talk with Principal Sterns and the Secret Service, okay?" the sheriff said. "You ride your bikes and let me be the detective."

He wheeled around his enormous horse around and rode off. We stared at the wake of dust his steed left behind, feeling hopeless.

Chase drew his lips back and got a determined look on his face. "Looks like it's up to us now. We'll meet at the tree-fort in the morning. Odyssey said she will tell us what to do, so we must be prepared for anything. I've got some fireworks."

Gio made a fist like he was ready for a fight and said, "I'll bring a blowtorch from my dad's auto shop."

Eduard strapped on his helmet. "I'll bring some pepper spray."

Gio shook his head. "That's not going to work; zombies aren't affected by pepper spray."

"How do you know? They have to see, don't they?" Eduard argued.

"You have to chop their heads off!" Gio replied.

Jax got up on her bike. "This is *so* stupid. I'm not bringing anything to our meeting tomorrow except a front-page story about the toxic waste cover-up going on at our school."

The girl of my dreams began riding away.

"Suit yourself," Gio shouted after her. "Zombies can't read!"

She hollered over her shoulder at Gio, "You're impossible."

The rest of us got on our bikes to ride back to our houses. When I caught up to Jax, she half-whispered over to me, "Oliver, we need to do this on our own."

"What do you mean?" I said back in a quiet voice so the others couldn't hear. "We can't fight the aliens and zombies without help from the other guys and Odyssey."

"No!" she said, sounding frustrated. "Oliver—I know you can't buy into this whole stupid paranormal thing. I'm talking about breaking this story of the toxic waste in the school's basement."

"Uh… uh. Well… uh… are you sure? What about the guys?" I mumbled, afraid of what she might suggest.

"You know they don't believe me, and this is a major story—which we could break together," Jax answered.

"Together" was all she had to say. I'd do anything now that she wanted me to do.

"Yes—you're right. Okay, what do you want to do?" I asked.

"The school building is closed now, but we could meet first thing in the morning before school starts—say, one hour earlier. That should give us plenty of time to get into the basement before class."

"What about the Secret Service? The President is here tomorrow, so Eduard's right: They'll have the entire school buttoned up."

"We're members of the press, right? We'll just tell them we're there to set up for the President's visit—then slip into the basement."

"You don't think we should tell someone—like Sheriff Graves, or—"

"We just tried to tell him, but thanks to Chase and his stories, he's not going to believe us without some evidence. Ollie, c'mon, there's no time to waste. The press will be there in full force tomorrow—imagine the exposure we'll get!"

Jax was excited about the possibility of breaking a story—her first story. And I was excited about the possibility of being a part of anything she was a part of.

"We'll meet at the tree-fort tomorrow morning about an hour and a half before school starts?" she asked me.

"I'll be there," I vowed.

"Don't be late, or I might break this story without you! Who knows? We might win the Pulitzer Prize—together," she said.

Still smiling at me, she rode off into the sunset.

I was in love, but that was old news.

CHAPTER FORTY-ONE

LATE FOR A DATE

BARNEY'S DISTANT CROW and the early sun's rays woke me the next morning. I hurried out of bed with a smile on my face. I was meeting Jax this morning to embark on a romantic thriller of a day—uncovering the evil acts of Principal Sterns and saving the environment, all while having Jax at my side. I imagined her falling into my arms after it was over, exclaiming, *"We did it, Oliver—you and I!"*

It was going to be a great day, and I couldn't wait to get started.

Then, like a runaway freight train, this thought hit me: *It was too early for the sun to be up, wasn't it?*

I jumped out of my skin and scrambled for my alarm clock... *No! My alarm had not gone off!*

The blood drained out of my head as I realized—I had set my clock for p.m., not a.m.

I was *late,* not early.

I raced over to the clothes I had set out for this morning and threw them on. Then I ran to the phone to call Gio. I told him to sound the alarm; we had an emergency, and we all needed to meet at the fort immediately. I quickly told him about Jax's plan of going into the basement before school—with or without me. I raced towards the front door.

My mother stuck her neck out her door with a toothbrush in her mouth, yelling, "Oli-er, I f-ought you were tha-paso-thed t'be at th-chool wa-hite now for an early morning project." Then she took out her toothbrush and spat in the sink. "Isn't that what you told me last night—that's why you couldn't walk Adam this morning?"

"I'm late! My alarm didn't go off! I've got to go!" I shrieked.

"Want me to drive you?" she offered.

Wow. That was nice, and unexpected.

"No," I said. Driving would be faster, but my mother wouldn't understand my meeting Jax at the tree-fort and not the school. "Thanks, Mom, I'll get there in time. Love you!"

Her words, "Love you too—be careful!" chased me out the door.

I rode Gio's bent, wobbly bike as fast as it would go, hoping that Jax would still be at the tree-fort waiting for me, or one of us could stop her before she left by herself.

The boys all arrived at our tree-fort at the same time. Jax was not there. There was a note stuck to the outside of the tree that read:

> *Gone to school to break story. See you in class or on the news tonight!*

I quickly filled them in on Jax's plan to go down into the basement to find toxic waste evidence. We scrambled up inside the tree-fort. Gio dashed to open the evidence box. "She took the key and left without us!" he yelled.

Eduard shook his head. "She doesn't know what she's getting herself into!"

Chase rubbed his forehead like he had a headache. "If Sterns finds Jax down in the basement, who knows what he'll do. She'll blow our cover too!"

"We've got to do something—stop her somehow," I said.

My stomach was in knots, and I was shaking and sweating.

"We've got to go after her," Chase said. "Let's gear up, so we're prepared for anything."

"Gear up?" Eduard questioned. He frowned as he looked around. "With what?"

"Lock-picks, disguises, rope, and weapons," Chase rattled off.

"Weapons?" Gio squeaked. "You mean the cattails?"

Chase shook his head no. "Not strong enough. We need the fireworks and a knife."

Eduard huffed. "The school's on lockdown today because of the President's visit. The Secret Service has closed every entrance, except the front, where they are running metal detectors. They are going to search every student as they go in. We're not going to be able to bring any equipment or weapons inside with that security."

"Well, I guess we're just gonna have to smuggle it in," Chase said. He looked straight at Gio and asked. "You in?"

Gio looked down at his half-fake leg and smiled. He then looked up and said, "Yep."

Chase smiled back. "Let's get you loaded up."

I knew what was going on too: Since Gio's half-fake leg was hollow on the inside, it could serve as the perfect place to hide anything that we didn't want the Secret Service to find. And the Secret Service would be fooled into thinking it was all the metal joint parts on Gio's fake leg that set off the metal detector, and not the metal items hidden inside—like the pocketknife. After all, who was going to make a kid with one and one-half legs take off his half-fake leg just to see if anything was inside?

I grinned inside. Even though getting caught sneaking fireworks and a knife into the school during the President's visit might mean getting more than just suspension, I knew Gio was excited that his half-fake leg was now going to be our secret hiding spot.

Once we placed all our secret items inside Gio's leg and put it back on, we slid down the ladder and mounted our bikes. Chase led the way to school, with Gio standing on the back pegs of Chase's dirt bike. It was a short enough ride to our school from our treefort, but we couldn't ride fast enough. No telling what Jax was up to or where she might be.

The gargoyles watched us approach, knowing we were arriving too early for the normal start of a school day.

We spotted several black vehicles parked in the front of the school. Their passengers—men in dark suits—were walking the school grounds. It was the Secret Service making final preparations before the President's visit later in the morning.

As we rode closer, we spied Jax's pink bike chained to the rack on the side of the building.

"She's here!" Chase said as Gio jumped down from his bike. "Maybe the Secret Service can help us find her!"

We left our bikes and ran up to the school's entrance. Two clean-cut, dark-suited men with wires coming down from their ears met us with cold looks. One of them, a tall suit, motioned for us to slow down.

"Whoa, there," he said. "Good morning. Looks like you're in a hurry, but we're gonna have to ask you to walk. We have security procedures in place for today. These are for your safety, so please cooperate by walking through the metal detector inside here—then you may go on to class."

Breathing hard, Chase panted, "We want to report that the President's in danger and our friend is missing!"

"What?" the tall suit asked.

The other suit pressed a button on the wire hanging from his ear. "Foxtrot, we have a situation. Stand by."

The tall suit bent down, preparing to listen closely to Chase. "Go on, son. Tell us why the President's in danger."

As Chase caught his breath, he began, "The President's in danger from alien abduction!"

The tall suit crinkled his nose and frowned. "What? What kind of joke is this?"

"No joke, it's true!" Gio squeaked. "The cooks, who are aliens too, have been poisoning the school lunches to create an army of mindless zombie children!"

Eduard spoke in the most excited tone I ever heard him speak. "They're going to kidnap the President and overtake the earth if you don't stop them!"

I followed up with, "And our friend Jax is inside the school now! She's probably a zombie already!"

Suddenly, I felt lightheaded. My mouth went dry. I hadn't thought about the possibility that Jax might be a zombie until it came out of my mouth.

What would I do if she were now a member of the undead; would I even recognize her? She'd still be cute in her own way, I'm sure, but would I have it in me to destroy her if I had to?

I shook my head frantically. I couldn't bear the thought of it.

"Stand down, Foxtrot—false alarm." The tall suit took his hand from the wire hanging from his ear and placed it on his hips. "I see… we'll look into it. Thank you for the information."

"You've got to believe us; it's true!" I whined.

"Listen, kids, this is no time to be pulling a prank," the tall suit scolded. "It's a serious offense even to talk about harming the

President of the United States, and making false alarms or statements will get you in deep trouble. Now, I don't want to ban you kids from attending school for today's event with the President, so I'm only going to give you a warning this time. Next time, I won't be so generous. We don't have time for games. The protection of the President is a serious matter—one of national security. Now, if you want to go inside, go through the metal detectors over there."

"But, what about Jax—" I started.

"Come on—let's go," Chase interrupted, pulling me through the front doors under the watchful eyes of the Secret Service.

Inside, there were more agents in suits. I noticed Mr. Doyle's substitute, Miss Lexington, was off to the side, talking with the Secret Service. She had her hair down today and wore a black miniskirt with matching black high heels. Around her waist, she wore a black belt with a large star buckle. The suits were looking through some papers and shaking their heads no.

Just then, Principal Sterns appeared seemingly from out of nowhere. Apparently, he was coming to her rescue.

"Excuse me, gentlemen. Miss Eva Lexington is not on the *permanent* faculty list because she is a substitute for Charles Doyle, who is not here. She will be taking his spot today. I added her to the guest list. See right down over here?" the principal said smoothly, pointing with his finger.

"Yes, I see her name now. Okay," one suit said. He gave a wide smile to Miss Lexington. "Please place your purse and belt on the conveyor belt, then step through the metal detector, Miss."

Miss Lexington smiled at our principal as she did as directed, then stepped through the detector. "Oh, thank you, Principal Sterns. For a minute there, I thought I was going to miss all the excitement!"

"That would have been so unfortunate," the principal replied. "I wouldn't want you to miss out on this historic occasion."

After Miss Lexington's purse had gone through the x-ray machine, one suit asked, "What is this, Miss?"

He opened her purse and took out a small canister with a mouthpiece.

"Oh, that's my inhaler. I may need it to breathe. With all the excitement about to take place, I might pass out!" she said. She batted her eyes at him before clumsily tripping on her high heels.

The suit behind the x-ray machine reached over a steadying hand, then inspected the canister with its mouthpiece. He gave it a quick test, smelling the air that came out, before placing the inhaler back in her purse. He handed her back the purse and her belt, saying, "Thank you, Miss—have a nice day."

This made me realize how strict they were; they were even examining poor Miss Lexington's inhaler. *Would they examine Gio's leg that closely?*

Another dark suit standing by the conveyor belt turned his attention to us and asked, "Any weapons or illegal material in your pockets, young men?" He motioned for us to empty our pockets and place the contents on the conveyor belt.

At that moment, I was glad I didn't have nun-chucks or Chinese throwing stars, just my nice pens.

"No, sir," Chase answered for us. "Just a magnifying glass."

Chase pulled the glass from his pocket and placed it on the conveyor belt with my pens.

"What's this for?" the man asked, examining the glass.

"Helps me see things better, you know. I'm legally blind," Chase quipped as he pointed to his pop-bottle-thick glasses.

"Okay, go ahead and step through the metal detector, one by one, and collect your items on the other side," the man directed us, as the belt sent our items through the portable x-ray machine.

We all moved towards the large metal frame detector that had been set up for us to walk through. Single-file, Chase, Eduard, and

I all walked through with no beeps. But when Gio started through, the machine started beeping.

"Step over here, young man. Anything metal in your pockets?" the suit asked.

"No, sir," Gio replied in his squeaky voice.

"Raise your arms out to your sides," the man said.

When Gio did so, the man waved a metal-detecting wand around Gio's body.

I began to think of what would happen if they found the secret stash of items inside Gio's leg. We hadn't talked about a backup plan if he got caught.

Should we run? Confess? The Secret Service won't be very understanding since we already had made reference to the President being harmed.

The expression on Gio's face confirmed he was thinking the same things as me.

The wand passed over his leg with a *beep-beep-beep*.

"What's on your leg?" the agent asked.

"It's my prosthetic, see?" Gio said.

Gio rolled up his pant leg, revealing his fake plastic leg and showcasing the metal parts of its joint while making a few grunting noises as if doing so was an ordeal. He was being dramatic—but he had to be.

This was it, I thought, *the moment we planned for. And if this goes wrong, we're all going to jail. But how could I save Jax if I was in prison?* I worried. *Maybe I could deny I even knew Gio, and the plan to smuggle in contraband?*

Thoughts spun through my mind; I wasn't sure what I was going to do.

Then, the suit looked up, and said, "Oh… I'm sorry. Okay, young man, you are clear. Pick up your items at the end of the conveyor belt and have a pleasant day."

It worked! Just like Chase said it would.

I let out a sigh, realizing I had been holding my breath the entire time.

Rather than delay another second, we quickly walked off down the hall. We tried to act normal as we strode right past our lockers.

Several people whom we didn't know passed us by, but they didn't pay us any attention. They looked like they were frantically setting up for the President's visit.

I noticed one particularly beautiful woman standing off to the corner. She was dressed in a black business suit with heels and had her black hair pulled back in a ponytail. She was wearing dark sunglasses fit to her face, and I thought it was odd she was wearing them indoors.

We were able to move quickly through the hallways, as they were still void of any students. We passed Professor Wetherby's classroom, catching a glimpse of him furiously writing on his blackboard. He didn't notice us.

Hurrying around a corner, we ran headfirst into dreadful Miss Crabtree. She was carrying a cup of coffee.

"Ohh!" she gasped as the coffee jumped from her cup onto her nice business jacket.

"Excuse us—so sorry," Chase apologized.

She pursed her frowning lips, "Watch where you are going, students! You know the rules—no running in the hallways!"

Around the next corner, we found Coach Conley and Miss Ivy. They were walking together towards us and chatting.

"Good morning, students," Miss Ivy greeted us. "Here a bit early, aren't you?"

"Miss Ivy, have you seen Jaclyn this morning?" I quickly asked.

Coach Conley furrowed his eyebrows, as Miss Ivy raised hers. She answered for the two of them.

"No, why?" she questioned.

I wanted to tell her everything—but with Coach standing next to her, I couldn't risk it.

"Uh… study group," I said.

We pressed on and passed by the empty cafeteria. The basement door was in sight near the end of the hall when I heard a clicking noise coming up behind us.

Click-click-click.

"Sterns is coming! Quick, hide!" I whispered.

We ducked into a classroom as the principal walked by. He was clicking his pen while talking on his mobile phone.

We heard him say, "I've got no time for this. Deal with it! All the preparations have been made. There's no changing our plans now. This cannot fail!"

When the hallway was clear and silent, we poked our heads into the hallway and looked down. Chase gave the nod, and we hurried in single file to the basement door… *locked!*

Eduard straightened his glasses. "Why would Jax lock it *behind* her?"

"She wouldn't," Chase answered slowly.

When he said this, I started to sweat all over again. And that's when a faint blood-chilling scream arose from down behind the door.

"That was Jax!" I grabbed at the handle and tried to turn the locked knob. *No-go*. "We've got to get help!" I screeched, my voice loud, not hushed.

I turned to run back for the Secret Service, but Chase grabbed me.

"Slow down! Who's gonna help?" he said to me. "We don't know who's in cahoots with Sterns now, and the Secret Service doesn't believe us!"

He was right.

"What are we gonna do then?" I demanded, unable to think straight. My love was in danger, and I had to save her!

"Give me some cover, and keep a lookout," Chase said to Eduard and me. "G—open your leg, and hand me my tools."

Gio nodded, then rolled up his pant leg. He loosened a strap. He managed to pull his lower fake leg off just enough to reach inside and pull out Chase's lock-pick set. Chase wasted no time working on the lock while we served as a cover for him.

Chase had to stop when Mrs. Huntley walked around the corner. She gave a startled gasp, then a nervous smile. "Good morning, my friends. Early to school so you don't miss the President's visit?" she asked us.

"Uh… yeah. We didn't want to miss anything today," I said, nodding my head.

She looked us over with suspicious eyes I hadn't yet seen from her, then retracted her smile. "That reminds me; I forgot something. All right then, I'll see you in class." She turned and hurried back in the direction from which she had come.

Chase continued his tiny manipulation of the keyhole.

"Hurry, Chase," I said, looking down both directions of the hallway.

"Almost there… one more pin… ha!" he said, giving a grunt of satisfaction.

The lock opened, and we swung open the door. But rather than dashing down the stone steps that disappeared in the dark, we all paused.

"Flip the light switch," Gio said nervously.

Eduard did so, sending down a garish light from atop the entryway. Hesitation took hold of each of us again, as we waited for the other to proceed first.

Finally, Chase started down. "Be ready for anything; who knows what's down here," he whispered over his shoulder.

"Zombies?" Gio squeaked.

"*Anything,*" Chase reiterated.

Thoughts flooded my brain as I stood for a moment longer. *Should I tell the guys about everything I had seen, heard, and felt—the shadow at this doorway yesterday, the image of the boy I saw during gym class and in the boy's bathroom mirror, the gargoyles moving, and the sounds of the woman wailing?*

But there was no time. One by one, we began our descent.

CHAPTER FORTY-TWO

DESCENT INTO DARKNESS

I FOLLOWED RIGHT behind Chase. The stairs were a long, narrow descent of twisting stone and pale light. My knees trembled, and it only became worse with each downward step.

I screamed Jax's name at the top of my lungs—but only in my mind. My mouth was sealed shut.

"This doesn't feel good," Eduard whispered.

He was right. The air hung about us with a pungent, musty smell that reeked of the undead. Coming down here with a group of guys was hard enough, and it made me wonder how Jax had the courage to come down here alone.

If we heard one groan, moan, hiss, or boo, I thought, *the group of us would run right back up the stairs screaming.*

We reached the end of the stairs, then entered the giant stone room of the basement. Here, the air was cool, heavy, and musty.

Metal shelving units by the walls were filled with school supplies, old furniture, extra cooking supplies, and old tools.

Two single light bulbs in the center of a wood trestle ceiling were covered in cobwebs. They gave out light so dim it was unable to reach the corners of the room—helping to conceal any creatures or ghosts there that wanted to spring to life and devour us.

None of us spoke; I wondered if any of us was even breathing. We had heard a cry for help from Jax only minutes before, but now there was no sign of her. *How could she disappear so fast?* I thought.

I looked about. There was no way out of the basement except for the stairs we had just come down.

"Jax?" Chase whispered. "Jax, are you here?"

I was a mixture of fright and worry as I moved to look into the dark shadows of the room. "Where is she?" I asked.

"She's not down here," Gio squeaked in a soft whisper.

Eduard's voice began to tremble, "M-maybe she's s-s-somewhere else, and w-what we heard w-w-was an echo. The v-v-vents could be playing tricks on our ears."

I noticed a large table with massive wooden legs pushed up against a wall. "Is that Horace Tanner's poker table?" I wondered out loud.

We huddled together and stared at the dusty table. It seemed to stare back at us.

Was the gambling ghost sitting there, waiting to play a game with us?

Chase spotted something on the floor by the table. He reached down and picked it up. "Look! It's Jax's notepad—she was down here!" he whispered. "But where is she now?"

I grabbed at her notepad and opened it. I flipped through some of her pages to see if she had written us another note while noticing her perfect handwriting that was so cute. "There's nothing new written in here—no note for us," I said, feeling dejected.

"W-w-where is she?" Gio said.

I looked over at him; he was shaking with fright.

Eduard looked terrified, as if he was going to run up the stairs at any given moment. "She's disappeared!" he yelped.

Chase bent down to look at the floor near a large metal shelf against the wall. "Look at these scratch marks on the floor—"

Gio interrupted him. "Claw marks!" He raised his voice and shrieked, "It's the zombies! They are clawing out of the ground!"

Eduard took several steps backwards, towards the stairs. "Let's get out of here and get some help!"

Chase didn't move. "The marks on the floor go under this metal shelf," he said in a level tone.

"Who cares!" I snarled; my patience shot as I worried about what had happened to Jax. I looked around the room again. "Where *is* she?"

But Chase was in his own world now. "G, give me the lighter," he said.

"What?" Gio squeaked. "Why? There's plenty of light to see, and we've got a flashlight. We need to get out of here while we still can."

There was no time to waste arguing about it; we had to find Jax. So I snapped, "Just give him the lighter, G!"

Gio listened to me. He quickly rolled up his pant leg, unstrapped his fake leg, reached down into it, and produced a small lighter, then threw it to Chase.

Chase gave it a few flicks, and when the flame ignited, he started walking about slowly and methodically. The flame flickered and drew towards the wall and shelf.

Chase slowly walked in that direction, and when he came close to the wall, the flame flickered intensely, as if something was blowing on it.

Was this Charlie Hackett's ghost trying to blow out the flame? I thought. *Did ghosts not like fire?*

"What is it?" Eduard asked. "Why are you standing next to the wall? Is there a reason?"

Chase let the flame die as his thumb came off the lighter. He tossed the lighter back to Gio, who quickly returned it into his hollow leg before strapping the prosthetic back onto his thigh.

"Give me a hand," Chase said, right before he grabbed at the large metal shelf, and tried to pull it away from the wall. Once we all moved in to help him, the metal shelf scraped across the floor to reveal an open hole in the stone wall behind it. The air behind us whooshed into the small opening.

"A secret passage!" Eduard exclaimed.

We slowly peered into the dark void, our eyes straining into the abyss. I felt a new sensation, and I came alive inside with excitement. "Jax is in there—I know it!" I declared.

"Along with who knows what else!" Gio squeaked. "This is classic zombies!"

"We need to get help! We have proof now!" Eduard said.

"No time," Chase said as he stood in front of the hole. "G, give me the flashlight."

Trembling, Gio complied after accessing his secret storage compartment. "I don't think this is a good idea. What if something happens to us?? Who will be alive to tell the Secret Service?"

"It won't matter at that point. C'mon—there's no time left," Chase said.

He sounded like our commander-in-charge, which, I guess, he was.

Chase pointed the flashlight into the dark like a sword, challenging anything that might be hiding in there. Chase took a deep breath and stepped inside, allowing me to take several deep breaths before I hesitantly followed. Gio was right behind me, gripping onto my shirt, and Eduard was gripping onto Gio's.

It was a small passageway, but large enough for us to stand in. The floor inside was moist and muddy, while the rock and clay walls were heavy with condensation.

Soon enough, we tunneled in farther than the basement light could reach. Our flashlight cut a stark path through the darkness, exposing every rock and stone. We moved in a silent formation, with careful, quiet, timid steps. Our eyes jittered back and forth from side to side as we looked for danger.

The cavern twisted and turned, taking us deeper and deeper. After a while, we had no idea how far we'd gone, what was waiting for us, or what we'd do once we found it.

"We need weapons," Gio whispered.

"Yeah. A machine gun would be helpful right now," I answered.

After we took several more twists, turns, and frightened steps, the tunnel of dirt and rock opened up to a much larger cavern, with high ceilings and different tunnels going in different directions. These tunnels were braced with large timber, giving the appearance we were inside… an old mine.

I looked down each tunnel, seeing the same amount of darkness greeting us from everywhere. "Which way?" I breathed.

Suddenly, I thought I heard a whisper—a soft whisper coming from down the passage to our immediate right. The other guys must have heard it too, as they stopped, and we all looked at each other.

It could have been the breeze echoing through the tunnels. But it could also be—something else.

Chase squinted his eyes. "Let's stick to the right," he said.

I knew he'd say that.

The old timbers that held up this tunnel gave a wider and more comfortable passage through it. They allowed us to walk side by side, and we held onto each other's shirts as we continued forward, Gio in the middle.

The smell ahead of us became more rank as we came to another open cavern with high ceilings. The tunnel continued to our right, and revealed, to our left, a steep drop-off into a pit of darkness.

Chase pointed the light down, and we peered down from the ledge into the pit. The smell was awful and caused us to cover our noses. The light couldn't quite reach the bottom, but we could make out rubble, and maybe a lump of something that looked like a sack.

"Wonder what's down there?" Eduard asked.

"Zombies, of course," Gio whispered back.

I tugged on Chase's shirt. "Let's get out of here."

He nodded, then ran the beam of light back up the walls—when suddenly, a shadow moved away from the path of light. The sight made us gasp.

Did we just see something?

Chase moved the stream of light back and forth, trying to uncover the source of the shadow. He found nothing but darkness.

I heard the echoing whisper again. It caused me to take a step back and lose my footing. Flailing my arms, I fell. I grabbed at the dirt but slid down into the hole.

I couldn't help but let out a scream. "Help me!" I shrieked as I tumbled down. The light faded from my eyes until I was in complete darkness.

My feelings of being afraid left me, and I closed my eyes. I was in my bed… I was dreaming now—dreaming of Jax and me in the tree-fort watching the sunset. The sun's rays enveloped us both like a warm blanket, as we watched the light fight off the oncoming darkness.

I heard a faint whisper. It sounded like my name.

"Oliverrrrr…"

Slowly, I opened my eyes.

"Ollie! You okay?" Gio and Chase yelled down at me.

I lay motionless for a moment, not knowing where I was. Then I began moaning. My hands and face stung, and my head ached. I surely would have many bruises by the next day.

I spotted the flashlight casting its faint light around the pit I was in. I could feel something touching my face. I turned in the dim light to see—*it was a hand.*

I recoiled from the touch of the cold digits. The hand dropped lifelessly to the ground, and I found myself looking at the lackluster eyeballs… *of a corpse!*

"Ahhh!" I screamed out in terror, kicking the corpse while frantically scooting away. The mouth of the corpse fell open as if to talk, and I screamed even louder. "Get me out of here now!"

"Hang on, Ollie!" Chase yelled down.

I moved back against the wall of the pit, shaking uncontrollably at the sight of the decaying body and rotting eyeballs staring at me. The faint light danced back and forth on the corpse, and I screamed again when I recognized the body: It was Mr. Doyle, dressed in the same brown tweed blazer and khaki pants he had been wearing last week.

The smell of the decaying flesh was awful, and I wanted to barf right then and there, but I was too scared to move. All I could think of was: *The stories were true! Mr. Doyle had lost a bet, and the gambler ghost had taken Mr. Doyle into the mine forever.*

The end of a rope landed next to me as Chase yelled down, "Climb up it, Ollie!"

I grabbed the rope and climbed up it faster than anyone had ever climbed a rope in the gym. Chase and Gio helped me to the top, grabbing onto my shirt and arms and asking, "What was down there?"

"Dead… b-b-body!" I cried. "Mr. Doyle's!"

"What? We've got to get out of here now!" Gio said in a panic. "This place will be crawling with zombies any minute!"

We turned to run back in the direction we had come from, but a large shadow moved along the cavern wall. "Where d'ya think you're go'n?" it asked.

A low grumble echoed through the cavern.

We stopped and went motionless as the shadow revealed the figure of a man. We turned to run in the other direction, but we came face-to-face with another man in our path. He grabbed us by our shirt collars and threw us to the ground.

"What are we gonna do with these brats?" the man asked in a sour tone that was… familiar!

It was the repairmen from the school! I looked up at them, then drew in a sharp breath at the sight of them pointing guns at our shaking bodies.

"Why you down here?" the younger man, Finnegan, asked as he pointed his gun at my face. "Answer me, ya brat."

I quickly stammered, "We… we… we're looking for our friend."

Chase shook his head at me not to say any more.

Finnegan looked around. "Who else is down here?"

"No one," Chase answered. "Like he said, we just were looking for our friend. But, uh, he's not here anywhere."

"Oh, you are? Well, let me help you," he sneered, then grabbed Chase by his shirt collar and pulled him to the edge of the pit I had just crawled out from. "I think he's down there—"

"Finnegan, stop! We need them alive," the tall repairman, Santos, scolded with his accent. "They might come in useful as hostages later."

"We don't have time to babysit, Santos!" Finnegan snarled.

Santos looked at his watch. "Let us bring them back to Murdoch and let him decide what to do with them."

Finnegan thought for a moment, then gave a snort. "Okay—get up, brats. Let's go!"

They marched us single-file down the cavern tunnel, Finnegan taking the lead with his light, and Santos following with his gun. This was way worse than marching to the principal's office because this trip might mean permanent detention.

Our shadows followed us down the cavern tunnel—and that's when a shadow darted in front of us, causing Finnegan to stop and turn his head.

"Did you see that?" he asked, narrowing his eyes.

Santos looked around. "I saw nothing—why?"

Finnegan got close to Gio's face. "There's no more of you brats down here, are there?"

"No… no… just us," Gio wailed.

"Come on, it was nothing! We have no time for this," Santos snapped impatiently. "Murdoch will wonder what happened."

With a quick once-around of his head, Finnegan continued his quick pace down the cavern tunnel.

We could just see a faint light ahead. It looked like sunlight and grew brighter with every step. *Could we be heading out above ground?* I wondered.

I was wrong: The tunnel opened up into a giant cave that was illuminated by sunlight coming through an airshaft in the ceiling. We were not going above ground after all.

This cave was littered with all kinds of equipment. Several black equipment cases were stacked around the cave; some were open, showing electronic equipment inside, and wires connecting with other wires. A large machine with what looked like a giant corkscrew on its end stood in a corner.

Near the center of the massive cave's floor lay a large mineshaft. It looked like a black hole in space. A pulley without a rope was affixed to the ground near the mineshaft's edge. On the opposite side of the mineshaft was a makeshift desk, with several television monitors, computers, and papers on top of it. Sitting behind the desk was the other repairman with gray hair—Murdoch.

He sat motionless and stared at us with hateful eyes. "What is this?"

"We found them wandering the tunnel," Finnegan said. "Thought they might be useful as hostages, like we're doing with the girl. If not, we can throw them down the pit."

"Your timing is priceless," Murdoch replied in a sarcastic tone. "Tie them up, and make sure they have nothing in their pockets—like phones or the like."

That's when I saw her. The beauty of the world. She was next to Murdoch's desk, against the cavern wall in the shadows.

Jax's hands were tied to her feet, and a gag was around her mouth. She looked at me with helpless eyes, awaiting me to rescue her.

My eyes filled with rage. Gone was the terror I had felt before.

I will rescue you, my love, I thought. *I will, somehow.*

Finnegan and Santos lined us against the opposite wall of the mineshaft and tied our hands behind our backs. They patted our pockets, seizing anything they found. No nun-chucks or Chinese throwing stars from me—but they confiscated my very best writing pen.

Finnegan pulled Chase's magnifying glass from his back pocket and put it to his own eye, then examined Chase's face with it. "Let's have a look here, shall we?" he laughed.

Chase tried to look away as Murdoch barked out, "Enough games, Finnegan! We don't have much time."

"Yeah, okay. Sit down, brats!" Finnegan commanded as he pulled the glass away.

We all slunk to the ground against the wall as Finnegan tied up our legs.

"In case you get some stupid ideas of running," he snickered. He gave the ropes an extra cinch to make them hurt. Then he stood tall and stretched.

We sat bound against the damp walls of the mine and looking at each other. Gio trembled, Eduard wheezed, I sniffled, and Chase frowned. So much for saving the world, our school, or even my grades.

We lost all hope. No one knew where we were—and the President was going to be at the school soon.

"Everything look okay, Murdoch?" Finnegan asked the man sitting behind the desk.

Murdoch was busy typing on his laptop computer.

"So far. Vincent's in place right now. We just need the guest of honor to arrive," he answered.

I strained to see what was going on in the array of television monitors set up by his desk. I could see different parts of the school on them, and men in black suits walking around.

"Look at 'em, would ya?" Murdoch smirked. "They have no idea what's about to happen."

Murdoch sat back in his chair, picked an object off his desk, and began fiddling with it. I took a second look: It was my great-grandfather's pocket watch! He must have taken it from Mr. Doyle!

I made a slight sound at Chase to get his attention, and when he looked over at me, I nodded towards Murdoch. Chase gave me a nod back in acknowledgment.

Chase spoke up now. "I can tell you your plan won't work."

"Shut up, before I gag you like your little girlfriend over there who wouldn't shut up," Finnegan chortled.

"What makes you say such a thing?" Murdoch asked Chase in a curious tone.

"We've told the sheriff and the Secret Service about your plans," Chase answered.

"Oh, you did?" Murdoch scoffed. "And just what are our plans?"

"You're not really air conditioning repairmen, and this whole time you've been setting the school up to... execute your plans for kidnapping the President," Chase said.

Murdoch, Finnegan, and Santos all paused and looked at each other.

Murdoch raised his eyebrows. "You told the sheriff and the Secret Service this?"

"Yes, and we told them we know you're planning on... selling the President to the aliens," Chase said.

"Ha-ha-ha," Murdoch laughed. The sound of it was so loud it echoed through the cave. "No, not quite. I don't think they'd be interested in dead weight."

"What? Are you going to kill the President?" Chase asked in horror.

"No, no," Murdoch responded. "Not as long as we get our demands met. Otherwise—"

Gio blurted out desperately, "The Secret Service will stop you!"

"Oh, I don't think we need to worry about them. After they get a taste of my chemical mixture, they'll be sound asleep," Murdoch said with a satisfied nod of his head.

Eduard cocked his chin up. "Ah-ha, I knew it! You've been poisoning the school's food!"

"Ha-ha-ha. Not quite. But actually, that's not a bad idea, young man. No, when the President and all his men are gathered in the auditorium, I'll just turn on the school's air conditioning. That's when they will start to feel a little sleepy," Murdoch boasted as he pointed to his computer. "That will release an undetected mixture of Nitrous Oxide and Xenon gas into the air ducts."

"*N2O*—for Nitrous Oxide—and *Xe*—for Xenon—a mixture of knockout gas!" Eduard exclaimed.

"You're smart, kid, but that's not all," Murdoch smiled in

satisfaction. "When everyone falls asleep, we have people on the inside who will cut the power to the building—turning out the lights. Then they will simply take out the trash."

He pointed to a television monitor displaying another repairman, who was bald and dressed in gray coveralls—Vincent. He was pushing a wheelchair with a small air tank strapped to the back, down a hallway of the school.

"Vincent will bring the sleeping President out, down through the tunnel you nosey kids came through. He'll wake up far away from his Secret Service. We'll be long gone with the President by the time the rest of those idiots wake up and try to figure out what happened. No one's ever kidnapped a sitting President, until now," Murdoch boasted.

"But what if something goes wrong?" Chase asked. "Like the gas doesn't release, or the Secret Service agents aren't knocked out—then what?"

Murdoch bristled at the idea that something could go awry with his plan.

"If things get out of control, we have an insider close to the President with orders to assassinate him on the spot," he said sharply. Then he looked over to a different monitor. "Looks like the party's about to begin."

We could just see on one of the monitors a procession of long, black limousines pulling to the front of the school. The President of the United States had arrived.

I thought about the timing: *If the President was arriving, it meant the school day had started already. That meant we all were absent from Miss Crabtree's class.*

Would we be missed? I wondered. *Miss Crabtree had seen us all at the school earlier, so maybe she would think to send out a search party?*

But then I answered my own question. I heard Miss Crabtree's voice in my head saying, "*Numbers don't care about kidnappings.*"

Murdoch grabbed a walkie-talkie and spoke into it. "Okay, we're on the clock. Everyone should be at their job site and ready to start."

"Roger that. Ready to start work," answered a man on the walkie-talkie.

Murdoch began typing on a computer. The rest of us watched silently as the President got out of his limo, surrounded by dark-suited Secret Service agents and reporters taking photos.

Principal Sterns was waiting there to greet him.

We could hear an audio of our principal saying, "Mr. President, on behalf of Raven Ridge Academy, the State of Colorado, and students everywhere, let me say what an extreme honor it is to have you here. I am one of your biggest supporters. If there is anything I can do to make your visit here more comfortable, please let me know."

The President, dressed in a suit and tie, shook Principal Sterns' hand, and said, "Thank you for your kind words and wonderful welcome. I've been looking forward to this visit for quite some time."

The President turned and spoke louder, making sure the press could hear him. "I believe children are our future—we must let them lead the way!" Then he smiled and waved before walking into the school building while reporters shouted questions at him.

"I believe the same thing!" Principal Sterns shouted out.

The press ignored him.

CHAPTER FORTY-THREE

BURNING DAYLIGHT

"ALL RIGHT, SANTOS and Finnegan, time to get—" Murdoch stopped, interrupted by what sounded like the soft whisper we had heard before. "What was that—the wind or more kids?"

Finnegan spun around to us and put his face right in front of our faces. "You said no one else was down here!" he snarled.

A shadow flitted across the cavern wall near the tunnel from where we had come. The sight caused Murdoch to stand up from his chair.

"Santos, Finnegan, go check the entrance again, and this time, don't bring home any strays. Go!" he ordered.

The two men picked up their guns and flashlights, then quickly headed back down the rock passage.

I mouthed silently to Chase, *"Odyssey?"*

He shrugged his shoulders and whispered over, *"I don't know—maybe."*

"I hope no more of your classmates followed you down here because otherwise, I'll be throwing all of you down this here bottomless pit," Murdoch said.

To reinforce his words, he tossed a rock into the large mineshaft near the middle of the cave. No sound returned as the stone disappeared into the black. We all looked at each other with worry as Murdoch turned back to his desk.

We sat helpless, watching Murdoch track everything on his television monitors as he fiddled with my great-grandfather's pocket watch.

The cameras showed the President moving to Mr. Doyle's classroom for the sit-in with Ana Rahela Balenovic. I wasn't sure which was worse: being kidnapped or having to listen to Three-Name's boastful tone as she brown-nosed the President.

Maybe being kidnapped wasn't so bad after all.

The small circle of bright sunlight from the airshaft in the ceiling slowly inched over us, like a sundial keeping time. That's when I noticed Chase shaking his head as if he had water in his ears. I watched his eyeglasses plop off his head and into his lap.

Chase squirmed until his glasses were between his knees. He whispered for Gio to turn his back to him and put out his arms near his eyeglasses. Gio looked confused, but quietly turned and did as directed.

"Right there, G. Now, don't move," Chase whispered.

I knew what was going on: Chase was attempting to use his glasses to magnify the sunlight coming through the airshaft to burn the rope.

Whenever Murdoch turned to glance over at us hostages with a suspicious eye, he found us silent and smiling. Gio's body fully blocked Chase's attempt from Murdoch's view, so Chase could continue on with his burning task.

As for me, I worried about what we would do, and what

Murdoch would do, if we escaped from our bonds. But I had to trust that Chase had a plan for this, too.

I looked at my fellow classmates. Chase's tongue darted out the side of his mouth as he maneuvered his knees with great precision. Gio did his part, holding his arms as steady as could be. Soon, a small smoldering started from behind Gio—the rope was burning!

The smoke rose behind Gio's back, circling in the still air. I glanced at Murdoch, worried he might smell the burning rope from across the cave. But he was mesmerized by the events on the monitors.

I saw Gio's arms move out and forward. He was free from the rope!

Murdoch sniffed the air and looked around. "Stupid Finnegan! I told him not to smoke down here!" Shaking his head, he glanced over at us with a quick squint before going back to his monitor.

Gio moved his hands down to his legs, then untied the rope that bound them up. His movements were slow and smooth, for too much movement would cause Murdoch to look over and discover he was untied. After a few final twists, he was completely free from his bindings.

Jax saw what was happening and kept Murdoch's attention by making sounds under her gag.

Murdoch looked at her, annoyed. "What is it? You have something to say?"

Jax nodded her head, yes.

"You're not gonna scream again, are you? You know no one can hear you down here anyway."

Jax shook her head no, and Murdoch got up to draw down her gag.

Meanwhile, Gio slowly removed his fake leg, which contained our equipment. He took out the pocketknife and slowly opened it. Gio slid it over to Chase, and then he resumed sitting still to avoid Murdoch's attention. Chase quickly began cutting at his own bindings.

Jax coughed a bit before saying in a sweet tone, "I think you should reconsider. If you leave now, the consequences for your actions might not be as severe. You might not even get caught at all."

"Humph… you know what? You're right, and I've reconsidered," Murdoch said while looking at Jax. "I think we'll just forget this whole thing and be on our merry way—no harm, no foul." Murdoch stretched out his arms behind his head and said, "Now shut up before I gag ya again." Then he turned back to look at the monitor.

By now, Chase's hands were free, and he was quickly cutting the rope around his feet. He slid the knife to Eduard while nodding to Gio that he wanted something else from his secret leg compartment. Gio showed him the lighter and some of the fireworks; Chase nodded yes. Gio slowly pulled the M-80, pop bottle rockets, and smoke bombs from his leg.

Eduard was now free of his bonds, and he slid the knife over to me. I grabbed the knife and was fiddling with it, trying to position the blade just right before the first slice, when it fell from my grasp and skipped over a rock. Chase quickly grabbed it up. The noise wasn't loud, but it was enough to bring Murdoch's glance in our direction.

Murdoch did a double-take when he noticed Gio's leg off. "What the?" he snarled as he threw himself off his chair.

We all continued to sit as if our hands were bound behind our backs as he stormed over to us.

"What's this?" he snipped at Gio, who started to shake in response.

"It's my… my… my leg," Gio stuttered.

"Yes, I know it's your leg, ya freak, but what's it doing off?"

Murdoch looked at the rope lying untied and cut on the ground. "Oh, thinking of going somewhere?" His eyes flashed fury as he kicked Gio's fake leg hard across the cave. It scattered the inside contents on the ground before it toppled into the abyss of the deep mineshaft. "Now you won't have such an easy time of it!"

"No!" Gio screamed, flinging his arms out in desperation.

It was too late: Gio's prosthetic was gone.

"How'd you get out of your ropes?" Murdoch snapped, grabbing Gio by his shirt collar and hauling him up. He then looked at the rest of us.

Chase waited until Murdoch met his eyes, then swung the pocketknife he clutched hard into Murdoch's thigh. Murdoch gave a scream of pain, let Gio go, and grabbed for his leg.

Gio scooted away from Murdoch while Chase and Eduard scrambled to their feet. I wiggled on the ground, trying to get up, but the ropes defeated me. Eduard rushed over to untie me. Chase had grabbed the lighter and a few pop bottle rockets before he ran around the mineshaft's edge over to Jax.

Murdoch pulled the knife from his leg. The blood gushed out, and he grimaced when he held the walkie-talkie to his mouth. "Santos, Finnegan—get back here! We've got a problem!" He then pointed the knife at us, mashing his teeth. "Do anything, and I'll cut every last one of you!"

Eduard finished with my ropes, and I scrambled to my feet. Flinging Jax a desperate glance, I saw Chase had freed her.

Gio got up onto his one good leg, and he hopped towards Eduard and me.

Murdoch wasted no time charging the three of us with the pocketknife. He lumbered forward, limping on his leg.

Chase yelled, "G, throw me the bomb!"

I knew he meant the M-80 near Gio.

Gio grabbed for the ground as Murdoch swung at his little

frame. Gio rolled and grabbed the firework, then threw it over to Chase. His throw was short, and the firework rolled on the ground near the edge of the mineshaft. Jax darted around the mineshaft and dove for it, catching it before it disappeared into the black pit.

Murdoch stumbled around, whining in pain. The rest of us looked around for anything to fight him with.

Gio picked up a piece of wood, Eduard found a long metal bar, I grabbed a rock, and Chase had a pop bottle rocket. Murdoch, however, grabbed Jax.

She dropped the M-80 near the edge of the shaft and squealed. Murdoch silenced her with a firm grip over her mouth. Breathing heavily, he flexed his grip on Jax, tightening it the more she struggled. I could tell he was sizing us, his competition, up.

Chase lit the lighter, then aimed the pop bottle rocket at Murdoch. "Let her go!" he ordered.

Murdoch stared Chase down. "I wouldn't do that if I were you—if you want your girlfriend here to live," he panted. "This here is a bottomless pit. None of us knows how deep it goes, but this girl is going to find out if ya don't start cooperating. Now put that DOWN!"

Chase looked at us; I nodded to do what Murdoch had said. Chase took his thumb off the lighter, then lowered the firework he was holding in his other hand.

Just as Gio, Eduard, and I dropped our weapons, Jax bit down hard into Murdoch's hand. He gave a loud yell and released her. There was blood streaming down his hand, and he grasped the bite mark with his other hand. Clearly, he was in pain.

Jax darted away from her captor, and in a rage, Murdoch charged forward at her. But Chase had lit the fuse of his firework already, and he let the missile go. With a burst of flames and a *whoosh!*, the missile raced straight out of Chase's hand into the face of Murdoch. The firework exploded with a loud *bang!*

Murdoch screamed, grabbing at his face, and stumbling backwards. Somehow, his flailing hand managed to grab the material of Jax's dress, and he brought her along with him—back, back, back.

His feet found the edge of the mineshaft, and I saw the look in Jax's eyes as her captor fell in. Terror gripped me as she screamed and grasped at the rocky ground.

Her attempt failed. She was dragged along by Murdoch—and she too tumbled over the side.

"Noooo! Jax!" we boys all screamed.

But she was gone.

None of us moved. The mineshaft was a bottomless pit, and Jax would never be seen again.

My heart quit working; I felt like I was going to collapse. "No! No! No!" I yelled. My Jax was gone! I felt like flinging myself over the edge of the shaft in grief.

In a group, we all raced to peer over the edge. There was only darkness.

Breathing heavily, we were otherwise silent, completely stunned. And that's when we heard a faint whimper coming up from the darkness.

"Jax?" I yelled.

"Help me!" she called back.

Eduard ran over to Murdoch's desk and grabbed up his flashlight. He ran back and shone it down the shaft.

The thin beam of light found the tiny hands of Jax hanging onto a wooden beam that jutted out from a side of the bottomless shaft. Eduard moved the light over, and we could see her. She was alive and crying.

"Hang on, Jax!" I called down, my heart filled with happiness and joy.

Chase grabbed the ropes used by our captors and tied them together into one long piece.

But would it be long enough?

"Hurry, Chase!" I panicked.

Chase flung the rope over the side, and it seemed to be enough to reach her. We looked at each other. *Who would climb down and get her?* I wanted to, but I knew it should be Chase.

"You go," I said. "You're the best climber."

He nodded as Eduard, Gio, and I grabbed hold of the rope. Since he only had one good leg, Gio sat on the ground as an anchor.

"Don't let go," Chase said right before he slid down. "I'll be right back."

I found superhuman strength; nothing was going to move me from my spot. The rope was cemented in my grasp and would not be pried out. Kryptonite would not weaken me.

I could hear Jax whimpering softly, "Help me, help me, please! Don't let me fall."

Chase climbed down until he was right above her. "Grab my hand!" he said. He stretched down one arm while holding onto the rope with the other.

"I can't! I can't let go," she gasped out.

"Lower me—more rope!" he shouted up to us.

There wasn't much left. In order for us to give any more, Gio had to let his portion go, and so it was now up to Eduard and me. We widened our stances as we let Chase go lower. Gio hopped over and reached to hold on to Eduard's waist as Chase came down next to Jax.

By pushing off the wall with his feet, Chase made a few light swings until he came even closer to her. He finally grabbed her by the waist and said, "I've got you! Hang onto my neck, and they'll pull us up."

With a frightened yelp, Jax released the log and threw her arms around Chase's neck in what must have felt like a death hold. Chase grabbed back onto the rope with both hands before yelling, "I've got her! Bring us up!"

Our muscles strained as Eduard, and I pulled up with all our strength. Gio continued to pull back on Eduard's waist, leaning away with his one leg. Finally, we pulled up just enough rope to permit Gio to grab hold of the end of it and help pull even more.

This went on and on. The process seemed endless, but none of us gave up. When Chase and Jax finally came up to the lip of the edge, Gio hopped over to help Jax climb over Chase's back. Chase heaved himself up and sat down next to her.

Safe. They were both safe.

Jax reached over and hugged Chase. "You saved my life—thank you!"

She then got to her feet and came over to hug each of us. "Thank all of you!"

Chase picked up the M-80 that was lying next to him near the edge of the mineshaft. He looked at it, gave a deep sigh of relief, and then looked back down into the pit.

Murdoch was gone forever, down a bottomless pit, along with my great-grandfather's pocket watch. But Jax was here with me, with us, and that's all that mattered.

Chase looked over at the tunnel passage we hadn't gone through yet. "That must lead to the outside. We've got to get out and warn the sheriff about their plans before it's too late."

We nodded in agreement, and Jax went over to the makeshift desk and picked up a flashlight. I gathered up some of the fireworks still on the ground.

Gio looked steadily at the rest of us. "You're gonna have to go without me," he said, looking down at his half-leg.

Gio was right. He wouldn't be able to get out of here with one and one-half legs, no matter how hard he could hop.

Chase quickly shook his head. "No one gets left behind."

"Murdoch?" A voice drifted into the cavern. "What's going on?"

Finnegan and Santos emerged from the dark tunnel on the opposite side of the cave.

"You little brats, where's Murdoch?" Finnegan demanded.

We stood for a moment, looking for something to say, when Chase winked at me. "Smoke bomb," he whispered over.

I tossed him the smoke bomb, and he lit the fuse. He threw the fuming bomb between the men and us. The cave quickly filled with thick smoke, blocking the sunlight coming through the ceiling. Curses cut through the smoke as the men stumbled towards us, no doubt being careful of the mineshaft that lay in the middle of the cave's floor.

In the confusion, Gio sunk unnoticed behind Murdoch's makeshift desk. He whispered, "Go! I can hide here till you get back."

After a pause, Chase nodded his head. He yelled at Jax, Eduard, and me, "Let's go!"

Jax wasted no time turning and running up the tunnel with her flashlight. Eduard hesitated, looking over at Gio, but Gio waved him on. Satisfied Gio was concealed from the intruders; Eduard turned to follow Jax. I raced after Eduard—but Chase was not quite finished.

He lit the crown jewel—the M-80. Its fuse sparked through the clouds of smoke. Jax, Eduard, and I looked back over our shoulders as we hauled up the tunnel. Chase tossed it on the ground and smiled at Gio, who plugged his ears. Then Chase turned to run himself while also plugging his ears.

The men yelled, "Stop, you brats!"

KA—BOOM! rang out behind us when the M-80 exploded. The noise it made seemed to echo forever. I looked back to see Chase right behind me, running, too. The men were on their knees, covering their ears from the explosion of the M-80. The unexpected attack had dazed them and helped to put a little distance between us.

Jax made no effort to keep the light in her hand steady as she ran, so we all kept tripping as we dashed forward into the darkness to escape.

A light shone from behind us, and there was the sound of curses. The curses from behind became louder and louder, as did our breathing. We gasped frantically in the damp, dingy air of the tunnel. We had no idea where this tunnel led to, but we didn't care as long as it got us away from our pursuers.

Finally, we could see a faint light ahead. This gave us the hope we needed. The tunnel grew wider and wider until finally; we ran into an enormous cave.

There were giant iron double doors pressed into the opposite wall, and slits of sunlight peeking through the cracks showed us the way out.

As we hurried through this giant cave, we spied Mr. Doyle's classic car, the white work van, and my blue piece-of-crap bicycle. All were parked inside! But there was no time to take in the fact that these items were in here.

Jax and Eduard furiously unlatched the door's iron bolts, and Chase and I pushed the mighty doors open. This flooded the area with blinding sunlight and filled our lungs with fresh air.

Chase yelled to me, "Ollie, get your bike!"

I hesitated. "My bike?" But I grabbed my bike and pushed it at Jax, hollering, "Jax, get on!" She looked at me for a brief moment, and I gasped out, "You can ride fast and go get help! Go on—we'll be right behind you!"

She hopped on my blue piece-of-crap bike, and with a helpful shove from me, she was off, riding down the dirt road ahead of our running feet.

Ride like the wind, my love! I thought to myself. *Ride for our love!*

CHAPTER FORTY-FOUR

NO TIME TO LOSE

NO SOONER HAD Jax begun down a hill on my bike than the two repairmen chasing us emerged from the tunnel behind us.

"There they are!" they yelled. "Stop 'em before they get to someone!"

Chase, Eduard, and I jumped off the side of the road into the weeds and brush, then ran through Old Man Owens's fields. There was no need for words. We knew where we were going—straight to our tree-fort!

The men were close behind us when a gunshot rang out. We ducked into the tall grass and weeds and ran in zigzag patterns.

More shots rang out. My lungs burned, and I didn't know how much further I could run, but I knew we needed to keep them away from Jax—and that gave me strength to keep going.

We reached the edge of the thick brush and the forest of trees leading to our secret tree-fort. We crashed through the thick bushes, snapping branches, and barely noticing the scraping of our faces and tearing of our clothes.

Our pursuers followed relentlessly.

We saw our posted warning signs, and continued on, carefully avoiding our traps. Our tree was waiting for us in the clearing, its branches stretching wide and calling us to climb to safety. Eduard was up the rope ladder, followed by me, while Chase held the ladder steady from the ground.

The tree thickened its armored bark, ready for the attackers.

The men must have been able to see us climbing the ladder, because one of them hollered, "There they are! Shoot 'em!"

Eduard reached the platform above us. He unhooked the booby-trapped door and climbed inside. I was only halfway up—an easy target clearly out in the open. I fumbled to find footholds and looked back toward the voices—only to see a gun pointed in my direction.

I panicked and missed a rung of the rope ladder with my foot. This mishap twirled me about in the air.

As I spun and wiggled on the rope ladder, Finnegan stepped forward for a better shot. But he stepped directly onto a tripwire, causing a log to drop—pulling a rope behind him. The rope tripped him flat on his back, and he fired his gun into the air.

The log hit a board, launching a bucket of green primer directly onto him. Finnegan was covered completely with lime-green slime. He let out a moan, then struggled to his feet.

There was no time to admire the beauty and effectiveness of Eduard's trap. I continued my climb and reached the safety of the platform. Chase, however, had no time to climb at all, as Santos was almost upon him. He quickly raced off to the north, Santos in close pursuit.

"Get him!" Finnegan yelled. "I'll take care of the others!"

Santos followed after Chase while Finnegan rose to his feet. "I'm gonna make it real painful for ya's!" he snarled.

We quickly pulled up the tree's rope ladder, leaving only the booby-trapped ladder in place. Finnegan insisted on using it, but he cursed with every rung he climbed.

Eduard and I huddled in the corner of the tree-fort, clutching cattails. When Finnegan reached the halfway point, the rung we had half-cut broke beneath his weight, sending him crashing to the ground.

He grabbed his leg in pain and yelled, "Ahgh, I broke my leg! You brats!"

Chase was leading Santos to the north while carefully stepping over the tripwires. Santos saw what he was doing and was prepared, stepping over the same wires Chase had. However, Santos was not prepared for the second set of wires, which he tripped.

The wires released the thorny branches that had been pulled back. At once, these struck Santos in the face, and sent him, with a scream, wobbling backward.

Now Santos tripped the first wire. The released wire pulled the trigger of a lighter, igniting a pop bottle rocket. It shot up and hit him on his butt, causing him to run forward.

In the meantime, Finnegan had hobbled to his feet. Limping, and despite the paint dripping into his eyes, he saw Chase and aimed his gun. He fired—but Santos ran in front of the bullet.

Santos spun around in disbelief and sputtered, "You… you shot me!" He fell to the ground.

Finnegan snarled and pressed forward. "I'll kill you, brat!" he threatened. He pointed his gun squarely at Chase again. Eduard and I rained down cattails on him, causing him to shrug when he pulled the trigger—and miss.

Chase darted to the east, and Finnegan pursued him with the fury of a bull elephant—a lime-green, limping bull elephant. In his rage, he failed to see Chase step over another tripwire, which he proceeded to hit. It released a slingshot of more green primer into his already paint-covered face.

Finnegan staggered and began wildly shooting as he stumbled forward. "I hate you! I'll kill every last one of you!"

His choice of footsteps was unfortunate. He hit another tripwire, which lit the fuse of another pop bottle rocket. The rocket fired off and streaked into him. It exploded and ignited the primer.

Ablaze, Finnegan ran around in panic. Burning and screaming, he dropped to the ground and rolled, extinguishing the flames. But his roll set off yet another tripwire, releasing a large branch, which swung around and hit the hive of bees. The angry army took flight to attack the smoldering intruder.

"No! Ahhh! I'm allergic to bees!" Finnegan shrieked.

Finnegan hopped up on one leg, waving his arms, and quickly limped off. The bees chased him away into the distance.

Eduard and I scampered down the rope ladder and stood next to Chase.

"Let's go!" Chase yelled. "We've got to get to the President before it's too late!"

Without another thought, we ran toward the road.

We emerged from the brush at the main road. It was empty of people or vehicles. The school was a mile up the road, and it would take some time for us to get there. We were exhausted, but there was no time to rest.

As we struggled forward, I worried about what had happened to Jax: *Did she make it to the school? Did the Secret Service listen to her?* There was still the other repairman, Vincent, on the inside, and he would assassinate the President if we didn't get there in time.

Bang-bang-bang! echoed through the air.

Were there more attackers chasing us? Or were they shooting at Jax?

Dust rose over the hill, and a flash of gray streaked down the road. It was Spencer's car!

The classic Mustang screeched to a halt in front of us as Jax waved us in from the window.

"Hurry—get in!" she cried out.

The door flew open, and we piled into the back seat. Spencer mashed the peddle into the floorboard, spinning the tires, and sending his car hurtling forward in the direction of Raven Ridge Academy.

Aspyn said in an angry tone to Chase. "This had better not be one of your stupid stunts, dork!"

"No—this is the real thing," Chase said, panting.

"If it weren't for your girlfriend here, I wouldn't have believed any of it," she snorted.

I instantly interjected, "She's not his girlfriend."

"Hey… ugh… watch it, Spencer!" Aspyn said, grabbing onto a handle in the car as it hit a bump.

"Sorry—the road is bumpy," Spencer whined.

A siren rose behind us. Then came flashing red and blue lights.

"What? Oh, great, it's the sheriff! Where was he hiding?" Spencer whined as he slowed his car to pull over. "I'm gonna be so busted going this fast—and it's all your fault!"

"What are you doing?" Chase gasped. "We've got to keep going! The school's just down the road—the sheriff will understand!"

"Spencer can't lose his license again, dork—he's got to pull over," Aspyn said as she put a sympathetic hand to Spencer's cheek.

"Well, then, we'll run the rest of the way!" Chase protested.

Aspyn glared back at Chase. "Running from a car just pulled over by a sheriff is never a good idea—no way, little brother. Mom'll kill you."

The Mustang shot out two loud bangs as it rumbled to a stop on the side of the road. Sheriff Graves got out of his car and placed his large-brimmed cowboy hat on his head. He walked over to Spencer's window.

"Morn'n, son… in a hurry?" he drawled while looking carefully at the occupants of our car.

"Uh, sorry Sheriff, it was 'cause of these dorks in the back," Spencer said, giving us up.

"Sheriff, please listen to us!" Chase screamed. "You've got to warn the Secret Service—the President is in danger!"

"Oh? From what now? More space aliens?" the sheriff said, shaking his head.

"No—that's what we thought at first, but we just escaped from men posing as repairmen who are planning to capture or assassinate the President!" Chase said.

"Please believe us!" Jax begged. "I almost died!

"And Mr. Doyle did die; I saw his body in the mine!" I hollered.

"And one of the men just shot his partner while they were chasing us back by our tree-fort!" Eduard added. "It's true—we swear!"

At that, Sheriff Graves narrowed his eyes. He looked at us, covered in scratches and bloody, our clothing ripped. Perhaps recognizing something in our eyes, he gave a decisive nod, and ran back to his car, trying to talk on the radio before slamming it down.

"Damn electronics! I told Abe to fix this weeks ago—damn it!" he cursed. He continued to curse a blue streak. The louder his cursing got, the worse it got, until he finally said, "Follow me!" He jumped into his cruiser, and spinning the tires of his car, tore off towards our school.

"Awesome!" Spencer yelled, smashing the pedal down once again. This spurred the Mustang into a full sprint, and it chased after the sheriff's car.

The sheriff's cruiser screeched to a stop in front of the school, followed by the Mustang. Several men in dark suits raced forward and held their hands in the air, indicating we needed to stop.

"We have a problem," Sheriff Graves told the suits as he climbed out of his car. "These kids in that vehicle have some information about a potential attack on the President."

"Let me guess—space monsters?" the tall agent scoffed in a

sarcastic tone. "Yeah, they were here earlier, and I told them false accusations would get them in trouble."

"Yes, but this time I think they might have a case," Sheriff Graves said. He quickly recounted our story to the suits, who listened with some curiosity.

"It's true! You've got to believe us!" Jax pleaded when the sheriff had finished talking.

Sheriff Graves said, "How about I head back to where these kids say they were attacked, and see if there's any truth to their story? You have a radio I can borrow if I find anything? Mine's on the fritz."

The tall suit handed the sheriff a walkie-talkie. "It's on the right channel. Call if you find something."

As the sheriff ran for his patrol car, Chase yelled after him, "It was at our tree-fort, and the man who was shot is probably still there! But how are you going to find our tree-fort? You don't know where it is!"

"I'll find it," the sheriff promised.

Chase turned to the tall suit. "The guy on the inside is dressed as a repairman in gray coveralls, and he's bald."

The suits nodded to each other, then began talking in code into the wires hanging from their ears before looking back to us.

"The President is just about to give out his award in the auditorium," the tall agent said. "You kids come with us and point out this supposed attacker. If this turns out to be a false alarm, then each and every one of you will be going to the principal's office—for life."

We nodded our heads solemnly, then followed the agent through the empty halls of our school to the gymnasium, now functioning as an auditorium.

Inside, the bleachers were crammed with students and teachers alike. Flashes and snaps from cameras filled the air as the reporters gathered in hordes around the makeshift stage. Television crews were capturing every moment of this event too.

We moved to stand by the bleachers with the tall suit, then scanned the audience for the attacker. In the front row, we found the teaching staff: Miss Huntley, Miss Ivy, Professor Wetherby, Miss Crabtree, and Coach Conley. Standing on the stage with the President was Principal Sterns, Miss Lexington, *and, of course,* Ana Rahela Balenovic. We strained our eyes looking through all the bleachers, but there was no sign of the bald repairman Vincent.

The tall suit looked down at Chase. "Well, kid, where is he?"

"He's here—I know it," Chase gulped.

"He's not here now," Jax whispered.

The tall suit talked into his wired microphone once again. "Stand down—looks like another false alarm. Let the President finish his speech and give the award out." Moving his mouth away from the microphone, the agent looked down at the four of us. "I should arrest the lot of you here and now. But it's preferable that this all goes off without disruption, so, you can join your classmates in the bleachers. Otherwise, I will have the sheriff take you to jail. What's it going to be, kids?"

Our faces said it all: disbelief, dejection, and acceptance that no one was going to listen to us. We shrugged our shoulders and walked to the bleachers to take a seat. We had all seen the bald man on the video, but where was he now? The tall suit walked with us and stayed close as we found some seats, to ensure we would not make any more distractions.

At the microphone on stage, Principal Sterns was introducing the President.

"We here at Raven Ridge Academy are truly honored to have such a distinguished guest to speak to us today. Education is my passion, and I know the President shares my passion—the passion of helping our young people of today become the leaders of tomorrow.

"When I took this position as leader of this institution years ago, people asked why. Why would I want to bring my talents here, instead of pursuing success in the business sector? I simply answered with one word—*passion.* Today, my passion is reflected in our very own Ana Rahela Balenovic, who won the national essay contest on why she's thankful to be an American. We here at Raven Ridge Academy are truly thankful to have her here as a student. So now, it's my great privilege, and honor, to introduce to you… the President of the United States of America!"

The crowd erupted into cheers and claps as the President rose to his feet and shook our principal's hand. It seemed like Principal Sterns didn't want to let go, and finally, as the audiences snapped photos, and flashes electrified the air, the President broke free from the principal's grip and walked to the microphone.

"Thank you, Principal Sterns, and thank you, Raven Ridge Academy!" the President shouted to more claps and cheers. "The honor is truly mine to be among such young, energized, and great American talent. I am here today to give an award to one such talented individual. Ana Rahela Balenovic's essay on why she's thankful to be an American won the hearts and minds of Americans throughout this nation. Through her words, she reminds all of us how very fortunate we all are to live in the greatest nation on earth. Students and teachers, you have an elite school here in Colorado—you should all be proud. And now, before I present this award, I would like Ana Rahela Balenovic to please come forward and read her essay."

The crowd erupted in cheers again, and Ana Rahela Balenovic stood as the cameras clicked and flashed. Her head was in the clouds, probably because it had swelled to the size of a hot-air balloon. Our heads, however, continued to swivel about as we looked around the gymnasium for any sign of the man we had seen on the video monitor before.

I was beginning to worry that he had caught wind of what had happened and escaped. I glanced back to the stage only when Ana Rahela Balenovic began to read her stupid essay aloud.

I thought I might kidnap myself and go back into the mine to avoid hearing her stupid essay again.

I shuddered as Ana droned on and on. Just when I thought my head had swelled to the size of a hot-air balloon and was liable to explode, Jax elbowed me and pointed toward the reporters.

"Oliver, that's *him!*" she hissed. "We've got to stop him!"

My heart pounded, and I looked at the group of reporters closely. My mouth dropped open when I realized one of them was in a wheelchair—a wheelchair like we saw on the monitor inside the mine—it was Vincent! The repairman had changed out of his gray coveralls and disguised himself by wearing a wig and dressing in a suit and tie with a press ID hanging from around his neck. He wore an oxygen mask on his face as if he was sick—but obviously, it was to protect himself from the knockout gas. And right now, he was moving towards the stage!

Chase and Eduard had the same shocking realization when they saw him too.

Jax tugged on the arm of the suit, pointed at Vincent, and said, "That's him in the wheelchair—that's the guy!"

The suit frowned. "He doesn't fit your description at all: he isn't dressed like a repairman, he's not bald, and you all didn't mention a wheelchair either. What kind of prank are you all trying to pull now—trying to get some poor guy in a wheelchair arrested?"

"He changed clothes!" I insisted, backing up my Jax.

"We saw him on the monitors inside the mine. He was pushing the wheelchair down a hallway, but we didn't know he was going to be *in it!*" Chase explained.

"That's enough! I told all of you *no more stories*—now let's go," the agent commanded us. "I'm taking you out of here."

"But he's *the guy!*" Jax objected.

"Let's go—*now!*" the suit ordered again. Then he turned his attention and spoke quietly into the wire hanging from his ear. "I'm taking these kids into the office."

Chase whispered to Eduard. "Distract him somehow."

Cough-cough-cough.

Eduard fell to the ground and began holding onto his throat. "I'm allergic to peanuts. Was someone eating nuts?" He began choking.

Then, kids next to us looked down at Eduard and made a concerned circle around him.

The tall suit furiously pressed on his microphone again, saying, "We have a new situation; one of these kids is supposedly having a reaction to peanuts. Probably a stunt, but to be safe, we need an ambulance."

Chase took advantage of Eduard's distraction and quickly snuck off through some of the kids gathered around Eduard.

Eduard's actions got the attention of the President, who said from the stage, "It looks like we have a student in the audience who might have fainted. I hope everything is okay."

In the commotion, I saw Vincent moving his wheelchair near the climbing wall and getting closer to the right side of the stage. A few of the suits on stage moved away from the President to watch what was happening in the bleachers. They were not paying any attention to Vincent.

Now only Miss Lexington and Ana Rahela were standing in Vincent's way of the President. Suddenly, I was afraid that Miss Lexington might be harmed if something wasn't done soon.

Suddenly, the tall agent's walkie-talkie lit up with the voice of Sheriff Graves.

The kids are telling the truth! I've got a suspect with a gunshot wound!

The tall suit yelled into his microphone, "Code red—code red! Lock down the President!"

I watched helplessly as Vincent reached for something in his jacket. I was too far away to do any good! Then, seemingly from out of nowhere, a flying body struck him. It was Chase, strapped to a harness and swinging from a rope on the climbing wall. The blow knocked Vincent off his wheelchair, along with his wig, and a gun dropped from his jacket.

As one, a mass of Secret Service agents surrounded the President. In the process, the suits knocked Principal Sterns, Miss Lexington, and Ana Rahela Balenovic to the ground.

Vincent fumbled for his gun: it was on the ground next to his hairpiece. From all directions, agents pointed their guns at him—and at Chase, who was still swinging back and forth in the air.

"Hold it right there! Freeze!" the suits barked out.

The shouts coming from the Secret Service agents were louder than the screams and gasps in the gymnasium.

Chase held his hands up as he dangled in the air. A split second later, Vincent did the same. When he did, agents from out of nowhere grabbed him and pushed him down to the ground, where they forcefully handcuffed him.

The auditorium filled with gasps and whispers as Principal Sterns, Ana Rahela Balenovic, and Miss Lexington all slowly started maneuvering back onto their feet.

The tall agent was up by Chase now, and so was I. Pointing to Chase, he told the other agents, "This one's okay."

The tall agent then lowered Chase, bringing him down from the rope.

"There's one more," Chase gasped out as he scanned the room.

"What?" The tall agent pulled his gun out again. "Who? Where?"

"It's a staff member at this school," Chase said.

The agents followed Chase's eyes as he looked to the front row—at Miss Crabtree, who had pressed her lips together; at Miss Ivy, who was shaking with tears; at Professor Wetherby, who had cracked the pencil in his mouth; at Mrs. Huntley, who was shaking her head in surprise; at Coach Conley, who looked like he was getting ready to run; and at Frank, who was standing still by the equipment room.

Chase pointed to the stage and shouted, “It’s Miss Lexington!”

Miss Lexington gasped and stumbled backwards. “What! Oh my goodness, no! I had nothing to do with this!” With a frightened expression on her face, she took a few steps back and reached into her purse.

Dark suits with guns drawn walked en masse towards her. “Sorry, Miss. But we’re gonna have to ask you to come with us. Please show us your hands in the air.”

“There must be some kind of mistake,” Miss Lexington protested in a quivering voice. “I was just reaching for my inhaler—I can’t breathe.”

She raised her hands while dropping both her inhaler and purse. But when her purse hit the ground, the gas mask from her classroom spilled out of it, prompting everyone to gasp.

Ana Rahela Balenovic was still near the microphone, and she shouted into it, “I knew it! I knew all along she wasn’t a real teacher! I tried to tell everyone, but nobody listened to me! I *knew* it!”

Miss Lexington’s frightened look quickly turned to an evil one as she pressed a button on a small remote control she clutched hidden in her left hand. A low rumble shot through the air, and the lights in the gymnasium went out.

As the room went pitch black, the crowd screamed and screamed. People panicked, pushing, and shoving against each other.

There were shouts from the Secret Service agents next to me. “Calm down, everybody! Nobody move! Stay in your seats!” A few of the agents turned on small flashlights.

Moments later, rays of light shot into the room.

I looked over. Chase had opened the door from outside, letting light in so everyone could see—just as he had done in gym class.

The suits immediately shuffled the President out through the lit opening. No doubt, a limousine, or some other dark car, was waiting out there to whisk him away to safety.

"Where'd she go?" yelled out the tall suit.

He was looking for Miss Lexington.

"I know where!" Chase shouted. "Follow us!"

Together, Chase, Jax, Eduard, and I ran out of the gymnasium and into the hall, heading straight for the basement door. Three or four agents followed us.

I grabbed at the knob first, finding it locked. I yelled, "Chase, pick the lock! It's locked!"

"I can't! My tools were taken!" Chase shrieked.

"Stand back!" the tall suit ordered.

He began kicking at the door, but the iron door would not budge.

"I've got a key!" shouted a voice from behind.

It was from Frank. He put the key in the lock, then flung open the door. We raced down the stairs to the basement. The shelf was pulled open—Miss Lexington had gone into the tunnel!

"There's an escape vehicle, a white van, on the other end of this passageway. It's at the mine's entrance. She might get away!" Chase told the agents.

The tall suit began speaking into his microphone as we poked our heads inside. He then pointed a small flashlight and his gun into the darkness and ordered, "Stay here. We'll handle this from here."

Chase wasn't about to let our adventure end here.

"You'll never catch her—you'll get lost," he said. "It's a maze in there, but we can show you the way! We just came from in there."

The tall suit paused for a moment, and then said reluctantly, "Okay, that makes sense. But stay behind us."

We followed the suits and their small flashlight into the small damp tunnel. But this time, we moved quickly, shouting directions at them when we came to each intersection.

As we moved along, we saw a light down the larger tunnel with trestles. The light became brighter and brighter until the cavern opened up and we saw—*Sheriff Graves?*

He was standing there, pointing a flashlight down into the pit where I had fallen. At our arrival, the sheriff's flashlight came up to our direction—blinding us.

"Secret Service! Stand down, Sheriff! What's going on here?" the tall suit demanded.

Sheriff Graves pointed his flashlight back into the pit. The group of us moved up and peered over the edge. We could just see Miss Lexington huddled in a corner, trying to stay far from Mr. Doyle's body.

"Get me out of here!" she screamed. "I'll tell you everything—just get me away from him!"

I knew how she felt with those lifeless eyes staring at her. But she deserved it, and I didn't.

The sheriff said in his low gravelly voice, "I followed up on the kids' story when I heard y'all's talk on the radio. I entered through the entrance into the silver mine. I searched the tunnels and found her down in this pit. She was pushed in there by this young hero."

That's when I noticed Gio, standing on one leg behind the sheriff.

"G!" we all shouted as we ran in to hug him. "You caught her! How'd you know she was coming?"

"I was watching on the monitors they had set up! I saw the whole thing with the President, and when she shut the lights off, I knew she'd be coming this way. So, I hopped on down here and waited for her," Gio said.

"I'm gonna need to talk with all you kids after we bring her up," the tall suit said, pointing his gun down towards Miss Lexington. "Sheriff, keep them close," he instructed.

Two of the suits picked up the rope we had left near the edge of the pit after pulling me out. They held it tight while another suit scaled down it to retrieve Miss Lexington. While they were apprehending her, we all turned our attention to Chase.

"How did you know it was Miss Lexington?" I asked curiously.

"It was the pocket watch," he said.

"What? How?" I questioned.

"When Miss Lexington handed back our quiz papers, Ollie pointed out there were smudge marks on all of them—the same kind of smudge marks left on papers when Mr. Doyle had the pocket watch. However, her fingerprints from the apple didn't match the prints on our quiz papers. This led me to conclude since she didn't have the watch, then someone else must have touched our quiz papers, and that person had Ollie's pocket watch.

"When we were hostages in the mine, I saw Murdoch rubbing the pocket watch. He must have gotten the pocket watch from poor Mr. Doyle; rubbing on it had stained his fingers. So, when Murdoch mentioned they had 'help on the inside,' I deduced that Miss Lexington was the only person it could have been.

"Miss Lexington may have posed as a substitute to get close access to the President, but from what she said in class, I could tell she knew nothing about history, the class she was teaching. Murdoch even answered a question for her during our history class, and he also explained that history was his hobby. So, she needed someone else to grade the papers—and that must have been Murdoch! The tarnish from the pocket watch tied them together.

"Furthermore, when Murdoch told us he was going to flood the school and auditorium with sleeping gas, it reminded me of her inhaler and the gas mask on the mannequin in her classroom. She and Vincent planned to use gas masks when Murdoch flooded the auditorium with sleeping gas, and then they would be able to kidnap the President with no interference. I jumped on Vincent when he made his move, and that forced the Secret Service to react."

"Genius!" Eduard exclaimed.

How could I have missed it? I thought to myself—*Eva... Evil? Lexington... Lex Luthor? I should have known from the start.*

"Looks like everything worked out," I said slowly, "except for poor Mr. Doyle and my great-grandfather's pocket watch. My mom will be devastated that it's gone forever, but I hope she'll understand."

Gio looked at me. "I don't think she'll mind at all. In fact, I think she won't even know it was ever missing."

"Uh, yeah, she will. Once this attention goes away—she'll care," I said, shuffling my foot in the dirt as I worried about what my mom would do to me. I'd probably be doing chores for the rest of my life.

Gio smiled and reached into his pocket. "Not if you put it back." He grinned as he slapped my great-grandfather's pocket watch into my palm.

"What?" I held it in my hand, rubbing the tarnish from the back and reading the inscription, "*Time Waits For No One.*" I looked back to Gio. "How did you—?"

"Murdoch left it on his table. When you all ran out, I saw it when I was hiding, then grabbed it."

"I... I...."

I didn't know what to say—but I didn't need to say anything. Best friends know what the other one's thinking.

CHAPTER FORTY-FIVE

ODDS AND ENDS

A FEW WEEKS later, the President made a return visit to our school, to properly give Ana Rahela Balenovic her stupid award, and to give the five of us awards, too. Much more important awards, I might add—for saving the President, and possibly the world.

The President stood at the microphone as we stood in a group behind him.

"Today, it gives me great pleasure to thank these heroes who saved my life and also averted disaster for this country. This grateful nation and I will forever be in your debt. I thank each and every one of you."

He then bestowed upon us each a medal with a ribbon around our necks and shook each of our hands.

Stupid Ana Rahela Balenovic also received a medal. She claimed she was a part of our investigative unit and therefore had something to do with the capture of the bad guys.

I knew who the actual heroes were, though.

Principal Sterns stood behind us as cameras flashed their bulbs.

"We are very proud of our students here," he said, "but not surprised by their heroics. I train them to use their minds at all times. *Always keep alert*, I tell them, *and report any suspicious activity at once*."

Mr. Doyle did, in fact, win *Teacher of the Year*. He deserved it, having lost his life during the kidnapping attempt. Despite his faults, he was an excellent teacher. He will be missed—especially by Ana Rahela Balenovic.

In appreciation of his service, Gio got a new half-fake leg from the government. It was an upgraded version from the one that Murdoch kicked down the mineshaft.

Gio now claims that zombies took his old one.

Since our big day, Eduard has been conducting research on the gasses the kidnappers had planned to use. He thinks he can invent a knockout gas detector for the Secret Service to use in the future. He still believes aliens use the gasses for their spaceship rockets, and to knock people out for their devious experiments.

Jax has not let the idea go that there is a toxic waste cover-up going on, even though the government did more testing on the local water and found it to be safe.

Chase has continued with his investigations into the many paranormal happenings at our school and is accepting new clients at this time.

I returned my great grandfather's pocket watch back to the display case without my mother knowing it ever left. My Monte Christo project actually did earn me extra credit, despite me not covering the entire room with fabric.

As to the kidnappers: Finnegan was quickly caught while trying to escape—it wasn't hard spotting his lime-green-covered body. He was put in jail, along with Miss Lexington and Vincent. Santos also was jailed after he recovered from being shot by Finnegan. Murdoch's body was never found since it fell down into the bottomless pit.

At the end of our school day, the five of us started on our way back to our secret tree-fort to soak in our new status as heroes with medals. That's when the sound of hoofs came from behind us—it was Sheriff Graves on his horse.

"Hold up, y'all," he yelled.

What now? I thought.

The sheriff's horse trotted up beside us and let out a snort. Looking down from under his cowboy hat, Sheriff Graves asked in a low twang, "So where y'all think you're going?"

Not knowing if we were in trouble or not, Chase hesitantly replied, "Well, sir, back to our home base. There's still trouble in the world that needs our attention."

"Of course. Well, I never had time to thank you kids for what you did. So—thank you, and I need to apologize for not listening to you. Seems you're quite the detective after all, young man—even if you are a dirt bike detective."

"Not a problem, Sheriff," Chase said back with a smile. "That's what we're here for."

"Y'all stay out of trouble—ya hear?"

The sheriff wheeled his horse around and trotted away.

Even though we weren't able to save poor Mr. Doyle, we did save the President, my great-grandfather's pocket watch, and, I'm sure, a few of my grades. There were still some unanswered questions: the image of the boy I saw, the gargoyles; the whispers, Odyssey, and the faceless agent. However, we would leave all that for another day.

We were a team now. A team of best friends who would stick together for the rest of their lives, led by the Dirt Bike Detective.

There was just one problem; *since I had so many best friends, who would I ask to be my best man at Jax's and my wedding?*

I guess I still had time to figure that out.

The End

EPILOGUE

AFTER WE HAD split from our meeting, Chase told me he was riding his dirt bike alone on a long, hot, country road, when a low rumble echoed through the air. A cloud of dust rose from the dry, dirt road ahead… it was a motorcycle, screaming straight towards him!

Chase pulled to the side of the road and stopped his dirt bike, waiting for the rumbling iron horse to pass, but instead, it slowed. Chase could see the flowing blond hair of its rider.

Could it be? he thought to himself.

The red lipstick and mirrored sunglasses confirmed what he hoped: *Odyssey.*

She pulled beside him, revving the bike's loud engine.

Hers was a large, glossy black chopper, with the engine, handlebars, and long forks all plated in shining chrome. Red and yellow flames painted on the tank engulfed intricately airbrushed playing cards of the queens of hearts, clubs, diamonds, and spades.

Odyssey gave Chase a stern look before shutting the bike down.

After a moment, a smile broke her expression. "Is this more appropriate?" she asked.

"Um-hmm," Chase nodded.

"Well, I see you made it in one piece, and a medal from the President to boot? Nice work, kid."

"Thanks to you," Chase said as he got off his dirt bike. "That was you in the mine—wasn't it?"

"I don't kiss and tell," she said as she flipped her long hair back. "Let's just say I had your back, and you did just fine. I knew all along you could do it."

After checking her lipstick in the chopper's mirror, Odyssey dismounted. That's when Chase noticed her tight black leather pants, knee-high boots, and guns strapped to her thighs were back.

"So, tell me, how did you come to your conclusions?" Odyssey asked the dirt bike detective.

Chase explained. "The kidnappers, who were part of the Earth Warriors organization, wanted to kidnap the President and hold him hostage until their demands were met. They had been plotting to abduct the President for a long time, waiting for a moment when they knew exactly when and where he was going to be. When it was announced that the President would come to Raven Ridge Academy to present the National Essay Contest award, they decided to execute their plan. They thought the small town of Raven Ridge was hillbilly and rustic, providing them with the perfect setting to catch the Secret Service off-guard.

"They had months to prepare, and during their planning, they realized the old, abandoned silver mine near the school gave them a perfect hiding spot to set up operations. When they pulled up old records and maps of the mine, they discovered there were old tunnels that came close to the school. They then spent the entire summer digging a new tunnel that led to the school's basement.

"Then, posing as repairmen, they made a sweet deal with Frank, our school's maintenance man, to fix any problems with the school's air conditioning that might come up in the future. And they made sure there would be problems! They vandalized the electrical panels in the basement to cause power outages. This prompted Frank to call them in for service, giving them access to the basement and a chance to dig through the basement wall and connect up with one of the long-forgotten tunnels. They installed a remote-controlled gas release mechanism into the cooling units of the school so it could blow knockout gas in through the vents at the proper time. Because Nitrous Oxide and Xenon gas are not explosive and can be used inside air conditioning units, they counted on their gas tanks being overlooked when the Secret Service performed their bomb sweeps of the building.

"During the awards assembly, Murdoch planned to release the Nitrous Oxide and Xenon gas mixture through the air conditioning units, causing everyone inside to go to sleep. The only ones who wouldn't be affected were their two operatives, who had gas masks concealed. Those operatives would also shut the school's power supply off, which meant all lights in the one area of the school with no windows—the gym—would go out, and the area would plunge into pitch darkness. If anyone tried to enter, they would not be able to see what was going on.

"The plan was to abduct the unconscious President by placing him in the wheelchair that Vincent was posing in, then take him down through the basement and into the escape tunnel they had dug to the mine. Once in their operations center, they would bring him into their van and leave with him. When everyone woke up in the dark, the President would be gone, and in his place—complete chaos."

"So why did they involve Mr. Doyle?" Odyssey asked.

"Well, Mr. Doyle was Ana Rahela Balenovic's teacher, so it would be natural to presume he would be on the stage too. The President was also scheduled to sit in on Ana Rahela's class, and therefore, Mr. Doyle's class. If they replaced Mr. Doyle with one of their own, that imposter, Miss Lexington, would end up right next to the President—better positioned to help capture or assassinate him. Therefore, they needed to get rid of Mr. Doyle.

"During lunch on the day he disappeared, the kidnappers asked to have Mr. Doyle move his classic car, which was parked next to their work van in the teacher's parking lot. Finnegan and Santos were hiding inside the van—waiting for Mr. Doyle to come to his vehicle. However, when Mr. Doyle came out to move his car, Principal Sterns began an argument with him—it was the argument we had overheard during recess before we ran around the building. After the two finished their argument and Sterns was out of sight, Mr. Doyle walked to his car, where Finnegan and Santos jumped out of their van, knocking Mr. Doyle out and quickly throwing him into the backseat of his classic car. Then Finnegan drove Mr. Doyle's car away with Doyle unconscious in the back seat while Santos followed in the van.

"They planned to hide the classic car inside the old mine, but the penniless Mr. Doyle had not filled it with gasoline, and so they ran out of fuel on the side of the road. They quickly transferred Mr. Doyle into their van that was following—which is why we saw footprints that disappeared into the middle of the road. The drag marks on the ground were from Mr. Doyle's heels as they dragged his limp body from the back seat. The van then tore off to the mine, spraying the hood of the car with gravel. Our original theory was that it might be jet propulsion that kicked up the dirt.

"In their haste to conceal Mr. Doyle, someone dropped the crude map of the tunnel they were digging with the markings *N2O*—for Nitrous Oxide—and *Xe*—for Xenon gas—gases they planned on using to put everyone to sleep when the President visited Raven Ridge Academy. They also dropped a key to the basement they got from Frank to perform work down there. The gray button Oliver found was torn off one of their gray uniforms while they were getting Mr. Doyle's body out of the backseat.

"The map with the chemical formulas was the clue that made us think the gasses were linked to aliens, and wonder if the map led to where abductions took place. However, Jax believed the map was a drawing of a toxic waste location, which was contaminating the school. She concluded that the chemical formulas on the map—along with the school's history of incidents, comments from the teachers, and the tanker exploding with unknown chemicals—all added up to a toxic waste cover-up going on in the school's basement. She took the key we found and went down to the school's basement that morning to get proof, but instead encountered the kidnappers, whom she surprised near the tunnel's entrance. They didn't know what to do with her, so they took her as a hostage in case they were caught.

"The kidnappers had parked their work van inside the mine's entrance as an escape vehicle, along with Mr. Doyle's classic car and Oliver's bike—which they confiscated, thinking the bike's owner had slashed their tires. But I think it was Nick who had slashed the tires on their work van, in retaliation for them running over his football.

"The men threw Mr. Doyle's limp body down a pit inside the mine, where he died.

"When Mr. Doyle didn't show up for his class after lunch, Principal Sterns—not knowing where Doyle was—had to fill in until Miss Lexington *just happened* to be stopping by looking for substitute work. Principal Sterns jumped at the offer of assistance from the beautiful substitute, and he immediately hired her to take over Mr. Doyle's class until the school figured out what was going on with him. This gave the group their inside person to be on stage with the President, with only one problem: Miss Lexington knew nothing about history. It was Murdoch who was the history buff. However, it wasn't as likely that Principal Sterns, who was known for appreciating the ladies, would hire Murdoch without a background check, which our principal overlooked with Miss Lexington. Miss Lexington did her best to muddle her way through class, and when it came time to grade a quiz, she had Murdoch do it since he knew the correct answers.

"Because Murdoch had taken the tarnished pocket watch from Mr. Doyle and fiddled with it, the tarnish was on his fingers, and it got onto the quizzes while he handled them. Oliver noticed the smudge marks from the watch on our papers, but when we asked Miss Lexington if she'd found the watch, she told us she hadn't seen it. This made us think she was lying. I used an apple to acquire Miss Lexington's fingerprints. However, my fingerprint analysis revealed the smudge marks on our quiz papers were not from her. At first, I thought they might be from Mr. Doyle or his ghost, but when I saw Murdoch with the pocket watch in the mine, I knew he had handled the papers, and *that* connected him with Miss Lexington, therefore identifying her as an accomplice.

"Miss Lexington brought in a gas mask on a mannequin to school. She said it was to provide the class with information about our nation's indiscriminate use of chemical weapons. But her actual plan was to use the gas mask when the sleeping gas was released. And the inhaler she showed our class, and to the Secret Service, wasn't for her breathing problems. Instead, it was simply filled with oxygen that she would use to help her avoid the knockout gas until she could put on her own gas mask.

"When everyone else inside the school was put to sleep, she would turn off the power to the building with a remote control, and help Vincent put the sleeping President into the wheelchair that Vincent was posing in. Then they planned to push the President to the basement, where Finnegan and Santos were waiting to help carry the President through the escape way they had dug. If anything went wrong with the kidnapping, Miss Lexington was close enough to assassinate the President by using the star belt buckle she wore during the ceremony, which turned out to be a Chinese throwing star laced with poison!

"Miss Lexington went out of her way to portray herself as a klutz—dropping books, spilling papers, bumping into things, and tripping—when, in fact, she was a highly skilled assassin. My first clue should have been when I fumbled the apple onto her desk, and she snatched it out of the air with lightning reflexes."

"Humph," Odyssey objected. "She was an amateur, and she had no fashion sense either." Odyssey flipped her hair. "So, how did you find out about the secret passage?"

"When we were looking for Jax in the basement, I knew there had to be a secret passage, since she was nowhere to be found. The scrape marks on the floor, and the air flickering the lighter told me right where to look."

"Bright boy," Odyssey said, giving a half-smile. "And what about the other faculty members you suspected? Were any of them involved?"

"Frank, the school's maintenance man, became one of our prime suspects when he had a confrontation with Mr. Doyle about the vandalism and the antiques stolen from the school's basement. It became apparent the two did not like each other, and Frank wasn't at all upset when Mr. Doyle went missing. Frank's dislike of the government and his suspicious behavior when we surprised him in the equipment room increased our suspicion of him. However, I had a feeling he was not directly involved when I noticed the red mark on the back of his head, and I was right. Frank had been in the equipment room taking a nap on the mats—and that's what left an imprint on his bald head. Frank believed the kidnappers to be legitimate repairmen, and they offered a fair price to fix the electrical and A/C problems of the school, so he received permission from the office to hire them. He had no clue as to their true motives. So Frank is clear of any involvement in this case."

"But he still seems to have some involvement with Sterns in other matters," Odyssey said with a suspecting tone.

Chase continued. "Miss Crabtree was a suspect because of her mean attitude. Her actions never gave us a really good reason, but she seemed a possible accomplice to Principal Sterns when we overheard the mention of *aliens* in their conversation, and we still don't know what that was about. Yes, she seemed uptight when asked about Mr. Doyle, but I guess she's like that with everyone. While she is cleared in this case, something else is going on with her—I just know it."

"Another one that could use a little fashion help," Odyssey said. "Although, she does have nice purses—I'll give her that."

"Professor Wetherby became a suspect when he was seen arguing with Mr. Doyle in the hallway over an equation that did not work. But other than Professor Wetherby helping to create mind-controlling food for aliens and his obsession with the universe, it is hard to come up with a motive for him. So, Professor Wetherby is clear in this case of Mr. Doyle—but not in other matters related to aliens."

"Of course," Odyssey agreed.

"Coach Conley became a prime suspect when we spied him jogging along the railroad tracks. At first, he denied being out there—probably because he wasn't supposed to be trespassing on Old Man Owens's property. He also claimed he didn't see Mr. Doyle's car—but as we knew he had been jogging on a path that would take him right by it, this made us think he was lying. It turns out he was telling the truth! He hadn't seen Mr. Doyle's car because after we had run away from it, the kidnappers returned, filled it with gasoline, and moved it—hiding it inside the abandoned mine entrance. So, Coach was just out jogging after all. He didn't want to explain the cut on his leg and arm to us because he had fallen rock climbing, and since our class was climbing the rock wall that day, he thought it might ruin our confidence. Coach Conley is clear in this case.

"Miss Ivy became a suspect when the flowers on her desk matched the ones we found in Mr. Doyle's car. Apparently, Mr. Doyle was in love with her. The poem and the flowers in his car were intended for her. He had been collecting the same flowers he had already given her from the school's flower garden because he was penniless and couldn't afford to buy some. She hesitated about telling Jax that the flowers were from Mr. Doyle because she knew he had picked them from the school's flower garden. But Miss Ivy did not have feelings for Mr. Doyle. She considered him a dear friend, and nothing more. When he went missing, she was worried that her rejection had pushed him over the edge. She is cleared in this case.

"Mrs. Huntley became a person of interest when we heard her disagreements with Mr. Doyle in the hallway. She used phrases like, *'Is it something alien that frightens you?'* and, *'Can't you see this is not just about the transformation of the Earth, but of minds as well—the minds of our youth?'* She also said, *'Don't worry about repaying me, because you'll be dead to me.'* She raised my suspicion of her the morning of the President's visit when she acted oddly in the hallway.

"As it turns out, in her argument with Mr. Doyle, she was referring to the *alien* nature of the Christo project—in that it was so *different* and unusual. She thought Christo using fabric to cover the river would not harm the environment but instead, would *transform* people's minds in terms of seeing the Earth differently. So, if the project didn't go through because of Doyle's opposition, she would view Mr. Doyle as *dead to her*.

"The reason Mrs. Huntley was at the school early that morning was to help set up decorations for the President's visit. Seeing us in the hallway made her remember she had forgotten something in her classroom. So, she is cleared in this case. However, she claims to see, and sometimes have conversations with, ghosts in the school—so it's still unclear if she is, in fact, in touch with the paranormal."

"She may have a screw or two loose," Odyssey smirked.

"As for the cooks? Principal Sterns gave the cooks the day off when the President visited, and we still don't know why. Although I can't prove they had anything to do with this particular incident, I'm still not comfortable eating their food. We must, of course, still consider the possibility they are aliens disguised as cooks and poisoning the student's lunches with mind-controlling food."

"Obviously," Odyssey agreed. "And smart to stay away from the food—you won't be missing anything anyway."

"Mr. Doyle had a gambling problem, and it became worse every time he won because then he would disregard every time he lost in the past, and continue to wager, going further and further into debt. He always thought if he could just win one big bet, everything would fall into place. He looked to other people for advice, thinking he could gain some advantage over the odds. That is when and why he turned to Coach Conley and Professor Wetherby.

"Having played football in college, Coach knew the game and had given good picks to Mr. Doyle in the past. When Mr. Doyle asked Coach which team he thought would win the football game that night, Coach was confident about his ability to pick. Nevertheless, he warned Doyle about the dangers of gambling.

"Professor Wetherby's claim of being able to create an equation from known factors that could predict the future attracted Mr. Doyle. So, Mr. Doyle gave Professor Wetherby all the statistics he could find on the two teams playing, so the professor could create his winning formula for that night's game. Professor Wetherby only guaranteed *a high probability of winning*, but Mr. Doyle heard what he wanted instead.

"Combining the advice from Coach Conley and the scientific

data from Professor Wetherby gave Mr. Doyle what he was looking for: a sure bet. So, Mr. Doyle called his bookie and placed *the wager of his life,* betting everything he had—and didn't have—on that night's football game. The only problem was—it didn't go his way. Luck failed him, and an unforeseen fumble by his team cost him everything.

"Devastated and broke, Mr. Doyle didn't know what to do. Knowing Coach had been involved in a gambling ring during college, he tried to pressure Coach Conley into *talking with his people.* He thought Coach Conley might buy him some time in terms of having to pay up. However, Coach wanted nothing to do with it, saying, *I'm not a part of that world anymore.* Mr. Doyle was out of money and options—so the pawnshop owner became his new best friend, and he began selling his precious antiques.

"The pawnshop owner wouldn't tell us what Doyle pawned. So even though Mr. Doyle did have access to the basement, we don't know if he was the one who took the antique items missing from there, such as Anastasia's vanity mirror. Nor do we know if he intended on pawning Oliver's great-grandfather's pocket watch.

"Principal Sterns, who was our chief suspect in the disappearance of Mr. Doyle, acted strangely and gave suspicious answers to our questions. We discovered that Principal Sterns needed Mr. Doyle, who is chairman of the Raven Ridge Historical Commission, to approve the expansion project for the school, but that Mr. Doyle was opposed to it. The two argued during lunch, and Principal Sterns implied he would get rid of Mr. Doyle if he didn't change his mind. Soon after that, Mr. Doyle went missing. Now we know he disappeared because the repairmen abducted him in the parking lot, and not because of Principal Sterns.

"Then there was the note I relocated from Principal Sterns' desk. It ended with the letters *COD,* and this made us believe there was a conspiracy afoot to kidnap and sell the President for *cash on delivery*. However, the letters *COD* did not stand for *cash on delivery* but instead, were Mr. Doyle's initials—*Charles Othello Doyle*—as he was the writer of the note.

"When Mr. Doyle wrote in the note, *alienate members of the faculty and create a toxic environment,* he meant Sterns was trying to get the rest of the staff members against Mr. Doyle in an effort to get him to quit. However, Mr. Doyle wouldn't change his *opinion* on the expansion. The part about, *focus on my star,* and, *arrangements for the President,* was in reference to Doyle's *star student*—Ana Rahela Balenovic—and *arrangements* meant arrangements for the awards ceremony with the President.

"Many questions remain about Principal Sterns. We still don't know what Mr. Doyle meant when he threatened Principal Sterns with exposing some cover-up at the school, which he warned would *haunt him*, or about the *visitors* Doyle said Sterns was hiding. We still don't know whom Sterns was whispering to during lunch, or what the talk about *blackmail* means, or his relationship with the cooks. But it turns out Principal Sterns, who was our chief suspect, doesn't have any connection to the presidential plot at all, or Doyle's disappearance. He's innocent."

Odyssey shook her head a bit at Chase when he concluded. "You don't have everything figured out," she said. "Sterns's innocence in this matter doesn't make him innocent in others. Something's going on with him, so he still should be a suspect."

"I have a lot of other questions still," Chase confided in Odyssey. "Like, who or what destroyed our tree-fort; what's responsible for the mysterious light in the bell tower; who stole Anastasia's mirror; what evidence remains as to ghosts and aliens in the area; and who or what is the faceless agent? But the biggest question is… who are you? Do you have any answers for me?"

Odyssey shrugged. "Sorry, kid, maybe some other time. I've got to go," Odyssey said as she mounted her chopper.

"So, Odyssey, what now?"

"This, my boy," Odyssey said right as she started her chopper and revved the engine, "is where it gets good."

As she rode off, her hair seemed to wave goodbye to Chase behind her. Chase watched her leave, thinking the adventure was over.

The truth was—it had just begun.